Salt People of the Cloud Houses

The Story of Sarah Rapalje and Dutch Manhattan

Fawn Brokaw Doyle

for my family,

especially my mom

and my many grandmothers

who led me here

Preface

New Amsterdam was multi-cultural and multi-lingual from the beginning. To convey the diverse backgrounds of its inhabitants, I've used many Dutch, French, Munsee Algonquian, and Norwegian words. Please note, I've included a glossary at the back of this book.

A bibliography, character list, family tree, full-color maps, and blog posts that explore my research for this novel can be found at: www.fawnbrokawdoyle.com.

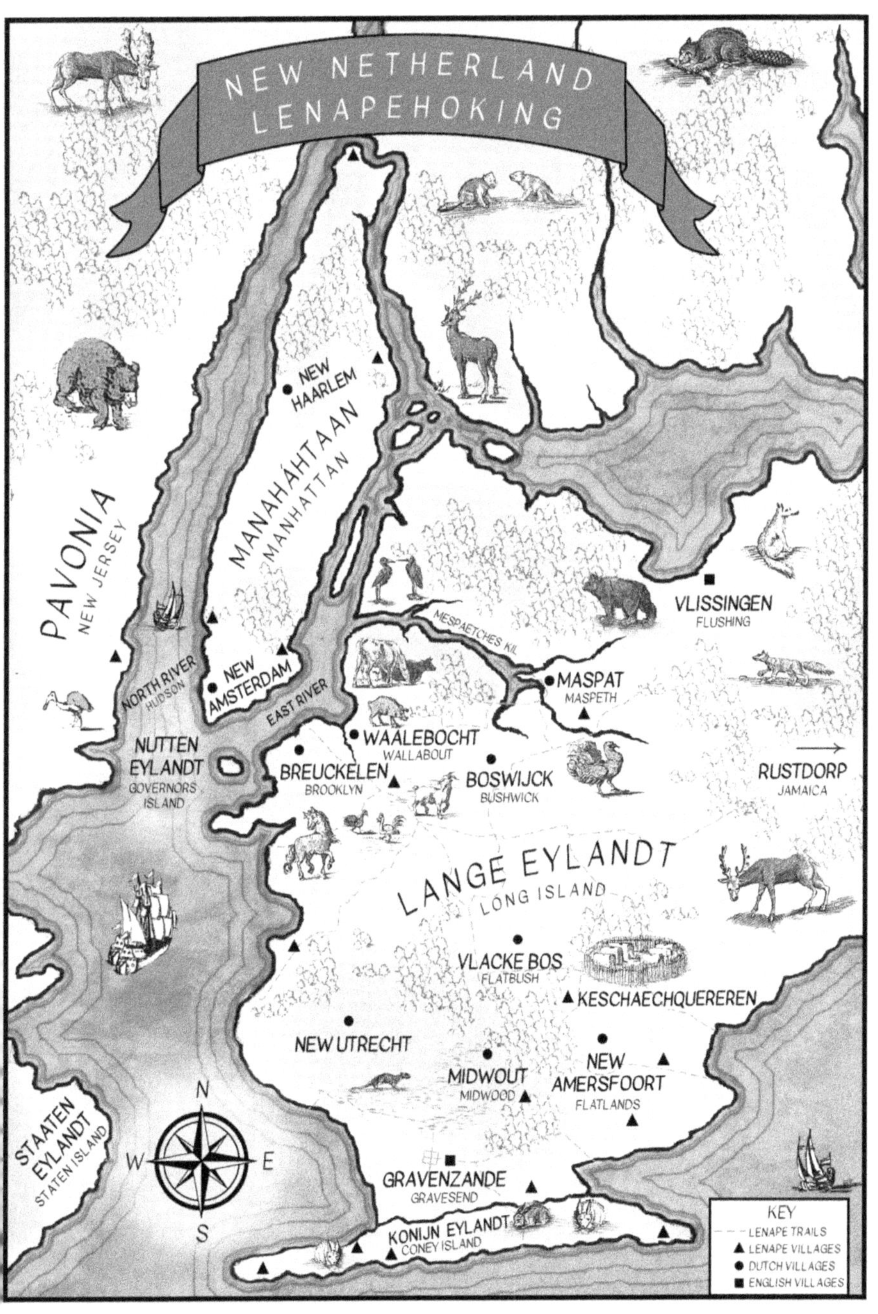

NEW NETHERLAND
LENAPEHOKING
PAVONIA
NEW JERSEY
MANAHÁHTAAN
MANHATTAN
NEW HAARLEM
NORTH RIVER
HUDSON
NEW AMSTERDAM
EAST RIVER
NUTTEN EYLANDT
GOVERNORS ISLAND
BREUCKELEN
BROOKLYN
WAALEBOCHT
WALLABOUT
BOSWIJCK
BUSHWICK
MESPAETCHES KIL
MASPAT
MASPETH
VLISSINGEN
FLUSHING
RUSTDORP
JAMAICA
LANGE EYLANDT
LONG ISLAND
VLACKE BOS
FLATBUSH
KESCHAECHQUEREREN
NEW UTRECHT
MIDWOUT
MIDWOOD
NEW AMERSFOORT
FLATLANDS
STAATEN EYLANDT
STATEN ISLAND
GRAVENZANDE
GRAVESEND
KONIJN EYLANDT
CONEY ISLAND
N
W E
S
KEY
LENAPE TRAILS
LENAPE VILLAGES
DUTCH VILLAGES
ENGLISH VILLAGES

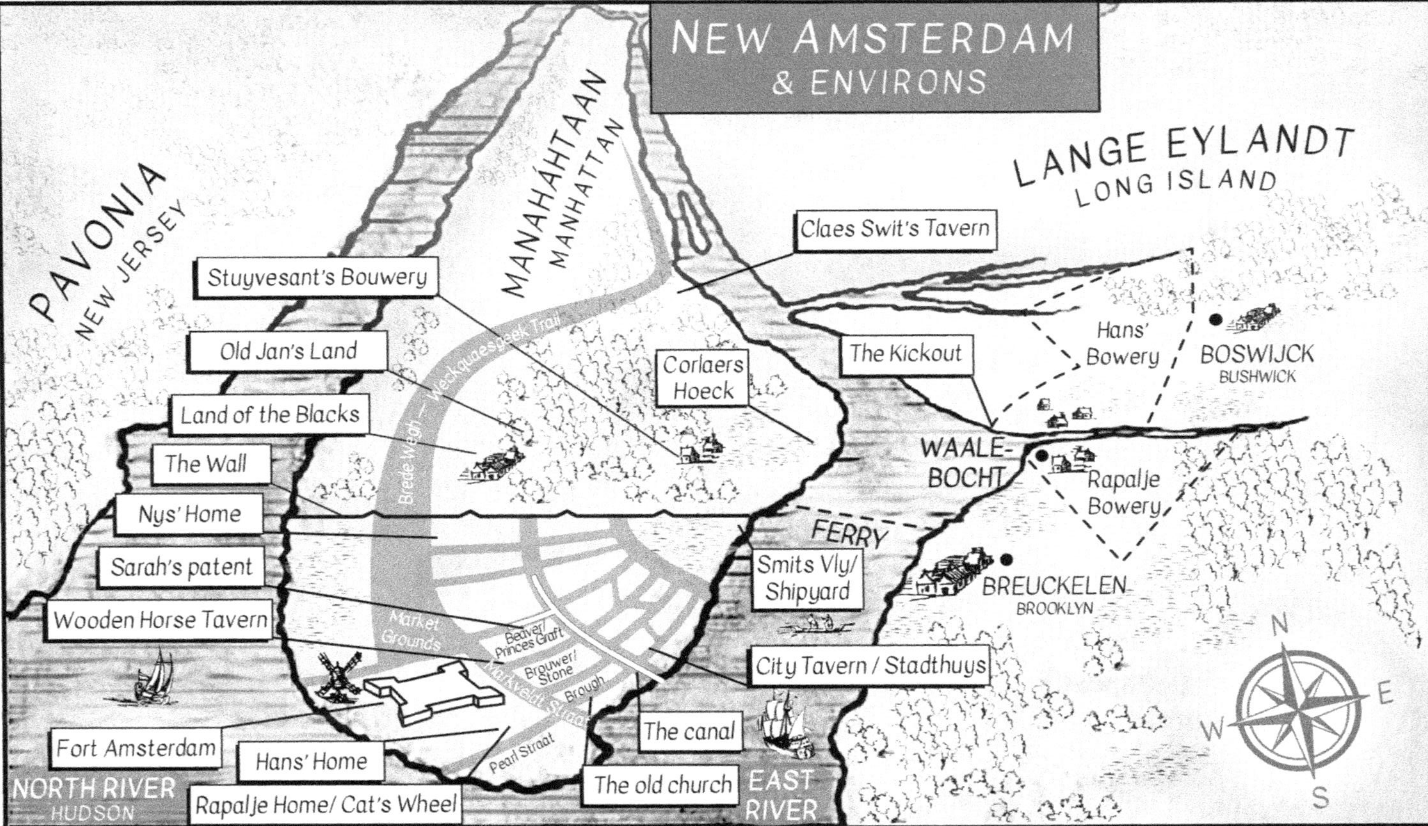

NEW AMSTERDAM & ENVIRONS
LANGE EYLANDT
LONG ISLAND
MANAHAHTAAN
MANHATTAN
PAVONIA
NEW JERSEY
BOSWIJCK
BUSHWICK
Hans' Bowery
Rapalje Bowery
WAALE-BOCHT
BREUCKELEN
BROOKLYN
FERRY
Claes Swit's Tavern
The Kickout
Corlaers Hoeck
Smits Vly/ Shipyard
City Tavern / Stadthuys
The canal
The old church
EAST RIVER
Stuyvesant's Bouwery
Old Jan's Land
Land of the Blacks
Brede wegh — Weckquaesgeek Trail
The Wall
Nys' Home
Sarah's patent
Wooden Horse Tavern
Fort Amsterdam
Hans' Home
Rapalje Home/ Cat's Wheel
Market Grounds
Beaver Graft
Princes Graft
Brouwer/ Stone
Marktvelt Straat
Pearl Straat
NORTH RIVER
HUDSON
N
E
S
W

Prologue

June 9, 1625

Fort Orange (Albany, NY)

Sarah entered the world during a moonlit summer night. Her hearty wail notified twelve other Walloon families, several Dutch fur traders, and the Mahican village across the river of her arrival.

In the past year, since the first French-speaking Netherlanders arrived, their tenuous colony had dwindled from illness and repatriation. For once, they added another soul to their numbers with Sarah Jorise Rapalje. Her cries lifted their hearts. The new life kindled hope that their colony would survive and grow.

New Netherland's firstborn child was also the firstborn of her parents, Catalyna and Joris. Their faces mirrored awe and joy in the dim, precious candlelight that barely illuminated their dugout bark-clad dwelling. They were impulsive teenagers when they'd married four days before their ship departed Amsterdam: besotted, wide-eyed adventurers with nothing to lose.

With poignant clarity that only occurs at the portal of life or death, Catalyna murmured, "Now we have something to lose."

PART ONE: NECESSITY

1639–1642

Is he a native? No, his extensive nature
is spacious and it rises from either sphere:
one skilled in weaving the willow bough
must know the root of the willow too.

– Rainer Maria Rilke –
"Sonnets to Orpheus"
Translated by Martyn Crucefix
Part 1, Number 6

Chapter 1

1639

New Amsterdam (Southern tip of Manhattan)
Sarah rushed to strain cheese curd. Distracted by the raucous chatter of merrymakers gathering outside, she poured the steaming whey too quickly for it to drain through the linen. It overflowed onto the table. She soaked it up with her apron, hoping her mother didn't see. Sarah pinched off a piece of the silky curds sticking to the linen cloth. Her impatient fingers and tongue were slightly scalded, but the creamy, furtive bite was worth it.

Her mother clicked her tongue in disapproval without even taking her eyes from the risen dough she punched down and kneaded.

"No more tastes. We're going to need all this bread and cheese to settle customers' booze-addled stomachs later," Catalyna said, shaping the dough into wooden bread troughs.

"*Maman*, the parade will start soon. May I go now?" Sarah asked as she twisted the linen around the curds. She set the bundle in a basket with a stone on top to drain the excess whey from the cheese and took off her dirty apron. Today was the culmination of three days of celebration. Tomorrow, Lent began, but Shrove Tuesday promised to be a zenith of amusements.

"I don't want you to go alone. Wait for your father to return and he'll go with you."

"He's playing *glückshaus*. Who knows when he'll return? I'm thirteen, *Maman*. I don't need *Papa* to accompany me. Phebe will come with me."

She gestured across their great room where pallid, mousy Phebe played marbles with Sarah's four younger siblings. Phebe's yearning, dark brown eyes pleaded with Sarah's mother. Sarah knew her mother trusted Phebe because her upbringing in the Puritan Massachusetts colony had made her inherently dutiful. Not like the Netherlander children of the colony that always balked at chores in favor of some fun. It was why her mother kept Phebe on as a nursery maid to the younger children when she needed her eldest daughter's help to run their tavern.

"We could take the children..." Phebe said.

"You could have the afternoon in peace before customers arrive later," Sarah added.

"*Bof*, you think two thirteen-year-olds add up to twenty-six?" Her mother laughed. "Promise you'll keep a good grip on Jean. He'll be toddling off at every distraction."

"Promise," the two best friends said in perfect unison.

"*Oui*, you may go."

The day would have been chilly, except the high sun shone down from a cloudless sky. Sarah squinted as her eyes adjusted to the bright light. The amber flecks in her blue-gray eyes, illuminated like sunrays, made her eyes appear green.

As the narrow cow path of Pearl Straat led them onto Markveldt Straat, the colorfully dressed merrymakers multiplied. Entertainers drew crowds at each of the jutting stonework corners of Fort

Amsterdam. A juggler gathered an audience at one while a sword swallower competed for attention at the adjacent corner.

Sarah, taller and more solidly built than Phebe, led the way through the crowds carrying her brother. Phebe followed, holding Sarah's sisters' hands. The walls of the fort were in crumbling disrepair. Onlookers perched on the slope of debris from the wall to get a better vantage point. Sarah helped her siblings and Phebe scale up the rise.

"Have you ever seen so many people?" Phebe asked in wonder. It was only her second Shrovetide in New Amsterdam.

"Many more than last year!" Sarah yelled to be heard as she scanned the crowd.

The parade began with drummers. The onlookers hushed. Standard-bearers marched forth with the orange-white-blue Dutch *Prinsenvlag* and the monogram flag of the Dutch West India Company who ruled the colony. The recently appointed Director General of New Netherland rode horseback while rows of marching soldiers followed. The crowd cheered with enthusiasm for him. Sarah noticed Director Kieft sat with formality, but had an amused twist to his mouth under his auburn mustache. Sarah thought his trimly pointed beard resembled a fox snout. Rows of polished brass buttons on his red woolen cassock and breeches glimmered in the sunlight.

Men dressed like caricatures of European kings and queens followed the procession north of the fort, where the rest of the day's festivities would be held. Flutists led men fearlessly draped with snakes. A man dressed in a bear pelt led a live baby bear on a leash, and a large group of men swathed in peltry trailed behind. Mobs of disparate merrymakers followed.

The spectating crowds followed the parade up the street. Sarah, Phebe, and the children had no choice but to follow. Sarah tucked her blond plaits into her festive blackwork-embroidered coif so no one could give them a playful tug. They slowly heaved forward en masse.

Past the fort, the street yawned open to the immense breadth of the Brede Wegh and comfortably took in the crowds. There were vendors where the weekly market set up. Sarah's sister Maria tugged her toward the *oliekoeken* stand. Sarah relented, but she haggled on the price. Her mother had given her a small amount of *sewant* shell beads, the common currency. She knew she had to spend wisely and there were several *oliekoeken* carts competing for business. The vendor agreed to her price, and she bought each of them a doughnut filled with brandy-soaked raisins and cherries.

At the end of the market, there was a crudely constructed stage for performances. They meandered until they found a perfect spot where they could watch while they ate their doughnuts. The first show had puppets. The next featured the baby bear and men dressed as women. Both shows told folk tales full of bawdy jokes the children didn't comprehend. Sarah laughed along with the adults, although she didn't quite understand the humor either.

Sarah pointed out a group of men who sang in rousing harmony as they danced, swathed in various peltry. Beaver pelts, the raison d'être of the colony, were the most abundant.

"Why do they dance covered with so many pelts?" Phebe asked.

"A worn beaver pelt, the *castor gras*, is worth more money. They wear off the outer coarse hairs and their sweat makes the undercoat easier to scrape off and work into hats," Sarah explained, as her father had told her.

"What games are they playing up the Brede Wegh?" Sarah's middle sister asked, prompted by a roaring cheer up the street.

"Cruel games with animals," Sarah told her, the corners of her lips curling in revulsion. She decided they would avoid watching the sport of "pulling the goose." She had seen it when she was younger and it disturbed her long after. A greased goose, or sometimes a rabbit or eel, was suspended from a rope stretched across the street. Men on horseback rode at full gallop and tried to tear the animal loose. "Kitten in a cask" was another sport Sarah found too unsettling to watch. They would hang a cask and beat it until it broke open, freeing the cat trapped inside. They then would chase away the cat to ward off evil. The cat usually lived, but Sarah couldn't endure its terrified yowls in the process.

The day turned to evening. Two-year-old Jean was on the verge of wailing. They'd placated him with more *oliekoeken*, but he was the lit wick of a firelock, threatening to discharge fury.

"We should have taken him home for a nap a long time ago..." Sarah said distractedly to Phebe and her sisters.

"Sarah! Your cat jumped out of the broken cask! She's run off over there," a neighbor's son shouted and gestured between two houses on the far side of the street. Sarah's stomach flipped with wild hope that it was her mother's dearest cat who had been missing for the past week.

"Phebe, take the children home," Sarah said. "I'm going to get Perle. I'll catch up with you."

Sarah zigzagged through the throngs. A man nearly crashed into her, sloshing his tankard of beer onto her dress. He grabbed her around the waist and swung her around to join the dancing that had begun. She jabbed him with her elbow and slipped from his grasp. Another man reached to dance with her, but she ducked through the crowd, reorienting herself to the alley where she hoped to find Perle.

She rounded the corner of the house where the neighbor boy had pointed. She slowed and searched every nook where the marbled tan and white cat may have hidden.

Suddenly, a corpulent figure bumbled into the alley between the houses. It was Cornelis van Tienhoven, Secretary to the Director General. He was dressed as a Native and had painted himself red. It appeared he had just finished relieving himself as he adjusted the deer hide that hardly covered his most private parts. Sarah's surprise turned to alarm when he looked her up and down like he was starving and she was a hog on the spit.

"What's this? A Shrovetide angel?" he drunkenly lisped. He snatched her toward himself. She screamed, but it was buried in the music and laughter of the festival.

CHAPTER 2

1639

Van Tienhoven tried to press his lips to hers, but he was so drunk, his open mouth slobbered her from cheek to ear. He clutched the cropped woolen partlet covering her shoulders. She took advantage of his imbalance and spun away from him, back to the festival, leaving him holding her partlet.

Pulse racing in her ears, Sarah weaved through the crowd, hoping for concealment and looking for any familiar face. It was mostly men. Merchants, sailors, fur trappers, and soldiers. Their scarred and stubbled cheeks blazed red and their mouths gaped in laughter and singing. Their sour breath, body odor, and alcohol fouled the air. She saw a woman she knew. It was her neighbor, *Mevrouw* Beeche, but she was drunk. She cackled as she fumbled with the breeches of a young sailor. She kept trying to untuck his shirt as he blushed and slapped her hands away.

Sarah reached the spot where she had left Phebe and the children. They were already gone. How quickly the crowd had turned belligerent without her friend and siblings next to her. Dusk had settled, and the temperature dropped with the sun. She looked behind her and locked eyes with the determined Van Tienhoven, elbowing his way toward her.

She skirted the crowd, hoping to make faster time. Then she weaved through the food vendors, hoping to lose him in the maze of carts and stalls. She found the *oliekoeken* vendor she had bought from earlier. She ducked behind the cart. The vendor shrieked.

"Out of here! You wastrel!" The woman thwacked her in the back with a spoon.

"Please…"

"Buy something or leave. No scraps for you!" Another thwack on the back.

She made it to the first corner of the fort and slowed. Surely she had lost him. Breathing deep to steady herself, she realized she was shivering without her partlet. She wrapped her arms around herself. Almost home. She just had to get home.

Suddenly, she was jerked backward by a hand on her arm. She let out a yelp.

"My Shrovetide angel," Van Tienhoven whispered, his voice thick, spraying spittle in her ear. She grimaced and braced herself to kick him with her wooden clog.

"Is that Sarah Rapalje?" A voice boomed behind Van Tienhoven. "Your mother asked me to fetch you."

Her neighbor, Hans Bergen, plucked Van Tienhoven off Sarah forcefully. Van Tienhoven's girth was no match for Hans's height and strength. Hans was the tallest man in the colony. Hans moved Van Tienhoven as easily as a trictrac backgammon piece.

"Secretary Van Tienhoven, I believe you are lost. The strumpet street is that way," Hans said derisively as he took Sarah's partlet from his hands and shoved him toward another street. "Wouldn't want this kind of behavior getting back to Director Kieft, would you?"

"Humph…" Van Tienhoven uttered as he lurched in the direction Hans sent him.

"Come, Sarah. Let's get you home," Hans said.

Mortified, she didn't know what to say. She followed him toward Pearl Straat in stunned silence. She'd always tried to get the attention of her handsome neighbor, but he had always treated her like the child she was, like an annoying black fly to be rebuffed or outright ignored when there were more important tasks at hand. Now, he stopped walking to face her.

"Your mother didn't really send me. I happened to see you could use a hand with that muttonhead. I don't have to tell her... as long as you're all right."

He gently touched her lip, then swiped with his broad hand.

"Ah, it's just red paint from that fool. I thought your lip was bleeding," he said, swiping again, his palm as rough and gentle as Perle licking her cheek. His thumb ran over her lower lip again. And again, softer.

"Thank you, Hans. I'm fine," she rushed to say. She wanted to say how foreign her town had become to her that night or ask why the evening had turned so abruptly hostile to her. She wanted to cry. They resumed walking.

"Did you see the show with the little bear? That was my favorite. And I'm deathly afraid of bears." He laughed.

She looked up at him and couldn't help but smile. Even in the dim light, his deep blue eyes still shone bright as the sky on a clear day. His mustache had the same feathery wings as his blond hair, like a dove taking flight from his lips. She wanted to feel his fingers on her lips again.

He held open the door to her parents' tavern for her.

The warm smell of pepper, cloves, nutmeg, mace, and cinnamon greeted them as they entered Cat's Wheel. Venison stew sputtered on the hearth, filling the room with the aromatics that Dutch traders brought from the East Indies. Her father entertained half a dozen customers waiting for food and drink, wringing the last conviviality from the day. By his boisterous tone, she assumed his dice games had gone well earlier. Her father only ever gambled on Shrove Tuesday, and it was his ritual superstition that, win or lose, his Shrove luck foretold the rest of the year.

"The four men at the back are waiting for stew. They already have bread and cheese," Sarah's mother instructed her as she filled tankards with beer. "Hans, I suppose you will want some, too?"

"*Ja*, Catalyna. With thanks," he said, taking a seat by Sarah's father at their long table.

Grateful to be back home and in the familiar rhythm of tavern work, Sarah ladled the stew. She served Hans first, but he paid her no more attention than usual with a glance and his congenial smile. She thought she must have dreamt up the longing look in his eyes when he had wiped the paint from her face.

Their customers eventually dispersed. Sarah cleaned their bowls and cauldron in the side yard with water from the cistern and scouring rushes. A meow came from near their storehouse. Sarah took her lantern to investigate. Perle crouched by the storehouse door, trying to get in. Sarah scooped her up, cooing, "Are you all right, *ma petite puce*? Was it really you in the cask?" Perle seemed unscathed.

When she returned inside, her parents sat together by the hearth, looking contented. Her sisters readied for bed. Jean was already asleep in the bassinet that he hardly fit in anymore.

"*Maman*, I found Perle!" Sarah exclaimed.

"*Bien fait*, Sarah! Bring her here!" her mother said with outstretched arms.

"*Papa*, will you tell us a story of the old country?" Sarah's sister Jannet asked, sitting impatiently as her mother combed her hair. "*S'il vous plaît.*"

Sarah glanced at Phebe. She sprinkled sawdust where spilled beer had puddled and then swept it up. Sarah's family spoke in their native French dialect as soon as their customers left. Sarah assumed Phebe had learned their French as quickly as she learned Dutch. Phebe had a good ear, but, by nature, she preferred listening to speaking.

"All right. All right…" He leaned back in his chair and lit his pipe. "We are Walloons, descendants of the fierce tribes of Gallia and the great artisans of Burgundy. Do you know why they call us Walloons?"

"Why?" Jannet and Maria asked in unison. Sarah restrained herself from replying with her little sisters. She had heard this call-and-response tale many times. Perhaps she was too old for these childish stories. Sarah began to comb the tangles from Maria's hair as her mother combed Jannet's.

Her father continued, "We are called Walloons because when the ancient people of Gallia were traveling the length and breadth of the earth, they had asked each other…"

"*Où allons-nous?*" her sisters answered.

Where are we going? Sarah wondered if her people would ever have a real homeland if they identified themselves by such a name. Her father had told her their people embraced the derisive names given to them, like "the strangers" or "the beggars," in defiance and pride. Her parents were among the first to settle New Netherland, so she could understand why they liked the wanderlust interpretation.

"The people of Gallia settled in the *Pays-Bas*, the Low Countries. They were as skilled in craft as in sword. Julius Caesar sent his soldiers to conquer the *Pays-Bas*, and what did he call us?"

"The bravest," Sarah said reflexively with her sisters, eager to claim that portion of her heritage.

"I have to tell you what happened," Sarah whispered to Phebe, beside her, in their shared *bedstee* bunk above her sisters. Phebe often slept at the Rapalje home, bunked with Sarah. Her father John, or Old Jan as he'd become known, had a rough lodging north of the settlement that was hardly suitable for Phebe. "I looked for Perle but found Secretary Van Tienhoven." Sarah went on to explain the whole story as quietly as she could into Phebe's ear.

"Hans rescued you? How chivalrous!" Phebe feigned swooning, with her hand to her forehead.

"I didn't need to be rescued. I was about to kick his shins and run. Although... if I had to be rescued by someone, I would choose Hans." Sarah mimicked Phebe's swoon but then grew serious. "But he's our neighbor. He was just being kind."

"Chivalrous," Phebe insisted. "It can't be a surprise if he's looking at you as a woman now."

"Do you think he heard about... that?" Three months ago, at the end of the school day, she stood up and there was a bloodstain on the bench.

"I don't know, but it's plain to see... you're grown."

Everyone remarked that she looked like a woman now. Her friends said it with envy. Sarah's mother said it as a complaint as she outgrew her clothing. Her mother had recently made her stays that laced. It supported her new bosom and easily adjusted as she grew.

Her bearings in the world had had slowly loosened over the past year, and Shrove Tuesday shed her childish naïveté like an old snakeskin. Both she and the colony seemed changed from when she was a child, leaving her feeling unmoored.

What was the next stage of life supposed to be? She felt ill-prepared to fend off the attention of men that now far outnumbered women in the colony. She tried to remember that her people were the bravest. They fought off Caesar's army. She could fight, but she just didn't know how to fight growing up. She yearned to be the grown woman everyone saw her as, while fearing what that would entail.

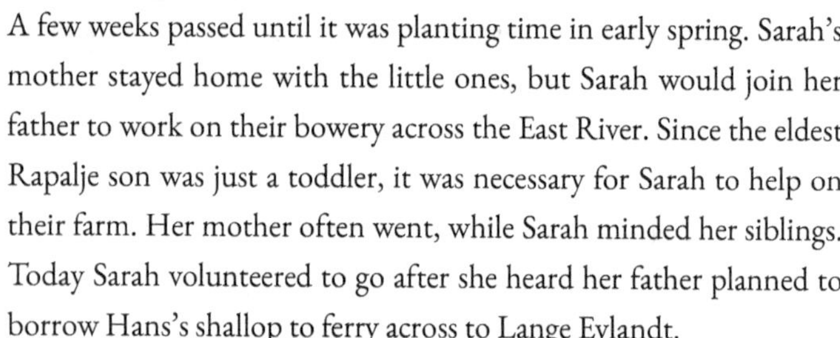

A few weeks passed until it was planting time in early spring. Sarah's mother stayed home with the little ones, but Sarah would join her father to work on their bowery across the East River. Since the eldest Rapalje son was just a toddler, it was necessary for Sarah to help on their farm. Her mother often went, while Sarah minded her siblings. Today Sarah volunteered to go after she heard her father planned to borrow Hans's shallop to ferry across to Lange Eylandt.

Her father pulled their wagon cart, loaded with sacks of seed, hoes, an adze, and a rake, to Smits Vly, where Hans worked as a shipwright. As they neared the shipyard, Sarah spotted Hans sawing logs near the river's edge.

"Hallo, Hans!" Sarah's father called out.

Hans greeted them with a wave. With sleeves rolled to the elbow, his forearms were nearly as thick as Sarah's thighs. Her mouth went dry. It was a chilly spring day, but his face shone with perspiration from sawing. He took a handkerchief from his jerkin to wipe his face.

"The shallop is waiting for you, there." Hans pointed out into the water. "I'll take you out to board in the *wey schuyt*."

Her father helped her into the birch bark canoe, placing her in the center of the hull with the seed sacks. He took a seat at the bow, Hans at the stern. They silently paddled out to the shallop. Sarah yearned to turn around to talk to Hans, but she couldn't think of what to say. She watched ducks at the river's edge as they dove into the water, popping up unpredictably. Finally, she thought of something.

"What are you working on today, Hans?"

"Repairing a privateer's ketch."

"Oh," was all she could think to say. She searched her mind desperately for a way to continue the conversation, but then they were already at the shallop. Her father swung himself aboard, and Sarah passed the seed sacks to him.

"Let me help you, Sarah," Hans said.

She turned to face him as a wave hit the broadside of the freeboard, sending a spray of water across Sarah's face. One of Hans's forearms hooked around her waist to steady her and the other was there in an instant to wipe the water away from her eyes with his handkerchief. She tasted the sweat from his brow on it. She laughed nervously and her cheeks grew hot.

Sarah's father held out his hands for her, and Hans lifted her by her waist to the larger vessel. She was too stunned to hear any parting words, if there were any. She watched as Hans returned to the shipyard and her father opened sail. Hans looked back once. He waved to her.

"I see Wunita and Cholena," Sarah's father said, waving at the Native man and woman as they drew near the inlet estuary that marked the beginning of their land. Her father made a deal years earlier with the *sachems* of Wunita and Cholena's Canarsie tribe to farm the land there. Wunita traded pelts with her father and Cholena helped them farm for a share of the crops.

"Joris! *Nitap*!" Wunita called out as they drew closer. Sarah knew *nitap* meant Wunita welcomed their continued friendship. There would be an exchange of gifts that day to reaffirm their alliance and her family's permission to farm the land.

She spotted Wunita's daughter, Weenjipahkihelexkwe, in the distance up the creek called Remegakonck Kil. Weenji, as Sarah called her, had watched over Sarah during planting and harvest season since she was a toddler. Now, Weenji was like an older sister that Sarah looked forward to seeing during the planting season. She taught Sarah to make cordage, weave baskets and mats, forage for mushrooms and medicinal plants, and taught her to swim. Sarah learned some of the Munsee language from her and taught her Dutch and French in return. Once on land, Sarah ran to greet her. Weenji's mother sat, legs crossed, weaving slender branches into a rectangular frame.

"Weenji, *nitap*!" Sarah called out.

"Girl Who Slips On Eel Grass! *Nitap*!" Weenji called her by her Munsee name and gestured for her to hold one end of a woven weir. It was one of the smaller gate-like portions that trapped fish when the tide ebbed and flowed. Sarah held the portion closest to shore while Weenji hopped in the water to secure it into the creek bed. Her tawny cheeks gleamed with the reflections off the water. Weenji wore a wrap skirt of animal skins that was so well oiled the water rolled right off it. Sarah marveled at how the porcupine quills on her skirt looked so much like lace in the distance.

Weenji and her mother, Cholena, were skilled at cultivating corn, beans, and pumpkins. They grew their native crops on the land they shared with Sarah's family. Her full name, Weenjipahkihelexkwe, meant "Girl Touching Leaves." Her mother's name, Cholena, meant "Bird Woman," but there was a significance to its meaning that Sarah knew she couldn't quite grasp. Gaps in understanding between them were common, but not a hindrance to their friendship.

Sarah helped Weenji climb up the embankment.

"What do you plant today?" Weenji asked.

"Crops for the Company. Spring wheat, barley, and oats," Sarah said. "Did winter pass well for you?" Sarah hadn't seen her since the fall harvest. Weenji smiled.

"I married a Massapequa man. I met him at the Gathering of Blessings. I call him Tiyas because of the blue jay feathers in his hair. He brought my family lots of meat over the winter, and we have many pelts to trade with you."

"*Wa-ni-shi*," Sarah told her—*may the path be good to you*—as that was the closest phrase she could think of in Munsee that was appropriate. "I brought you a gift."

Sarah brought forth a linen handkerchief edged with lace. It was a practice piece of *passementerie* she learned over the winter. Weenji took it with both hands. Her fingertips glided over the lace edges. She pressed it to her cheek.

"*Wunneet.*" Weenji told her it was good and smiled. She nodded toward their fathers. They set off to begin a long day of planting.

Chapter 3

1639

In late summer, the market in New Amsterdam thrummed with activity. Sarah wiped beads of sweat trailing down from her linen coif cap. Stray strands of her golden blond hair clung to her face and neck from the humidity in the air. Impatient for her mother to be done haggling for pins, thread, and needles from one market stall, she wandered to the next.

They sold exotic birds from the Caribbean. She marveled at the vibrant colors of their plumage and delicate gilt cages. One stood on a turned wood post, cocking his sapphire head at her quizzically. His foot was lashed to the post. She had the urge to pull loose the leather thong and let him decide his own fate. He suddenly let out a squawk and yip. It startled her backward, bumping into someone. A voice came from behind her that made the hair on her arms stand up.

"Hallo, my Shrovetide angel."

She spun to face Van Tienhoven. Her heart pounded in her ears as she remembered him ripping her partlet off as she escaped him during the Shrove celebrations. Although now, he presented a stately appearance in his black doublet and lace falling collar in stark contrast to how she had last seen him dressed. In the broad light of day she could see the creases around his eyes and gray hairs encroaching into his sideburns.

"How fitting to find you among these colorful beauties, yet your comeliness exceeds them. I've often thought of you since Shrovetide. I do apologize for my appearance to you that night. You must have been frightened that I was truly a *wilden*."

It had been months since the Shrovetide incident. She was shocked he remembered her, considering his drunken state that day. In all those months, she had done her best to not remember their encounter.

"*Nee*, think nothing of it. Excuse me, my mother is waiting," Sarah said quietly and strode back to her mother's side, silently willing her to cease bargaining so they could leave.

"What was the Secretary Van Tienhoven speaking to you about?" Sarah's mother asked as they walked home. Sarah hoped her mother hadn't noticed.

"He was admiring the birds."

That evening, there was a knock at the door. Her mother answered. It was the court messenger.

"*Mevrouw* Rapalje, Secretary Van Tienhoven requests a visit from you and your husband this evening," he said.

"A court summons? This evening? Why?"

"No, at his home. He didn't give a reason," the man replied.

Sarah's stomach twisted. She bowed her face toward her mending work and prayed the meeting had nothing to do with her.

Her parents went to Van Tienhoven's and returned without any explanation to Sarah. She was too afraid to ask the purpose of their meeting. Her parents discussed the matter late that night when Sarah should have been asleep. They whispered, but she could hear bits through her *bedstee*. She heard Van Tienhoven's name. They argued.

Her mother's exasperated tone battled against her father's patient reasoning.

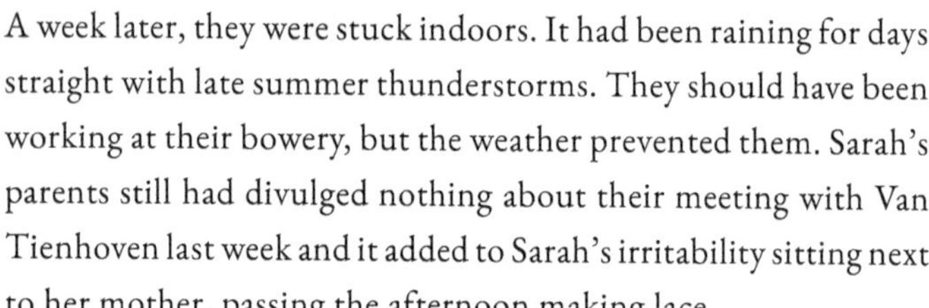

A week later, they were stuck indoors. It had been raining for days straight with late summer thunderstorms. They should have been working at their bowery, but the weather prevented them. Sarah's parents still had divulged nothing about their meeting with Van Tienhoven last week and it added to Sarah's irritability sitting next to her mother, passing the afternoon making lace.

Sarah set down her *passementerie* pillow in frustration, the bobbins clattering against each other.

"I hate lacemaking. It's too... fiddly," she said to her mother.

"Sarah, *passementerie* saved my life when I was a young girl. Wealthy people will pay good money for it, if you do it well. The skill meant my survival—"

Her mother was likely to go on with the lecture when there was a knock at the door. Sarah jolted, relieved at the interruption. Perhaps just an early tavern guest?

Her mother swung the door open to see the Director General. She let him in, drenched and dripping on their floor.

"Director Kieft, what an honor! Please come in," her mother said. "Would you like something to drink or eat? Sarah, go fetch some of the best cheese... smoked pork sausage and... pickled eels from the storehouse."

"Dreadful weather. I apologize I come unannounced..."

Sarah ran from their back door to the storehouse in the torrential rain. As she returned, she paused behind her parents' *bedstee* and the stairs to the garret so she could listen to their conversation before she entered the great room. Drenched, arms full of their best provisions, she willed her breathing to slow so she could hear them better.

"This colony needs more married men. They're better behaved. It's not only Sarah. I'm advising this to all with daughters of age. Best to pick soon before the most desirable bachelors are betrothed. I don't think she could have a better prospect than my secretary," Director Kieft said.

"Maybe the behavior of the men is *their* responsibility, not that of young women who should tame them," her mother said in a measured voice. "Or perhaps it's the responsibility of their leader and *baas*?"

There was a heavy pause. Her mother argued this way with her father, occasionally. She couldn't believe her mother would argue with the Director. She held her breath.

"I intend to enforce ordinances against public drunkenness and brawling," Director Kieft replied. "Even so, what's better than a wife to keep men home, rather than out carousing in taverns and cavorting with strumpets?"

"Does your secretary frequent the taverns and strumpets, then?"

"*Mevrouw*, if she won't accept Cornelis's offer, I'd advise you to choose someone, or you won't hear the last of my secretary. He asks for a betrothal, but I'm afraid he'd just as soon claim her another way... bribery... blackmail... I don't mean to say he's a rogue. Merely, if he wants something, he does not accept refusal. He can be very persuasive when determined."

"My daughter will marry. In good time," her mother said as the door closed.

Sarah hurried into the great room with the provisions, alarmed.

"*Ma petite puce*," Sarah's mother said and embraced her with a blanket to dry her drenched shoulders. "Sit down and dry off. I'll make us some tea."

Sarah tried to discern her mother's thoughts from the herbal concoction her mother chose to brew. Hawthorn and borage.

Heartbreak and courage. Catalyna sat and Sarah slunk down beside her.

"Van Tienhoven proposes to marry you. Your father suggests... an open mind, while he agrees that... he thinks we'd do well to at least consider the benefits. Van Tienhoven is well educated and his prominence is rising."

"*Non.*" Her face contorted in horror. "How could I marry him? He's older than *Papa.* You need me here to help with the tavern, my sisters, and Jean. I cannot marry him."

"Legally, you were of marrying age last year. No one gets married so young back in *Patria*, but things are different here. Maybe this is an opportunity. Your life doesn't have to be as hard as ours." Her mother stared at the floor, silent for a moment.

"Why did you decide to marry *Papa*?" Her father had told her that the Spanish occupied their lands in the *Pays-Bas* and her parents fled north as teenagers. They met at the Walloon church in Leiden and her father said it was love at first sight.

"Your father and I married for a shared goal. To come here. We were desperate for a new life. He persuaded me with his dreams of this New World, and love grew from that. We've worked *so* hard, Sarah... it's more than a miracle we're still alive... that you're alive."

"I don't want to marry..."

"Think on it. You may change your mind. According to Kieft, you *must* change your mind. Van Tienhoven suggested the wedding could take place after the harvest, so we have until then to consider."

The harvest season went too quickly. Sarah's consideration time was drawing to a close.

Just past dusk on a chilly October night, Sarah swung the ax hard as she split logs into kindling behind their house. A waxing moon lit the yard. The rhythm of iron splintering wood began to soothe her frustration and panic that the harvest season was nearly over and she had to give Van Tienhoven an answer. She gathered the kindling into a sling. She had made more than they needed. Pigeons flew out of the elderberry shrubs and startled her.

"Hallo there, Sarah," Hans called out in his affable way. "Shouldn't there be your father or English maid to do such work?"

"*Nee*, all's well. Phebe is visiting with her father. I can chop wood just fine," Sarah replied, setting down her ax and stooping to the woodpile. She immediately regretted her tone with him. She didn't mean to sound so abrasive toward Hans.

"Please," he said. "Let me..."

She straightened to face him. He suddenly stood so close, more than a head taller than her. She inhaled his scent of sweet, grassy hay, sawdust, and the salty musk of his work clothes. The memory of tasting his salty kerchief made her mouth water.

He reached down for the wood sling. As he leaned his face to her height, Sarah impulsively kissed him softly on his lips.

He stood upright and muttered something in Norwegian. He assessed her with his deep blue eyes. Hans was several years older than her, but a decade younger than Van Tienhoven. She had always dreamed of a kiss with Hans, although she imagined his mustache would feel softer.

"I must marry soon," Sarah whispered. "I didn't want Van Tienhoven to be my first real kiss."

Hans suddenly wrapped his arms around her, pulled her close, and kissed her deeply. She melted into his embrace and couldn't move. She didn't *want* to move.

He pulled away and locked eyes with her, searching. He was silent for a moment that felt eternal to Sarah.

"What if you married *me*, Sarah?"

Her heart raced. Could he be serious? Everyone adored Hans. He was a shipwright, carpenter, and tobacco farm overseer. He kept his own taproom when the crowd at Cat's Wheel spilled over. Despite all that, he wasn't wealthy. He had no education other than woodworking. Their common language of Dutch was neither of their first languages. But he was very handsome, charming, and capable.

"Are you asking…?" she breathlessly uttered. She almost finished the sentence with "out of pity."

"*Ja*, will you marry me?"

His swift reply made her hesitation vanish. She pulled his face to hers and kissed him again in reply.

He scooped up the wood sling with one arm and his other around her waist and started walking toward her house.

"Let's tell your parents and get their blessing."

Sarah's mother had tears in her eyes, but she smiled at the news.

"You're a good man, Hans," she said.

"I don't disagree," her father said. He clapped Hans on the back, a bit rough, but with paternal affection. "You should consider the ire of Van Tienhoven, however. He will take umbrage with the man who stole his intended."

"Should I send him a bottle of gin? A strumpet?" Hans asked. "He already has all he wants of those."

"That's why Kieft was pushing the marriage," her mother said, eyes brightening with a realization. "Go to the Director. Ally with him in telling Van Tienhoven. Perhaps he'll have an idea to deflect Van Tienhoven's wrath."

Sarah's stomach churned with giddiness and nerves. How could she ask such a favor of the Director?

Chapter 4

1639

Sarah clutched Hans's arm as they made their way to the Director's quarters in the fort. The aftertaste of her mother's decoction for courage was still on her lips. Sage, borage, and brandy were not unpleasant, but her belly burned from the liquor. She did not feel courageous, but she drew steady breaths that belied her trepidation.

A soldier conveyed them into the great room and bade them to wait. They silently stood by the cold hearth. Hans took her hand. He breezed his thumb over the ridges of her knuckles before giving a firm, confident squeeze. She smiled and her cheeks grew hot. They were in this together. They would be wed. It still felt like a dream.

Director Kieft entered. They bowed their heads deferentially.

"Hans Hansen Bergen and Sarah Jorise Rapalje..." Kieft said, head slightly cocked in surprise. He paused to regard them. Sarah's cheeks burned under his scrutiny.

"Director, we came to seek your approval and esteemed advice," Hans said. "I intend to marry Sarah. I know your secretary also had that intention..."

Hans paused to let Kieft speak, but he remained silent.

"I wish to marry Hans but not offend Secretary Van Tienhoven," Sarah spoke up. "We hoped you could advise us on such a matter."

"Do your parents approve?" the Director asked her.

"*Ja*, but they advised us to consult you."

Director Kieft considered.

"My secretary will undoubtedly despair at his failure to court you," Kieft said with a frown. He paused, pulling his pointed beard contemplatively, and paced back and forth. "I know someone who might be more amiable toward Van Tienhoven. I shall convince him that it is a more advantageous match. Indeed, it is. She's more equal to him in station, and her stepfather is eager to rid his house of stepchildren."

"We would offer our humble gratitude, Director," Hans said.

"Are you *sure* you wish to marry a carpenter rather than a secretary?" Kieft asked Sarah.

Sarah looked at Hans. Hans's face fell at the Director's implied criticism of his station.

"*Ja*," Sarah said without hesitation.

"Fine, then. I only ask that you invite me to the wedding celebration," Kieft said, with an amused twist to his mouth.

"Of course," Sarah and Hans said in unison.

The day before their wedding, Hans gave Sarah a silver medallion as a marriage gift.

He presented it to her on a *knottedoek* embroidered dowry cloth. The medallion was as wide as her palm. He could have given coins, as was customary, but the medallion was particularly fine. On one side was the bas-relief figure of a man and a woman, being married by a Domine. Encircling was the inscription, in Dutch: "Behold this young woman whom I love and none other. She is my true one, my love, and is next to God alone." The reverse side depicted a man and a woman in a garden, encircled with the sentence: "Behold, the creator of flesh and blood, created two out of one." After allowing her a moment to admire it, Hans gathered the fabric around the medallion and tied it up loosely with a braided silk cord.

"Pull here and tighten the knot, if you will accept me as your husband," Hans whispered to her. She did as he bade and smiled proudly at her parents, who watched the formal presentation.

Sarah and Hans were to be wed on a Friday, November 18, 1639, at the Dutch Reformed Church. She had six bridesmaids to help her prepare for her wedding. Her oldest friend, Sarina du Trieux, was also a Walloon. Saartje Roelof's parents were Norwegian, like Hans, but she'd been born in the Netherlands. After the death of Saartje's father, her mother married Domine Bogardus, who would perform the ceremony. Phebe and Sarah's little sisters Maria, Jannet, and Judith also joined the bridal party.

Sarah's aunt Marie in Amsterdam, whom she'd never met, had sent her parents fine fabrics over the years. Her parents traded the fabric, which was in short supply in the colony, but her mother had stowed some bolts for special occasions. Sarah ran her hands over the dark blue silk skirt laid out on their table.

"*Maman,* this is too fine," Sarah told her mother.

"*Bof,* you should have seen what I wore to marry your father. All I had was my mother's old dress. I've saved this fabric for your wedding day. Don't you like it?"

"It's the most beautiful fabric."

"Then let's help you into it."

It took her mother and all six of her bridesmaids to help the skirt over Sarah's head and adjusted on the hooped *fardegalijn* that gave shape to the swathes of silk. Her ochre-colored silk stomacher created a long triangle down her front and displayed her bust in a low, rounded neckline, topped with a borrowed millstone ruff. Over it all, she wore a deep blue damask *vlieger* cape with matching sleeves.

"Only a *mevrouw,* a married woman, wears the *vlieger,*" her mother explained as she tied the sleeves to the cape.

Sarah knew her uncle was a silk merchant and her mother, although not a professional dressmaker, was a proficient enough seamstress to make her clothes. Yet Sarah imagined she had an ethereal benefactor, enchanting her in such finery.

Her mother secured the starched white *passement* lace-trimmed diadem cap atop her head. It radiated into elaborate pinnacles and framed her plaited blond hair in a halo. Sarah made it herself.

Her mother presented her with a chatelaine belt of dainty silver chains from which hung a pair of scissors, a knife in a leather sheath, a needle case, a silver-bound pincushion, and a pomander scent ball filled with lavender.

"The chatelaine holds everything you will need at hand as wife and lady of your own house," her mother told her, smiling proudly.

The church was the second story of the gristmill. It had a spartan interior and no spire. Some referred to it as "the Holy Barn." The juxtaposition with their humble venue only made Sarah's clothing look more radiant.

Hans wore a dark brown woolen doublet with voluminous sleeves, slashed to reveal his goldenrod chemise, accented with lace cuffs Sarah made for him as a wedding gift.

"In the Massachusetts colony, Hans's sleeves would get him banished for breaking the Sumptuary Laws," Phebe whispered to Sarah, with a smile.

Sarah stiffened. She knew Phebe meant it in jest, but it made her feel self-conscious. Sarah worried that someone would accuse her of dressing above her station. She held her head high, projecting the demeanor of a stately, proper lady even though her heart jittered as fast as hummingbird wings.

After the Domine Bogardus performed the sacraments, Sarah's bridesmaids sang Psalm 127. A tear streamed down Sarah's cheek, and Hans's rough palm brushed it away as he tenderly cradled her cheek in his hand.

Afterward, dozens of their neighbors and friends joined the celebrations hosted at the Rapalje home just down the street. Sarah heard Van Tienhoven held his own party that night, which the most affluent merchants and landholders attended, including his newly betrothed, Rachel Vigne. To Sarah's surprise, Director Kieft attended Sarah and Hans's wedding rather than Van Tienhoven's soiree.

The guests spilled between the Rapalje's and Hans's houses and partook in rich foods, spiced wine, beer, Dutch gin, and French brandy. A cinnamon-brown milch cow grazed, leashed to the front of Hans's house, adorned with garlands of dried blue cornflowers strung on straw.

"I made provisions in my lease of the Company's cows that my daughter would receive the first heifer calf," her father explained. "I have one more gift for you."

The wedding guests stroked the cow's nose and kissed it for good luck. Sarah's father took her hand.

"A person without money is like a wolf without teeth." Her father quoted the Walloon proverb as he fastened a bracelet on her wrist. It was made of three rows of alternating white and purple beads. "With this bracelet, you'll always have some teeth at the ready."

"*Papa*! Are these the *sewant* we made two winters ago?"

He nodded and squeezed her hand. She recognized the shell beads, used as currency in the colony, as the ones they had made together. They were so imperfect.

She fondly remembered that winter they spent cracking the white whelk and purple quahog clam shells, sanding shards into cylinders, and making holes with the bow drill. She had never heard her father curse so much as when he drilled holes in *sewant*. It had been their shared obsession that winter. Her mother wagered she'd make more profit in *passementerie* than their counterfeit *sewant*. Indeed, she had. She sold a set of lace cuffs to one of the wealthy *patroon* landholders and made as much as half a Company sailor's annual salary. That was the end of their *sewant*-making endeavor, and when Sarah began to learn lacemaking.

"And now a toast!" her father announced.

The guests raised glasses of *kandeel*, a celebratory cocktail made with cream, sack wine, eggs, sugar, and spices.

"My darling daughter, Sarah, and my new son, Hans... To love is not to only gaze into each other's eyes, it is to join your gazes on the horizon of your shared future. May you be blessed with children as sweet as you. May the fish jump into your canoe. May your roof be tiled with tarts. *Que Dieu vous bénisse*! I wish you every blessing!"

Everyone laughed and cheered at her father's jumble of French, Dutch, and invented proverbs.

"*Skål*!" Her mother shouted in Norwegian for her son-in-law and raised her glass. "Cheers!" Phebe shouted. "*Proost*!" Domine Bogardus chimed in, his speech already a bit slurred, the party having hardly started.

"Cheers to the couple!" Director General Kieft bellowed. "My wedding gift: To the eldest child of New Netherland, I shall be godfather to your first child." He gave a benevolent bow.

"*À votre santé*!" Joris hollered. "Let the dancing begin!" He signaled to the musicians waiting with string instruments, flute, and jaw harp.

Hans, joined by a man with a voluminous head of chestnut curls, approached Sarah and Phebe for a dance.

"Phebe, this is Nys. A good friend of mine," Hans said. "He has a bowery near the tobacco plantation I oversee."

"Hans helped me finish my house there, just in time for winter," Nys said.

"Are you going to have a housewarming?" Phebe asked, her lips loosened with the *kandeel*. She reddened as if she just realized she had spoken aloud.

"If you'll come visit, *ja*, I will," Nys replied with a smile.

Nys held his hand out to Phebe. She looked at Sarah for reassurance. Sarah urged her on with raised eyebrows and a smile. They spun away. Hans took Sarah by the waist and pulled her close.

"Dance with me," he whispered in her ear.

She melted into his embrace. He could have said jump into the river with me, and she would have. She twirled with Hans, glimpsing blurred snippets of her friends and family, enjoying the evening. Her cheeks hurt from smiling.

The party went on until dawn. Sarah, buoyant yet exhausted, watched the sunrise from the strand. Her bridesmaids, Sarina and Saartje, had gone home. Just Phebe, Nys, and some of Hans's friends were left. Sea lions began to bark on the island off in the distance in front of them and monstrous pelicans patrolled the water in between.

Sarah held Hans's hand as they stumbled back up Pearl Straat. Phebe walked ahead of her with Nys. She marveled at the growing coquettishness Phebe used on him as the night turned to dawn. They'd kissed at least twice, that Sarah saw.

Phebe said goodnight and opened the door of the Rapalje home. In her befuddled state, Sarah imagined she would follow her, and they'd whisper in their bunk about the night.

Hans held her hand tight and her body was jerked into remembering her new life. She was Hans's wife and would now live in his house. She felt silly that she hadn't anticipated this moment. What before had seemed like no change at all suddenly felt like a chasm to cross, even though his house was next to her childhood home.

Hans didn't give her a moment more to think about it. He swept her up, kicked his door open, and carried her to his bed. Their bed.

Sarah woke at midday after their wedding to find they had fallen asleep fully dressed. Hans still slept. She stripped down to her chemise and went back to bed. When she awoke, it was evening. Hans, dressed in his everyday attire, heated sausages on a pan over the hearth.

Sarah went to her trousseau that held all her worldly goods.

"Come here, Sarah." Hans called out. "Don't dress yet."

She strode to him, self-conscious in her thin linen chemise.

He put his arms around her, kissing her neck. His hands grazed over her. She breathed heavily into his hair as he continued to kiss her neck and decolletage. The sausage sputtered loudly on the pan and startled them both.

"Let's eat first," Hans said. Sarah nodded. She turned toward her trousseau and put on the linen skirt and stays she usually wore.

They ate, and Sarah felt more at home already. She rose to take Hans's plate to clean up. He pulled her onto his lap and kissed her.

"*Min kvinne mitt alt*," he whispered in Norwegian.

"What does that mean?" she asked.

"My woman, my everything."

He unlaced her stays and stood up with her to remove her skirt. She began to undress him, slowly opening the laces of his jerkin. They both stood, arms-length apart, in their linen undergarments for a moment.

Her mother spoke to Sarah before her wedding night about wifely things. Her mother explained there was a carnal conversation that happens between husband and wife that makes babies. Their Domine preached the importance of physical affection as the foundation for a Godly union, with fornication in abundance to provide the "Godly mortar." He also stated that the woman should enjoy and be satisfied as much as the man. Sarah had seen animals couple. She imagined the carnal conversation was something like that, but somehow more divine. Sarah let out a nervous laugh, unsure what to do next.

Hans smiled. He swept her up and carried her to his bed. He removed her chemise, slowly kissing her skin as it was unsheathed. His mouth on her skin exceeded any other pleasure.

Like the feel of kissing Hans's mustache, the culminating act wasn't as she'd imagined. It brought to her mind a tree struck by lightning: a thunderous, surprising burst that left a smoldering split. He held her close afterward with their legs entwined. His warm body encircled hers, comforting and protective. She radiated the heat of one who'd been touched by lightning.

The next morning, Sarah rose to milk their cow and churn the butter from yesterday's milk. They had a simple breakfast of bread and butter, and then Hans left for work at the shipyard.

Sarah was alone for the first time in her new home. She was unused to complete silence.

She put on her chatelaine and examined it, as if it would reveal some secret of being a *huisvrouw*. She inspected her trousseau. It held no answers either, unless clothing, bedding, table linens, and little sachets of herbs and spices were the keys to being a housewife.

Curiosity overtook her unease. First, she would inspect her new home. The layout was the same as her childhood home. The great room held an open-jamb hearth on the right, table to the left, with bench seating and two chairs. A *kast* held linens on the left wall. The *bedstee* was tucked behind stairs to the garret. The garret was bare except for extra bed rolls and straw pallets for guests. She peeked inside a trunk hidden in the corner. It held Hans's spare clothes. Breathing deeply, she smelled them. A bit musty, but mostly she smelled the cedar wood of the trunk. She made a note to check later if anything needed mending. Going back downstairs, she followed the length of the house to the back door. The back corridor was empty, except for a basket of whittled figurines of animals. She smiled at a little bear that looked like the one from the Shrovetide performance.

Exiting to the backyard, she meandered through the neglected kitchen garden to their cow grazing at the far end of the yard abutting the fort. Sarah observed earlier when she'd milked her that the kitchen garden was entering its dormant winter season. Not much tending was needed until spring. She'd have time to discuss with Hans what she would need to plant.

"Hallo, Cow. It's just you and me here. Are you lonely, too?" Sarah asked, wrapping her arm around the docile beast. "I should find a better name for you than Cow... How about Cinnamon, for your pretty brown coat?"

The cow chewed, ambivalent. She briefly looked at Sarah through her thick lashes before returning to graze. Sarah took that as her agreement with the name, and she returned to the house, feeling a minor task was accomplished.

Sarah appraised the interior again. The house did need tending. It was obviously the home of a bachelor. The valance curtain along the hearth was filled with soot. The floors needed sweeping, and the furniture needed dusting, and polishing. She didn't begrudge Hans for not wanting to polish furniture after coming home from a day of carpentry.

She looked for a broom or polishing oil but was at a loss. Distracted, she thought how she could make some nice rag rugs to make the place cozier. It also seemed to echo more because there were no herbs drying from the rafters. She decided to fetch supplies from her mother.

She felt sheepish returning home for help so soon, but it was too convenient to be stubborn about it. Maybe she could get Phebe and her sisters to come back with her to keep her company. She needed a break from the silence.

Chapter 5

1640

A few weeks later, during the first week of January, Sarah and Hans joined the Twelfth Night festivities at her parents' home. It was an eagerly anticipated occasion to gather family and friends mid-winter and a continuation of the New Year's festivities. They ate pancakes and waffles. Beer flowed liberally. There were stories and songs.

Her mother brought forth the king cake, and everyone took a portion, men from the left and women from the right, as was the tradition at Cat's Wheel.

"I will be queen this year!" Sarah's little sister Jannet declared as she destroyed the chewy, spiced honey cake to find the hidden bean that would grant her such honor.

"I'm the king!" Hans's friend, Nys, announced, proudly holding up his bean. Sarah's mother put a wooden bowl on his head as a crown. His curls matted down over his eyes. Cheers erupted at the ridiculous sight of him. He readjusted the hat with a cavalier tilt and shot his chin up to look more regal. "The king of misrule!"

Sarah laughed and searched her slice. Nothing but dried fruit dotted hers. She looked at Phebe, who delicately pinched the bean from her cake.

"Phebe's the queen!" Sarah shouted. Jannet groaned. Phebe paled at the attention, eyes wide like a spooked deer. Sarah's mother adorned Phebe with a pierced tin lantern whose bottom had fallen out. Phebe held it on her head as she bowed to the accolades with crimson cheeks. "I shall check the power of the king of misrule!" She shot a sly glance at Nys.

Sarah suddenly didn't feel well. She ran out the front door to retch into the snow.

"Are you ill?" her mother asked when she came inside. Everyone else held rapt attention to Hans telling a story.

"I have had bouts of stomach upset, but it passes," Sarah replied, overly cheery.

Her mother raised an eyebrow.

"You haven't had your monthly," her mother whispered as she looked at her knowingly. It wasn't a question.

Sarah didn't know the last time she had her monthly flux. Her cheeks burned. She worried her mother had inferred just how much Sarah had come to enjoy her and Hans's carnal conversations. They took pleasure in their union daily. It no longer felt like a lightning strike but reminded her more of Hans's carpentry, like the satisfaction of two staves joining, snugly slotted into position. Yet, she hadn't expected to be with child so soon. Sarah felt her mother's studying gaze, and the heat from her cheeks radiated to the tips of her ears. She was so warm, beads of sweat gathered on her upper lip. Her mother's expression vacillated from smug appraisal, to tender empathy, and finally a broad, proud smile.

A dizzy elation made Sarah's head swim. She was with child. Surely becoming a mother would solidify her adulthood, fill her quiet home with sounds of new life, give her a more significant purpose than to merely polish the furniture.

Her mother's smile boosted her confidence.

"You have your own hidden bean," her mother said as she rubbed Sarah's back. "I'm glad I know. I'll make you a tea to ease your roiling stomach. It will ease as the weeks go on."

Sarah's attention shifted to Hans, who was retelling the story of a tense encounter with the Weckquaesgeek, the Natives who inhabited the upper part of Manhattan, while he was overseeing his friend's tobacco bowery near Corlaers Hoeck.

"By the time I saw them, it was too late. The warriors were after me, with low whoops and high screeches at my heels. I climbed up a tree and tried to hide in the dense branches. They taunted me, threatening to let loose their tomahawks. I was defenseless, desperate, and sure I was in my final hour. I started singing '*In Mijn Grootste Nood O'Heere.*'"

Hans then sang the Dutch psalm, "In My Greatest Need O'Lord," for his audience. His voice was powerful and moving. It was so beautiful, tears streamed down Sarah's cheeks. Hans loved to tell the story of how his singing saved his life, placating the Natives and persuading them to leave him in peace. Sarah had heard the story countless times, same as everyone there. But her emotion was impossible to control as she thought of Hans singing to their baby.

Two days later, Phebe paid Sarah a visit while Hans was at the shipyard. Phebe eyed Sarah.

"You certainly look radiant, and not just the usual cheer you have when I visit."

"I'd say the same about you!"

"Well, I've happy news to share," Phebe said coyly.

"Me too! You go first!"

"Nys asked me to marry him," Phebe said, shyly beaming. "I said yes, of course."

"That's wonderful!" Sarah rushed to embrace her and kiss her cheeks in congratulations.

"Now your news…"

"I'm with child," Sarah whispered. Phebe gasped, embraced her, then put a hand to her belly.

"Well, at least you aren't so far along that you can't dance at my wedding and celebrate with me."

"When will it be?"

"Three weeks. As soon as the banns are proclaimed. Nys is in a hurry. I can scarcely believe the effect I have on him. He asked me not to touch him, not even his hand, in the next three weeks or he won't be able to wait to bed me."

Phebe's glow now blazed and she averted her eyes in embarrassment at divulging such a personal detail.

"How did your father react?"

"As you may guess. Gruff. That's why Nys is so perfect—he took no slight. Only proffered him more affable charm. It didn't take as long as I expected for my father to give his blessing."

Phebe's father was an odd fellow, even among New Netherlanders, who were made of similarly rough, beleaguering stock.

Three weeks later Sarah, engrossed in her bridesmaid duties, prepared Phebe for her wedding.

"This color suits you so well," Sarah told Phebe as she helped with plaiting and pinning her hair. Phebe wore a russet red silk dress, a wedding gift from Sarah's mother. "I've never seen you glow like this. I don't believe you're the same person as that pallid Puritan child who appeared at our tavern just a few years ago."

"That was a lifetime ago," she said wistfully. "Will you weave this into my hair?" She pulled a scarlet silk ribbon from her discarded apron. "If I'm to break Puritan Sumptuary Law without rebuke, I may as well gild the lily."

"There's certainly no law against flaunting finery here. You could wear my diadem cap, if you'd like," Sarah offered.

"No... this ribbon... my mother had a ribbon this exact color that she used as a bookmark in our family bible. I want to wear it... in memory of her."

"Of course," Sarah said. Phebe had told her that her mother and baby sister died on their sea voyage to Massachusetts. She gave Phebe a moment in her reverie before she tried to lighten the mood. "Do you know what Nys's wedding attire will be?"

"He has a black mock velvet doublet, but he spent most of his money on the biggest brimmed castor hat that he could find. He said it will be passed down by our children for generations—never mind that it cost a half of his year's earnings." She laughed before continuing in earnest. "He does look fine with it. It somehow balances that enormous cloud of curls."

Sarah finished weaving the ribbon through her hair. Sarah's mother joined them. They stepped out into the cold February air and set off for the church.

They met Phebe's father out front. Sarah greeted him. Old Jan did his best to clean up. He wore a dark brown wool doublet. He had cut his gray hair and beard short. On the few encounters she'd had with him, he had a much longer, scraggly beard. A woman with a pinched, dour face stood next to him.

Her father approached Phebe in a solemn, wistful mood.

"I didn't think I'd live to see this day, much less to give you away to a Netherlander," he said loudly, snorting, but then dropped his voice to a whisper. "I feared this day. I thought Master Coggeshall would marry you off to some zealot and I'd never see you again. I never told you, Phebe, some years before they'd let us go, I escaped. I went to the Natives and we were going to snatch you away. Imagine... we could be living amongst the heathens now! But then, half the Natives there died of the pox. So, I returned to that bastard, Coggeshall. I thought you and I would never get away… and yet we did. And I'm damn proud you're marrying a Netherlander and not a Puritan, nor a heathen."

"I'm Maria," the pinch-faced woman introduced herself to Sarah, as she strained to hear what Phebe's father said. Maria gestured to Phebe. "Phebe's stepmother."

Sarah knew Old Jan had recently married a widow. Phebe told Sarah she was glad her father had a companion. He had a cantankerous soul, but Maria could handle it. She reveled in bickering with their neighbors as much as Old Jan. Sarah wanted to hear what Old Jan was saying, but Maria prattled on.

Phebe didn't like to talk about her past in the Massachusetts colony, but shortly after Phebe started working at her parents' tavern, Sarah found her crying. Phebe explained the long story which led her and her father to New Amsterdam. Shortly after they'd arrived from England on the Winthrop Fleet, Phebe's father took corn and clapboards from their neighbors, claiming they'd had an agreement. Nevertheless, he was charged with thievery and sentenced to work as an indentured servant for a man named Coggeshall for three years. Phebe was indentured to the same man until she was of age to marry.

They were released early, just before Coggeshall was banished from the colony for being a supporter of the heretic, Anne Hutchinson. Anne was banished and forced to walk for days, pregnant and alone. Her child was born, deformed and stillborn. Phebe had heard the news of Anne's fate the day Sarah found her crying. Phebe said she had felt closer to God when she went to Anne's bible studies. She wondered how a woman who made her feel closer to God could have been bedeviled. Phebe worried she damned her own soul for revering Anne. She fixated on her damnation when she arrived in New Amsterdam, but she found solace in the Dutch Reformed Church, and the threats of the Puritans had slowly loosened their grip on her.

"It all turned out fine though, didn't it?" Phebe replied to her father, looking for his approval.

"Yes..." He stared off a moment and almost looked like he might have tears welling up, but stalwartly blinked them away. "Yes, fine."

By the following summer, Sarah's family and Hans resided mainly at their bowery farmhouses at the Waalebocht, across the East River. Hans staked his claim to the land north of her parents, where the farmland was fertile.

Hans had just finished building their home there. Staying there to tend the land was much more enjoyable in the hot summer months, and they would yield a good profit on the grains, corn, and other vegetables they grew. They rented out their home in New Amsterdam to transient traders for the summer and would return there in winter when the farm was barren and too desolate.

Mid-July, Sarah's belly was enormous. The baby was due any day. Nesting like a Dutch woman, Sarah polished the new wide plank floors because being on her hands and knees was the position she found most comfortable.

Plank floors were an incredible luxury in their new summer home. She showed gratefulness for the expansive pine planks with every swirl of linseed oil pressed and buffed into the grain.

Hans worked diligently to ready their new home, with the flooring and a *bedstee* box bed. Wood was plentiful in the colony, but the tools and skill of carpentry kept Hans in constant demand for his craftsmanship. It was difficult for him to finish personal projects.

The front door opened behind her. Hans was home. That morning, he left for work at the shipyard at Smits Vly, just across the river. He returned carrying a large object, wrapped in red duffel fabric.

"*Min kvinne mitt alt*," he said softly in Norwegian. "I finished making what you wanted."

She pulled off the cloth. It was the perfect bassinet. Made of cedar, it had two sturdy rocker feet, and a little canopy on one end, decoratively scalloped on the edges.

Warmed near the hearth, the cedar would smell heavenly.

"Hans… it's perfect." Her eyes welled up as she set it by their hearth.

"The baby can come now." Hans smiled. Sarah laughed nervously. She stood on her tiptoes to kiss him. He rubbed her belly, then pulled open the drawstring of her chemise. Her breasts were swollen, and they ached under Hans's tender massage.

"Will you lie down with me a moment to rest?" Sarah asked. He readily agreed, and they climbed into their *bedstee*. Sarah was so content to lie next to him, feeling the baby moving. But Hans's brow furrowed with worry.

"What troubles you?" She smoothed his brow with her thumb. His face softened.

"Nothing." He paused and sighed. "No matter to us, I hope. I saw Director Kieft giving orders to the soldiers. He said there was a group of Naraticong Natives who stole hogs from the De Vries bowery on Staaten Eylandt. Kieft is sending a company of one hundred soldiers, led by Van Tienhoven, to punish them."

"They might think Van Tienhoven to be one of the missing hogs." She immediately regretted her uncharitable comment. "I just feel sorry for Rachel Vigne." She meant she felt guilty that her refusal meant Rachel had to marry Van Tienhoven. Rachel's parents were Walloons that had lived in the colony as long as her parents. Sarah had been schoolmates with her, although Rachel was a few years older. Sarah didn't worry about the Naraticong. Her father had good relations with the Canarsie in their area. The Naraticong wouldn't dare attack their part of Lange Eylandt. Doing so would start a war with the Canarsie, too.

"Rachel's stepfather, Jan Damen, has been angling with his cronies in Kieft's ear as well. He prefers military action to diplomacy," Hans said. "I know Director van Twiller had his issues, but it was never violence with the Natives."

Sarah knew Hans and the former Director had come over on the same ship. Hans considered him a friend, so she said naught of what she'd heard about that spoiled, money-grubbing, incompetent drunk being far worse than Director Kieft.

"The former Director realized conflict wouldn't be as profitable as peace," Sarah said at last. "Let's hope we don't have to see that proven before it's believed by our new Director."

Sarah winced at a sharp spasm in her belly. She'd been having them for days, but it had been happening more frequently that day.

"What is it?" Hans asked, concerned.

"I don't know. Fetch my mother. She'll know," she said after the spasm relaxed.

"The baby is coming," Sarah's mother said. "Be patient. First babies take their time."

Her mother was at her side with Sarah's little sisters, Maria, Jannet, and Judith. Sarah benefited from seeing her mother give birth five times. She understood how it looked, but not what it felt like.

Every time her belly tightened, the pain came like a wave, threatening to never let her breathe again. Then she was above the wave, gasping for air before the next menaced to take her under. Night came, and the contractions fully took over her body. She writhed to escape the pain, her screams unconsciously sounding like "HAAAAANS" every time the pain was most intense.

The door opened. Her mother was in conversation with someone.

"*Bof*, are you sure? It's not usually done. But... out here, on our own... things are different. Joris attended Sarah's birth as well," her mother said.

Hans was suddenly at her side, concern in his eyes. He wiped the wet wisps of hair off her forehead. He was supposed to be at her parents' house, being distracted by her father's hunting stories. Husbands were not birthing attendants. She closed her eyes tightly as another wave came.

"*Min kvinne mitt alt*, were you calling for me? Do you need me?"

"HAAAAAANS!" she gasped.

Her mother helped her onto her hands and knees on the pallet on the floor. Catalyna showed Hans how to press on her hips to relieve the pressure.

"*Ja*, Hans. I need you. Keep... doing that."

"The baby will be here soon. The waves are coming quick. Not much longer," her mother said.

CHAPTER 6

1640

Catalyna had Hans flip a sheet over a rafter. She helped Sarah stand. "Hang on to this, Sarah. Hans is behind to support you."

Sarah wore one of Hans's chemises, her legs mostly exposed, half crouched, clinging to the bed linen.

Hans cried out as Sarah felt the warm liquid stream down her legs. She looked at her mother, alarmed.

"That's good, almost there," her mother said, sopping up the birthing fluid with wads of linen.

Sarah's sisters stood ready with hot water and clean cloths, softly offering encouragement.

"Hans, do you want to catch the baby or hold Sarah?" Catalyna asked him.

"Hold Sarah," he said quickly and decisively.

Sarah clung to the sheet and bit into it. She screamed, her mouth full of linen, so it was muffled, "I can't do this. It's too much pain. I am bleeding. I will die."

One more wave of exertion and the floodgates of what held her together popped open. She worried all her organs would flow out. Relief abruptly followed. Her mother brought the baby into view. It wailed with new life, indignant to leave the warm, dark interior of Sarah. Her mother wiped the baby clean. It was a girl with Hans's deep blue eyes and white wisps of blond hair like corn silk.

Sarah took her baby, both of them bloodied and crying, still attached by the cord. Her mother guided her to lie on the pallet and helped the baby latch on to Sarah's breast. Sarah felt sweet relief flow through her body until another wave came.

"That's good, Sarah. Here comes the *arrière-faix*, and then you're done," her mother said.

Passing the afterbirth was not as painful, but Sarah winced as her mother pressed her abdomen to ensure it was entirely expelled.

"What is *that*?" Hans asked as Sarah's mother placed the organ in some linen and prepared to tie off and cut the cord linking their baby to it.

"It was the baby's first bassinet. The red is vibrant. That means your baby is strong."

Sarah was overwhelmed with emotion, watching her daughter's deep, dark blue eyes as she nursed. Those remarkably alert eyes surprised Sarah, but as she nursed they closed. Sarah looked at the mass of tissue her mother and Hans spoke of. From her vantage point, she thought that it looked like a birch tree. The cord was stark white and wound its way into branches that were held together by a thin membrane. The tree was cut by her mother, and her baby was left with a stump at her navel.

"It will fall off in a few days, and you may need to apply some of the calendula tallow salve to the navel."

Sarah's attention returned to her baby's eyes as her daughter's drowsy lids fluttered and shut. Sarah felt herself relaxing, her body begging for sleep. She looked to Hans. He held the baby's tiny fingers in his enormous palm. There were tears in his eyes.

"You did it, Sarah. You're a mother. Well done, *ma petite*," her mother said. "We will leave you in peace with Hans and your daughter. Get some rest. She will awake with hunger again soon enough." Her mother shooed her other daughters toward the door.

"*Merci, Maman.* You are now a *grand-mère*!" Sarah called out. Her mother beamed with pride, blew a kiss, and shut the door.

One week later, they traveled back across the river for the baptism of Aneken Hansen Bergen at the church in New Amsterdam. It was a sultry, warm day, and Sarah wished she could remain half nude with her baby at the Waalebocht instead of wearing her Sunday best. But it was an event that needed to happen. Director General Kieft sponsored as godfather and Sarah's mother as godmother.

"For my goddaughter," the Director said as he handed an oblong box to Sarah and Hans. It was about the length of Hans's hand. Hans opened the small silver swing clasp to find a beautiful silver spoon nestled in pink silk.

"We're so honored. Thank you," Sarah said.

"She's a fine daughter of New Amsterdam." He smiled, gazing at Aneken. "May she be the first of many children!"

"That was very kind of him," Hans said to Sarah once the Director turned away to speak with Sarah's parents. They were in serious discussion immediately, but Sarah's thoughts focused on Aneken.

Sarah's throat tightened and her eyes gleamed. Her emotions were like a knife on a honing block, sharpened against the harsh demands of mothering. The days and nights had blurred together. As an eldest child, comforting a baby was second nature, yet mothering was far different from being a big sister. She never slept more than an hour, interrupted by endless cycles of nursing and changing soiled clouts. There were times she should have slept but was too enraptured examining Aneken's perfect, tiny features.

After the baptism, Sarah and Hans walked to their home on Pearl Straat. Aneken fell asleep along the way. Once home, Sarah laid her in the bassinet. Sarah had thought it was unnecessary that they brought it for the trip to town, but now she was happy to have it. She hoped Aneken would sleep long enough for her to pack a few things to take back to their Waalebocht home.

"Sarah, don't pack. We aren't returning to the Waalebocht. We're going to stay here," Hans told her.

"Why?"

"It's out of caution for you and Aneken. I can't go to work at Smits Vly and leave you and Aneken alone at the Waalebocht. It's too isolated and dangerous."

"It's fine, Hans. I can take care of myself and Aneken. My parents' house there isn't very far away."

"*Nee.* Your father and I spoke. They aren't returning either. Van Tienhoven's campaign against the hog thieves went badly. The soldiers killed the Naraticong *sachem*, among others. The *wilden* retaliated and attacked boweries on Staaten Eylandt and Pavonia. They're negotiating peace talks now, but Kieft insists they pay him a tribute of corn. Other tribes are angry about the corn tribute, too. I won't endanger you and Aneken. We're staying here."

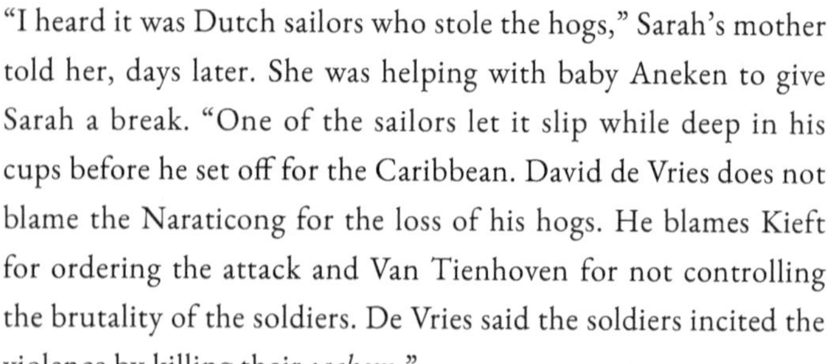

"I heard it was Dutch sailors who stole the hogs," Sarah's mother told her, days later. She was helping with baby Aneken to give Sarah a break. "One of the sailors let it slip while deep in his cups before he set off for the Caribbean. David de Vries does not blame the Naraticong for the loss of his hogs. He blames Kieft for ordering the attack and Van Tienhoven for not controlling the brutality of the soldiers. De Vries said the soldiers incited the violence by killing their *sachem*."

"Was his bowery on Staaten Eylandt among those attacked...?"

"*Oui.* They killed four farmhands," her mother said. "Somehow, De Vries has established a tentative peace. He's always had Natives peacefully staying on his bowery when they'd come to trade. He's been a friend to them. I'm shocked that the Natives killed his farmhands. If only they let De Vries handle things instead of Van Tienhoven..."

Sarah felt fatally exhausted from Aneken's incessant needs enmeshed with anxiety over a possible war. This is adulthood, she realized. The bitter revelation turned her yearning fire to ashes. Her mother read her mind.

"Sarah, you and Aneken will have an easier life than I had when you were a baby. You were born on the dirt floor of our dugout lodge at Fort Orange. A rag rug and a bearskin were the most advanced degree of comfort we had. And then we were ordered to leave it all behind and start over on Manhattan because of violence with the Natives. Your father and I had peacefully traded with the Mohicans and Mohawks. We owed our survival to both tribes, but they were at war against one another. A Company commander joined a Mohican attack against the Mohawks and was killed," her mother explained. "There are always men who are eager to wage war. But we survived, and you're in a much better situation than we were. You'll protect your family when you need to. Don't let it steal the joys of motherhood from you. It's hard enough to be a new mother. It gets easier. Don't worry, *ma petite.*"

"How did they convince you to leave and start over again?"

"I was coming back from the fields because you were wailing with hunger. As I approached our home, there was an unfamiliar Company man coming out with a corn biscuit in his mouth, the last scrap of food I had prepared. I drew my knife and called him a thief. He explained he was the new Director, Pierre Minuit. He came with news we must move to Manhattan. I was outraged! Then he offered to give me a cow for the stolen biscuit—and land for it to graze."

"That was Mabelle?" remembering their old heifer.

"*Oui*, but I said a cow downriver wouldn't cease your wailing at that moment. He offered to help make more biscuits. By the time they were ready, your father had returned from the fields. Director Minuit convinced us to abandon the crops we had planted in exchange for a cow and clapboard house. I always wonder how different our colony would be if Pierre Minuit was still our director. He knew how to make proper treaties with the Natives."

Sarah marveled, imagining Catalyna as a young new mother, like her. Strong-willed and fierce, like Sarah wanted to be.

Part Two: Safety

1641–1653

What did we once glimpse with our eyes
staring at the hearth, its slow-burning coal?
Visions of life – forever lost to us.

– Rainer Maria Rilke –
"Sonnets to Orpheus"
Translated by Martyn Crucefix
Part 2, Number 2

Chapter 7

1641

Sarah didn't return to the Waalebocht the rest of the summer or harvest season. But the following spring, peace held with the Naraticong. They were able to plant their fields across the river. Sarah, Hans, and one-year-old Aneken spent much of their summer there, only returning to town for Sunday Mass.

In late August, they began to return to New Amsterdam more often with the first harvests of corn, squash, and beans. They loaded Hans's shallop and stopped at the Rapalje bowery to add her father's early harvest to their transport. He joined them on their crossing.

"This sweltering day makes me tempted to swim across," her father joked, fingertips skimming the water.

"Hans and I have swum in Remegakonck Kil every day to cool off. The rains and heat have been good for the crops at least," Sarah told her father.

Being out on the water was almost as enjoyable as a dip in the creek. A cool breeze caressed the back of Sarah's neck. Aneken chortled at the occasional surprise of spray when a wave hit the hull.

"See how the Director spends Company coin?" Her father nodded toward the large timber-frame building with brick edifice on the southern shore of Manhattan. "A tavern before we even have a proper church built."

"Joris, you're just worried the City Tavern will steal away your customers," Hans said. "You've got your regulars that come through during the fur season."

They moored at the pier. Her father stayed with the boat while Hans went to retrieve their cart to transport the crops, accompanied by Sarah and Aneken. Before they reached home, they could see people gathering in the street by the fort.

"I don't want to keep your father waiting. I'm going to fetch the cart. Go see what all the fuss is about," he told Sarah.

She saw her oldest friend, Sarina Du Trieux, and waved to her.

"Sarah! I have so much to tell you!" Sarina said as they met and kissed each other's cheeks. "Do you want the happy or sad news first?"

"Happy," Sarah replied, unsure.

"I'm betrothed! To Isaac de Forest!"

Sarina and Isaac both came from well-regarded Walloon families. Sarah's parents credited Isaac's father, Jessé, for organizing their passage to New Netherland.

"That's wonderful!" Sarah paused. "What's the bad news?"

"You know the old tavernkeeper, Claes Swits? He was murdered by a young Weckquaesgeek man." Sarina's face turned solemn. "Director Kieft ordered Isaac's uncle to go to the Weckquaesgeek and demand they turn over the murderer. He's just returned. Their *sachem* refused. They claim the young man's kinsmen were killed by New Netherlanders fifteen years ago. They say it was an honor killing and justice has been served."

"Claes Swits killed his kinsmen? That's impossible. The only thing Claes could be guilty of is talking someone to death."

"I agree. It couldn't have been Claes, but maybe he looked like one of the men?" Sarina offered, puzzled. "Everyone is speculating, wondering if Kieft will send his soldiers against the Weckquaesgeek. They're worried it will be like the Pig War. If the soldiers attack, then more New Netherland boweries will be burned in retaliation."

"Poor Claes. What madness," Sarah lamented. "I hope this news doesn't rob you of joy in your betrothal. Isaac is a good man."

"I hold joy and worry in the same hand. Isaac's bowery is north, in Weckquaesgeek territory. He's building a house there with a palisade. We won't be married until it's finished."

The next day, Director General Kieft ordered the residents of New Amsterdam to the fort.

"We meet here today because a *wilden* brazenly slew an innocent Christian," the Director bellowed, his voice coarse with outrage. "The murderer's tribe has refused justice for Claes Swits. I propose we form a council to discuss the matter and determine a course of action. I leave it to you to suggest who among you should serve. Secretary Van Tienhoven will record your nominations. I will choose twelve men from among the nominees."

They formed a line to Van Tienhoven, who sat with rag paper and quill at an absurdly ornate desk in the fort yard. When Sarah and Hans reached the head of the line, she shuffled forward. She was reluctant to square up to the man she had spurned, but resolved to stand by Hans. Van Tienhoven's chin shot up and his eyes narrowed. She bowed her head to him.

"Out of curiosity, who would you vote for, Sarah Rapalje? Surely a young woman cannot comprehend such things." He laughed, snorting at her, just like a pig.

"I'm old enough to be a wife and mother," she said. "I would nominate Joris Rapalje."

"Your father? Very well. You aren't the first. I expected a foolish choice, like your husband."

Hans smiled down at Van Tienhoven and cast a vote for Sarah's father. Van Tienhoven ticked the paper next to Joris's name.

Van Tienhoven consulted with the Director before announcing the twelve men.

Sarah heard her father's name, and she let out her breath in relief. The fact that Director Kieft had formed a council impressed her, as it had never been done before. She was surprised that the men selected were a fair representation of their settlement, not simply the wealthy *patroon* landholders.

That evening, Sarah and her mother eagerly awaited Joris's return and news about the first council meeting. They held their breath as he entered, threw himself down into his chair, and wiped his face with his hand.

"Kieft plainly wants war and expected us to simply back his decision. I don't know if some of these men are intentionally blind or just stubbornly daft, but several are of the same mind as Kieft. To damnation with the consequences of a war—they welcome bloodshed. Part of me thinks they don't care if it's Native blood or ours. The sorrowful thing is, they say it's justice for Claes Swits, but they're just using his death as an excuse to show superiority and execute Natives so they can have more land."

Her mother brought him his favorite drink, peppermint tea. She was uncharacteristically silent as she waited for him to continue.

"There are sensible men on the council, though many of us are afraid to speak too freely in opposition," he said, pausing to sip his tea and sigh. "Actually, I think we triumphed because the majority did not agree with war. We'll delay further. Maybe with time they'll see the peril in the undertaking."

Sarah let out her breath. She was proud of her father. She twirled the beads on her bracelet, as she always did when she was deep in thought. Occasionally, her father's morals were gray, like when they spent one winter's doldrums making those beads from shells to make counterfeit *sewant*. He only gambled during Shrovetide, only drank to excess on Twelfth Night, and he never resorted to violence to solve a problem.

She wondered, had it been the verdant naïveté of childhood, or was life in the colony actually simpler when she was a child? When her parents were her age, they were living through the Dutch Revolt during the oppressive Spanish occupation of their homeland. They found freedom here though. She thought about the Natives before European arrival. She learned from Weenji that they also warred against one another. Weenji's people were forced to give tribute to stronger, more aggressive tribes. Perhaps war was a normal part of life no matter where or who you were? That didn't make it any easier to abide by the idea of it.

She looked at her daughter. Aneken, absorbed in rolling an apple on the uneven floor, was blissfully unaware of the adults' concerns. Sarah was not the child anymore. She was the mother and would shape the life her daughter would remember. How much had worries like this burdened her mother when Sarah was little?

Aneken's apple rolled into the jamb-less hearth, next to where Catalyna had bread baking in the Dutch oven surrounded and topped in coals. Sarah swept Aneken into her arms as her daughter dangerously inched toward the coals to retrieve her apple. That jolted Sarah out of reflection, and she realized she must get home to prepare their evening meal. She didn't have time for such reflective pondering. She had things to do.

The Twelve Men continued to meet with Kieft over the next few months. To Kieft's growing frustration, the council would not agree to attack the Natives. Attempts were made to track down Claes Swits murderer, but his fellow tribesmen would not hand him over.

On a bitterly cold dawn in December, Sarah was summoned by Nys. Phebe was in distress and due to give birth. Sarah called on her mother to come as well.

"Go, keep my husband and Hans company. Your wife will be well cared for," Sarah's mother told Nys after they arrived.

"You don't need anything?" Nys asked.

"No," resounded from Phebe, Sarah, and Catalyna. Sarah's mother pushed Nys out the door into the harsh, freezing day.

Sarah was glad her mother hadn't pushed Hans away during Aneken's birth, but Nys was a different sort of man under pressure. Sarah laughed to herself that they all knew he'd nervously talk too much and be a frustrating distraction to Phebe in her birthing.

"It began last night. It woke me from a dream of my mother. At first it was a good dream. I could smell the earthy, floral scent of meadowsweet she wore in a sachet at her waist. She held me, but I couldn't find her face. I was shrouded in a curtain of my mother's hair. I wanted so badly to see her face again. I swept the hair away with my fingers, but I couldn't find the edges. It became seaweed that tangled around my wrists, waist, and ankles. I was underwater. I tried to scream, but nothing came out. I awoke to a seizing pain that started from my belly and dug into my back."

"It was your body telling you the baby is coming," Sarah's mother said, palms gently pressing Phebe's belly to check the baby's position.

"It's scary at first, but the pains will form a rhythm like waves in the ocean. The seaweed is not tying you down. You need to be like the seaweed. Flow in the waves, but be anchored deep in the sea floor," Sarah told her friend.

Sarah's mother made Phebe an herbal tea that eased the pain a little. Sarah brought a bone broth soup with bread and butter for dinner. It was slow cooked for hours with herbs and vegetable scraps. During the end of Sarah's pregnancy, dipping the bread in the broth was the only thing she could eat without having the vile burn of her stomach creep up her throat, since growing a babe left little room for digestion. Phebe was shaking with nerves, but the food and tea made her relax.

"Rest. Your waves are still far apart. It will take some time, and you will need strength for later," Catalyna told her.

"I'm afraid to sleep. I'm afraid my mother is pulling me to her, lying at the bottom of the ocean." Phebe said. "Am I going to die?"

"No," Sarah whispered, lying next to her in bed.

"Every woman asks that every time they give birth," Catalyna said drowsily from Nys's chair. It wasn't an answer, but there was comfort in comradery.

The ground had been bare when they arrived, but in the morning the snow piled so high against the door that they couldn't open it. Sarah tensed upon the realization there was no way they could call the midwife, if needed, but she was sure her mother was as good as a midwife and everything would be fine.

Phebe's waves of birthing pains came faster by midday. She prayed and screamed oaths in English. She apologized to Sarah and Catalyna as soon as the pain passed and asked for God's forgiveness.

"It's all right," Sarah said. She held Phebe's hand through the waves. Phebe squeezed so hard, Sarah wanted to scream too.

Sarah's mother moved Phebe from her bed to the birthing stool she brought. It was low to the ground and had a hole in the middle. Her mother placed a basin underneath. As Phebe sat down, waters and blood streamed out.

Despite the long labor and the frightful winter storm, Phebe's baby girl arrived in great health. She had a ferocious cry and an immediate penchant for suckling. Once she had the birth grease and blood wiped clean and dry, it was apparent she had Nys's headful of curls.

Nys arrived that evening. He dug out the snow to free the door. Catalyna and Sarah made sure he warmed himself thoroughly by the fire before he held his daughter.

"I'll return tomorrow with some soup that will strengthen you and your milk supply," Sarah's mother said to Phebe as she kissed her forehead in farewell. "Nys, make sure she has a small bit to eat every few hours. And if you eat any of her soup, may the Lord deign to give you paps, and you can help suckle the babe."

Nys chortled, not taking his eyes off the baby.

"I'll bring you some soup, so you're not tempted," Sarah said.

"Thank you. Take the snowshoes outside the door, else it'll take you until dawn to get home," Nys said.

Sarah returned home to find Hans smoking a pipe by the fire. The relief on his face when she walked through the door warmed her heart.

"I missed you. I was worried about the storm... Is Phebe...?"

"All's well. They have a fine baby girl named Jannet." Sarah smiled. "I missed you too. Where's Aneken?"

"She's playing with your sisters next door."

"What did I miss while I was away?"

"We tried to keep Nys distracted at Cat's Wheel. We played trictrac. It went well for a while until Maryn and Jochem came in. Your father couldn't help himself. He had to vent his frustrations with their council meetings. That turned into some arguing."

"What did they say?"

"Everyone wants justice for Claes Swits, but your father and Jochem are against siding with Kieft's plan to show force. They brought up good points. There are a lot more *wilden* than settlers. Maryn's of a mind to side with Kieft and Jan Damen. I've known the man for a long time. I think he owes some debts to Jan Damen, so I think he'll need to side with him."

"What do *you* think?"

"I think it was a sad and horrible end for such a kind-hearted fellow. Claes deserves justice."

"Does justice mean killing more innocent people to find the murderer?" Sarah narrowed her eyes at him.

"I'm not saying burn the murderer's village, like some want. Intimidation. Show them their place."

"What is their place? They're our neighbors who share their land with New Netherlanders. One of theirs killed an innocent man. How many Netherlanders are here because, back home, they'd be in jail?"

"If we do nothing, it means Natives can kill anyone who looks like someone who wronged them. My thoughts are on keeping our family safe. I'm not willing to fight over this. I missed you—don't make me regret that," he said with a smirk and open arms.

She went to him and melted into his embrace. She felt safe wrapped in his arms, and she let her heavy head drop into the crook of his neck. Unease and quarrelsome thoughts still pricked at her, but she tried to push the worries away.

CHAPTER 8

1643

A year passed, the conflict with the Natives at a stalemate. Sarah gave birth to their second daughter, Rebecca in July. Her new baby and precocious toddler distracted Sarah too much to have time for worries about the conflict anymore. She only remembered when she overheard her father's complaints.

Joris had argued and dissuaded against Kieft's war plans for the past year and a half with the Council of Twelve Men. They tried putting forth issues other than attacking the Natives, like improving streets and proposing new wells.

Last week, in early February, Kieft disbanded the council and forbade them from meeting. Her father told her he supposed Kieft was giving up on the council, but not on war.

Catalyna and Hans returned from the baptism of Sarah's first nephew, her sister Maria's baby. Sarah's mother entered with her brow furrowed, shaking her head. Sarah was supposed to have been her nephew's godmother, but she, Aneken, and six-month-old Rebecca had the winter sickness. The ill humors would not stop flowing from their noses, so it was prudent Sarah stayed home with them. Catalyna and Hans had been the baptismal sponsors.

"*Maman*, are you cross with me for not going? The girls have been clinging to me in such bad tempers. I applied the poultice that you made to their chests and gave them the valerian tincture. It eased them enough to sleep for now."

"*Non, ma petite*... Adrienne Cuvelier has lost her wits," Sarah's mother said.

Adrienne was Rachel Vigne's mother and among the first Walloon settlers with her parents. Sarah knew her mother's opinion of Adrienne changed when she married Jan Damen after her first husband died. She allowed him to evict all of her children from his house, which forced her daughter, Rachel, to marry Van Tienhoven. Adrienne's husband was part of the Twelve Men with Sarah's father. He was in the minority who wished to attack the Weckquaesgeek.

"The woman rudely distracted from the baptism," Hans said.

"Adrienne was raving at the back of the church," her mother explained. "She kept saying, 'Lord, smite them. Drag them to the deepest caverns of Hell' and other spiteful prayers. After the ceremony, I went to speak with her. She barely recognized me. I took pity on her and told her I would help her home. But then she told me we must pray for the vanquishment of the *wilden* who infect the land and that an attack was imminent. She refused to leave."

"What has her so agitated? What attack?"

"She lost herself once like that before, when we lived at Fort Orange. A group of Company men from our fort joined a Mahican attack against the Mohawk. Adrienne heard rumors the Mohawk had killed and eaten the Netherlanders. A frightful tale. She raved similarly then, but I cannot guess the cause of her current madness."

A week later, Sarah awoke to the most horrific, yet faint, sounds of hell. She tried to reason that it was merely the shrill screams of coyote pups fighting over the evening meal their mother brought home.

But no, there were the distinct booms of gunfire. She felt beside her. Hans wasn't there.

Every hair on her body stood up and her stomach cramped.

She quickly shuffled to light a candle from the dying fire. Aneken and Rebecca were still sleeping on their trundle bed beside their parents' *bedstee*. The tightening fear in her chest relaxed just a little. The horrific screams and booms continued, though.

Sarah took their iron fire poker to use as a weapon. She smelled tobacco smoke, so she went to the door and cracked it open tentatively.

"Hans?" Sarah whispered.

"*Ja.*" He sat on their stoop, nervously sucking on a pipe. She stepped outside and closed the door quickly, so as not to let the grotesque noises into the house. "Are the children still asleep?" he asked with concern knit across his brow.

"Yes, but what is that dreadful noise?" Sarah asked urgently, as if knowing would make it stop. The screams and gunfire came from multiple places. It resounded off the hills, making it more difficult to discern. An eerie glow of a massive fire reflected onto the low clouds in the night sky. Its origin seemed to be across the river.

"Director Kieft ordered an attack against the *wilden* encampment at Corlaers Hoeck and... looks like Pavonia."

"An attack? Why? How do you know?"

"David de Vries just ran by to the strand. He was helping two Natives that escaped the attack at Corlaers Hoeck."

"What do we do?"

"Go inside and comfort the children if they wake. I'll keep watch out here tonight." He rose, and she saw he had his rapier and firelock with him. He put his arms around her, kissed her forehead, and pushed her back inside.

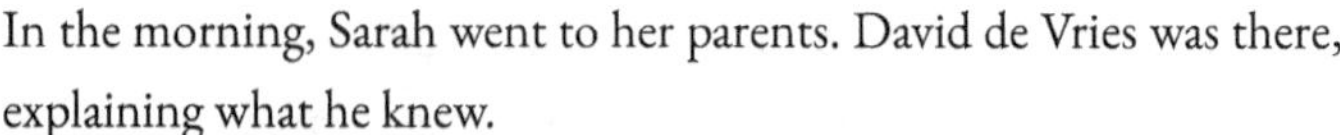

In the morning, Sarah went to her parents. David de Vries was there, explaining what he knew.

"I told Kieft, 'You will also murder our own nation, for none of the settlers in the open country are aware of the danger this will cause afterward,'" he explained, eyes bloodshot from lack of sleep. "One couple escaped and came to the fort. They asked us for help because they thought it was the Mohawk that had pursued them. I put them off in a canoe to Lange Eylandt for safety," De Vries said, shaking his head. "God help them."

"Kieft is so damned wrong that this could be justice for Claes Swits or that this could solve problems with the Natives. This massacre could easily unite all the disparate tribes against us," her father said.

"This morning the soldiers returned, boasting of what they'd done. What they recounted would move a heart of stone." He looked to Sarah's younger siblings. "I won't repeat what they said in this company, but it was brutal and indiscriminate of women and children. The soldiers were proud of this, and Kieft congratulated them on their Roman valor! Some Natives sought shelter with farmers near Corlaers Hook... It's just unspeakable... worse could never happen!"

"What horror, so ruthlessly inflicted," Sarah's mother said, eyes wide and unfocused.

"This has gone much too far already. I'm writing to the States General to enumerate Kieft's rash and dangerous governance. I will plead for his removal. The Company board members won't listen, but perhaps they will when the highest powers in government get involved," De Vries said.

David de Vries was a *patroon*, a large stakeholder in the Company. His bowery had already been laid to waste during the Pig War. Sarah hoped he had enough influence that they would listen. Letters would take months to have any effect, whereas the Natives' reaction to the massacre could be immediate.

Sarah worried about Phebe. Nys's bowery and their home was near Corlaers Hoeck. Most of all, she worried for Sarina, living far north on the island after her marriage to Isaac de Forest. They had a palisade fence, but that was hardly impervious to attacks.

"Sarah, come to the fort," Hans instructed. "They've posted the petition that prompted the attack."

Her mother and father greeted her on the street. Hans and Joris couldn't read, and Sarah was more proficient than her mother. They needed her, and she burned to read it.

"Aneken, go next door and help your aunts. They're making cinnamon bread," Sarah's mother instructed. Sarah carried Rebecca and started toward the fort.

They saw people gathering at the southeastern bastion, where a wheat-pasted broadsheet attracted everyone's attention.

Sarah carefully read aloud, "The whole of the freemen respectfully represent that though heretofore much innocent blood was spilled by the *wilden* without having had any reason or cause therefore, yet your Honors made peace on condition that the *sachems* should deliver the murderer into our hands (either dead or alive), wherein they have failed up to the present time, the reputation which our nation hath in other countries has thus been diminished, even notwithstanding innocent blood calleth aloud to God for revenge; we therefore request your Honors to be pleased to authorize us to attack the *wilden* as enemies, whilst God hath delivered them into our hands for which purpose we offer our persons. This can be effected at one place by the freemen and at the other by the soldiers, Your Honor's Subjects, Signed Maryn Adriaensen, Jan Damen, Abraham Verplanck, under the authority of Cornelis van Tienhoven."

"The whole of the freemen? God's blood! The liars!" Sarah's father shouted. She could count on two hands all the times she'd ever heard her father curse, and they were mostly when making *sewant*. She'd never heard him take God's name in vain in public, nor shouting slanderous accusations.

"They signed this on Shrove Tuesday!" someone shouted. "Likely lost in their cups!"

"These men saw the Natives sheltered nearby as an offering of revenge from God?" Sarah asked no one in particular as she tried to discern the signatories' logic. "Is the murderer of Claes Swits even among those killed? Surely the women and children of that man's tribe were innocent."

"The murderer would have thought twice before he killed Claes if he knew it meant his whole village would die for it." Hans said.

Sarah stared at Hans, speechless and horrified. Did he really think slaughtering a village would dissuade violence?

A few weeks after the massacres, Sarah sat with the women and children at the new proper church that Director Kieft had finally erected. It was still spare and unassuming, but built of stone, and didn't smell like a barn. Sarah missed the smell of the freshly milled grain. She had thought it was inextricable that God and grain were linked as givers of life.

The only scent in the church was the heavy scent of smoke. A constant companion throughout the settlement. The Natives burned boweries following the massacre in Pavonia and Corlaers Hoeck.

Displaced families surrounded her in the church. The only clothing they owned still reeked of their burnt houses and crops. A growing number of people, with nowhere else to turn, sought refuge at the fort. The smell of smoke only grew stronger daily.

Sarah struggled not to involuntarily wrinkle her nose at the stench, lest she offend her displaced neighbors. She shifted Rebecca on her lap and held her tighter as she returned her focus to the sermon. Domine Bogardus's past few services used his pulpit to defend Maryn. Director Kieft blamed the Shrove petition on him, as he'd been the first to sign. Last week, Maryn charged into Kieft's quarters and tried to shoot him, but he was disarmed and arrested. The next day, one of Maryn's servants tried at the task his *baas* had failed. He was shot and killed. His head hung from the gibbet at the southern tip of the island. Maryn was sentenced to face trial in *Patria* for his assassination attempt.

"... Maryn Adriaensen will return triumphant!" the Domine shouted as soldiers started to drum right outside the church. The church was located within the fort, so at first Sarah wasn't surprised to hear drums.

The din quickly overtook the sanctuary, and Sarah could feel the spite in it. Director Kieft was attempting to drown out the Domine.

"If Kieft will not behave himself, I will give him such a shake from the pulpit as would make him tremble like a bowl of jelly!" Domine Bogardus cried out above the discordant clamor.

How childish, Sarah thought, disappointed. These men are the leaders of our community and yet they comport themselves like bickering children.

Chapter 9

1643

Sarah kneaded the dough with vitriolic gusto. She punched it down so hard, her fist hit through to the table. Hans had just told her he signed a petition to attack the Lange Eylandt Canarsie. The cosigners of the petition had wealthy *patroon* connections. One was his *baas* at the shipyard. Under normal circumstances, Sarah could see why he'd be hitching his wagon to theirs, but not when it meant jeopardizing the safety of their bowery.

"I'm trying to keep us safe. It may be a gamble... but my friends have persuaded me it is a reasonable action to protect our boweries," Hans said, determined, but a slight hesitation showed he was not wholly clear of conscience.

Rebecca wailed. Sarah slapped the overworked dough into a bread trough and picked Rebecca up to nurse her.

"Your desire for powerful friends will lead to our ruin. Don't you understand you can't just frighten the Natives into submission, and you can't kill them all? Do you forget Wunita, Weenji, and Cholena? They have always been friends to us."

"Perhaps friends to you, but do you forget I was chased up a tree, fearing for my life? Haven't you ever been afraid of them?"

Rebecca's mouth popped off the pap, and she wailed when they raised their voices.

"*Nee*. Not our Canarsie neighbors. They weren't the Natives who chased you up a tree," Sarah said, quietly resolute.

They stewed in silence, distractedly watching two-year-old Aneken play with corn husk dolls she'd received from Weenji.

Eventually, Rebecca nodded off and Sarah transferred her to the cradle Hans made.

Sarah switched tactics and softened. She was tired of fighting. The dough made, Rebecca fed and napping, Sarah just wanted to be comforted. She went to Hans and sat on his lap, the bosom of her dress still open.

"Promise me you won't go if Kieft authorizes to attack. You can't put yourself in harm's way. You can't leave me and the girls alone to face the retribution," Sarah pleaded while she kissed his neck. Her seduction distracted from the forced promise, and he agreed.

Sarah sought her father that evening. She found him in her family's storehouse. He was just standing there, lost in thought.

"*Papa*?" She startled him. "Are you busy?"

"*Ma petite puce*! What brings you by?"

"I'm troubled by a petition Hans signed. He joined Van Couwenhoven asking Kieft for approval to attack Lange Eylandt tribes, preemptively."

"I've heard." His brow furrowed like a hatchet had struck between his eyes, up his forehead. "I went to the Waalebocht today with gifts for Wunita to reaffirm our friendship. I asked if he'd talk to *sachem* Penhawitz. Tell him not all *Swanneken* want war. Remind him that the people at Remegakonck Kil have been their friend and lived peaceably for many years."

"What did he say?"

"Wunita didn't take the gifts. He said he had to talk to his *sachem* first. He told me I should go to my *sachem* and ask that they spare the Canarsie of Keschaechquereren village."

"Will you go to Kieft?"

"I would... but since I did not do his bidding as a council member... he's not going to listen to me."

"I'm sorry Hans signed that petition," Sarah apologized, but her father was lost in thought, staring at the crocks of dried beans, corn, grains, pickled vegetables, jams, and smoked meats.

"I love our home and land there. The dark rich loam, the prairies, the creek, forest, and cripplebush marsh. I worked so hard to establish our crops... mostly without oxen or horses to clear and till the fields... years of backbreaking work might be rendered futile. Can we survive if we can't harvest this season? How long would our stores last? My advice is to go home and consider your stores."

Sarah had another plan in mind.

"Hallo, I'm here to see Director Kieft. This is his goddaughter, Aneken," Sarah said to the soldiers as she stood at the iron lattice entry to the fort.

They considered her and her child. Aneken looked like a toddling doll with her *passement*-trimmed coif.

"On what business?" one soldier asked.

"As I said," Sarah said, feigning the annoyance she thought an entitled lady would have. "This is his goddaughter."

"All right. Follow me," the soldier finally conceded.

The soldier led them to the Director's house inside the fort. He instructed her to wait while he announced her. Sarah swallowed hard and took a deep breath. She clasped her hands to still their tremble.

The soldier led them into the great room of the Director's quarters. Kieft sat at a table, papers strewn before him. He was pale and greasy-faced in the stale air that smelled of tobacco and rag paper. The scene explained how he occupied all his time, holed up in the fort. The room was a carefully arranged chaos of books, papers, maps, and casks of wine and beer, tapped and ready to draught.

"Good day, Director. Aneken insisted we visit her godfather as we passed the fort. I see you're busy. Our apologies in disturbing you..." Sarah said, voice honeyed with deference, turning to leave.

"Not at all! Please, stay," Kieft said, pleasantly surprising her with his warmth as he gestured for them to come in.

Sarah nudged Aneken forward. She smiled shyly and gave the little curtsy she had practiced.

"Hallo, *mijn meisje*," Kieft said to Aneken. "Do you want to see a pretty picture?"

Aneken nodded, and he motioned for her to come closer. Sarah followed, curious what papers he was looking over.

"These are journal pages from a man who went deep into *wilden* country ten years ago. I'm determined to find a weakness, a key to their subjugation, but I was distracted by these drawings of spring flora."

He lifted Aneken to his lap to see. It was a simple drawing of odd-looking flowers adorning an arching stem.

"He called them Dutchman's Breeches," Kieft said.

"Do you see, *Maman*?" Aneken laughed and looked to Sarah.

"Yes, they do look like breeches hung upside down on a clothesline," she replied. She tried to act amused, but Kieft's mention of finding the Natives' weakness quickened her pulse and made a perfect segue to the true purpose of her visit.

"You can spend more time on your floral distraction, for I can tell you the Natives' weakness," Sarah declared.

Kieft dropped his smile and looked at her with an arched brow, waiting for her to continue.

"It's the same as the Netherlanders' weakness…"

"Booze?" he interjected, scoffing, as he heartily sipped from his fine silver tankard. He wiped his mustache and reshaped his pointed beard with elegance.

"No. Trade," she replied in earnest. "Peaceful, secure trade for the items that are commonplace to us, but are the things where our craftsman exceed those of the Natives. Knives, iron pots, steel traps, axes, adzes, hoes, rakes, blankets, coats. Give them a favorable trade agreement for these simple things. In turn, we receive the pelts that fill the Company coffers with guilders… Your pockets as well. We will have peace and prosperity."

"Trade does not make them respect us. We must show force." He snorted, looking at her with pity for her simplistic, girlish notions. Sarah, undaunted, tried a different argument.

"Lord General, you are on an island surrounded by Natives. Their tribes are as different as Spain or England is to *Patria*. The Lange Eylandt Natives are not so different to the *Pays-Bas* before the Dutch Revolt against Spain. The Natives call Lange Eylandt *Paumanok*, 'the island that pays tribute.' They are subjected to excessive taxation from the northeastern tribe, the Montaukett. Defend the smaller tribes against the Montaukett and they will pay *you* tribute and join with you in your war against the Naraticong and Weckquaesgeek."

"Child, you presume to know a great deal. Alas, a subjugated tribe does not make a great ally. They will respond only to force. And if they will not show respect, we shall show no mercy. I will protect this colony. Your good husband agrees. He petitions to attack the Lange Eylandt *wilden*."

"I am not a child. I am a wife with two daughters. I have lived here my entire life. My husband, nor you, understand that those *wilden* are our neighbors and business partners, not our enemy." Sarah's indignation escaped unchecked. She witnessed the effect of it transform the man in front of her.

"Insolence! Do not presume higher authority to decide such things!" he shouted, his cheeks flushing with his rising anger. "They are godless heathens, and I am the Director General! No one has more power to cower the *wilden* or insolent colonists! They laugh at justice, and I intend to uphold it! I am my own master, for I have my commission not from the Company, but from the States General!"

"If the Natives band together, our colony will be outnumbered!"

Aneken, still on his lap, began to wail with the shouting. Sarah gave a loud *Shhh* directed to both her child and Kieft. She took Aneken in her arms before the man vaulted her off his lap as he stood to face her.

"Perhaps I shall send you to the stocks for your insolence..."

"Director General, I do not mean to offend. I humbly offer my perspective," Sarah replied, eyes demurely downcast, trying to charm him back with graceful steadiness. "In your wisdom, with God's will, our colony will flourish."

"You are your father's daughter," he mumbled and sat back down, turning attention again to his papers. "I shall think of your family's safety and gratitude when the *wilden* are vanquished."

Sarah let herself out.

A fortnight later, Hans burst in the door with a broad smile. Rarely had Sarah ever seen him so giddy.

"The Director has granted my land patent," Hans said. He brought forth a rolled document and handed it to her.

She unfurled and read it aloud for him.

"Director Kieft gives and grants to Hans Hansen Bergen a piece of land located upon Lange Eylandt bordering Joris Rapalje to the southwest..." she glossed over the lengthy details of boundaries "...containing two hundred *morgens*..."

"Director Kieft denied our petition to attack the *wilden*. Instead, he made agreements with them to secure land patents across the river." Hans beamed. "Though Kieft did say, in case they evince a hostile disposition, every man must do his best to defend himself."

She had not told Hans about her meeting with Kieft. A secret fire swelled in Sarah's chest. It tickled at her breastbone, like a spark illuminating a pile of tinder. A small thing that floods the darkness with light. Perhaps her words to the Director had made an impression.

That brief light of hope and peace was snuffed out a month later.

"They were defending themselves," Hans said. "I heard the Mareckkawick threatened a group of New Netherlander farmhands."

Sarah didn't trust the story told of what precipitated the attack, but it didn't matter. The farmhands attacked the Mareckkawick village north of her and Hans's bowery across the river.

Her mother told her she heard Hans's petition cosigners planned the attack in order to steal corn. They knew Kieft would not punish them and would be happy to stock up Company storehouses. The farmhands plundered two wagonloads of corn, killing three Natives who attempted to stop them.

In consequence, the Mareckkawick, Massapequa, Matinecock, Merrick, Rockaway, and Secatogue bands made common cause with the other Lenape. There were now twelve tribes united against the Dutch colony, surrounding Manhattan in every direction.

"Was this attack organized by your petition friends?" Sarah asked.

Hans sat at the table, stuffing his pipe. He lit it and sighed out a cloud of smoke. He shrugged and wouldn't meet her eyes.

"Why are you so beholden to them?"

"Lambert Mol is my *baas* at the shipyard. Jacob van Couwenhoven was my shipmate on the voyage over. Plus, Jacob's a cousin of Kiliaen van Rensselaer. Why shouldn't I want to be among the company of the most rich and powerful *patroon* of New Netherland?"

Sarah didn't know what to say. She remembered Hans's wounded look when Kieft implied he was a lesser man than Van Tienhoven before they wed. Perhaps Hans was trying to make up for that. She understood his ambition, but not at the cost of loyalty to the people who had been critical to her and her parents' survival, like Weenji and her tribe. She saw clearly how opposed she and Hans's friends were and how little she could do about it.

CHAPTER 10

1643

By midsummer, Sarah longed for a swim in the stream at the Waalebocht and a cool reprieve from the heat. She didn't argue with Hans's decision that they would remain in town. Weenji's tribe hadn't joined the other Lenape allied against the Dutch, but she knew it was too dangerous to live there.

She reposed under the shade of their apple tree in their kitchen garden, trying to avoid exertion during the hottest part of the day. Her daughters dozed next to her.

Rebecca's chest moved rapidly, panting for air in the heavy humidity. Aneken slept sprawled out like a starfish, as if each of her limbs needed maximum breathing room. Sarah wanted to sleep but couldn't. Rivulets of sweat kept her irritably alert.

A great commotion came from the pier. Men's voices carried through the air. Perhaps a merchant vessel unloading. Drumming started. A military parade?

Rebecca woke as the drumming grew louder. Grumpy and confused because of her abbreviated nap, she started to cry. Aneken awoke, angry at her sister's cries. Then she heard the drums and shot up, like she had overslept and the party started without her. Sarah carried Rebecca and followed Aneken as she sped through their house to the street.

Her mother and her siblings emerged from their house and joined them as they went to Markveldt Straat to see what warranted an unexpected parade. Their neighbors filled in around them.

The drummers led, followed by the standard-bearers. Sarah expected to see Director Kieft, but she couldn't see who commanded the soldiers. The rear lines of the soldiers held pikes. Sarah squinted to identify the orbs sitting atop each pike. Squash? Melon? No. She gasped. They were the severed heads of Natives.

"Aneken, look away!" Sarah pressed Rebecca's face to her bosom and whirled Aneken by the shoulders to face her skirts.

Sarah looked at the spectators. Many had paled, horrified expressions. A few cheered for the soldiers. Adrienne Cuvelier was among those in vocal appreciation.

One soldier tripped, which sent his pike tilting, and the head atop it came free. It hurtled to the ground at the feet of the spectators.

"Damn the heathens to Hell!" Adrienne screamed as she charged the head and kicked it up the street, sending coagulated gobs of blood flying to the crowd's astounded disgust.

Sarah dragged her girls away. Her mother joined her. They were both too stunned to speak.

"How can they call Natives the savage ones after such a barbaric display?" Sarah whispered as they neared home.

"No one looks for others in the oven who have not been in there themself," her mother quoted the Walloon proverb.

Sarah and Hans lay in bed that night, discussing matters in whispers. It was still infernally hot, even at night.

"The Mareckkawick set fire to two boweries north of ours," Hans told her. "In response to that, the Director sent the soldiers to attack the Mareckkawick village."

"How has it made us any safer to escalate to war?" Sarah said.

"Despite you having a friendly relationship with a small band of *wilden*, conflict has been brewing and was bound to happen. This attack, though brutal, may be the end of the conflict."

"How? Kieft only gives them more reason to rally together against us. They have grudges against each other—as much as my father does against the Spanish—but given a common enemy, they will far outnumber us. They surround us from every side." Sarah's breathing grew pained. She couldn't take in enough air.

"*Min kvinne mitt alt*," he said languidly, brushing her damp, matted hair from her forehead. He pressed his thumb between her eyes, at the bridge of her nose, and stroked upward. She slowly relaxed and her breathing returned to normal. "It will be all right. We're safe. I will keep you safe."

She rolled onto her side to face him. He cupped her cheeks with his broad palms and kissed her. She reached for his hips to come to hers. She wanted to forget her worries, if only for a little while.

One week after the brutal parade, Sarah's mother popped her head in their half open Dutch split door.

"Sarah, come over. Your father has news," her mother said quickly and disappeared just as fast.

Sarah was in the middle of cooking their evening meal. Beans were simmering. Squab plucked but not yet dressed. She checked the beans had enough liquid, took the poker, and knocked down the wood under the bean pot from a medium to low heat. She picked up Rebecca. Aneken had already followed her grandmother next door.

Sarah's father sat at the table, head in his hands. Her mother's eyes were glazed and bloodshot.

"Tell her, Joris," her mother said as tears streamed down her cheeks.

"Our bowery is ruined," her father began. "I thought Wunita was acting odd all day. Skittish. He was looking around, scanning the horizon, instead of at the work at hand harvesting the corn. Cholena and Weenji weren't there. The farmhands and I got into the shallop with the day's harvest. We were halfway across when I saw smoke billowing from the far end of the wheat field. By the time we were across to Manhattan, flames engulfed all our fields. There was smoke rising from your bowery, too," her father whispered, barely audible.

"Where's Hans?" her mother asked Sarah.

"At the shipyard," answered Sarah. "He went to our bowery at the Waalebocht yesterday. He said things were fine."

"Hans wasn't at the shipyard. I looked for him," her father said.

Hans was still not home hours after he usually returned from work. Sarah put the girls to bed and fetched her mother to watch them.

"I have to go find Hans. I'm sick with worry," Sarah said. She calmed herself by thinking of the possibilities. Either their bowery had burned, or it had not. Hans was alive, or he was not. She could handle the destruction of their bowery as long as Hans was all right.

She checked with her neighbor first, where Hans's *baas* lived.

"Is your husband home? Hans didn't come home from work. I was wondering if Lambert knew when he left," Sarah explained to Lambert's wife.

"*Nee*, he's not home, but that's not unusual. You can likely find him at the City Tavern or the Wooden Horse Tavern." She thought a moment. "I hope Hans doesn't start following Lambert's habit of getting stinking drunk after work every night."

Sarah thanked her and set off for the Wooden Horse.

She braced herself and stepped into the smoke-clouded tavern. Men from the tables nearest the door eyed her. One requested she join them. She didn't acknowledge them as she scanned the room. She saw a familiar face.

"Nys!" Sarah called out to Phebe's husband.

"Hallo, Sarah! What—"

"Have you seen Hans?"

"*Ja*, he's upstairs playing trictrac."

Sarah lifted her skirts and ran up the stairs. Her heart pounded faster than her steps. She didn't know what she would say to Hans. *Why didn't you come home? Why are you gambling? Did you know our farm burnt? Why did you make me worry you were dead?*

She entered the room and saw him. His back was to her. He was hunched over the game board.

His *baas* saw Sarah and nodded to Hans to look behind him. Hans was bleary-eyed. Drunk. Had he been crying? Her relief at seeing him tempered her anger and disappointment.

"Hans..." Sarah started.

"Let's go home," he said, rising as soon as he saw her.

"You owe me for that last game and likely this round, too!" Lambert called after him. Hans shot him a look that made him wither. "I'll let it pass this time, on account of..."

Once in the street, Hans leaned on Sarah like a crutch. She stayed silent as she struggled to support him. Her mind screamed questions. Hans spoke first.

"It's gone. It's all gone. The tobacco, grain, corn ... and... the house. Gone. Gone. Gone..."

"It will be all right." The words surprised her as they left her mouth. They came out confident and reassuring, neither of which she felt. She wanted to scream.

"I saw Joris's land burning from Smits Vly, but ours was already an inferno. There was no chance to save it. I'm sorry."

"We're safe. It will be all right."

CHAPTER 11

1643

On an early September morning, a heavy fog wrapped around the southern tip of Manhattan. Sunlight filtered through the opaque air, casting an eerie, wan yellow of an impending thunderstorm. The distinct smell of petrichor wafted in their open window, making Sarah's nose tingle. She, Hans, and their daughters ate bread and butter to break their fast.

There was indistinct shouting nearby, followed by screams. Sarah froze and strained to listen.

"Sarah, get in the *kast* with the girls!" Hans threw the linen out of their enormous oak armoire, removed the shelves, and pushed her and the girls inside.

"Don't worry, *mes petites*. We're safe, but we must stay quiet."

Luckily, the girls were too stunned to have any reaction yet. Sarah's belly was swollen with child. Crammed in with her girls pressed against her, bile rose in her throat. She thought she heard her father's voice scream, "... my son!" He said it again, and again. She couldn't breathe in the *kast*. Once the breathing fit started, it only grew worse. She felt like she was drowning. Her throat burned. She burst open the door and gasped in air.

"*Maman...*" Aneken said, eyes wide with worry. Sarah took a moment to regain herself.

"It's all right. I have to go help *Grand-Père*. I'll be right back. Stay in the *kast*."

Sarah knew she was doing the wrong thing, leaving the *kast*, but she couldn't stop. She opened the door. The roof of the storehouse down the street was on fire. She heard gunfire at the strand. Hans led a Native boy toward the fort. He had a bloodied nose, his skin was purple-tinged, and he looked barely conscious. Sarah caught the briefest glimpse of her father as he raced to his front door.

"Sarah! Stay in the house!" Hans called to her as the sky cracked with thunder, releasing a deluge of hard rain. It quickly doused the fire of the storehouse roof. She went inside and froze. Something was wrong with her family. Her father's voice crying out "my son" replayed in her mind. Without thinking, she opened the door and dashed through the rain to her parents' house.

Their door was open. Her mother cradled Sarah's four-year-old brother, Jacob, in her lap just inside the door. Her father threw himself over them protectively when Sarah approached.

"It's just me. What—?"

Her father pulled back to reveal Jacob had an arrow piercing through his chest, precisely through his heart. Sarah's mother pressed her apron around the wound, trying to staunch the bleeding. Her mother's eyes did not leave Jacob's face.

"*Maman*," Jacob faintly said. His eyes rolled back in his head. Her mother shook him to wake up.

Sarah realized her siblings huddled under the table, too shocked to move, watching their brother bleed out. Sarah went to them. She took four-month-old baby Jeronimus and gathered her other three little siblings into her embrace.

"Come with me," she whispered. They quickly darted through the rain to her home. She got Aneken and Rebecca out of the *kast*.

"Let's all get into the *bedstee*," Sarah suggested.

"Is Jacob dead?" her sister Judith asked.

"I don't know. Let's pray for him."

The prayers turned into scripture and then folk tales. Sarah chose ones where all seemed lost, but then a magical element showed up that made everything all right. It soothed them, or at least distracted.

The door opened. They held their breath and exhaled collectively. It was Hans.

"Judith, can you tell the next story?" Sarah asked her sister.

Sarah went to Hans. She hung her arms around his neck and began to sob into his chest. He led her away, out of earshot of the children.

"What happened?" she asked.

"It was a small group that attacked, mostly young Naraticong. I went outside and saw your father choking a *wilden* boy into the dirt with his rifle across his neck. He screamed that the boy shot his son. When your father saw me, he ordered that I take the boy as prisoner to the fort. A few were captured and the rest got away with some wheat, corn, flax, and beer. The only death was your…"

"*Nee,*" Sarah whispered, choking back a sob that made her entire body heave. Hans wrapped himself around her so tightly, it stilled the wracking sob.

"I'm sorry, Sarah. Your father said you came to get your siblings. You were mad to leave the house! But your parents are… Your brother… It's not something children should see."

"Are you sure Jacob's dead? I should have fetched Surgeon Kierstede. Why didn't I think to fetch the doctor?"

"He's dead. He was shot through the heart. There was nothing that could've been done to save him. I'll go see if I can help your parents. You stay with the children for now. Prepare to go stay in the fort. They've opened an area for women and children. I don't want to take any risks while you're…" He rubbed his hands over her belly. "Thank God nothing happened to you."

"Are you coming?"

"*Nee*, it's just women and children. Plus the outlanders whose houses were burned."

"I won't leave you."

"It's not a request, Sarah. Your brother... It's not safe here." His eyes pleaded with her, tinged with love, regret, and shame to admit such a thing. "They killed Cinnamon, too. What if you had been in the garden milking her? Thank God nothing happened to you. You'll be safe in the fort."

As fall turned to winter, Sarah couldn't believe Jacob was gone. She didn't know what was worse: that he was gone or what was left behind. The Rapalje family all had glazed eyes and twitching reflexes. But they were hardly alone. Many in the fort had that look. Haunted eyes. Unblinking, far off gazes.

She grew up thinking her family was invincible. Every time there was an epidemic or failed crops and famine, they had survived when others did not. She felt so foolish for thinking they were impervious to the tragedies that befell others.

As the eldest daughter, she felt somehow responsible for not protecting her little brother. She read the same emotions on the faces of her mother and father. It stabbed her heart to see the weight of guilt and grief upon them.

The wracking, whole body sobs came and went. It gave her stitches in her side and made her retch her empty stomach. She couldn't tolerate seeing her parents' grief. Eventually, she avoided them, especially her mother. She couldn't look at her without redoubling her own fit of sorrow.

Sarah thought to seek out Kieft and ask, "Do you still think my family will be grateful for your war?" but she hadn't the energy.

She consigned herself to the area in the fort cordoned off for pregnant women, children, and babies.

Company midwife, Tryn Jonas, tended to them. Tryn was calming and some of the best company to be had while they waited out war, winter, and childbirth. Her granddaughter, Saartje Roelofs, had been Sarah's classmate and bridesmaid.

"Saartje recently married the surgeon, Hans Kierstede." Tryn tittered, obviously pleased.

"My best wishes for them both. I haven't spoken with Saartje in a long time. How is she since...?" Sarah asked, enjoying the distracting, light conversation, as if there wasn't a war. She nearly ruined the illusion of normalcy by bringing up the attack.

"Saartje's offered to help in peace negotiations. She had plenty of experience working as a Munsee Algonquian translator at the market before the war. They pay little heed to the girl though," Tryn whistled reproachfully. "She and Dr. Kierstede are a well-suited pair. She's been teaching him about medicinal herbs she learned from the Lenape."

"She's a bright girl. No doubt a help to her husband—and negotiations—if they'd let her," Sarah said.

Phebe was also sheltering in the fort with her toddler girls and seven-month-old boy.

Her baby seemed to not get enough milk. In tragic, divine providence, Tryn knew a woman who had just lost her baby. She agreed to nurse Phebe's son. Tryn had Phebe introduce a watery *sappaen* cornmeal porridge when the nursemaid wasn't available.

"I think I'm with child again. I pray for mercy and ask forgiveness for not wanting another baby. Not right now," Phebe confided to

Sarah. "Yet, sheltering here with you, other mothers, and Tryn is a blessed opportunity the war brought."

Sarah empathized with Phebe's situation. Having three children under the age of three was absurdly arduous without other women kinfolk to help.

"You're strong, Phebe. I should have visited you more often... but this war..."

"... makes everything more difficult."

A few days later, Sarah saw Sarina had arrived at the makeshift mothers and children refuge in the fort. She was hugely pregnant as well. Sarah hadn't seen her since before her and Isaac's wedding. Sarah smiled and waved like a little girl at her childhood friend.

Sarina looked nervous and uncomfortable as she entered, but as she saw Sarah, her face lightened, like a great weight had been relieved.

The two pregnant women tried to embrace and kiss each other's cheeks, but their bellies forced them to go on tiptoe to reach. They settled into a hug, their bellies touching side to side with their torsos entwined. Suddenly, they both wept. Tears of sorrow, joy, loss, friendship, nostalgia.

"You must tell me everything that's happened since I saw you last," Sarah said.

"Isaac built a beautiful home for us. We only lived there a few months before his uncle, Johannes, said it wasn't safe. We live on Markveldt, just around the corner from you."

"How did I not know?"

Sarina's face fell. She pressed her fists to her eyes.

"I was with child and felt the quickening when we moved back to town. Shortly after, I stopped feeling the baby move and fell ill. I was very unwell, with a fever," Sarina said, looking distantly at the ground. "Tryn came and gave me a remedy of herbs decocted in white wine, sweetened with syrup of mugwort and cinnamon water. She massaged my belly, and it was the most painful thing. I didn't think I could endure." She took a deep breath. "Finally, I birthed my tiny baby. He could have fit in my hand. I saw him before Tryn covered him in a shroud. I instructed Isaac to tell no one we moved back. I didn't want to see anyone."

Sarah could hardly breathe or blink.

"The fever left, but I had this heavy sickness on my mind. And then the massacre... I heard the massacre in Pavonia echoing off the hills across the river. I couldn't stop hearing it. And I thought maybe the Lord did not want my child to hear such things, so He took him into the grace of Heaven."

"Oh, my dear Sarina," was all Sarah could say, breathlessly, and hugged her.

"*Mon Dieu*, your brother," Sarina said, clutching Sarah, as she realized she wasn't the only one living with a wounded heart.

"Jacob..." Sarah said it on an exhale, like she'd had the wind knocked out of her. They held each other wordlessly, tears streaming quietly onto one another for a long time.

"Hopefully, the Director will destroy our enemies," Sarina whispered and crossed herself.

Sarah stiffened.

"I hope the Director will broker a peace without more bloodshed," Sarah said.

"Either way, an end to it."

Sarah looked to the corner of their area where the young children and babies were playing. Her daughters were being watched over by Phebe and other pregnant mothers. Sarah realized how resilient the children were. Would they even remember her sullen mood and crying fits or simply that they got to have more playmates during this time?

Sarah was among her girlhood friends, comforted in the irony of their joyous reunion abutting anguish.

"Sarina, come meet my daughters. Soon enough, the babes in our wombs will be their age and causing mischief together," Sarah said, without too much cloying hope in her voice that it may be true.

Sarah began her birthing travails the first week of November. Tryn checked on her, but with experienced mothers she wasn't as involved. She let their own feelings guide them and offered support as needed.

Sarah was grateful that her mother came. She realized how much she missed her steadying presence.

"Finding myself with purpose is respite from sorrow," her mother said with a sad smile.

Sarina observed, grateful to see her friend go through it before her. Saartje even showed up for a time, before she was taken by Tryn to help with more urgent midwifery needs. Phebe sat by and helped with Aneken and Rebecca.

As Sarah labored, she went inside her mind, tracing the paths of unsettled land she'd loved when she was little.

Run up the Weckquaesgeek trail, 'til there, the crooked tree, turn and run to the pebble beach on the stream, strip naked and float in the clear fresh water. The water tickling her, like Hans's kisses while undressing her, but everywhere at once.

She'd repeat this, over and over through each wave of birthing pain. Although, one time, she ran to the stream, and little Jacob sat at the water's edge. He looked pale and sad. His eyes were downcast. Dead squirrels, birds, and rabbits encircled him. "The waters are foul. We cannot swim today. Come away with me, away from the dead," she dreamt she said to him.

When at last her baby boy was born, she called him Jacob.

Chapter 12

1644-1645

Stomachs growled with hunger and Native attacks continued throughout the colony that winter and into the new year, bringing more refugees to the fort. Wet, wracking coughs echoed throughout the refugee encampment. Sarina's baby, Jessé, was born a week after Sarah's son. He died a month later. Sarah no longer saw Sarina. She had retreated home, despite the risk.

Sarah and Jacob fell ill with the winter fever and also moved back home to recover. They could not live in the crowded fort any longer.

Tensions were high after such a desperate winter. In March, Director Kieft announced there would be a day of thanksgiving, observed with fasting and prayer.

Sarah went to her parents for more information.

"What is the occasion for thanks?" Sarah asked her father, confused. "No one is thankful for his new taxes. People are without homes and basic necessities. Our crops were torched. Fasting is a convenient order when our storehouses are empty."

"The taxes pay Commander John Underhill. The thanksgiving is for that sadistic Englishman, just returned from a rampage. He reported that they slaughtered over six hundred Natives from seven tribes, brought together at their annual gathering," her father said with disgust.

"Why did Kieft hire an Englishman?" Sarah asked.

"Underhill built his reputation on the Pequot War in the English colony ten years ago. It's not the first time he's massacred hundreds of Natives. They surrounded them and burned their village to the ground, with women and children inside. If further evidence of that man's black soul is needed, I overheard Underhill tell Kieft 'the most wonderful thing was that not one was heard to cry or scream.'"

"I cannot imagine. Are the English always so brutal?" Sarah asked, eyes wide.

"Unless you are a Puritan."

"Yet they even treat fellow Puritans cruelly, like Phebe's neighbor, Anne Hutchinson."

"I heard the Hutchinsons are now living in New Netherland, quite far north, in Bronck's Land. A man in town was saying he tried to sell them guns for protection, but they refused."

"Do you think Wunita's tribe was at the gathering where Underhill attacked? Weenji said that gathering was where she met her husband."

"If they weren't there, they may have fared no better. Underhill and the soldiers marched through Lange Eylandt and burned villages along the way before they found the gathering," her father said in a low voice. "Wunita's *sachem* Penhawitz was among the Native leaders entreating for peace, though. They may have been spared."

Sarah wondered about Weenji's Massapequa husband. His tribe joined in the Lenape alliance against the Dutch, but in marriage, he was now part of Weenji's tribe. She wondered at the conflict that must have brought between Weenji and her husband if he wanted to fight with his tribe or make peace with hers.

"The recent ship returning to *Patria* was full of settlers desperate to leave. It will soon be as empty as when we first settled, but ash and blood have replaced the vast swathes of greenery." Her mother said and grimaced.

"Would you return?" Sarah asked. "At what point will this colony be abandoned?"

"*Non*," her father declared. "There's nothing for us across the ocean. The Company may abandon us as an unprofitable trade outpost, but we will remain."

Many houses were empty. There were no tavern guests. The Wappinger attacked ships laden with beaver pelts coming from the northern territory. It was too much of a risk to plant at the Waalebocht. Her father borrowed money to broker for grain sent from Rensselaerswyck in the north. Luckily the Wappinger did not attack those ships.

Hans still had work in the shipyard. He still courted the favor of men Sarah detested. One such man was a newcomer. Paulus van der Beeck was a Company surgeon. Her husband began to have Paulus over to the house every Friday to give Hans a shave.

"I finished serving in Curaçao and thought New Amsterdam could be no worse. I'm ready to settle down, and there are many properties available... and plenty of widows to choose from," Paulus said.

It made Sarah think of one of her father's proverbs. *Where the carcass is, there fly the vultures.*

"Beyond a shave, I can lance a boil, blood let for fever, stuff gauze in a wound, and twice I have amputated limbs. I thought my services will be sorely needed and well rewarded in your war with the *wilden*."

"Did the amputees live?" Sarah asked, genuinely interested how he fought the pestilence that often overtook such a wound. He ignored her, as if that were beyond his concern.

"I know how to break the rebellious nature of those whom God deigns to be subjugated to us. In Curaçao..." he continued.

Unfortunately, Paulus was also related to Sarah. Her sister Jannet married the blacksmith, Rem van der Beeck. Paulus was a cousin of

Rem's, but they couldn't have been more dissimilar. Whereas Rem was genial and modest, Paulus was condescending and verbose, his ego elevated by his profession.

Sarah bit her tongue many Fridays until she no longer could.

"Director Kieft is right," Paulus orated as he shaved Hans, who could not speak whilst under the straight razor. "We should not look at what we've lost but how many *wilden* we've rid ourselves of. When I was in Curaçao—"

Suddenly, that was it. Sarah could be silent no more.

"What do you know about them? What do you know of our losses? You've been here mere months. Stop talking like you know anything. You're not in Curaçao," she said, getting close to his face and talking in an angry but hushed voice, so as not to disturb her children.

Without hesitation, he swiftly passed his straight razor to his other hand and slapped her, twice, about her face. Sarah reeled back, stunned. No one had ever hit her before. Ever.

Hans shouted in Norwegian and shot to his feet, towering over the barber surgeon.

"*Ach*, sit down, my friend, or your shave will be lopsided all week," Paulus said, dismissive and annoyed.

"You may *not* hit my wife," Hans said and stood for a moment before he reluctantly sat back down for his shave.

"If she will not speak to me in such a manner, I will not," Paulus said curtly and re-involved himself in the task of shaving.

Enraged by the incident and Hans's lack of tepid reprisal, Sarah went to her mother. She explained what had transpired.

"*Non*," her mother said before flying into a fit of whispered French epithets. "He will not abuse you in your own home, in front of your husband who does nothing."

"Should we talk to Rem?"

"*Non*. A man like that will not listen to his cousin's chastisement. Rem is too kind to make an impression."

"Should I forbid Hans to bring him back into our house?"

"*Non*. I have an idea. Come with me." Her mother pinned on her finest partlet to go out.

Catalyna went through town. She stopped and chatted with each one of Hans's friends she saw. She asked them how their business was, what were they working on. They were conversations utterly banal and normal for her mother, who prided herself upon knowing everything about her community. Except for the last part of the conversation. She urged them to visit Hans on Friday afternoon when they could get a fresh shave from the barber surgeon Van der Beeck.

"*Maman*, what are you planning?" Sarah asked.

"*Bof*, nothing. You needn't worry," was all her mother would say.

Next Friday, Paulus came again. Catalyna was there to help Sarah with the children while Sarah ground rabbit with apples, onions, spices, and dried herbs into sausage. Egbert van Borsum and Willem de Key, master carpenter and merchant respectively, stopped by to have a chat with Hans and stayed for a shave.

The men discussed business and waylaid shipments due to the war. Catalyna chimed in now and then, which was not unusual. Her opinions were respectfully heard, especially among these younger men. She'd lived there longer than anyone and was as well versed in numbers as in the social capital needed for transactions.

Paulus was obviously annoyed by her and kept trying to cut her off and speak over her. Sarah finished her task, packed the sausages in a basket, and left toward the back door to hang them in the smokehouse in their yard. The tension in the room was making her feel ill. She froze at the door when she heard her mother speak up.

"Paulus, why did you beat my daughter?" Catalyna confronted him in an even tone.

"*Ach*, I did not. You're a liar," Paulus said.

"You're a villain and a liar, Paulus," Catalyna shot back.

"You're a liar, a whore, a *sewant* thief..." Paulus struck her across the side of her head as she raised her arms to defend herself.

"Leave my house," Hans bellowed at the man, now that he'd hit not only his wife but his mother-in-law.

"But your shave..." Paulus said meagerly as Hans pushed him out the door. Hans didn't respect him with a reply.

"Are you all right, Catalyna?"

"My honor is more wounded than my head," she said.

Hans and the two other men continued with their talk of business, though the men looked disappointed it didn't come with a shave. Sarah came back into the room. Her mother gave her a nod.

Three weeks later, on January 12, 1645, Sarah's mother had her day in court with Paulus van der Beeck. Sarah accompanied her mother. Paulus's face grew grim when he saw Egbert van Borsum and Willem de Key there as witnesses.

"Catalyna Trico, plaintiff, vs. Paulus van der Beeck, defendant, for defamation. Plaintiff demands satisfaction for the injury done to her character, which she proves by two witnesses," Van Tienhoven read. "Defendant is ordered to prove what he said, or, if he cannot do so, defendant shall acknowledge that he knows nothing of the plaintiff that reflects on her honor or virtue."

Paulus cleared his throat and paused before saying, "I know nothing of the plaintiff but what is honest and virtuous."

"Defendant declares that he cannot prove the slanderous remarks made to her. For the blow struck by the defendant he shall pay two and a half guilders and is warned not to do so again on pain of a more severe punishment. Dismissed," Van Tienhoven said hurriedly in a bored monotone.

"Did you intend for this all to happen?" Sarah whispered as they walked home.

"Perhaps I baited the man, but he's guilty of his own reaction. I knew we needed witnesses other than you and Hans. I wanted to teach that pompous newcomer a lesson," her mother explained. "Wins are hard begot these days, and personally, I needed one."

CHAPTER 13

1645

Winter dragged on. Kieft's War dragged on. Hans's salary as Company shipwright had been cut. He silently brooded, his brow constantly furrowed. Yesterday, he left, saying he would be away for work for a few days. Sarah hadn't questioned him. She knew they needed the income for grain they had to buy from *patroons* up the North River. Sarah had sold all her wedding clothes, except the *vlieger* cape, which now served as a duvet for her children.

Her mother's court victory the previous week assuaged Catalyna's agitation, but not Sarah's. She had barely left the house in the past two years, since her little brother was killed. Sarah could no longer stand it. Her three young children and six-month-old baby were driving her mad, and the walls of their house were closing in on her. Little hands tethered her down, constantly greedy for her attention. She wanted to scream. She needed to escape.

Considering where she could go, Sarina came to mind. Sarina recently had a healthy baby girl, Susannah. But Sarah knew she needed to selfishly vent her ire, and visiting a newborn wasn't the place. Phebe and Nys had moved closer to the fort and she hadn't visited their new home yet. Phebe was the perfect person to vent to.

Her little sister stopped by, and Sarah took the opportunity.

"Watch the children, Judith. I have to go see Phebe."

"But it's not safe!"

"It's a fine, sunny day. If Natives were to attack, I'd see them a mile away and be able to duck into the fort. I won't be long. If *Maman* asks, tell her I had to take something to Phebe."

She set out for Phebe's with babe Jan swaddled to her chest under her thick duffel cloak.

She swiftly skirted past the fort on Markveldt to Brede Wegh. She felt a little guilty passing Sarina's house on the way. The crisp, cold air cleansed her lungs and invigorated her. She welcomed the longer walk. The muddy ruts of Brede Wegh were frozen solid, filled in with packed snow that made walking easy. She smiled to herself, enjoying the freedom of being outdoors.

Sarah drew near Phebe and Nys's new home, situated across from the Company gardens. The split door and the shutters were closed up tight. It looked like no one was home, but smoke came from the chimney. Sarah went to the door and knocked their secret knock.

"Sarah! Just a moment," Phebe said, muffled through the door.

It took a while for Phebe to open the door. Sarah saw why as she entered. Phebe struggled with the heavy slab of wood that barred the door as her youngest child, Marrietje, clung to her leg. The baby was standing but clearly wobbly on her own. Sarah rushed to embrace Phebe and squeezed baby Jan between them. Phebe's eyes were red and her skin mottled pink.

"Are you all right? I'm sorry it's taken me so long to visit you at your new home. I hope you've settled in well," Sarah said as she noticed the barred clapboard shutters. Their new home was certainly more fortified than their last. It was dim but cozy inside with the fire burning and one wall sconce lit.

"I'm overwrought with grief. My father died. My stepmother is living with us now," Phebe said as she nodded to the garret.

"What happened? Were they attacked?"

"No, it was an injury that festered." Sarah held her as she whimpered. "He cut himself with his ax while chopping wood."

"Oh, Phebe. My heart breaks for you. That's dreadful news."

"Upon that loss, we heard that Siwanoy Natives attacked Anne Hutchinson. They slaughtered her and her family. Their house is a pile of charred bones. Anne said she spoke directly with the Lord. How could He smite her thus? The Puritans were so cruel as to exile her, forcing her to walk for days, pregnant, in the snow. Only to find such an end as...? Why did Kieft grant her lands so far out? They didn't even believe in owning any weapons to protect themselves..."

"Phebe, slow down. I'm saddened for the travails of Anne Hutchinson, but her end was due to the war of men, not God." Sarah looked deeply into her dear friend's eyes. "The saintly are often horrendously mistreated and given ignoble deaths."

Sarah thought of Saint Catherine, the patron saint of the Walloon church in Leiden where her parents met. Saint Catherine's symbol was the emblem and namesake of her parents' tavern, Cat's Wheel. The wheel with skinning knives was meant to torture the saint, but miraculously, it broke when Saint Catherine touched it. Escaping the wheel, she was then beheaded. Sometimes the saintly are despatched just when it seems they've escaped such a fate.

"There's as much blame in my heart for her fellow Englishmen in exiling her than for the *wilden* who killed her. I can never decipher His meaning. Why does He allow such things? Was she truly a heretic? How do you know if you have been damned? Maybe I am—"

"Faith and Grace are His unconditional gifts. You're a good wife and mother, blessed with these four children, and I swear that is enough to worry over. You needn't add deciphering the Lord's ways to your concerns."

That snapped Phebe out of her abstract thinking and back into her own life. She sighed and wrung her hands. "I know," she said, looking at them playing around her. "I am blessed by my family, even when they are such rascals!" she said with concern as she caught sight of four-year-old Jannet climbing a chair, reaching out for the crock full of honeycomb. Phebe scooped up her little girl and the crockery right before she toppled it. She set Jannet's rump on the bench at the table and got a wooden spoon to give her a little taste of honey.

They both nursed their babies by the fire. The children played with whittled wooden animals and corn husk dolls around their feet. It was a serene moment that made Sarah sleepy and content. She forgot the thorn in her heart that was the whole reason for her visit.

There was a knock at the door. Phebe rose to answer it. Her stepmother barged through the door as soon as it was unbolted.

"I've decided," she declared to Phebe. "I'm going to marry the widower Thomas Grydy. He wants to move to Gravenzande. I like the idea of a community founded by an Englishwoman."

Sarah realized she referred to Lady Moody, who had founded her own Anabaptist community on the southern tip of Lange Eylandt after she was banished from Massachusetts for being a "dangerous woman," like Anne Hutchinson.

"What perils are you walking yourself into? How can you move so far away after the Hutchinsons' massacre? You can stay here," Phebe said, alarmed.

"Your husband would rather I leave. Nys is paying Thomas two hundred guilders to take me. You'll inherit your father's land. He stated in his will that if I remarry, the land goes to you. Thomas wants to leave as soon as possible. I know it's not been long after your father's death, but I'm too old to worry about impropriety. I want to be among the English again, not living under the roof of your Dutch husband."

Jan began to fuss. Sarah worried she imposed on their family discussion as Phebe's stepmother eyed her whimpering baby.

"I should return home," Sarah said. "If I walk with him, he's likely to fall asleep."

Sarah kissed each child and Phebe from cheek to cheek before she left. Her heart was lifted, and she longed be with her children once again, taking her own advice.

Remember the blessings.

In August, the settlers were called to the fort. Sarah's heart leapt with hope for good news. She had heard there were several *sachems* in Fort Amsterdam discussing a peace treaty. There were perhaps two hundred settlers gathered, less than half the population before Kieft's War began.

Director Kieft addressed the crowd.

"We negotiated a firm and inviolable peace with the assembled Native leaders, twenty of whom have signed our treaty. We have agreed to settle future disputes by discussion rather than violence," Kieft bellowed, gesturing to the *sachems*.

The settlers cheered and a weight lifted from Sarah. Peace at last!

Kieft smiled now. He announced food would be served, courtesy of the Company storehouses. Some of the Natives stayed to break bread; others retreated, wary. Sarah learned the names of the sachems who stayed. Oratany of the Hackinsack, Sesekemu of the Tappan, Tackapausha of the Matinecock, Willem of the Rachgawawanck, Mayauwetinnemin of the Nyack, and Weckquaesgeek *sachem* Aepjen Eskuyas representing the Wappinger, Weckquaesgeek, Sinsink, and Kichtawank, among other smaller tribes. Sarah scanned the crowd for any of the Canarsie. She hoped to see Weenji and her family.

The Native's favorite meal, the cornmeal porridge *sappaen*, was dished out in oyster shells as big as a man's hand. Dutch favorites like *koolsla* cabbage salad and many types of *koekje* cookies were served. There was fresh bread and spit-roasted venison. Everyone eventually relaxed, ate their fill, and shared in communal pipe smoking, which the Dutch and Natives were equally fond of.

"*Kwey, nitap.*" Wunita approached Sarah's family. He grasped her father, brotherly, on the shoulder. "You live. I live."

Wunita didn't smile but there was warmth in his eyes. His face was thin and wizened. He broke away from his group to talk with Joris. Sarah strained to hear as she looked for Weenji, but did not find her among the remaining Natives.

"There is much loss and sadness," Wunita continued. "Our Keschaechquereren village burned. Many died. *Sachem* Penhawitz was killed. Many of my wife's family were killed." Wunita turned to face Joris. "Your house stands, but fields and barns burned. Mareckkawick clan burned it, not my clan. I stopped the fire before it took the house. It stands."

She saw the pain and relief on her father's face. She was relieved Wunita did not say Weenji or Cholena died.

Sarah was distracted when she spotted Sarina, carrying her baby Susannah. She waved her over to where she, her mother, and Phebe's collective brood gathered. Their children, around a dozen altogether, played ninepins on the bowling green. Most of them had a *koekje* in hand, even the bowler.

"What a rare beauty—those dark lashes!" Phebe exclaimed.

"May I give your arms a rest?" Sarah's mother asked, holding out her arms, and upon receiving her, expertly bounced and swayed the baby, to Susannah's delight.

Sarah was grateful to see Sarina and her baby doing so well after losing poor Jessé, and their loss before that as well.

"She's wonderfully interested in the other children, isn't she?" Sarah exclaimed, watching Susannah's eyes dart around at them. "Isn't it glorious we can go outside and gather freely again?"

"Yes. It's as foreign to Susannah as it is for us, to gather like this," Sarina said with a small smile.

Sarah felt strange. It was intoxicating being gathered with other women and children and not having to fear. Yet her heart raced and the familiar impulse of anxiety crept up. She swallowed it down. Like heartburn, it still lingered.

Suddenly, they heard Director Kieft's orders. He called out for a three-cannon salute. They braced for the noise and instructed the children to cover their ears. The cannons fired, the boom reverberating in the pit of Sarah's stomach.

In the deafened aftershock, shouts rose. Something was wrong.

Sarah spun to look up at the fort. The northwest-facing cannon had exploded. Sarah saw pieces of the cannon and the gunner had fallen to the ground just steps away from them. Sarah heard screams, and it took her a moment to realize they were her own. She grabbed to gather her children as the horrified women rushed their lot away from the fort and the bloody bits of the gunner.

The fatal accident crushed the revelry of peace and made everyone whisper that it was a bad omen.

CHAPTER 14

1646

On a frosty November day, the hearth's fire crackled peacefully in the early evening as Sarah mended the stockings of her two little boys. Her task rested conveniently on her pregnant belly.

She was trying to finish the work before Hans came home and it was time to serve the quail braising with carrots, cabbage, currants, and cinnamon in the Dutch oven. She had to take time to do the mending correctly though or else the well-worn areas at the knees of the stockings would just rip open again after a few days of wear.

Her children were busy shelling dried bean pods from the kitchen garden, ruining the knees of the stockings they currently wore as errant beans skidded across the room and they crawled after them.

There was a knock at the door. She was not expecting anyone, and the interruption startled her. Hans would be home soon, but he would not knock. She rose and opened the upper half of her Dutch split door.

"Saartje! What a surprise. Please come in!" she exclaimed, immediately delighted and intrigued by the reason for such a rare visit. Saartje was now a much more prominent citizen since she married Doctor Kierstede and rarely had time for social calls.

"My apologies for visiting unexpectedly... and with a request." Saartje kissed her cheeks, quickly getting to the point. Her hurried forcefulness meant it was not a request, but a necessity. She distractedly spun a large gold ring on her middle finger.

"I need to help my grandmother with a birth, but I'm also obliged to help my stepfather. Domine Bogardus has tasked me to help a special girl study her catechism. She will be the first African to perform the full confession of faith in the colony, which is a very important achievement to my stepfather. Her name is Susanna Negrin. You were educated on it as well as I, and you're the only person I could ask at such short notice," Saartje explained.

"Of course," Sarah said without a second thought. "When?"

"Oh, thank you! It was supposed to be in an hour at the church. I forgot you were pregnant too, but you needn't leave your house. I'll send word to have her come here," Saartje rushed to say. "My apologies, I must be off to help my grandmother with haste."

Hans came home minutes later. Their children ran to greet him.

"I need to help a girl with her catechism, so we'd better eat our evening meal quickly," Sarah explained.

"Who is it?"

"Susanna Negrin."

"An African?"

"*Ja*, Saartje asked as a favor."

"All right, as a favor to the doctor's wife, but I hope she doesn't make this a recurring chore." He sat down, face drawn in exhaustion. She knew he dreaded trying to put the children to bed without her.

A little over an hour later there was a knock at the door. Sarah opened it to find a young African woman with a cautious expression.

"*Mevrouw* Kierstede told me to come here," the young woman said a bit defensively, as if she expected to be interrogated on the fact.

"*Ja*, of course. Susanna, right? Come in. I'm Sarah."

"Thank you," Susanna said. She looked nervously at the garret above, from where loud scampering noises emanated.

"That's just my children," Sarah explained, pointing up. "They're getting ready for sleep, but they tend to have a burst of energy right before settling in."

Susanna relaxed except for her tight-lipped smile. A few years younger than Sarah, she held herself with rigid posture. She dressed in a modest but freshly pressed kirtle dress in dark brown duffel with a black partlet around her shoulders. Her gloved hands were clasped at her waist.

"So, you're learning the catechism? How may I help?" Sarah asked.

"*Ja*, I intend to be baptized next year. I practice answering the questions with *Mevrouw* Kierstede." Susanna spoke fluently in Dutch, but with an accent Sarah seldom heard, a mixture of Portuguese and African.

"I commend you. The 129 questions of the Heidelberg Catechism are not easy to perform," Sarah stated.

Susanna said nothing in reply. She stiffened slightly and stood resolutely, with her chin held a little higher, and handed Sarah a slim volume that was her study guide. Sarah took it and indicated they should seat themselves on the bench by the hearth. She opened it to the page bookmarked with a ribbon.

"Shall we start with Lord's Day 30?" Sarah asked. Susanna nodded as she took off her gloves and held them tightly in her lap.

"Question 80: What difference is there between the Lord's Supper and the Popish Mass?" Sarah asked.

"The Lord's Supper testifies to us that we have a full pardon of all sin by the only sacrifice of Jesus Christ, which He Himself has once accomplished on the cross; and that we by the Holy Ghost are ingrafted into Christ, who, according to His human nature is now not on earth, but in Heaven, at the right hand of God His Father, and will there be worshiped by us—but the Mass teaches that the living and dead have not the pardon of sins through the sufferings of Christ, unless Christ is also daily offered for them by the priests; and further, that Christ is bodily under the form of bread and wine, and therefore is to be worshiped in them; so that the Mass, at bottom, is nothing else than a denial of the one sacrifice and sufferings of Jesus Christ, and an accursed idolatry."

Susanna spoke with a clear, confident voice and without stammering to remember the wording. They continued, and Sarah wondered if Susanna really needed to study at all since she nearly flawlessly performed the answers. They reached the Lords Day 32, and Sarah sensed Susanna's throat was growing dry and becoming hoarse.

"Shall we take a break? I'll make us some tea," Sarah suggested, as she took out a box that her mother asked Hans to make. It had dividers for different dried herbals, roots, and berries. Sarah chose some marshmallow root to soothe a dry throat and some spearmint, rosemary, and lemon balm for memory. She tossed them into her kettle and hung it from a chain, rotating the iron arm of the trammel potholder until the kettle was positioned above the flames. They sat in silence, watching the fire for a moment, although Sarah felt the silence wasted the opportunity to learn more about Susanna.

"You're doing very well. Do you know how to read, or are you memorizing it from recitations?" Sarah questioned her before she remembered the girl's defensive tone upon arrival and added, "If you don't mind me asking."

"I can read. My mother secured a labor contract for me five years ago under the condition I would be taught to read. I am a servant to the household of the glove maker, Albert Wantanaer," Susanna stated proudly. She looked at Sarah and thought a moment before continuing to share. "My father and mother received their manumission from Director Kieft two years ago. My siblings and I were not included in that. I intend to petition for my freedom, as a devoted, faithful congregant of the church. Even if I do not succeed in manumission, my faith in God grants my spirit freedom, whether or not my body is free."

Sarah didn't know what to say. Many people were indentured for several years to the Company, repaying their passage and land grant, or beholden as tenant farmers to the *patroons*. She'd never considered how the indenture of the Africans could be unending. Sarah remembered seeing the first Africans arrive in the colony when she was a little girl. For a long time, she thought that's what Portuguese people looked like, because she'd heard a sailor call them their "Portuguese prize."

Sarah took the kettle off the fire and poured two cups. She opened the honey crock and swirled a small portion into the steaming libations and handed one cup to Susanna.

"Please come by again if you want to practice, though I suspect you could perform it perfectly today, if given the chance," Sarah said, handing her the cup of tea. She realized she contradicted Hans's request not to make this a habit, but she felt called to help Susanna in her mission. "I think you will also persuade Kieft for your freedom. I'd vouch for your sincere devotion," she added.

"From your lips to God's ears," Susanna said with a wide smile that showed off her brilliant white teeth. It changed her demeanor completely, like the sun coming out for a moment.

There was a knock at Sarah's door, weeks later, in December. Sarah wondered if it was Susanna returning to practice, but when she opened the door, it was her old friend Sarina.

"Sarah! My apologies I haven't visited sooner. Congratulations on your baby boy!" Sarina said, rushing in from the cold and unwrapping her bundled toddler. Her daughter was eager to play with Sarah's children. Sarah brought them toward the warmth of the hearth, bedecking them both with kisses.

Sarah picked up her one-month-old baby, Michael, from the bassinet to show off the new addition to their family.

"Thank you. My mother was right. It gets easier. Michael slipped out in an afternoon," Sarah said, smiling at her baby as he barely opened his eyes and dozed again.

"I pray that's true... I'm with child again," Sarina said in a whisper, as if proclaiming it to the world would curse her.

"That's wonderful news!"

"I'm at the quickening now. Midwife Tryn prescribed lots of liver, red meat, and beer infused with sage. And my mother gave me this coral talisman to help the baby stay caught in the womb," Sarina explained, brandishing the trinket from a cord around her neck. It was a smooth, pinkish-red that forked like an antler.

"I've heard coral helps. Can I make you some tea? My mother makes a wonderful blend with raspberry leaf that she and I both swear by for strengthening the womb."

"Yes, of course I know your mother's tea. She hawks it to every woman in the colony." They both laughed. "But it is remarkably tasty. Better than sage beer."

Sarah handed Michael off to Sarina as she prepared the tea. The two comfortably sat in silence as they watched their children play and the tea brewed. Sarina's gaze transfixed on baby Michael in her arms. Sarah thought Sarina's cheeks were plumper, with a glow that she lacked during the war.

The tea served, Sarina shot a sidelong look at Sarah.

"Might we talk gossip now?"

"Of course," Sarah said, taking Michael, settling him back in the bassinet, and sitting down to inhale the sweet, astringent vapors of her beverage. She leaned toward Sarina conspiratorially.

"Did you hear about Schoolmaster Adam?" Sarina asked, referring to their old schoolmaster.

"No..."

"He's a wicked man!" Sarina whispered. "Adam went to see Herck Syboltsen, but finding only his wife Wyntje home, he forced himself on her. He left marks on her body, fondling her breasts... and trying worse." She paused as Sarah gasped. "He will be flogged next week. He was supposed to be banished as well, but Kieft took mercy on his four motherless children. It being the dead of winter, banishment was postponed. It's better treatment than he deserves. "

"How awful! Poor Wyntje!" Sarah exclaimed, her outrage in a whisper as well. "That man who so self-righteously taught us to read bible verses!"

"A swine," Sarina said, staring off into the fire, sipping her tea. "He was always so arrogant. I would never send my daughter to be educated by a man like that."

"As he taught us: 'Pride goes before destruction, a haughty spirit before a fall,'" Sarah said sardonically. "Speaking of Bible verses... Saartje asked me to help Susanna Negrin study the catechism. She plans to be baptized and petition Kieft for her freedom."

Sarah expected praise, for Susanna and even for herself in helping the girl. Sarina was silent. Sarah turned to her with her head cocked, waiting for some response.

"Do you think that's wise? If the Africans become full members of the church and gain freedom, won't they just leave? There are so few able-bodied people remaining in the colony. We need their labor more than ever to rebuild."

"Other colonists work off their contracts in six years. Isn't it only fair that would apply to Africans same as to Walloons and Netherlanders? They could still labor, but for wages."

"I don't like to dwell on such questions. Maybe Susanna is an exception, if she is true in faith to the *Reformeé*."

Chapter 15

1647

The following spring, Hans said he would be away a few days for work. He seemed distracted and worried in the days before he left.

Sarah felt a mix of curiosity and anxiety over his vague responses for his absence. After he left that morning, she immersed herself in work at her parents' tavern and eavesdropped to distract herself. Usually, their customers were fur trappers, but lately, a handful of current and former council members gathered at Cat's Wheel. Sarah's father served them beer as well as his opinions.

"The Company does not understand New Netherland differs from their other far-flung trade outposts," her father said, refilling men's beer steins. "It's not just merchants, soldiers, and sailors here. We have families. Our fate should not be tied to the whims of one man who never leaves the fort."

"We made great sacrifices, and many paid an enormous price for Kieft's War. The population is a third of what it was. They should be thanking those of us who persevered," Cornelis Melyn argued. He was *patroon* of a large portion of Staaten Eylandt. Not long after he arrived from *Patria*, the conflicts started. His bowery had been ruined and was uninhabitable for the past four years because of Kieft's War.

"This colony has much potential to grow and be profitable, but I'm afraid the Company does not see it that way," Adriaen van der Donck observed with a plaintively honest expression. "We could petition for the style of government offered to even the smallest villages in *Patria* if we were under the governance of the Dutch Republic and not a private company."

Van der Donck was Director Kieft's lawyer and translator. Kieft granted him such a vast swathe of territory north of Manhattan that the citizens called him *Jonkheer*, an honorific for nobility. He surprised Sarah. Despite his preferential treatment and prominence, he seemed genuinely invested in fighting to persuade the Company to remove Kieft as Director.

Sarina's husband, Isaac, and his former neighbor in the north, Jochem Kuyter, agreed with Van der Donck and pounded their fists on the table. They'd also had their boweries destroyed in the war.

The next evening the men met again at Cat's Wheel. This time, Van der Donck had a petition drafted. He unfurled the document on the table. Sarah was grateful she had thoroughly cleaned the tabletop just before the men entered.

"Melyn and Kuyter—since you two are currently on Kieft's Council of Eight, I think you should sign it," Van der Donck said. "A ship leaves for *Patria* tomorrow. This remonstrance shall be sent to *de Heeren XIX* and the States General."

"Who are *de Heeren XIX* and the States General?" Sarah whispered to her mother.

"The Nineteen Lords are the board of men who control the Company. The States General is the highest government of the Dutch Republic. They represent the seven provinces of the Netherlands."

The colonists continued to grumble in her parents' tavern, wondering if their arguments would have any effect. Sarah thought of all the men in charge of the Company and the governance of the Dutch Republic. Faceless men across an ocean held the fate of the colony in their hands.

In the spring of 1647, Susanna Negrin successfully performed the catechism and confirmed as a full member of the church. Sarah looked on in admiration of her new fellow congregant. She congratulated her after the ceremony.

"Thank you, but it's not time to celebrate yet. Pray that Kieft will be impressed enough to hear my petition," Susanna told her. "Will you come and vouch for me?"

"*Ja*, although I don't know if it will help."

On the appointed day, Sarah went to Fort Amsterdam with Susanna. Saartje decided against joining them because of her stepfather, Domine Bogardus, and Kieft's adversarial relationship. Hans was conveniently away for another job. Sarah doubted he would have agreed with her decision to go before Kieft, and she didn't intend to tell him.

"I am Susanna Negrin, daughter of freeman Gratia D'Angola, the first and only African to become a full member of the Reformed Church. I humbly request that you consider my manumission. My father has died. I request my freedom so I may inherit his land and take care of my younger siblings."

Sarah could smell gin on Kieft as if he had slept in a cask of it. She watched his face as emotions flicked through, from rage to despair. He obviously churned something over in his mind that had nothing to do with Susanna.

"*Mijn Heere*, I humbly submit to vouch for her sincere devotion to the church," Sarah said.

"Your father owned property in the Land of the Blacks?" Kieft asked Susanna. He had granted land to free and enslaved Africans north of the colony. Sarah heard he considered the African settlement the first line of defense against potential attacks from the north.

"*Ja, mijn Heere.*"

"All right," Director Kieft replied. "I already granted a divorce and pardoned a debt this morning—Why not give this African girl her manumission? That way she will be *my* benevolent legacy, not Domine Bogardus's."

"All right?" Secretary Van Tienhoven asked him, expecting more formal elaboration.

"*Ja*... write it however you want. *Sssusanna* is free," Kieft made a slurred whistle at her name.

"She will, of course, need to pay an annual tithe to the Company, correct *mijn Heere*?" Van Tienhoven interjected. Kieft hiccupped in affirmation.

Susanna bowed to them, deep and solemn, as she gave thanks. She wasted no time as she turned to leave before Kieft changed his mind or van Tienhoven added any more stipulations.

"Susanna! You did it!" Sarah whispered in exuberance as they left the gate of the fort. Only then did Susanna turn and flash her full, brilliant smile.

For all Kieft's failures, Sarah thought perhaps there was still some good in him.

Less than a month later, a ship anchored, and word spread that a new Director was aboard. The Company ordered Kieft to return to *Patria*. The petition Van der Donck drafted had succeeded. The whole town gathered to greet their new Director with high hopes as he disembarked his ship. Sarah wore her finest clothes. She and her whole family stood in the crowd to catch a glimpse of their new leader.

Director General Petrus Stuyvesant and his wife Judith Bayard were announced as they disembarked. If Kieft was a fox, Stuyvesant was a bull, Sarah thought. He had a broad face with a long, sharp nose, ample lips, and a staunch, stately countenance. Thick-necked, face freshly shaven clean, and very notably, a wooden peg leg ornamented with silver bands. Rumor was that he'd been hit by cannon fire in an attack on Sint Maarten and continued to command his men as they amputated his leg. Sarah winced as she saw that the horrific rumor must be true.

With pomp and formality, the transfer of power took place beside the fort with one windmill and the harbor as a backdrop. The windmill was in such neglect of repair; it didn't run even when winds were favorable and was a tremendous source of frustration.

Stuyvesant began a speech. He did not take off his castor hat. His thin brown hair hung just above his shoulders and framed a large forehead, like a taut white sail atop his visage that the hat hardly obscured. A grim smile curled his lips at the corners.

"...I vow to look after you, like a father over his children," Sarah heard him pontificate in a booming, stern voice.

Kieft then made a flowery farewell speech, which sounded like pure farce to those gathered who had experienced his tenure in power. He made the mistake of pausing for the colonists to reciprocate thanks and farewells. That's when Kuyter started the heckling, reviling to the effect of what Kieft deserved instead of thanks. He was joined by Melyn and many of the colony's most respectable men. Sarah heard her father join in. She gave a faint smile at her feelings being put to words by her fellow colonists, but she restrained herself from joining in. She privately cursed Kieft for his war, but he had also granted Susanna freedom and he was still Aneken's godfather.

Stuyvesant finally commanded the attention of the crowd, which was then quieted instead of devolving further into chaos.

"A formal review will be conducted on these claims. Under the new administration, justice will be applied equally and swiftly," Stuyvesant declared, ending, for now, the discourse and ceremony.

Morning began on a day in mid-June with the rhythmic singing of hammers and nails, nearly a constant symphony as of late. A new era had begun. Homes and businesses were being reconstructed and new structures were being built. It was the day Stuyvesant set to make his ruling over the claims of Melyn and Kuyter against Kieft.

Sarah went to Cat's Wheel that evening to learn what had transpired. Van der Donck was there. Melyn and Kuyter were conspicuously missing.

"They presented their argument. Stuyvesant had not expected such a robust legal document," Van der Donck explained. His face held mild satisfaction, though not triumph. "Kieft called their claims libel and sedition. Stuyvesant adjourned the meeting to review the documents. When we reconvened, and Stuyvesant stated his view that Melyn and Kuyter's claims were, indeed, treasonous. He recited the Articles of War: 'To utter words tending to mutiny and rebellion demands capital punishment.'"

Sarah saw his audience's faces pale as they realized Stuyvesant's governance would not be as they'd hoped. Van der Donck continued.

"I advised Stuyvesant against rash action. He agreed the two men would be allowed to appeal before the States General and ordered them to depart by the first ship available."

In the early harvest season, Sarah and their five children accompanied Hans to their land at the Waalebocht. He spent the summer rebuilding their house and sowing the fields. The crops thrived again after everything burned during the start of the war four years ago. Sarah had stayed in New Amsterdam with her children all summer. It was her first time seeing the rebuilt house.

"Hans, the house looks wonderful. Almost exactly the same," Sarah exclaimed as she walked in the front door, treading on the wide, pine plank floors. She carried nine-month-old Michael, and Hans carried a cast-iron Dutch oven. Her older children carried in the linens. Hans set the oven on the stone hearth. Their home looked complete.

Sarah opened the window shutters and noticed Natives pulling nets out of the creek in the distance. Sarah thought it might be Weenji and Cholena. They had a little boy with them. Sarah went outside and waved. She hadn't seen her childhood friend since before the war. Weenji walked toward their house alone with an uneven gait. Sarah's stomach cramped in anticipation of their reunion, unsure what the effects of the war meant to their old friendship.

"Hallo, Weenji! *Nitap*!" Sarah cried out. Weenji did not wave or smile. She walked soberly toward Sarah, with a slight limp to her gait.

"Your man comes and builds and plants, but he does not greet us or make offerings of friendship. He is not a friend to us. I wear scars from the day your tribe burned my village. Your *Swanneken* tribesmen murdered my husband and over one hundred of my clansmen," Weenji said bitterly, not concealing her anger. She pointed to her feet. Purple gnarled skin was visible above her moccasins and traveled up her leg. Sarah could tell from the shape of her close-fitted moccasins that she was missing toes. Sarah was speechless for a moment.

"So much sorrow, Weenji. I try to stop attacks... not able," Sarah pleaded in bewildered, rusty Munsee words. "My little brother... killed... Our bowery and house burned."

"It was not my tribe..."

"I know. Your father told us. Nothing can replace those lost... but wait here."

Sarah ran into the house and took the linens. She placed them in Hans's arms, whispered, "Give them to Weenji," and pushed him out the door. "Call her *nitap*."

"Hallo, Weenji," Hans said in Dutch, emerging from the house, looking uncomfortable. She accepted the linens. "*Nitap*? What do you need? We will get it for you."

"*Wunneet*," she thanked him, paused a moment, looking at him coolly. "Guns."

"We cannot give guns, by law, but I will give you good, sharp knives. I will have a *schepel* of wheat for you once it's harvested," he promised.

"Is that your son?" Sarah asked, looking toward Cholena and the boy. She saw Weenji's brow soften for a moment.

"*Ja*, Mehakachtey. He is called Coal From the Fire."

"Will you share a meal with us? Mehakachtey looks about the same age as my son Jan. This is Michael," Sarah said, bouncing Michael in her arms until he smiled.

"*Nee*, we must go back to our village now," Weenji said, her stern tone returning.

"Next time," Sarah replied. Weenji paused, considering.

"*Ja*, next time we will share gifts and a meal," Weenji said in Dutch, looking at Hans, and turned sharply to leave, her long black braid following her like a whip.

A surge of empathetic pain coursed through Sarah, making her hair stand up, as she thought of Weenji's scars and missing toes. She felt sick. How could she ever repair their friendship with trade goods when Weenji had lost her husband and kin?

CHAPTER 16

1647-1649

It was a busy day at the market in the late fall when a ship arrived, and word spread like wildfire. Shipwreck.

The *Princess Amelia*, the ship which carried Kieft, Melyn, and Kuyter, crossed the Atlantic uneventfully. But the captain mistook the Bristol Channel for the English Channel. It hit rocks and smashed to bits off the coast of Wales.

Anneke Jans sobbed. Her husband, Domine Bogardus, was also aboard that ship. Sarah's mother comforted her old friend, who was now twice widowed.

Saartje held her younger sister as they grieved their stepfather. Sarah tried to comfort them, but words caught in her throat. Saartje looked too stunned to hear her anyway.

"Hans!" Sarah exclaimed, delighted at his surprise entrance to her parents' home. He had been away for a job the past week.

She ran to him and he lifted her up to kiss her. Deeply inhaling his delicious, gamey scent, she then exhaled all the worry she'd had over his prolonged absence. His beard growth tickled her cheeks. She wanted to burrow herself into it. Their children rushed to Hans as well. He stooped to collect them all in his enormous embrace.

"I've only just returned. I need to bathe. Sarah, can you heat me some water while I unpack?"

"Children, stay here and finish helping your aunts prepare the pretzels. You're almost to the fun part of shaping them." Sarah's mother winked at Sarah.

As soon as Sarah and Hans were outside, he whispered in her ear, "*Min kvinne*, I *need* you."

Sarah needed no further cue to run back to their house. They wrenched their outer layers of clothing off themselves, no more languid undressing by one another. It was late winter and there were a lot of layers to get through. No time or desire for completely undressing. This was the most intimate moment they'd had in a long time. She missed him so much while he was away.

Things had been strained between them since they lost their son, Jacob, that winter. They'd all fallen ill with grippe and recovered, except poor Jacob. His little body purged more than it had to give. She lost her baby born in the fort during wartime. Sarah was tormented afterward, searching for meaning. Sarina had lost Jessé much sooner. Maybe naming their wartime babies after lost loved ones had cursed them into an endless echo of loss: Jessé gone, Jessé gone, Jacob gone, Jacob gone. It still haunted her. Using the names of the deceased was a tradition meant to keep the deceased living, not perpetually dying.

Their carnal conversation was quick. Sarah wasn't quite done with their private moment, though. She put her arms around Hans and drew him back to stay in bed. It was cold in the house, as the banked fire from breakfast that morning didn't give much heat. They embraced wordlessly for a long minute before Sarah broke the silence.

"I know you say it's a job. I am curious what business it is that keeps you away for so long lately," Sarah said, eyes locked on Hans for a substantive answer. He'd been evasive about the topic ever since these extended trips began. She couldn't take it anymore.

He opened his mouth, but nothing came out. Was he debating whether to tell her or how much to tell her? Another woman? Illegal business? Espionage on the English or Swedish colonies?

"It's nothing nefarious, *min kvinne mitt alt*. I swear. I'm doing work for one of the major merchants," he said finally. His eyes were direct and sincere, but he was still holding something back.

"Can't you tell me who or what work?"

"I was selling coats to the Natives in Southampton," he said finally, hoping to end it at that.

"You're working for Govert Loockermans then? The man who was just accused of being a smuggler, among other cutthroat deeds?" Sarah grilled him, but she knew she was right by the look on his face. Sarah heard that Loockermans was accused of killing the Minquas's *sachem* on an expedition to the South River. Loockermans claimed he only roughed him up. There was precedent for Loockermans getting away with being a loose cannon because of his prominence in trade. Sarah's pulse beat in her ears with fear and outrage that Hans conducted such shifty business without telling her.

"The Natives receive a gunpowder bonus for every additional coat purchased. We're not smuggling it to them—" Hans gulped. "Although what got Loockermans in trouble was that he promised to sell them guns and lead shot if they cut off trade with the English completely. But we didn't sell them any guns this trip."

"Hans," Sarah said chidingly. "*This* trip?"

"Loockermans is a prominent merchant. He's on Stuyvesant's council. There's nothing to fear," Hans tried to reassure her.

"What about you, though? Would he throw you under the bow if it came to loggerheads?" Sarah asked.

She wanted to thrash his head for not speaking to her about this *before* he started such dangerous ventures.

"*Nee*, the man has few scruples in business, but he's fair with the people on his side," Hans said confidently.

"All right." She paused a long moment. "Thank you for telling me," Sarah said as she returned to his embrace and whispered, "If anyone asks, I shall promptly forget I ever heard such things."

"*Jeg elsker deg,*" he said, shooting her his most charming smile, the one that melted her anger and mistrust every time.

"*Je t'aime,*" she answered.

There had always been obvious, vast chasms between them, like how they said "I love you" differently or how they processed the grief of Jacob: Sarah, having a lying-in period of sobs and prayer for meaning, and Hans, jumping into dangerous new business prospects.

Ultimately, Sarah reconciled these differences because they had a love and physical alchemy. Their bond somehow always prevailed and reconnected them. She loved him and she had to trust he knew what he was doing.

Sarah went to visit Sarina and Isaac's new, larger home on Breuers Straat. Sarah meant to visit for some time, but the final brutal cold snaps of winter kept her home. Today's unseasonable warmth felt like summer in comparison. She had her coif bonnet pulled forward to shade her pale cheeks but still felt like she would get a sunburn.

The ice-laden streets had thawed into a consistency that varied between bread dough and pancake batter. Sarah's clogs slid through the mud and she almost lost hold of the package she carried.

Her fitful movement startled some hogs that reveled in the mud. They squealed at her before going back to their contented soft snorts as they rooted. One had a ring through its nose. Director Stuyvesant had issued an ordinance that all hogs should have nose rings to dissuade them from digging through the streets. It hadn't deterred this one.

She regained her footing and turned the corner onto Breuers Straat. Sarah was surprised to see Sarina standing in the street with her neighbor Anneke Loockermans, Govert's sister.

Half a dozen of Anneke's servants and hired workers were laying down cobblestones in front of her home. A second team of laborers followed, shoveled sand, swept, and tamped the paving flat. The number of cobblestones awaiting their placement was astounding. The mountain of them blocked off the street, halting traffic for Anneke's construction project.

"No more filth bespattering my tulips and roses!" Anneke declared to Sarina. "I'm tired of wearing clogs or patten overshoes to keep my hem from getting dirty. Clogs are for fishwives! The pattens are more elegant than clogs, but I feel like a clomping horse on stilts."

"I agree. I loathe leaving my home for that very reason."

Sarah came upon them, her footsteps quieted by the mud. They were so concentrated on overseeing the servants' work and the clamor of tamping, they hadn't heard her approach. She thought for a moment she would just turn and walk back home, embarrassed of her muddy clogs, fit for a fishwife, but Sarina turned and saw her.

"Sarah!"

Sarah curtsied to the women.

"Is this a bad time, Sarina? I brought you some apple butter and cinnamon bread as a housewarming gift." She held out the linen-wrapped package. Anneke did not acknowledge her, still fixated on overseeing the paving.

"No, not at all. I'd love to show you our new home. Please excuse me, Anneke."

"Sarina, tell your husband to pave your portion! Let's inspire everyone to do their bit. I've petitioned Director Stuyvesant about the poor state of the streets but received no reply," Anneke called after her.

"Isaac is at the court almost every day. Perhaps he can inquire why the petition stalled," Sarina suggested.

As soon as they were out of Anneke's earshot, Sarina turned to Sarah and spoke in a low voice.

"Isaac works tirelessly between civic duties, running his tobacco farming and exports, as well as his brewery, but Anneke and her husband eclipse our wealth. Captain van Cortlandt has plenty to spare on his wife's penchant for paving. We do not," she said, swinging open the door to let Sarah enter. "We did, however, finally get some upholstered seating for our great room."

Sarah left her muddy clogs at the doorstep.

She strode across the room to the damask upholstered seating. Her hands grazed the finely turned arms. Sarina's home made hers look like a drab hovel in contrast. She sunk down into the comfort of the blue and white floral padded seat. Sarina and Isaac lost their baby Gerritt to grippe around the same time Jacob died. Right after that, they moved. Sarah hoped the new house brought her friend some consolation, or at least distraction.

"Your home is beautiful," Sarah said. "As are your neighbor's tulips and roses. I understand why she is so protective of them." There was a hint of sarcasm in her tone.

"Thank you. I hadn't considered how much more sweeping and dusting a larger home needs, though. No wonder Anneke has so many servants. You know... those red and white striped tulips are the variety that once fetched five thousand guilders ten years ago. Now, they're not worth much more than the dirt that bespatters them. I just placed an order for some."

"*Bof*, I think I prefer red endive. At least you can eat it!" Sarah laughed. She continued in sincerity. "Good for Anneke getting her paving done. These New Netherlanders born in *Patria* certainly have different expectations than those of us born here, not that I would object to more paved streets."

"Would you like a *kleinbier*? It's from a fresh cask Isaac brewed. You'll like it. He flavored it with ginger, caraway, and cinnamon instead of hops."

Sarina didn't wait for Sarah's reply before she poured some of the beer from a tankard on the table into a green *roemer* glass.

"*À votre santé et à la maison!*" Sarah toasted her friend's health and home, raising her glass high before drinking. She made an appreciative murmur. It was very good.

"Have you heard Melyn and Kuyter returned?"

Sarah's next sip nearly came out her nose.

"What? They're alive?"

"They survived the shipwreck, continued to the Hague, and were vindicated by the States General. Isaac told me Melyn carries a letter from Willem II to deliver to Director Stuyvesant. The Prince of Orange warns Stuyvesant to leave them to enjoy their lands and take the order without objection."

"Astounding... divine provenance that they survived and were pardoned. Resounding vindication. What of Kieft and Domine Bogardus? Did they survive?"

"Apparently, divine provenance was not in their favor. Kuyter said that as the ship sank, Kieft approached him and admitted his wrongs. Neither Kieft nor the Domine were seen ashore."

"That's heartbreaking."

"Kieft deserved worse."

"Perhaps," Sarah said, recalling the horrors of the war. "But asking for forgiveness before the face of death can move a heart of stone."

Three months later, Sarah sat in the back of the courthouse in the fort. She nervously twirled the *sewant* beads of her bracelet. She didn't hear the other cases presented in the court that afternoon. Her thoughts focused on prayers for Hans. The open windows let a gentle May breeze flow through the room, but her underarms and palms were damp with perspiration.

"*Fiscal ex officio*, plaintiff, vs. Hans Hansen Bergen, defendant, on account of smuggling military guns," Van Tienhoven read the charge, taking unveiled satisfaction at the severe accusation against Hans. "Plaintiff demands harsh punitive recourse... Hanging would befit such a crime."

Sarah gasped, along with the rest of the courtroom.

"I admit I helped transport them, but I didn't know they were military guns," Hans replied. His hair was neatly combed back, hat in his hands. His brow furrowed slightly and his blue eyes were wide with innocence, as if this was all just a misunderstanding. One that he was very sorry for.

Loockermans stood to address the *schepens* of the court.

"I have many testimonies that speak of Hans's good character and standing in the community," Loockermans said, passing a dossier to the *schepens*.

They looked over the statements and discussed in whispers. Sarah held her breath.

"The charge is found to be of serious consequence, but inasmuch as Hans has maintained a good name and reputation during his fourteen years' residence in New Netherland, the aforesaid offense is forgiven, on condition that he beg pardon in this court of God and the *schepens*," the magistrate announced.

Sarah exhaled.

"I beg pardon of God and the *schepens*," Hans recited quickly.

"Wherefore the offense above mentioned is forgiven, further demand from the plaintiff is denied," the *schepens* ruled.

After they left the court, Hans half-astonished and half-smugly recited the deceased Kiliaen van Rensselaer's business philosophy to Sarah, which he'd often recited before to Sarah's consternation.

"One cannot accomplish as much by well-doing as by having friends in the game," he said and smirked at her like a rogue.

She allowed him a small, weary smile, but still she wanted to box his ears for the worry he caused her. Van Tienhoven had proposed his execution, and in the end, they didn't even make him swear he'd discontinue such smuggling.

CHAPTER 17

1649-1653

Soon after Melyn and Kuyter returned, Van der Donck gathered a crowd at Cat's Wheel.

"The States General requested Director Stuyvesant send delegates from New Netherland to the Hague, but the Director asked to make sure the delegates represent the will of the people. I've come to record testimonies as to Company rule in the colony," Van der Donck said to the rapt attention of people gathered at Cat's Wheel.

Sarah's father went first.

"Please state your name, age, and time in the colony before your testimony," Van der Donck requested.

"Joris Jansen Rapalje. I'm forty-five and have resided here twenty-five years. I was on the Council of Twelve. I advised against war with the Natives, and the consensus voted to that as well. Our advice was ignored and a minority's opinion was acted on. The soldiers massacred indiscriminately, killing women and children. That attack led to counterattacks. My four-year-old son was murdered on our doorstep during an attack. My bowery on Lange Eylandt burned. Things have gone on so badly and negligently that nothing has ever been designed, understood, nor done that gave appearance for the content of the people; but on the contrary, what good comes from the community has been mixed up with the bad business of the Company. We are in the highest degree beholden to the Natives, who not only have given up to us this good and fruitful country, for a trifle yielded us the ownership, but also enrich us with their good and reciprocal trade. We wish for peace with them."

"My son died in my arms, so near the ineffective protection of the fort and soldiers," Sarah's mother added.

"Thank you. My sympathies for the loss of your son," Van der Donck said. He already knew of their losses but still gave a moment of silence for them before he said, "Hans..."

"Hans Hansen Bergen. I'm thirty-five years of age. I've been a resident for fourteen years. My bowery on Lange Eylandt was also burned in the war. Our crops and home were destroyed there. At the beginning of the war, I thought a show of force was needed, but Director Kieft did not lead his soldiers. His orders only worsened losses for the colonists."

"I appealed to Kieft with alternatives to war, and he threatened to put me in the stocks." Sarah spoke before she thought.

Wanting to be heard by Van der Donck, she hadn't realized Hans was also hearing this for the first time. He looked at her, shocked.

When Sarah and Hans were alone, he reprimanded her.

"You undercut me by appealing to Kieft on your own. That was very foolish. You're lucky you didn't end up in the stocks," he said with a furrowed brow.

"Foolish? Not as foolish as the attacks on the Mareckkawick that led to them burning our bowery," Sarah said. She sensed all the muscles in his body stiffened, but she couldn't look at him, and he had no reply.

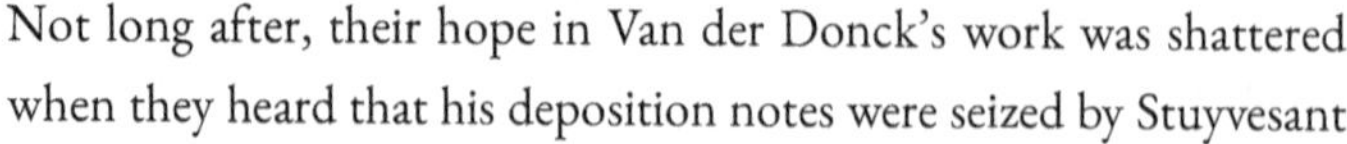

Not long after, their hope in Van der Donck's work was shattered when they heard that his deposition notes were seized by Stuyvesant and he was arrested on the charge of *laesae maiestatis*, an offence of defamation against the dignity of a ruling head of state. High treason.

Two days later, Stuyvesant gathered the entire population of New Amsterdam to the church. He held Van der Donck's folio, no doubt to read aloud what he considered seditious testimonies.

Sarah sat with her mother and the children near the front of the church, nervously wondering what would take place. The men stood in the back, whispering speculations.

Stuyvesant entered and a heavy silence fell over the room. Just as he was about to speak, Melyn rushed the pulpit, seizing the moment and lectern away from Stuyvesant.

"I have a statement given to me from the States General, to be read aloud," Melyn declared.

"Give it here. That is not the purpose of this gathering. It does not need to be read aloud," he said, wrenching it away from Melyn.

The document was torn in the struggle.

The crowd gasped. To Sarah, a state document fought over in a church seemed to be a double desecration.

In a moment, the crowd went from astonishment to eruption. Stuyvesant called the room to order and allowed the reading of the document to proceed. In scolding language directed at Stuyvesant by the higher office, it was a mandamus ordering him to appear before the court in *Patria*. When it was finished, Stuyvesant stood stiffly.

"I will obey their commands and send a delegate in my place to receive their legal pronouncement," Stuyvesant dryly concluded and promptly left the church.

Sarah couldn't stay away from Cat's Wheel. News swirled about the latest developments.

"Stuyvesant is certainly not swaying public opinion in his favor. His own Vice-Director is defying him," Sarah's father said.

"He sells muskets to the Natives while we have a shortage and are barred from doing the same. What hypocrisy! Hans was almost hanged for it!" Sarah's mother said.

"At least he's released Van der Donck. Stuyvesant told him to prove and establish, or revoke, what he wrote," Sarah's father explained. "He said he's going to ask the States General to take charge of the colony and to provide it with a suitable municipal government instead of the tyrannical rule of the Company. He's leaving next month with Jacob van Couwenhoven and Jan Evertsen Bout to present his appeal. Stuyvesant is sending Van Tienhoven as his delegate. All our hope for self-governance resides with Van der Donck."

It was hard for the colonies to keep up with the chaotic news out of Europe at this time, as they were always on at least a three-month lag, and it was especially sparse in the winter months. It was impossible to predict how the news they received would affect the colony or if the latest news was even still accurate. All they knew was that astounding things were happening in Europe, but it remained to be seen how it would affect them.

The following July 1650, Jacob van Couwenhoven and Jan Evertsen Bout returned. Sarah heard what had transpired directly from Jacob van Couwenhoven as Hans insisted hosting him for dinner several days after he arrived. He was an old friend, since he and Hans came to the colony on the same ship, but Sarah still mistrusted him for persuading Hans to sign the petition to attack Lange Eylandt Natives during the war.

"All of *Patria* was abuzz with endless celebrations for the Treaty of Westphalia when we arrived," Jacob said, relishing a circuitous explanation of their visit on his attentive listeners. Sarah didn't understand the significance to their colony. Her confusion must have shown on her face because he continued speaking more slowly, in the tone one uses with a child. "Spain formally recognized the independence of the Dutch Republic."

"That's great news for *Patria*, right?" Hans asked. "But does it affect New Netherland?"

"*Ja*. It means that the influence of the Company has been diminished. Their ships are no longer to be used as arms of war against the Spanish," Jacob explained, eyes shining. "The States General were ready to reconsider New Netherland and the Company's role. They received us with great interest and Van der Donck shined in his exaltation of New Netherland's potential."

"What took so long, if you were so well received?" Hans asked.

"Have you heard nothing of Willem II and his opposition to the treaty? The Prince of Orange threatened to pose a coup against the government with his mercenaries. It considerably distracted the States General from discussions of their overseas colony," he explained, chiding Hans for his ignorance.

Sarah bristled at his condescending tone with her husband. She knew about the Prince of Orange but didn't understand how the political intrigue affected them. In fact, she had heard the news in a puppet show and didn't even know if it was a farce or fact. She didn't understand European politicking. The stories sounded just like a fairy tale of a children's show—royals or nobility jostling for power.

"Then in April, after six months of appearing at the Hague to rally for our cause, finally a ruling came on our case," Jacob continued. "The States General renounced the Company's administration in neglecting and opposing our good plans for the increase of the country. They instructed Stuyvesant to return home and report himself, not a delegate. Jan and I brought home a copy of the papers and a shipment of guns for the defense of the colony. At the time of our departure, it seemed likely they will appoint Van der Donck as the new Director of New Netherland," Jacob concluded triumphantly.

⁕

The New Amsterdam colonists held their breath at every ship that arrived. What news would it bring? When would Van der Donck return? Would they ever be able to form their own government? Sarah, again, saw the news of Europe told in puppet show form at the market with her mother.

The tale of Charles I of England being beheaded the previous year was retold. He was portrayed with long dark curls, mustache with pointed beard, clothes that sparkled with baubles, and a long, upturned nose. Red silk ribbons spilled forth as the puppet's head was liberated from its body. A Puritan named Cromwell became Lord Protector. He had a humble appearance, dressed in brown, with a lump of a face, and silver pauldrons on his shoulders. It was a triumph over tyranny and an end to the English Civil War.

The second show told of further actions of the Prince of Orange. Willem II held government officials captive in a castle and attempted to take Amsterdam with a force of ten thousand men. He failed because of bad weather, and shortly after he died of smallpox. Sarah thought it a fantastic tale and doubted the veracity. According to what Hans's dinner guest said, that should be one distraction removed from the States General reconsidering the governance of New Netherland.

"Have you heard Van Tienhoven returned?" her mother asked.

"*Non.* What about Van der Donck?"

"He's still in the Hague. There's more about Van Tienhoven though. He abandoned his role countering Van der Donck's arguments because of a young paramour. He convinced some basket maker's daughter that he intended to marry her. Her father found out and they absconded on a ship home. Rachel met him at the docks when he arrived with the mistress, who apparently had no idea he was already married!"

"That's outrageous! What did Rachel do?"

"She convinced him to eschew the young girl and return to her and their children."

"She should have asked for a divorce from that adulterous swine!" Sarah said, appalled and full of sorrow for Rachel.

On February 2, 1653, the bells of the City Tavern rang in a newly formed government. Under pressure from the States General, the Company board members allowed Stuyvesant to form a municipal government with a *schout*, two *burgomasters*, and five *schepens*. The City Tavern would be rechristened the *Stadthuys*, where judicial court and governmental meetings would be held.

"This is officially the city of New Amsterdam now," Sarah said to her father as they watched the ceremony.

She held her one-year-old, Maria, on her hip and looked around. There were handsome, new brick homes, but she could see clearly in her mind's eye the dilapidated roughhewn homes abandoned during the war. She had a murkier memory of the site being a Native encampment in the summer months when she was a child.

"*Bof.* We're leaving New Amsterdam for the Waalebocht," her father said, shaking his head and walked away.

Sarina moved to stand by Sarah's side, her two-year-old son with her. Sarah set down Maria to play with Johannes.

"It should be a triumphant day, but my husband is as disappointed as your father." Sarina nodded to where Isaac stood among Stuyvesant's former council members as the new government officials were sworn in. "Isaac said Stuyvesant ignored the requirement of elections for government officials. He was hoping for a continued appointment with the new government. He was hoping Van der Donck would be our new Director."

"We've all had that hope dashed. My father can't stomach that the new war with England has secured the Company's control over the colony. He said he's moving to the Waalebocht. He just wants to be in the quiet countryside, some distance away from politics."

"Isaac feels the same disappointment, but he's not running off to bury his head into the muck of farm life."

"Well, you've got a good husband, Sarina. It's just... my father's been here longer than Isaac. He's tired of waiting for progress and ready for younger men to take up the fight."

"My father has been here as long as yours, yet he continues to serve as court messenger."

"Your father's role is different. He serves to uphold the law, not the Director's whims."

Sarina shrugged and Sarah continued.

"I remember welcoming Isaac to our tavern when he first arrived. Pimple-pocked and idealistic. I'm glad the pimples disappeared, but he's still an idealist." Sarah smiled and Sarina needled her pointy elbow into Sarah's ribs.

"Your parents should be proud that New Amsterdam is finally recognized as a city by *Patria*. They had some hand in that, same as my parents. There was nothing but *wilden* when they came here to settle. Now look at it! A civilized municipality!"

"If Europe's ongoing wars are any indication of civilized society, I'd rather not have it," Sarah said wryly of the Anglo–Dutch war.

She knew that in part her parents were proud of the colony being recognized as a city. They'd persevered. And she had, too.

CHAPTER 18

1653

It was Sarah's favorite time of year. In autumn the trees became enormous bouquets of gold, amber, crimson, and vermilion. Abundance reigned. She loved the gathering of the harvest, sweating in the cooling air, processing the crops, then organizing them in their storehouse. She wasn't able to do much of that this year though.

Her belly swelled larger than with any of her previous children, as did her ankles and feet. She was tired all the time. Lightning bursts of pain traveled from her groin up her back, making it impossible to wield a thrasher, a winnowing basket, or even stand for long periods to prepare meals.

Her oldest daughter, Aneken, now thirteen, helped care for their cows, hogs, and chickens as well as snaring rabbits and birds. Sarah wondered at how she'd taken over the role of an eldest son, but she realized she'd done the same at her age. Rebecca, at eleven years old, was responsible for her younger siblings. She doted on each of them like Sarah wished she could, given more time in the day.

On a pleasant afternoon in mid-September, Sarah sat on a barrel while she supervised her children pull carrots and cabbages from the garden. Four-year-old Joris, nicknamed Jorsey, pulled hard on a stubborn carrot. When it suddenly loosed from the earth, his heels went over his head as he tumbled backward. Dirt spattered his face and duckling-like blond hair. She laughed as he proudly held up a red

Hoorn carrot as fat as his wrist and as long as his face. A lightning burst in her womb choked off her laugh. She gripped her belly as her muscles thrummed with a birthing wave.

"Rebecca, fetch *Grand-mère*!"

Aneken helped Sarah to the house. She didn't need to be told to boil water and bring out clean old linens.

Time was amorphous in the pain. She could remember her mother arriving, but not how long it took until her baby was in her arms. A boy. Jacob. It was still light outside. She pushed again, expecting the *arrière-faix*, and the end. The waves continued, however, just as strong. A few more waves produced another head. Another push and there was a baby girl. Catalyntje.

Bewildered, with her son already latched, Sarah didn't know how to also hold her daughter. Her mother helped adjust Jacob so Catalyntje could latch on her other pap. Sarah realized then how small and frail Catalyntje was in comparison. She was sluggish to nurse and nearly dozed off without a first meal.

Later, Sarah thought she knew the girl would not live at that moment, but she couldn't allow herself to accept it. She did everything she could to get the girl to nurse. Jacob wailed in hunger as Sarah tried with all her might to give Catalyntje enough milk.

Hans nearly fainted when he saw there were two babies. Sarah saw agony on his face when he assessed their disparity in health.

They baptized the twins. Catalyntje wasted away and passed quietly not long after. It felt surreal to Sarah. She slept very little. When she did sleep, she would awake looking for both her babies, reliving the loss of her baby girl anew.

Sarah poured herself into hyper-vigilance over her children and delegating management of the household while she recovered from birth and death. Hans took the loss as quietly as their daughter left them. Sarah resented his silence. She interpreted it as indifference.

Hans retreated into his work and proffered excuses to be away from home.

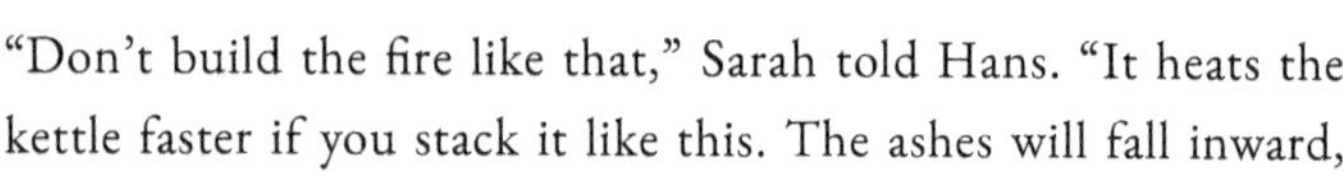

"Don't build the fire like that," Sarah told Hans. "It heats the kettle faster if you stack it like this. The ashes will fall inward, instead of spewing across the floor when the logs fall."

Hans kicked the wood and it clattered against the back of the fireplace. He walked to the other side of the room.

"I'm taking a job from Loockermans. I'll be gone a few days, maybe a week."

"Must you?" Sarah pleaded with him. She understood he needed a break from their household. She hated feeling like he needed a break from her. "Please..."

"*Ja*, Sarah, I must." He wasn't seeking her opinion or arguing. He shut down either option with his tone of voice.

"Please... be careful," she said as she held back tears. "Don't get called to court again. They won't be so lenient a second time."

A week after Hans left, a young man showed up at Sarah's door whom she'd never seen. His plain clothes gave no clues to what his business was, standing at her doorstep. He wouldn't meet Sarah's eyes.

"I'm sorry to inform you that... unfortunately... I'm sorry... I regret... that your husband, Hans, died on our trip. There was an attack. We lost Hans."

Her mind spun. Her vision went black.

Sarah came to with the young man shaking her awake. She was on the ground, flat on her back, with her children and the young man looking down at her. Pain radiated from the back of her head where she hit the floor. She shot to her feet and grabbed the young man by the shoulders. He was the same height as her.

"*Non. Comment? C'est vrai?*" She realized she was speaking French to a Netherlander by his blank stare. "How? Are you sure? What happened to him? Where is he?" she asked frantically as she shook him for answers.

"We lost him in an attack," was all he could say.

Sarah went to Govert Loockermans for more information as soon as she could.

"Hans was a great man. I am sorry for your loss, and I share in it. I have little information as I wasn't there, but the other men said smallpox ravaged the village they went to. They searched for survivors and saw no one. Then Hans's party was assailed by arrows as they returned to their canoes. Perhaps it was misplaced vengeance from afflicted *wilden*?" Loockermans offered, shrugging and shaking his head. His body shuddering and squirming looked like he was trying to shake any blame off himself. "The other man with Hans was found in their canoe with arrows in his back."

"But you didn't find Hans? How do you know he's dead?"

"They were last seen in the canoe together. The man with Hans was dead in the canoe."

"Maybe Hans swam away?"

"They searched."

"I can't accept that. Take me there. I will search for myself."

"I understand your grief. As I said, I share in your loss."

"What do you know of sharing in my loss? You lost someone who worked for you, who is easily replaceable. I have seven children who lost their father. Hans was everything to us... this... devastation..."

Sarah broke down. She didn't care. She wanted him to witness the ugliness of her pain.

"*Mevrouw*, you must understand, I valued him highly, above others. I know it is no consolation, but I will pay you what Hans would have profited from this trip," Loockermans offered.

Sarah choked back tears and tried to speak, but she didn't know what to say. How would that do anything to fill the void left by Hans?

He opened the door for her to leave. She dug in her heels.

"Did you report this to Director Stuyvesant? Perhaps he could send a search party?" Sarah asked, unwilling to drop the matter.

"*Mevrouw*, attracting Stuyvesant's attention would not be wise. My men reported a thorough search of the area. The only place they didn't check was the bottom of the river, and it's the only possibility for his final resting place."

"Hans has an uncle in New Sweden... Knut Martenson. What if Hans escaped and fled to Fort Christina?"

Loockermans looked at her with pity, shaking his head.

"I'll send an inquiry to his Uncle Knut," he said in a reassuring tone. "He should be notified of the death, in any case. I'll send my messenger boy to deliver Hans's wages to you and an answer from his uncle when I receive it."

She nodded and left, still crying.

There was no funeral. There was no grave. It was a long, dark winter. Some days, Sarah couldn't bring herself to get out of bed.

It was the first winter they spent at the Waalebocht. Since her father made the decision to move there permanently, Sarah followed to be near her family. Catalyna visited Sarah often, to take care of her children, and make sure Sarah ate.

"Is Loockermans sure that it was not retribution for him killing the Minquas *sachem* not so long ago? I heard Stuyvesant restricted Loockermans from trading in the South River area. No wonder he doesn't want to alert Stuyvesant of the attack," her mother said.

Catalyna brought up a fair point, but speculating motive changed nothing. Hans did not return.

Sarah received Hans's wages from Loockermans and a message from his uncle. She had to have her Swedish neighbor translate it. He expressed condolences and regret that he hadn't seen Hans since he was a boy. Sarah's last hope collapsed.

Weenji came to visit. She never usually visited in the winter. She brought her son with her. Mehakachtey was excited to show her children some *arakun* tracks. Sarah's son Jan and Mehakachtey didn't need any encouragement to go off together, and the younger children followed them. Mehakachtey had taught Jan how to find animal burrows and make rabbit snares over the past summer. Sarah found some satisfaction in their boys' friendship. In learning from each other, Sarah hoped they would somehow heal the divisions formed during Kieft's War.

With the children distracted, Sarah cried in Weenji's arms. Weenji also wept. She'd lost her husband too and she understood Sarah's pain. Weenji said little, but she helped Sarah wash her hair and sang her a song. It was a melancholy, breathy chant.

After Weenji combed and oiled Sarah's hair, she pulled her knife from her belt and cut a hand's length off the bottom. She threw it on the fire. The acrid scent of singed hair and the resinous, balsam-like oil filled the air. Sarah had no idea what these rites meant, but she didn't need to ask. It felt like a funeral. An acknowledgment of loss.

She wailed. It felt good to get those collapsing deep sobs out. Sarah slept a full night for the first time after that. Weenji looked after Sarah for several days before she left for the winter village of her tribe.

Phebe visited as often as she could, at least once a week. Sarina paid one brief visit. She also grieved. Her father and eldest brother were killed that past September. Sarah had missed the funeral because of the twins' birth and Catalyntje's demise.

"People whisper that *wilden* attacked them, but no one could figure out a motive or who was responsible. There's speculation it could have been someone who had come into conflict with my father's court messenger duties," Sarina said.

"My heart breaks for the loss and the unanswered questions—for your father, brother, and my husband. Not knowing is the cruelest grief," Sarah said.

"Why do you stay here at the Waalebocht? You should move back to town."

"*Non*, I want to be near my parents. My sister Maria and her husband run Cat's Wheel now. I prefer the farm."

"Will you remarry?"

"Sarina, I can't even think of it."

"Good. If any woman could make it on her own, it's you. You aren't so desperate as some widows."

Jacob slept in Sarah's arms. She laid him down in the rocking bassinet Hans made. She retreated and sobbed. Sarina went to her, and Sarah composed herself.

"How simple life was when Hans made that bassinet. Before the war. Before we buried two children. Before Hans left... How endless and bright our future seemed then."

PART THREE: BONDS

1654–1663

Seek transformation. O be eager for that flame
in which something escapes you, proud of change.
In overcoming the earthbound, that designing spirit
loves the zest of a figure at its turning point.

– Rainer Maria Rilke –
"Sonnets to Orpheus"
Translated by Martyn Crucefix
Part 2, Number 12

CHAPTER 19

1654

Sarah's dreams tormented her, but these wild imaginings of Hans's death came day and night.

The variations were endless. Hans sang "*In Mijn Grootste Nood O'Heere*" as an arrow pierced his throat. He was taken captive by Minquas, given as a thrall to the *sachem*'s daughter, and forced to fight a bear to the death for amusement. Hans escaped a volley of arrows, but drowned in the river. He tried to make his way back to her, but exhausted and starving, he curled up to rest in the hollow of a rotten oak and died.

In these diverse predicaments, he died over and over, carving an aching hollow at her core. She knew, even when she imagined a peaceful and painless death for Hans, it wouldn't stop her from driving the dagger of loss deeper. It was like compulsive pickings at a scab. So, she took up *passementerie* to escape her thoughts.

She used to hate lacemaking lessons as a child. She couldn't focus and sit still to find the rhythm of the weaving bobbins. But now, keeping her hands busy with methodical work was the only thing that stopped the visions of Hans. It took her whole concentration to get into a rhythm so the lace would be neat and even. She could count threads instead of reasons to despair. It was something she could do by candlelight, late at night, when she couldn't sleep.

She soon realized that she not only had a remedy for her grief, but also a source of income.

Her mother was right. The skill taught to young Catalyna in the orphan workhouse of Leiden would have to become a means for Sarah's survival. The city's population was growing again, and lace-trimmed linens were *de rigueur* for those who could afford it.

The market in New Amsterdam flitted with activity. The March snow fell softly, blown in meandering directions like the shoppers.

Sarah stood with her *passementerie* sample book in one hand, finished goods in the other.

"Lace cuffs, collars, and coifs! Pillowcases, table linens!" Sarah exclaimed to the mostly indifferent ears around her.

A young woman met her eyes from across the street and made her way to meet Sarah. She was not unlike many other Dutch women. She held herself with dignity and determination. Sarah braced herself for a forceful bargaining.

"These are exquisite. Do you import them?" the woman asked, skipping small talk.

"I make them. They are Valenciennes *passementerie*, taught to me by my mother," Sarah replied.

"I'm an agent for several merchants. I trade commodities, such as pins, for pelts," she said. "As I establish a household, I will need lace-trimmed linens though. What's your name?"

"Sarah Jorise Rapalje. And yours?"

"Margaret Hardenbroeck."

"Are you married or betrothed?"

"Neither." Margaret laughed. "Perhaps someday... sooner or later. I'll keep you in mind when I have need of household trimmings..."

"Are you in need of cuffs or perhaps a collar?"

Sarah did not suggest a coif because the woman wore a castor hat. The hat suited her.

"I'd like some cuffs. I would pay two hands of *sewant* for those," Margaret said, pointing to the cuffs in Sarah's hand.

"Five," Sarah countered.

Margaret shook her head and turned abruptly to leave. Sarah admired her confidence and envied her apparent ease with being unmarried, but she wouldn't let her walk away from the sale.

"I'll give you a deal if you can trade two hundred pins and eight skeins of fine linen thread," Sarah cried after her.

Margaret's head swiveled.

"Two hundred pins and *six* skeins of thread," Margaret offered.

"Deal," Sarah said.

That night after going to the market, Sarah laid in her bed, not asleep but not awake. It was nearly dawn. A muffled shattering cracked the silence. Sarah's eyes sprang open. The storehouse. Something or someone was in the storehouse.

She raced to don Hans's coat. She paced the room to retrieve their fowling piece, but she couldn't find the pouch with the powder, wadding, and shot in the dark. The ax would do instead. Jacob began to cry. All of her children were awake now.

"Stay here. Comfort your brother. I'll be right back."

The faint glow of predawn on the horizon gave enough light that every shadowed landmark of her yard menaced. A dormant shrub looked like a crouching gargoyle. The hitching post loomed like a wraith. The chickens made blathering nervous warbles in the barn.

Sarah inched her way to the storehouse. As she drew closer, she could hear something scratching and riffling.

What if it was a bear? It sounded smaller than a bear.

She kicked the door and it swung open. A second later, a rush of fur brushed past her ankles. The fat rumps and banded tails of a family of racoons bolted away from her. She turned back to the storehouse. A shaft of dawn light illuminated one raccoon left inside the storehouse, oblivious to danger, chewing a haunch of smoked venison. A primal rage overtook Sarah. She strode forward and swung her ax decisively, like her ferocious ancestors of Gallia. Racoon meat tasted like pork and would have to replace the filched provisions.

After sunrise, she assessed the losses. They'd smashed a large crock of dried beans, ate most of her sausages, a good portion of venison, and made off with some of the corn that hung from the rafters.

She found where they entered. There was a hole in the roof where they pulled off half a shingle with their devilish little hands. The Lenape word *arakun* meant "he scratches with his hands." Their clever little fingers had always made Sarah wary. The opening wasn't large. She was surprised they could fit their fat rumps through it. Sarah considered if she could repair it herself, but she would take no chances on the creatures regaining entry. Her father would have to help her fix it right away.

Thoughts of her father reminded her of deer hunting with him when she was younger. She placed a hand on the dead *arakun*.

"Thank you for your life," she said as her father taught her, as he had been taught by the Mahicans. "Sorry you paid for your family's meal with your life, but now you will help feed my family."

There was a rustle, and Sarah braced herself with the ax again, but it was only the storehouse cat, Grietje. She was a descendant of Perle, but nowhere near as fine a mouser. Grietje stretched and looked at Sarah with a sleepy, half-interested gaze.

"You slept through the whole thing, Grietje? You worthless creature!" Sarah stooped for the cat to rub her cheeks across Sarah's knuckles. "We'd be better off with a storehouse dog."

Phebe often visited Sarah that spring. She helped Sarah make bread and cheese, boil laundry, mend clothes, make tallow candles, soap, or other household necessities.

"I know you need distractions and company, so I brought all nine of my little distractions," Phebe said as she came in the door that day, full brood in tow. Sarah's children cheered at the sight of Phebe's.

"Oh, good! It's laundry day and my children's arms are already tired of cranking the wringer." Sarah winked at Phebe.

"Pitch in, children!" Phebe said.

Sarah started her usual frenetic ramble to Phebe.

"This morning I was wondering... should I sell some of our cows? But then we won't have as much milk and I've been bartering butter for thread to make lace. The money from the lace I'll use to pay some farmhands to plant and harvest. No, never mind. I'll ask Weenji to help with fieldwork and save some money. I can pay her in baked goods. She can't pass up my *koekjes* and baguettes. The children need new shoes. The sow will have a farrow soon. I can sell the piglets. I was thinking of getting a guard dog after those racoons invaded the storehouse and ate most of our meat..."

She always marveled at how talking her plans aloud to her friend always helped, although Phebe rarely interjected with solutions. Phebe surprised her by speaking up at that moment when Sarah took a breath and would have continued her ramble.

"Have you thought about remarrying? I know you can manage everything... but there's only so much you can do in a day," Phebe said gingerly, with caution.

"I can't say I haven't thought about it because my parents keep bringing it up. But I cannot imagine marrying again," Sarah said, shaking her head. "If only Aneken would become proficient with *passementerie,* I think we could nearly make as much selling lace as Hans did with his carpentry."

"I hate it!" Aneken said. "I'd rather muck out the animal stalls."

"Don't be so stubborn. You must learn to make lace *and* muck out the stalls."

"Sarah, she sounds just like you when you were her age," Phebe whispered and laughed. "You're just as stubborn now to not even consider remarrying."

"Who would I marry? No one could replace Hans."

"Don't think of it that way. Your bowery is a business, and you need a new partner to help you run it."

"The Company is a business and they only have one Director to run all of New Netherland."

"And how well has that been for its settlers? The truth is... Nys has been pushing me to introduce you to a new friend of his," Phebe confided. "He's a young man, energetic, solidly built—no stranger to hard work—and handsome too! I like him, Sarah. You should meet him at least."

Sarah gave her a wary look, scrunching her nose.

"Is he one of those men who keeps Nys out drinking at the tavern to all hours?"

"No, of course not. He makes Nys leave at a proper time. That's why I like him. In fact, I like when Nys brings him home to share in our evening meal because he's good company. He has a way with the children, too."

"Where's he from?"

"Same province as Nys. I think that's why my husband has taken such a liking to him."

"Is he a widower?"

"No."

"Then why hasn't he married by now?"

"You'll have to ask him. Next week, have your mother mind the children at your parents' house. I'll bring Nys and his friend. Just a friendly visit," Phebe pleaded with her.

"Does he know I have seven children? Will that scare him off when he finds out?" Sarah asked.

"He knows. I suggest you first meet him without the children because it might be less distracting," Phebe said. "It doesn't scare men off. On the contrary. It attracts them because they know it'll be a fruitful union."

"Did he say that?"

"No, but he yearns to be a father. I can tell. He didn't flinch when I said you have seven. I could see it in his eyes that he wants some of his own."

"Perhaps I'll meet him," Sarah finally agreed, "but please, no more talk of fruitful unions. Just a friendly visit."

CHAPTER 20

1654

The following week, Phebe came to visit Sarah with her husband and his friend. Sarah's stomach churned with nerves.

Even as she told herself she wasn't interested in attracting a new husband, her pride wouldn't allow her to be an ungracious hostess.

She fastidiously cleaned her home. A seafood stew with fish, pickled eel, smoked oysters, a sundry of root vegetables, and herbs sputtered over the fire. Rye bread, cheese, and freshly churned butter sat ready on the table.

She wore a pale woad-blue linen skirt and bodice she usually reserved for church, a black partlet, and a plain white coif over her plaited hair.

"Sarah, it's good to see you!" Nys jovially greeted her as they came in. "This is Teunis Gysbertse Bogaert. He's from a village near mine in Utrecht and practically my younger brother, if you count our similarities," Nys laughed.

They even had the same given name, except everyone called Phebe's husband by his nickname. Nys was a good man to break the awkwardness of the meeting, reliably gregarious and talkative.

"Thank you for having us to visit," Teunis said, more soft-spoken than Nys. "Your home is charming, and the food smells delightful."

Taking off his hat, he held it to his chest and bowed slightly with a boyishly shy smile. Sarah nodded to him, then kept her eyes on her hands, which sought inane tasks to stay busy.

She noticed how he and Nys had the same accent, slightly different from the other Netherlanders. She'd always thought the funny way Nys said his vowels was merely a personal quirk.

"Welcome. Please, have a seat," Sarah said, gesturing to the long kitchen table and benches. "How was the ferry over today?"

"A bit chilly, but not too bad. I brought some brandy to warm us up. May I?" Nys offered.

"Certainly," Sarah said, setting out her green *roemer* glass goblets that were reserved for special occasions.

She finally allowed herself to regard Teunis while Nys filled the air with idle chatter about the weather. She had to admit Phebe was right. He was handsome, though not in the same way as Hans. He had strikingly beautiful, dark brown eyes. Though not as tall as Hans, he was younger by ten years, closer to Sarah and Phebe's age. The peaks of his cheekbones were the healthy color of someone who spent their time outdoors. He had a tidy, tapered mustache and chin hairs. When he took off his castor hat, he revealed thick, wavy, light brown hair to the length of his ears.

He carefully undid the brass buttons of his dark brown duffel cassock. He had fastened it like a cape for the cold, but he opened it to the elbow to free his arms.

"Teunis has been in the service of the Company the past few years. He arrived not too long ago, coming from the Caribbean." Nys said. That may explain his tanned cheeks, Sarah thought.

"*Ja*, mostly in the sugar trade, although we had some confrontations with English and Spanish vessels. My brother-in-law, Aert, and I intend to settle in New Netherland. My cousins came ahead of us and have settled up north in Beverwijck and Catskill."

"Oh, is that where you intend to settle?" Sarah asked, sipping her brandy. The burn as she swallowed helped distract from the nervous tightness in her chest.

"Perhaps, but I've become rather enchanted by New Amsterdam. I think the northern territory might be too desolate for me. Nys understands." He shot Nys a sideways glance as Nys nodded. "I like your city. The stepped-gambrel brick buildings, the canal, the busy market, and the number of languages spoken in town make it feel a lot like Amsterdam. And yet there's still such a bounty of land for farming!" Teunis spoke animatedly.

Sarah smiled at him for admiring the "canal" that longtime residents derisively called the Ditch. People tossed their household refuse in it, and it usually stank terribly until high tide took the rotten vegetables, animal guts, and fish carcasses away. Stuyvesant recently ordered it cleaned and dug deeper. Perhaps it did deserve to be called a canal now.

"Sarah was born at Fort Orange, before there was the town of Beverwijck, but her parents had one of the very first houses on Manhattan. People call her the eldest child of New Netherland because she was the first born here," Phebe boasted of her friend.

"Really? That's remarkable! You must have seen so much change in the city," Teunis wondered dreamily.

Sarah felt her cheeks burn with embarrassment and vexation. She realized Teunis must imagine a wilderness come to be a city in a nice orderly progression, without knowing the horrors like Kieft's War that set them back and shattered the beauty of her early life here. She was jealous of that ignorance. He had a clean slate to appreciate the place. She wished she could see it like that again.

"How about some food?" Sarah changed the subject and began dishing out the stew into wooden bowls.

They ate heartily and drank some more brandy. The atmosphere was more convivial now that they all were full and a little drunk. Sarah cleared their bowls and brought out long clay pipes for each of the men and a box of tobacco leaf blended with aromatic herbs. She and Phebe shared a pipe.

"That was delicious. I couldn't believe the size of oysters for sale in town, some as big as a man's head!" Teunis exclaimed. He took off his cassock, revealing a stiffly starched linen shirt and worn, dark leather jerkin. More humble-looking attire than his coat, but Sarah liked how the snug, worn leather accentuated his broad chest.

Sarah took off her coif. The brandy made her feel overheated.

"The small ones are sweeter, but the large ones are delicacies in stews, like this," Sarah said.

"Quite good fried too," Phebe added, as she drew on the pipe and blew out a plume of smoke.

"What's your favorite crop?" Teunis asked Sarah. Nys looked at him quizzically, as if it was an improper question to ask a lady. Phebe laughed.

"Red amaranth. It's not a staple crop, but the flowers are beautiful and I love the grain," Sarah said without pause.

"Never heard of it. How about favorite fish?"

"One time, I saw men bring in a sturgeon from upriver. It was mythic in size! But to my taste, I could eat smoked trout every day."

"How about your favorite nut?"

"Chestnut."

"Favorite mushroom?"

"Chestnut."

"You just said that..."

Sarah laughed. "It's the name of a nut and a mushroom. You find the mushroom around oak, not chestnut trees though. There were some dried ones in the stew."

Teunis stared at her, grinning. She willed herself to hold his gaze, and he bashfully looked away. Sarah wondered if he was charmed by her or just drunk. The way his thumb lazily circled one prunt on his glass made her whole body flush. The raspberry-shaped raised dots were for a better grip on the glass. She had never thought of them as so suggestive.

She poured them all more brandy, hoping to get him to divulge something more about himself, but he beat her to the next inquiry.

"Tell me about your children," he asked and looked at her with intense interest.

Sarah stiffened. She suddenly felt guilty she had been having such a pleasant time.

"There are seven. Four boys and three girls. The youngest, Jacob, is six months old, and the eldest, Aneken, is thirteen," she replied.

"Such a marvelous woman must have equally marvelous children," Teunis said, looking at Sarah in a way that made her blush again, despite herself. "I'd like to meet them."

Phebe and Nys looked very pleased as they departed with Teunis to return home. Sarah bid them adieu from her stoop and went back into her empty house. The silence was unnerving. She considered taking up her *passementerie* to clear her head, but she realized she was too befuddled to concentrate.

There was a knock at the door.

She opened it to see Teunis had come back. Alone. They looked at each other, each hesitating to speak first. The wind blew an icy chill into the house.

"Come in, please."

"I... I forgot my gloves," he said in a low voice.

She looked around but didn't see them.

"Here they are." He scooped them up from under the table and nearly lost his balance.

She stepped close to catch him. They were both tipsy. He held on to her for a long moment before he drew back, embarrassed. Her impatient fingers had the urge to draw him close to her, run through his hair, and pull him in for a kiss. Instead, she also stepped back, embarrassed and horrified by her urges.

"That brandy was good, huh?" He laughed and broke the awkward moment. Sarah laughed too.

"Would you like to come for dinner again?" she asked. "Next week. You can meet my children."

"*Ja*, with pleasure," he answered, smiling with an eased expression. "Excuse me, I must catch up to Phebe and Nys to catch the ferry back. Thank you, again."

He paused, as if he considered kissing her goodbye. Instead, he tipped his hat and bowed before he closed the door after himself.

The next week, Sarah's little ones played catch with a straw-stuffed leather ball Teunis brought. Every time the little ones threw to him, he'd feign being knocked over by the force, making them squeal with giggles. He had a jester-like humor that easily charmed them.

The older children looked to Sarah as to how they should regard him. Sarah was polite and reserved, so they were too. Only Aneken interrogated him.

"Can you birth a calf?" she asked.

"*Ja*, I grew up on a farm. I've seen many calves come into this world. And piglets, colts, kids, puppies, and kittens."

"Are you good with a bow and arrow?"

"*Nee*, but I'm a good aim with a musket. And quick to reload."

"Have you ever killed a man?"

He paused a moment.

"*Nee*. I've shot at English and Spanish vessels, but I don't think anyone was fatally wounded."

"Did you fight pirates?" her son, Jan, chimed in.

"*Nee.* They steered clear of our ship. They were outgunned."

"Children, let the man be. He's a guest in our home, and we're not the Inquisition," Sarah scolded.

"It's all right," Teunis laughed. "It's only fair after all the questions I peppered you with during our first meeting."

When he prepared to leave, Sarah busied herself. She doted on her children, swept invisible crumbs from the table, tended the fire—all so she wouldn't have to put words to how much she would like to see him again.

She needed to feed Jacob. Her breasts were swollen and distracting in their ache.

Teunis said goodbye with a little bow and tip of his hat.

"Until next time," he called out as he closed the door after himself.

Sarah went to her parents' home the day after Teunis's visit. He told her he'd already visited with Catalyna and Joris. A feeling akin to panic tightened her chest when he said that. It meant his interest was sincere. She was curious but unnerved, wondering about their opinion of him.

Her mother met her and the children at the stoop, kissed their cheeks, and helped the little ones out of their muddy clogs. They went inside, where her father sat at the table, drinking peppermint tea. She sat down beside him and put her head on his shoulder.

"*Bonjour, ma petite puce,*" her father said, kissing her on the forehead. "You have a suitor! Teunis Bogaert came to ask for our blessing to wed you. I'm sure you guessed as much. What are your thoughts on him?"

"What are *your* thoughts on him?" she parroted back.

"*Très beau,*" her mother said with a sly, sidelong glance, her face not revealing much more as she joined them at the table.

"He's familiar with hard work. His hands have good calluses, and he's the son of a planter. He's well suited for taking on the bowery," her father considered with raised eyebrows, mouth scrunched to one side. "He spoke with much interest in crops and farming practices here."

"Is that why he would marry me?" Sarah asked suspiciously. "Does he want my land?"

"I got the impression he was smitten with you, not land. I was starting with the practicalities, but he mostly spoke of how well he regarded you," her father said, seemingly offended for the young man. "Beautiful and bright were the words he used."

"And he was quite ingratiating to us, having raised you," her mother said, smug in her approval. "Your father never goes about these conversations the right way, but I agree. He's a capable young man, quite taken with you."

"You could remain a widow, *ma petite*," her father said gently, "or you could be joined in all the woes and joys of life with a husband to share the load."

"Think of your children, especially your boys. They need a father." Her mother leaned close to whisper to Sarah. "You are lucky. A hardworking man that's not bad to look at... and clearly smitten with you *and* your children. I don't see how it's a difficult decision."

"We gave him our blessing, but the decision is yours, of course," her father said, looking at her with eyes that understood it was not a decision taken lightly.

"You are still so young," her mother said. "Your children are still so young."

"Well, he hasn't asked *me* yet," Sarah said and left it at that.

Sarah reluctantly came to comprehend that although she *could* remain a widow, life would be much harder without a partner. She thought shamefully of how she'd wanted to kiss him. The Domines would say it's better to marry than to burn with passion. She thought of Margaret Hardenbroeck and her independence, yet she hadn't the connections to become a she-merchant beyond selling her paltry lace. There were several other she-merchants, but she couldn't think of one who wasn't acting as agent for her husband or some other family member back in *Patria*.

She sometimes still expected Hans to walk through the door, half-heartedly believing he might be alive in Minquas territory, trying to get back to her. Would she be an adulteress then? A bigamist?

Sarah heard from Phebe and Nys that Teunis went upriver to visit his cousins. Several weeks went by. She thought perhaps his cousins persuaded him to settle up north. Relief from the pressure to remarry intermingled with disappointment.

She decided to sell their house on Pearl Straat. There was nothing for her there, only memories of her girlhood. And so much of Hans.

She set aside the money for her children. She resolved to work as hard as possible to survive as a widow without needing to use her children's inheritance.

CHAPTER 21

1654

One morning in July, Sarah opened the front door to go milk the cows and nearly tripped over a pair of wooden clogs on her doorstep. They were carved with her initials "SJR" and patterns of little flowers. How odd, she thought. Who would have left her handmade *klompen*?

She brought them in the house. Her children sat at the table, eating bread and cheese to break their fast.

"Where did these come from?"

They gave her blank stares.

Later in the day, Sarah heard strange noises. She went to the pigsty and found that the sow had birthed her farrow. The children gathered to look. Seven softly snorting piglets! Sarah sent a silent prayer of thanks to the Lord. The children helped position them into a row to nurse, so none were crowded out in their greedy jostling for the best position at the paps.

She felt it was a good sign there were seven, same as her brood. She vowed she would not lose a one of them. Their pink freckled flesh looked so vulnerable. She tucked a horse blanket over them, even though it was a pleasant, early summer day.

"Sarah?" someone called out.

It was Teunis.

He roved the yard, looking for her. Sarah, shocked to see him, froze, and stayed crouched down in the pigsty. She hadn't heard he'd returned to New Amsterdam. Suddenly, she realized she was acting like a coward, hiding in the pigsty. She popped up and waved.

"Hallo, Teunis!"

His face brightened and he smiled. She strode to meet him at the gate, but his smile turned to disappointment when she opened the gate and he looked down at her feet.

"What's the matter?" Sarah asked him, confused.

"You aren't wearing the *klompen*?" he asked her dejectedly.

She looked down at her feet, at her muck clogs that she always wore. She finally put it together.

"*You* left those for me?" she asked.

"I made them for you ... as my marriage proposal." He spoke in a whisper, cheeks turning red, and turned to leave.

The dam she'd built up around her heart burst with a wave of affection for him. It was such a sweet gesture, and she didn't understand how, but she had botched it completely.

He thought she refused him, and that made her realize that wasn't what she wanted at all.

"Teunis, wait!" She ran after him. She grabbed his hand to stop him from leaving. His hand was rough with calluses, as her father said, and his nails bitten short. He hung his head and looked at the ground. Her words tumbled out.

"I don't understand. What did you say? I thought they were too lovely to wear. I didn't know *you* made them. I didn't know..."

She stared at his hand and ran her fingertips along the hard ridges. Giddy exhilaration rushed through her, like she had with Hans that night she first kissed him, on the precipice of an irrevocable decision that exhilarated her. She wanted to feel those rough hands on her body, and her cheeks heated at the thought.

He took her chin with his forefinger and made her look up. His rich brown eyes searched hers for an answer. It felt like her stomach dropped through her womb and lit a fire that surged through every part of her. And yet, she froze in place.

"Will you walk with me?" he asked.

She nodded. He held her hand to lead her. She realized he did not know where he was going, so she pulled him down the path that overlooked the East River. They walked in silence, hands still intertwined. She led him to a rocky outcrop that overlooked the river to Manhattan. She faced him.

He removed his hand from hers, took off his hat, and crushed it to his chest. His lips parted, as if to speak. Her eyes fixated on his mouth. She drew nearer to hear him. He smelled good. One of his hands moved to the small of her back and pressed her closer. The hand on her back was enough to make her lose her composure. She ran her fingers through his hair, pulled his face to hers, and kissed him. He tasted like wild sweet mint. A weighty sigh escaped him as he returned her kiss, pulling her body to his. She nestled into him in such an easy way. He didn't have to stoop so low as Hans did to kiss her.

The thought of Hans made her arms go slack, and she stepped back. Her cheeks blazed and she stared at her muck-encrusted clogs.

"Why did you make me clogs?"

"It's tradition," he explained, naïvely expecting that to be self-evident. "The man leaves clogs for his beloved. Upon return the next day, if she is wearing them, then she accepts the marriage." He smiled shyly.

"Why do you want to marry me?"

"You're beautiful, but... you're also so clever and capable." He shook his head. "I don't think I can explain what draws me to you. You're what I picture when I think of a wife, but I've never met anyone like you. I just... want to be near you... wake up with you, eat meals with you... raise children with you."

"Have you ever been married?"

"I was betrothed." Now *his* cheeks burned. "During the announcement of our banns, I found out she was with child. Not *my* child. We never... She loved another man. A married man. That's when I left and became a sailor for the Company."

"That must have been difficult, but I'm a woman with another man's children, too."

"She didn't love me... and I didn't love her. I wasn't so interested in being a father then, as I am now."

"My children..."

"They don't have to take my surname, but I promise to treat them as my own. I want to be a father to them. My mother died when I was very young, and my father died when I was a teenager. I was sent to live with my grandfather, and then my uncle," Teunis explained. "I always felt I was a burden. I don't want your children to feel that way."

He looked so tender and vulnerable, reliving those memories. She wanted to hold him. She stepped closer to him, but reminded herself of what Phebe said. Marriage is business.

"Do you accept marriage according to *usus*? I will not be under your guardianship. My property will remain in my name. I will continue to sell lace at the market and conduct my own dealings."

"*Ja*," he said without hesitating. "Nys said that is the common manner here. I wish to be your partner, not your guardian. Your grief is still fresh, but I hope that in time, you'll find love in your heart for me. I aim to do everything I can to make it so."

His use of the word "partner" lifted a heaviness in her heart, and the word "love" went straight to an ache at her center. She was silent a moment, but took his hand again.

"I still think the clogs are too beautiful to wear. I put them on a shelf with my best majolica plates to admire them."

"As long as you will be my wife, you don't have to wear the clogs," he said, his eyes beaming with his affection for her.

"*Ja*, I'll be your wife."

She barely got the sentence out before he kissed her again, tenderly. She could feel him shakily restraining his fervent desires, and she allowed herself to melt into his embrace.

In August, the recently appointed Domine Polhemus married Sarah and Teunis in a barn that served as their church in Breuckelen. Their ceremony was small. Only Sarah's parents and Teunis's brother-in-law, Aert Middagh, attended.

Aert was a little younger than Teunis, about the same height and build, with less facial hair and a heavy brow that made him look contemplative, until he smiled. Since they first met one week ago, Aert always had a grin, with his apparent approval of Sarah.

She didn't need to look in her small mirror glass to know that she looked very different from when she'd married Hans. She was twenty-nine years old. No longer a maiden. The angles of her face had sharpened, and her belly had softened, ready to fill out again with child or, in its deflated form, serve as a pillow to her little ones. A few coarse gray hairs threaded in with her dark blond hair.

Sarah wore the same pale woad-blue skirt and bodice she had worn when she first met Teunis. Her hair was curled and pinned up with hair needle bodkins topped with her *passement* lace diadem cap. She wore the clogs Teunis made for her.

"You look so beautiful, Sarah," Teunis whispered with wonder in his eyes. "You're the most beautiful woman I've ever seen."

Sarah was flattered, even as she didn't quite believe him.

She surveyed her new husband. Teunis wore voluminous linen breeches the color of sage with his dark brown leather jerkin, black doublet, and lace falling collar Sarah had made for him. His dark eyes shone with passion for her. She surmised that they were a humbler sight than she and Hans on their wedding day, but not less handsome. Yet both times, married in a barn serving as their church.

Sarah's children, her siblings, Phebe, Nys, their children, and their Waalebocht neighbors joined afterward for a celebration feast at the Rapalje's house. They had turkey, hare, ham, pike, and bream served with *koolsla*, roasted oysters and clams, waffles stuffed with brandy-soaked berries, and apple cinnamon cake.

When it was time for Sarah and Teunis to depart towards home as man and wife, a pit of dread crept into her stomach. Her mother kept Sarah's children at her house, so the newlyweds would have privacy to make the mortar for a Godly union. The children had been eager for a celebration sleepover. Sarah wanted to fuss over them, but they were all too busy and contented to need her, and she was left facing the nerves she felt about being alone with Teunis. She thought of undressing in front of him. Her heart thrummed so forcefully she was sure her mother could hear it as she kissed her goodbye.

Teunis lifted her onto the seat of their horse-drawn cart to return home. He swung himself up beside her. Their thighs touched as the cart jostled on the rough road.

They didn't speak. She quickly countered her attraction to Teunis with thoughts of Hans and her children. It was her duty to her children to remarry for the stability of their family. It was her duty to her new husband to consummate the marriage. She repeated it these duties to herself until she drove herself into a state of agitation. Trying to convince herself she only felt obligation, not desire, toward her new husband was very tiring.

By the time they arrived, her emotions were blunted. She just wanted to rest.

She'd hoped Teunis would be shy. She tried the slow, ceremonious undressing of her and Hans's early repertoire, but Teunis was not so patient. Impassioned, he almost tore her dress as he removed it and took her onto the bed in her chemise. He tried to kiss her, and she pushed him away reflexively. The wounded look on his face made Sarah mortified at her knee-jerk reaction.

"My apologies if I'm overly amorous. You're just so beautiful... and now you're my wife," he said, both admiring and pleading with his eyes for her willingness.

"I'm sorry... I'm... I don't know. Not ready," she stammered.

"Sarah... wife... may I hold you?"

She nodded, slowly relaxing her body next to his. He held her with one arm, stroking her hair back, again and again. After some minutes, she turned her face to his and their lips met. His fingertips gently roved over her curves. He pulled back to look at her. She turned her head away to settle it on his chest, listening to his breathing and heart thumping until she fell asleep.

Sarah woke in the early dawn hours, startled when she realized the man in her bed was not Hans. She quickly remembered. The friendly visit, the clogs, the wedding. Teunis.

She studied his sleeping face. The straight slope of his nose, the slightly parted lips, the chin cleft under his facial hair.

Why did a sleeping person seem so endearing? The innocence of dreaming? The vulnerability of unconsciousness? It strangely stirred a willingness in her.

She brushed her lips softly against his. He roused immediately, smiled at her, and pulled her closer. It was like being sucked into a whirlpool. Part of her wanted to break away, like she had the night before, but she also wanted to succumb to the pull.

Before she knew it, he made her abandon self-consciousness and submit to the pleasure of it, the sweet sensation filling her up. She hadn't before realized how much she missed the carnal affection of a man. Imagining his strong hands on her bare skin was nothing compared to the real thing. She'd meant to close her eyes and think of Hans, but she never did. Teunis's need for her was too demanding and present.

With consummation complete, she felt adulterous, and even more conflicted that she enjoyed it with such abandon.

"Wife," he murmured, as the fog of passion lifted. Not a question, but a confirmation.

"Hmm," she replied in a noncommittal evenness.

Although she was relieved that they had a physical passion like she had with Hans, she simultaneously felt the weight of guilt. She felt it spill over her, staining every thought. Hans hadn't even been gone a full year. She couldn't allow herself to admit any happiness. Not so soon. The pleasure that her new husband brought her was foiled with a self-flagellating shame. She had succumbed too quickly to the temptation to move on with her life. She resolved to think of Teunis as a partner, not a lover. No one could replace Hans.

Chapter 22

1654

Teunis and Aert had shared a room at an inn in New Amsterdam, which Aert continued to rent while Teunis moved into Sarah's home. He had so few possessions, she barely realized he'd moved in. Being a sailor, all his belongings fit into a duffel sack.

Sarah's children missed their father, but this new man in their house—their stepfather—was a welcome distraction. Teunis indulged them with attention and curiosity. The children eagerly showed him around the farm and their property. Sarah chided them for prideful boasting when they called their chickens "the best egg-layers in New Netherland" or the wild grapes "the sweetest thing God gave us," but it also warmed her heart to see Teunis so engaged with them.

One morning, two weeks after they had been married and Teunis moved in, he came running toward the house as Sarah beat the rag rugs clean on the front porch.

"Sarah!" Teunis called to her, his eyes wide. He pointed across their fields to a solitary figure approaching, dressed in buckskin.

"It's all right. It's Weenji. She is an old friend," Sarah told him. "I knew she would come the week before the Corn Moon. Go greet her and give her this." She handed him four baguettes of white bread wrapped in duffel and followed behind him. She wasn't supposed to give white bread to Natives by Company orders, but this was Weenji and Teunis's first meeting. It was a special occasion.

"*Wunneet,*" Weenji said and gave him a string of fresh-caught bream. "Sarah, *nitap!*"

Sarah responded in turn, realizing she forgot to tell Teunis the word of friendship. Weenji gazed at her, clasping her arms.

"This is my new husband, Teunis..." Sarah started, but Weenji interrupted, gazing at Sarah.

"I see the fire dances in your heart again," Weenji said.

Sarah's cheeks grew hot and Teunis's cheeks reddened. Even though he didn't understand what she said, he must have felt her appraisal. Sarah was relieved that Weenji approved of Teunis and embarrassed that she saw the feelings Sarah was still loath to admit. They exchanged inquiries about the health of each other's families before Sarah brought up business.

"Will you help us with the harvest this year?" Sarah asked in Munsee. "We need to teach the new husband."

Weenji nodded.

"I will bring Mehakachtey in two days, maybe three," Weenji said. She stared at Teunis, making him blush again. She smiled. "Pleasure to meet you," she said in Dutch.

Sarah was content. The introduction went well. Weenji's approval of Teunis assuaged the guilt that gnawed at her decision to remarry.

After Weenji left, Sarah explained their Munsee conversation and her plans to Teunis.

"We can't afford to hire farmhands this year, but Weenji and her son will help us harvest," Sarah told Teunis after Weenji left. "We'll share a portion of the crops with her, mostly in baked goods."

"How do you speak her language?"

"I've known her since I was little. Our families are old friends. Her mother is a skilled planter, and we shared harvest time with her family for as long as I can remember. Her father and mine are good friends. And Weenji... I nearly drowned when I was three years old. I slipped on eel grass into a deep tide pool. Weenji saved me. She uses my given name now, but she called me "girl who slips on eel grass" for years when I was little. She taught me to swim after she saved me and just kept teaching me things over the years." Sarah took a long breath and slowed. "During Kieft's War, Dutch soldiers torched her village and killed members of her family and clan. That war left nothing but ashes, yet Weenji is still a friend to me. My parents credit the Natives for their survival in the early days. My father has always said they are better friends than enemies."

Sarah had never thought her stories were anything extraordinary, yet Teunis regularly had a look of wonder. She found it was endearing to see a grown man look like an astonished child.

"Are you afraid of them?" Sarah asked. "I'm not sure what you've heard, but they are not the wild men of folktales, although the Dutch call them *wilden*. They are the people who traded us this land, and we trade gifts to affirm friendship."

"I'm not afraid if they are your friends. Maybe you can teach me some words? I should thank Weenji for saving you from drowning and helping with the harvest, at least."

Sarah smiled, relieved.

That week, Sarah, Tenis, Weenji, and Mehakachtey harvested the corn, beans, and pumpkins. Teunis gave his thanks to them in Munsee.

"Why do you grow them in mounds, like this, all mixed together?" Teunis asked Sarah.

"It was the first thing my parents learned when they arrived. The Natives call them the Three Sisters," Sarah explained. "Corn is the big sister. She gives beans, the middle sister, a nice tall stalk to climb up. Squash, the little sister, has broad leaves close to the ground that shade the soil, so the roots are kept cool and moist."

"They help each other," Weenji said, in Dutch.

After the Three Sisters harvest, Teunis and Aert began the grain harvest. They both grew up on farms, so the rhythm was familiar to them. Aert wielded the scythe and Teunis the cradle, gathering it after cutting. Sarah and Aneken followed behind, tying the wheat, rye, barley, and buckwheat into bundles using the straw itself to bind them. Sarah stood the shocks upright to dry in the field.

Her sons, Jan and Michael, ten- and eight-years-old respectively, watched Teunis and Aert's rhythm with scythe and cradle, and took after them sometimes in the field as well. It was the first time they took on such tasks. Hans had always hired farmhands. The boys were tall and strong for their ages, and although young and awkward, proved capable. Teunis stopped to give them pointers and direction sometimes. Mostly, he garnished praise to keep them going when they grew tired or distracted.

When the grain was dry, Teunis and Aert took turns threshing, separating the edible part. With the front and back doors of their barn opened, the structure became a wind tunnel, winnowing as they threshed. Sarah liked to watch the clouds of chaff blow in the wind out the barn, like golden snowflakes twinkling in the light.

Threshing completed; Sarah raked away the straw to be used as bedding. She further winnowed the grain from the chaff and any pests in a shallow woven basket. Over the course of a few weeks, the younger children helped harvest the kitchen garden. They stacked apples, carrots, parsnips, onions, and cabbages in baskets.

When Sarah returned from the fields one day, there was a pitcher filled with amaranth stems. Their fuchsia, torch-like flowers created a grand centerpiece on their table. Aneken told her Teunis had brought them home.

"I was surprised you didn't have any growing, but your father told me he grew some. We'll plant the seeds next year. You shall have some of your favorite crop on our land," Teunis told her later. "Why didn't you have any growing, if they're your favorite?"

"Hans didn't want to grow it," Sarah said.

"Why?" Teunis asked, intrigued. After a moment, when Sarah didn't answer, he continued, "You don't talk about him much. You don't have to, but I want you to know it's all right, if you want to."

Her eyes welled with tears. She turned away.

She didn't want to tell him Hans never asked what her favorite crop was. Amaranth was not worth as much as other grains and, therefore, not worth the effort to cultivate.

"Do you want to know the real reason it's my favorite?" Sarah asked him as she turned back to him. He nodded. "The Spanish Conquistadors forbade it in the faraway lands of the south because the Natives used it in their religious practices. Dutch sailors bought some secretly from the Natives and sold it in the New Amsterdam market. That's why my father has some. He has an affinity for anything the Spanish would try to extinguish, like our Walloon brethren."

Teunis opened his mouth to ask questions but just looked at her, bewildered a moment. He smirked, drew her close, and whispered, "Three Sisters and now anti-Spanish flowers? You never cease to enlighten me, Sarah. I never knew crops to have so many stories."

"Maybe the crops never had so many questions."

"I love you, *mijn kastanje*." He kissed her tenderly. The words and the kiss made a deep warmth unfurl from her center. It was the first time he'd told her he loved her.

"Your chestnut? Why am I your chestnut?" Sarah laughed and deflected to that part of his statement.

"Because my chestnut is the answer to everything."

That October, Director Stuyvesant granted one hundred acres of land in Breuckelen to Teunis and Aert.

"Breuckelen is growing. We should build a sawmill," Teunis said. "People will need posts, beams, and clapboards."

"We could build it here?" Aert asked, pointing to a map unfurled on the table.

"*Nee*, here is better. Right, Sarah?" Teunis pointed downriver of where Aert had. Sarah was arranging herb bouquets to hang from the rafters to dry. She stepped down from the chair she stood on so she could look at the map.

"*Ja*. I think so. You could have a solid foundation there instead of soft, shifting marshland. Either way, you should make gifts to the tribes that hunt in that forest there before you start logging. Maybe offer to leave this section untouched." She pointed to the map. "If you give the right gifts, they'll help you amend the cleared land for crops. Ask Wunita. He'll send word to make arrangements. Ask him what they need. Likely metal tools and duffel fabric, but if you give a hoe when a jaw harp was wanted, you waste the opportunity to make a better friendship. Don't forget the *sewant* too—it's how they mark records of alliance."

Teunis and Aert contemplated the new information. She saw on their faces that they hadn't calculated on negotiating with the Natives.

"What a gem you have married," Aert whispered to Teunis, loud enough for Sarah to hear as she went back to hanging yarrow, marshmallow, and chamomile. "Praise the Lord she has more wits than the two of us combined."

The harvesting done, the dried goods stowed in barrels, all other provisions were pickled, salted, smoked, or made into jam and stocked in their storehouse and their kitchen. The newly formed family settled in for winter. As the first storm of the season rolled in, Teunis returned from a day trip to the New Amsterdam market.

"Considering the lack of a school out here, I bought the children two new books," Teunis said, unwrapping a package. There was a children's Bible with pictures and another with parables.

"The children will love these! Were you schooled?" Sarah asked. It hadn't come up before. They were preoccupied with the harvest. She expected, like Hans, he wouldn't have been very educated.

"I have a basic education. I can read, write, and cypher numbers. Were *you* schooled?"

"I can read. I'm not good with a quill, but my mother taught me to cypher. I teach my children with the embroidered *abécédaire* my mother made to teach me."

The children loved the new books and Teunis's attention in reading with them. Each evening, when waning daylight closed the day earlier and earlier, they put down their books and they sang psalms, finding their new harmony as a family. Teunis's voice wasn't as impressive as Hans's. He was more of a choir singer than a soloist.

As December drew near, Teunis animatedly told the children about Sinterklaas as they ate their evening meal.

"Soon he will ride over our house on his white horse, his red cape and white beard flapping in the wind, wearing a tall red hat," Teunis said as the children gathered around him. "If you leave a clog by the fireplace, with some food for his horse, he might leave you some treats, if you've been good boys and girls."

"Will Père Noël come too?" five-year-old Jorsey asked, confused.

"We call him by the Walloon name," Sarah whispered to Teunis.

"This is a Dutch colony. You *must* celebrate traditions the Dutch way," he whispered back.

"We celebrate *our* traditions," Sarah said firmly, then turned to the children. "Père Noël and Sinterklaas are the same. Your stepfather is calling him by his Dutch name."

"Will we get double the treats?" Jorsey asked, still confused.

Sarah turned to Teunis, frowning at the trouble he unleashed.

"*Ja*, if you're very good—and double the coal if you're naughty!" Teunis said, mussing Jorsey's hair.

"What about Fjøsnissen?" Jorsey questioned. Teunis was confused and looked to Sarah.

"He's the Norwegian elf who lives in the barn," Sarah whispered to Teunis, explaining the tradition that had been important to Hans. She turned back to answer Jorsey. "We'll still leave him some porridge and beer so he'll bless next year's harvest and watch over the animals... and maybe he will have a treat for you too."

The children chattered, delighted that they may get treats from a bevy of Yuletide visitors.

On December 5th, Saint Nicholas Eve, the children left hay and parsnips in their clogs by the fire. Sinterklaas came and left them each an orange and small cloth bag with chocolate coins and *kruidnoten* gingersnap cookies.

Teunis made sure to acquire the appropriate little treats for them from the market. There were many people selling such things because Sinterklaas was so popular with the children, even the non-Dutch were forced into participating by their envious, expectant children.

Père Noël left a red duffel sack by their hearth. They each took a turn pulling out a gift. There were two sets of adjustable ice skates, several spinning tops, new cornhusk dolls, whistles made from broken pipe stems, and a hobby horse with a broomstick body and a felted wool head.

When they were over the initial excitement of playing with new toys, dinner from their Dutch oven was ready: young turkeys stuffed with parsley and lovage, braised with carrots, onion, cabbage, and pumpkin smothered in a butter and sour grape juice sauce. It was served with a sweet white bread spiced with nutmeg and cardamum. *Sappaen,* aged cheese, and *koolsla* were already set out on the table.

"Don't forget about Fjøsnissen!" Sarah said and set out a mini wooden bowl-and-cup set on a tray that Hans had made specifically for the elf. The children took the offering out to the barn.

Sarah and Teunis rose extra early the next morning and quietly slipped out to the barn so as not to wake the children. As their treat for leaving the cornmeal porridge and beer, Fjøsnissen did the children's morning chores and let them sleep in.

Chapter 23

1655-1656

One day in the spring, Phebe arrived unexpectedly at Sarah's house early in the morning with her children. Teunis and the older children were out in the barn, tending the animals. Phebe's face was bone white with pale violet rings under her bloodshot eyes.

"Children, go find your friends. They're tending the animals in the barn or perhaps in the paddock," Sarah instructed Phebe's children after kissing each on their cheeks.

After they left, she sat across from Phebe at the table.

"You must tell me what's the matter. Are you unwell?"

Phebe looked dazed. She stared into the fire in the hearth, where Sarah hung a pot to boil water.

"I made myself look a fool… and I'm not sure I have regret. I went to the Wooden Horse Tavern last night to fetch Nys. I watched him smoking his pipe, telling some story that those former Company sailors have doubtless heard before. It was so dimly lit, the air so clouded with tobacco, I don't think he saw me until I was a hand's length from his face. And with all nine children in tow. All of us to bring him home," Phebe told Sarah.

Sarah breathed deeply. Phebe had finally confronted her husband about his late night drinking. Sarah knew it had been a growing irritation to Phebe as of late.

"What did you say to him?"

"I told Nys it was time to go home. I tried to stay calm, but then Philip Geraerdy tried to show me out! I told him if he didn't keep his place open past the drinking curfew, I wouldn't need to fetch my husband. I threatened to alert Stuyvesant's officers to send them *all* home if he made me leave without my husband. I made a terrible scene, but God's wrath upon Geraerdy for not abiding the curfew."

"And Nys followed you out?"

"Not at first. His drinking mates jeered him, and his rump was stuck to his seat in shock. Eventually, he stood, tipped his hat to his company, and followed. I didn't speak to him, mostly because the children cried the entire walk home across town. He fell asleep as soon as he hit the bed. This morning, I left with the children and came here without preparing breakfast or stoking the fire. Let him wake from his stupor, cold and alone, this morning."

Sarah had never seen Phebe so angry. She had become Dutch in many ways, but her Puritan dutifulness still pervaded deeply. She truly must be at her wits' end.

Sarah made her chamomile tea with a bit of the linden sleeping tincture for when her children were ill or teething. She put her to bed. Phebe woke at midday, groggy but refreshed. She and her children supped with Sarah, Teunis, and the children before they began the trip back home.

"Is something wrong with Phebe?" Teunis asked after they'd left.

"She's just tired and needed a break. She has no kin in town to help her. Nys stays out too late at the tavern."

They went to sit on their stoop to bask in the midday sun.

"Teunis, you've done so well with the lumber mill, but I wish Breuckelen had its own gristmill. Perhaps you should encourage Nys on such a venture. He's opportunity-minded, like you. Perhaps you could even persuade him to buy some land on Lange Eylandt. Wouldn't you like your friend to live closer? I would like to see Phebe without taking a ferry ride."

He looked at her, holding her hand, tracing and caressing her scars. Years of close encounters with the edge of a hot pan, spatters of scalding stew or hot oil, or a slipped knife. He pressed deeply between the callused mounds that formed at the top of her palm. She would have closed her eyes, but she held transfixed on how the sunlight turned his dark, loamy eyes to glinting honey brown. She could almost taste them. Nutty bitterness. Rich, smoky brown butter. A lingering, subtle sweetness.

"*Ja*," he said thoughtfully. "I will speak with him."

"Thank you," she murmured.

He leaned in to kiss her. Sarah had a moment of pleasure before the nagging guilt overwhelmed her. Why did this shame still surge up? Hans was gone. Teunis was her husband.

"I need to clean up after our midday meal," she said as she pulled away and went back inside.

In mid-September, the sky was overcast with clouds and birds migrating south, creating a cacophony of wing beats and flight calls. Sarah could not locate them by eye, except for darkening portions of steel-gray cloud cover becoming charcoal. She puttered around her kitchen garden, trimming bouquets of herbs for drying. Some patches had gone to seed and turned brown. She shook them to disperse the seeds for next year's garden.

The clatter of a horse and cart came up the path. She went to greet the visitor.

Phebe came into view, driving the cart. It had been three months since Phebe and Nys moved to Breuckelen. Sarah was delighted with her friend's more frequent visits and improved mood, but this time, Phebe looked distressed.

"There were attacks on Manhattan, Staaten Eylandt, and Pavonia!" Phebe exclaimed, lowering herself from the cart. Her children climbed out of the back.

"Who? When?"

"Hundreds of Natives, two days ago," Phebe said. "I ferried across in the afternoon yesterday to go to the market. I saw Isaac questioning people. He said the Natives attacked and took women and children. Stuyvesant appointed him Orphanmaster."

"Sarina...?"

"She's fine. Their children are fine."

"What tribe was it?"

"Isaac said it was several tribes combined. A coordinated attack. There's a rumor it started because a farmer shot a Native woman for eating peaches from his orchard."

Sarah was grateful that choosing to live on Lange Eylandt had spared her the experience. She thought back to the last attack on Manhattan, when her brother was killed while she hid in their *kast* with her two little girls and Jacob in her belly. Now she was heavily pregnant with her and Teunis's first child, and all the children would not fit in their *kast*.

Weenji told Sarah that Lange Eylandt Natives had not taken part in the Peach War, as it was now being referred to. After the attacks, a delegation from Weenji's tribe went to Fort Amsterdam to offer the Dutch absolute friendship and reaffirm peace. This eased Sarah's mind, but she had not forgotten the escalation of Kieft's War.

In the weeks following the attack, Stuyvesant chose diplomacy instead of brutality. Just when Sarah began to feel at ease, she noticed men in the meadow at the edge of their land. They mowed the tall salt grass that formed a wedge between where her property ended and her sister Jannet and her husband Rem van der Beeck's bowery started.

"Teunis!" She called for him in the barn where he and Aert were going over plans for the construction of their sawmill. "There are men at the edge of the property in the meadow. No one owns that tract of land. Please, go see what they're up to."

Teunis put on his hat and motioned for Aert to follow him. They arrived back at the house about twenty minutes later.

"It was Rem and his cousin, a man called Paulus van der Beeck. He said he's quitting the city for his land in Gowanus and looking for land he could mow for feed. He was surveying the property over there, next to Rem's." Teunis said nonchalantly, not knowing the stomachache it gave Sarah to hear such news.

"Not *that* man! He beat me and my mother!" She sat down, clutching her rounded belly. He'd been polite to her ever since her mother took him to court, but he still had a snide superiority. She felt sick at the thought of Paulus being her neighbor, prowling the edge of their property.

"He hurt you? By God's wounds, I'd put a turd through his teeth if he ever tried that again! That vile dog..." Teunis shouted. When angered, which wasn't often, he tended to let his sailor's mouth talk before he thought. Sarah's eyes widened with each curse. Teuns's eyes met hers and he tempered his outburst. He dropped to his knees and held her.

"Don't worry, *mijn kastanje*," he said in a soothing tone. "He didn't seem much impressed with the meadow. It's not convenient to his land in Gowanus. I'll talk to Rem. He'll encourage Paulus to find land elsewhere."

Sarah gave birth that December to a baby girl, Aertje. The birth was fast and easy. Sarah enjoyed Teunis's reactions to his first child, bewildered and delighted at the same time. Aertje was the bond that firmly affixed Teunis, inseparably, to the new family. He already doted on his stepchildren, but he fully embraced his status as a father now, with his new baby girl. Sarah watched his confidence grow.

Sarah appreciated how he devised a scheme to keep the children on task to complete their chores. He delegated in a way that they completed even the chores they disliked doing. It had been a point of contention with Hans because Sarah always had to be the disciplinarian and harangue her children to help her.

Instead of rote shifting of chores, he made challenges to see who was best at a task. If they were the best at something no one else wanted to do, they would get more leisure time. When granted new authority over a domain of the home or bowery, pride made them excel.

Aneken, who had always secretly prided herself on a well-mucked-out stable, had the least number of chores to do in return. Jan, who cared more than anyone about understanding the tides, oversaw the fish traps. Rebecca excelled at domestic arts and oversaw cooking, mending, and *passementerie*.

Whoever neglected to take pride in their chores was given the least desirable tasks, like emptying the chamberpot, upkeep of the outhouse, and pulling weeds. There were competitions of who groomed the animals best or who made the best pancakes, things they all enjoyed.

Their household and bowery ran better than ever. Sarah slowly relinquished her tendency to domineer the household, distracted with the needs of her new baby and Teunis's newfound leadership.

Only two months after giving birth, in late February, Sarah was required to appear in court. She'd missed the first appearance because the weather was so bad they'd stopped running the ferry that day. Someone sought repayment of a debt Hans owed for eighty-four guilders and five stivers.

"I knew nothing of the debt. It was not accounted for in the settlement of Hans's estate." Sarah requested a delay of payment until next harvest, which was agreed to by the court.

She realized they didn't know of her marriage to Teunis. The New Amsterdam court saw her as a poor widow. A plan set in motion in her mind, and she decided she would take action to prevent Paulus from becoming her neighbor.

The next time Sarah appeared in court was six weeks later, on April 4, 1656. This time, she had arranged to make an appeal.

"Sarah Joris Rapalje, firstborn Christian daughter of New Netherland, widow of Hans Hansen Bergen, petitions Director and Council for twenty morgens of meadows adjoining her land," Secretary Cornelis van Ruyven read. Sarah stood proudly, emboldened by the fact Van Tienhoven was not present in the court as *schout* that day.

"My neighbors mow the meadows in question and disturb me in their use of them. They have meadows adjoining their own lands," she stated. Looking plaintive, she continued. "I am burdened with seven children. Crop yields have been poor. I am also requesting exemption from taxes."

"The twenty morgens shall be added to your land, in honor of being the firstborn daughter of New Netherland. A tax exemption is denied, however. The tax remission of the past several years has concluded," *Schepen* Hendrick Kip ruled.

Sarah bowed her head to them and said her thanks. She had won the most important bit and was contented.

Later that night, they had waffles with early season strawberries and buttercream to celebrate, the children impatiently taking turns with the waffle iron.

"You're as bold as you are cunning and beautiful." Teunis lifted his pewter tankard to toast her.

"Sometimes, all you have to do is ask nicely." Sarah smiled at him, making her point as a lesson to the children.

"Children, ask nicely for your favorite fruit, and maybe next year we'll make that meadow a grand orchard. Bogaert means 'of the orchard' so it's only fitting," Teunis told them, smirking at Sarah while the children hollered the name of every fruit on earth at him.

CHAPTER 24

1656

On a Saturday in late November, Teunis, Aert, and Sarah took the shallop with their tithe crops and the excess to sell at the market in New Amsterdam. Sarah sold a pair of lace cuffs, garnered commissions for another pair of cuffs, and the hem of a baby's baptismal gown. It was a good day.

The men stayed behind to discuss plans for their sawmill with prospective builders and housewrights. Sarah had to return via the ferry to relieve her mother, who looked after her children.

As she walked into the house, Phebe and her children were a pleasant sight, but not a surprise. Sarah's and her mother's homes always had an open door for her since she'd moved to Breuckelen.

"Sarah!" Phebe met her at the door and kissed her cheeks. "I came by for a visit with the children, and Catalyna invited me to stay until you returned."

"She was welcome company. The children love to see their Nyssen playmates, too," her mother said. "They're much better behaved when they're having fun."

Her mother brought her two youngest as well. Sarah's youngest siblings, Daniel and Elizabeth, were five and seven years old. Catalyna swore that Daniel, her eleventh child, would be her last.

"The children asked to see the new kittens. I told them to wait and ask you," Phebe explained.

"Yes, you can go see the kittens. They're nestled up with their mother in the storehouse. Be gentle with them and mindful of their mother," Sarah instructed as the children ran out the door.

"That barn cat has the sharpest claws!" Catalyna warned before continuing the conversation with Sarah. "You'd never guess she descended from our sweet Perle. They just get more feral with every brood unless you let the children handle them when they're young."

"I had a very productive and pleasant visit to the city, and I want nothing more than to sit and gossip for a spell," Sarah said. Having taken off her clogs, she traded her cloak for her housecoat and relaxed into her chair. Catalyna brought her chamomile tea with honey and a bit of brandy. She put fresh coal from the fire into the footwarmer box and placed it under Sarah's feet.

"Tell us the news from town," her mother said.

"I'll save the scandal for last. But first—" Sarah took a sip of tea "—I saw Sarina. She's well and the children are well—her four little boys look healthier than ever—but Isaac is swamped with work. She says he practically lives at the *Stadthuys* with his *schepen* duties. When he's not there, he's tending to his brewery, tobacco farm, and exports. She's very proud of him, only worried he's wearing himself thin. She said Isaac is arranging a contract for a servant girl from *Patria*. I don't know how that will help with his workload, though."

"Maybe he wants a companion for Sarina while he's gone so much of the time," Catalyna wondered. "I am glad to hear that she and the children are well."

"I saw Susanna Negrin, too. She's putting the midwifery skills that Tryn taught her to good use. Rest her soul, Tryn taught her well. Susanna hasn't lost a single child or mother. She told me her husband was put to work on the construction of the palisade wall across the island. He overheard Stuyvesant ordered it completed because former Commander John Underhill went to the English colonies to raise an attack against us. What irony!" Sarah paused a moment to mentally trace how Underhill fought for Kieft, settled on Lange Eylandt, only to return to the English to conspire an attack on the Dutch.

"Have you heard about Thomas Baxter—the Englishman who sold the timber used in that wall—has now turned pirate for the English colonies and is attacking Dutch vessels?" Phebe exclaimed.

Her mother whispered expletives in French.

"I shall never trust an Englishman again," Phebe said, her face a stony facade with a torrent of emotion in her tone. "What rogues!"

"I also saw Judith Bayard," Sarah said.

"Stuyvesant's wife?" Phebe asked. Sarah nodded.

"She told me to send her greetings to you, *Maman*. I couldn't really speak with her, though, because a Jewish man beseeched her to speak with her husband. He wants a license for his butcher shop. Apparently, Stuyvesant's latest religious ordinance is too harsh on his people. The man argued they must at least be allowed to have their meat butchered, according to their beliefs. Those poor Jewish people had to flee their homes in the Dutch Brazil colony when the Portuguese took over. Judith is so kind, especially regarding the dispossessed. She said she would speak to her husband on the matter."

"Judith is empathetic because she's a Huguenot," Catalyna interjected, "and Stuyvesant is the son of a Friesland minister who never experienced the Inquisition under the Spaniards. To experience oppression makes it easier to practice toleration."

Phebe and Sarah nodded at her mother's wisdom.

"There are whispers that the Netherlanders in Vlissingen are writing a remonstrance for their English Quaker neighbors to have an exemption from Stuyvesant's ordinance," Sarah explained.

"The Company's policy is for religious freedom of conscience—although in private, not public," Catalyna noted.

"All I know is that Stuyvesant sees any religion other than his own as blasphemous... But all right, now the real scandal... Word is that Cornelis van Tienhoven is dead! His hat and cane were found floating in the river and he's nowhere to be found," Sarah said and then sat forward, "but since he's been under scrutiny for defrauding the Company, the disappearance seems dubious. His younger brother also vanished. Seems rather convenient timing to disappear."

"What a rogue 'til the end!" Phebe exclaimed.

"Truly. And what's worse, Rachel is pregnant. I can't believe after he came back from *Patria* with his mistress and was the laughingstock of town, he still found his way back to the marital bed," Sarah said, involuntarily shuddering.

"If you can't find love in a marriage, being a young widow of a wealthy man is the next best thing," Catalyna nonchalantly stated as she made them more brandy-spiked chamomile teas.

"Too bad Hans didn't leave me in the latter condition," Sarah retorted quickly, without thinking. The brandy had loosened her lips.

"What do you mean?" her mother asked, concerned. She set down their refreshed drinks. "Are things not going well with Teunis?"

"Oh no, I didn't mean that. On the contrary. It's just..." Her eyes welled up and she couldn't find the words.

"What is it, Sarah?" Phebe encouraged her.

"Two years have passed and I still feel like I'm an adulteress when I should be a widow... I don't want to diminish Hans in my heart... I don't want to love Teunis... but I do." She wiped her eyes and stiffened. "Who am I to complain, though? Poor me, blessed with two good husbands and Rachel hasn't even had *one*!"

"Oh, *ma petite*," her mother said, putting her arms around her. "It's natural. Everything you're feeling is natural."

"You can embrace both blessings, Hans and Teunis. It's not one or the other," Phebe said, taking Sarah's hand. "You don't have to choose. And Rachel Vigne might be blessed in other ways, as Catalyna said."

"If you love him, don't hide those feelings. Rejecting love doesn't shelter you from loss," her mother advised.

Sarah felt better, simply saying it aloud, but Phebe and her mother's words also helped. She loved Teunis. She needn't push the feelings away anymore. They'd been married two years and had a child together, but it was only in that conversation she felt she finally had permission to love him.

Later that night, after dinner was done, and the children put to bed, Sarah put on her cloak and went out to their storehouse. Teunis was separating out the goods he contracted to sell and would need to deliver, rolling certain hogshead barrels to the front of the room.

"Hallo, Sarah, everything all right?" Teunis asked her.

It was cold, but he was in his linen shirt and duffel breeches with his sleeves rolled up to the elbow. His tousled, wavy hair was half in his eyes as he looked up from rolling a barrel, and he brushed it back. His bare forearms of taut muscle, built up and tanned from the work of the harvest, rested akimbo.

She wrapped her arms around him and buried her head into his chest. She inhaled his salty musk.

"Teunis, it's been hard for me to say, but I just want you to know..." She looked up into his dark, velvety, umber-colored eyes. "I love you."

"*Mijn kastanje*," he whispered in her ear, "I'm happy to hear you say it... I could feel it though, even without the words." He looked into her eyes, smiled, and grabbed her rear, pulling her body into his with bawdy levity, and he kissed her. "I've loved you since we first met, and since then, I love you even more."

Teunis lifted her up and set her on a barrel. He kissed her neck as he found his way inside her skirts and she opened his breeches. His hands slowly stroked up her inner thighs and delight rippled from his fingers to every part of her body.

After, he held her with her legs still wrapped around him. She was unwilling to let him go. He made a soft laugh.

"What?" Sarah asked.

"I don't want to sell this barrel now." He grinned at her. "It's quite a romantic spot."

"There are plenty more barrels and plenty more romantic spots to be had." Sarah smirked at him.

CHAPTER 25

1658-1660

Sarah and Teunis's tryst in the storehouse resulted in Catalyntje, their little Catalyna. She was an absolute beauty and strong-spirited like her grandmother, with Sarah's color-shifting, light hazel eyes and Teunis's thick brown hair.

A year later, Sarah was with child again. Having many of her older children helping to run the bowery and tend their siblings made Sarah enjoy motherhood more than when they were all so young. She was thirty-three years old, pregnant with her tenth child, and she suspected the first of her children was soon going to be married.

Rebecca, her second oldest daughter, and Aert, Teunis's young brother-in-law, had been sneaking off with increasing frequency. Sarah had noticed, even though they tried to be stealthy. They requested to speak with Sarah and Teunis one evening, with comical formality until Aert blurted the news.

"I've proposed to Rebecca!" Aert announced, his smile stretched wide. He took Rebecca's hand.

"*Maman, Pater*, I'd like your blessing before I accept," Rebecca said with cheeks crimson as crab apples.

"Of course!" Sarah and Teunis exclaimed in tandem.

Sarah couldn't be more pleased. Rebecca was seventeen and Aert was twenty-five years old. Their temperaments were a good match, and it was the most natural union Sarah could think of for Rebecca. Aert was already a beloved member of their family.

"Where do you intend to settle?" Teunis asked.

"If you're agreeable, we'll build a house on the land Stuyvesant granted us. Near the mill."

"Being near the mill is sensible. We'll have a house raised for you in no time!" Teunis declared.

They were married in late summer of 1659. Sarah gave her daughter the silver marriage medallion that Hans gave her on their wedding day. Rebecca did not appear as happy to receive it as Sarah expected.

"I don't want Aneken to feel bad. Perhaps as the eldest daughter, it should belong to her?"

"Aneken cares less for such baubles. Or husbands," Sarah told her. "Perhaps your marriage will inspire her to think on the latter."

Sarah and Teunis had their third daughter, Neeltje, a month later. They named her after Teunis's grandmother. One grown child moved out, and the vacancy was quickly filled.

Sarah and Teunis sat on their stoop after their midday meal. Neeltje nursed at Sarah's breast, and they enjoyed the sweet, earthy smell of springtime. The afternoon sun thawed the dormant soil, and early shoots of greenery had begun to poke up in the past few days, drawn to the sun.

Despite the pleasant afternoon, Sarah had a headache over the news Teunis shared while they had eaten. There was a Native attack on Esopus and Stuyvesant ordered all outland settlers must move to palisaded villages.

"Why must we start over again because of a drunken brawl? Esopus is a day's journey away," Sarah argued.

"It started as a drunken brawl, but praise be that they have a palisaded settlement there, else the Natives would have done more than just destroy crops and kill livestock."

"Peace is sensible! Moving our household is not!" She was distraught over losing the home Hans built, yet again.

"Stuyvesant granted our proposal for a new palisaded village. Your father, Aert, Jean Clerq, and Jacob Kip agreed to the spot. The Kickout isn't far from our lands and fields here and it has a view of the city and harbor. It's where we first kissed. A beautiful spot."

"I don't want to leave this home."

"Don't worry, *mijn kastanje*," Teunis told her. "Right now, the conflict is far away. But if conflict looms closer to home, we'll be grateful to have somewhere safe to live. This is an opportunity to grow our holdings. Our lumber mill will be in great demand. We could build a larger home, too. Since they appointed me *schepen* of New Amersfoort and Midwout, I'll be held to a higher standard to comply with the order. I need to set an example."

"Is that appointment going to your head?" Sarah wondered at the shift in his ambitions. He was once contented to just be a planter.

"I'm a big fish in a small pond," Teunis told Sarah, humbly referring to the relatively small number of inhabitants of his jurisdiction.

"More accurately, in a large forest," Sarah retorted. She knew the cases brought before him as *schepen* were mostly disagreements over land boundaries in undeveloped wilderness, where the roads were mostly Native paths that one could easily lose track of.

"I have other news. Perhaps it will be more agreeable to you. I received a letter from my younger brother Abraham in Heykoop. He inquired if I would sell him the portion of land I inherited from our father," Teunis told Sarah.

"Do you want to sell it?"

"*Ja*, we can put the money toward paying off the mill or our new house. I'll need to go conduct the sale, though. Have you ever wanted to visit *Patria*?" he asked, smiling at her with a gleam in his dark eyes. She enjoyed that look from him, but she was still too upset to take the bait as he wanted her to.

"I've never thought about it." She looked at him, slightly puzzled by how she truly felt. Intrigued? Nervous he would leave and not return? Why did she feel a pang of jealousy? "Do you miss it?"

"Not really. I miss my brother and sister sometimes," he said, looking off in the distance. He looked back at her and kissed Neeltje's forehead. "There's much more for me here, though."

They fell into contemplative silence. Maybe she was merely afraid. She thought of the stories some settlers arrived with—tales of rough storms, pirates, and never-ending days on meager rations of stale or spoiled food. The *Princess Amelia* wrecked on the rocks when the captain accidentally veered off course. Phebe's mother and little sister died of illness on their journey. Her parents had a relatively easy crossing, yet they both swore they'd never do it again. Perhaps she was afraid that once she saw a European city, it would taint the majesty that she felt that this land had? Maybe she didn't want to go because she was simply content with her life as it was.

"I don't think Neeltje would do well on a sea voyage, nor Catalyntje. And we couldn't leave them," Sarah said.

"I can't leave you or the children for that long, especially when we need to move, and running the mill will be crucial," Teunis replied, furrowing his brow. "Maybe Aert could go as my agent? Would that cause trouble with Rebecca?"

"I don't want her to risk the voyage, but she might want to go with him. Ask them, and they can decide," Sarah told him.

Aert and Rebecca accepted the proposition and were excited as they prepared to leave that fall after the harvest.

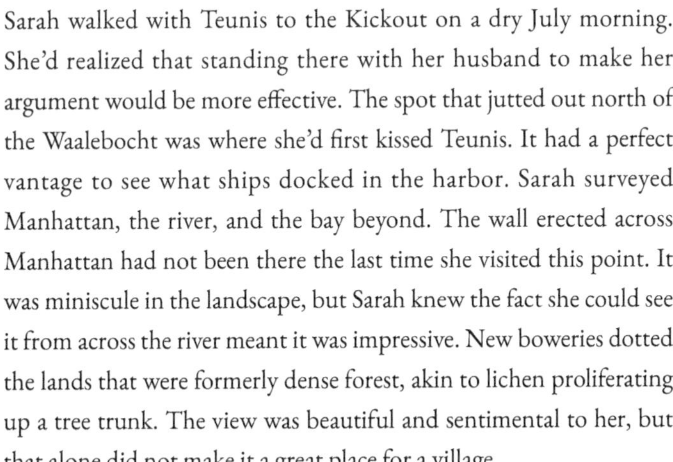

Sarah walked with Teunis to the Kickout on a dry July morning. She'd realized that standing there with her husband to make her argument would be more effective. The spot that jutted out north of the Waalebocht was where she'd first kissed Teunis. It had a perfect vantage to see what ships docked in the harbor. Sarah surveyed Manhattan, the river, and the bay beyond. The wall erected across Manhattan had not been there the last time she visited this point. It was miniscule in the landscape, but Sarah knew the fact she could see it from across the river meant it was impressive. New boweries dotted the lands that were formerly dense forest, akin to lichen proliferating up a tree trunk. The view was beautiful and sentimental to her, but that alone did not make it a great place for a village.

"It's as rocky as I remember. Good for goats but not a kitchen garden," she said, dismayed. "Where is the creek? It's nothing but caked earth. There's no water up here in the heat of summer."

"I know. I'm not unsympathetic to your arguments... but Stuyvesant commanded we fortify ourselves here."

"They've made peace. War has been averted. The tribes of Lange Eylandt even fought with the Dutch against the Esopus Natives. There's no reason for us to hurry to a palisaded village."

"Did Weenji's tribe join them? It's been a long time since we've seen her, not since she brought gifts of fish and cornhusk dolls after Catalyntje was born."

"Her Keschaechquereren clan moved east and joined the Poospatuck on the far end of Lange Eylandt," Sarah said somberly.

"We aren't the only ones forced to relocate," Teunis said. "The English are increasingly land-grabbing east and north of here. I hope they will allow her clan to remain there."

"Perhaps we should fear the English encroaching as much as the Natives. In case of either threat, why not propose a better position for this new village?" Sarah said.

CHAPTER 26

1661

The following February, residents of the Waalebocht and vicinity were notified they must comply with the Director's orders to remove to the village proposed the previous year at the Kickout between Kip and Bogaert's land. Sarah spoke with all of her neighboring fellow Walloon housewives and convinced them to cajole their husbands into signing the petition which her father and husband brought forth.

Her father, Teunis, and several other men met with Stuyvesant and his council in March. Joris presented a request to move the intended site of the village. Jacob Kip represented the position of keeping the village bordered on his land, although he didn't reside there himself. Sarah had Phebe look after her children so she could attend with Teunis and her eldest sons.

"The Kickout is wholly unfit for the purpose, partly because the woodland thereat, being stony, is not suitable for arable land," Joris testified. "Moreover, in consequence of the uncommon height of the land there, it is impossible to find good and sufficient water to make a well. The streams in the neighborhood are mostly dried up in summer. When people wish to water their cattle, they are obliged to fetch water in casks from Teunis Bogaert's well, which is most fatiguing and injurious for farmers."

"This drudgery I see daily performed by my neighbors with weeping eyes," Teunis testified. "We request to concentrate our village on Joris Rapalje's land. By nature, it's more defensible, and the water there is, by far, the richest fountain in the country. It is also more conveniently located to several existing boweries."

"There's plenty of water in Teunis's well for them," Kip countered. "And isn't there a risk of separation if Remegakonck Kil floods?"

"We expect to build a bridge over the creek. Each willing to settle there will have granted to them convenient lots for house and garden and hold the title for such. So that, under God's blessing, it may increase to a village," Joris responded.

Stuyvesant considered a moment and then conferred with his council. Kip had been his secretary, but Joris was a longtime resident and respected founding citizen of the city.

"Since Kip does not reside on his land at the Waalebocht, and the people who live there are unified in their desire to establish the village on Rapalje's land, permission is granted," Stuyvesant announced.

Following that ruling, her father, husband, and eldest sons petitioned for the wooded acreage next to Joris's land, as the timber would be conveniently used in building their new village. Stuyvesant approved the land patents.

Carel de Beauvois, a Walloon born in Leiden, was appointed by Stuyvesant for a sundry of duties necessary to the township of Breuckelen: court messenger, gravedigger, choir singer, liturgy reader, and schoolmaster. He arrived from *Patria* with a new bell for their church, for which he would add bellringer to his list of duties. Kindly, the coffers of New Amsterdam would subsidize his salary, serving the outlander towns. The man was around the same age as Teunis and Sarah. He brought with him his wife and three children who were the same ages as their children. They welcomed them with enthusiasm.

As much as Sarah begrudged having to uproot their household, she came to see the benefits of their Waalebocht village properly forming, now composed of twelve families. They would be closer to the Breuckelen market, church, and school. It was the first time her children could attend school and catechism studies. But they were a long way from enjoying those benefits.

Sarah sat with Teunis on the stoop, reviewing the steps to building their new home.

"We should contract a master builder," Teunis told her, holding forth a blueprint roughly drawn by his own hand. "We'll save money on the posts, joists, and clapboards, which our mill can provide. The boys can help me with the insulation, lime-washing the walls, and other finishing work."

"Do we need a master builder?" Sarah asked. She felt nauseous. "Can we afford it?"

Hans had single-handedly built their house without asking for any input from her. He hired his coworkers from the shipyard to help. She wished she'd paid more attention.

"It will be paid off when Aert and Rebecca return with the funds from selling my land to my brother. I have plans for a fine home, not a simple dwelling. We need a master builder."

Sarah rose and, with exerted calm and purpose, walked to the edge of their yard and purged the contents of her stomach into the hedges.

By the beginning of summer, the cost of the master builder and housewright exceeded the amount Teunis expected from the land sale. They had milled an excess of clapboards, though. Teunis contracted a sale of export to *Patria*.

"We can pay off the master builder and have plenty left over for the finishing work," he explained over dinner. "The structure is done. Insulation will take but a day or two. Then flooring. After lime-washing the walls, we'll move in very soon!"

Teunis was buoyant with the news, and Sarah was optimistic, but she couldn't shake the waves of nausea. She choked it down, but it made her head swim.

"Can we reuse these floorboards? Please. Pull them up and reuse them in the new house. It's the only thing I ask."

"*Mijn kastanje.* Do you feel all right? You're as white as limewash."

She had to run to the holly hedges again.

A fortnight later, Sarah accompanied Teunis to their new home, close to the homes of her parents, several of her siblings, and other Walloons. The palisade around the Waalebocht village was half raised.

"Wait," he said and stood to face her. He pulled forth a silk kerchief and tied it around her eyes.

"Really, Teunis? A blindfold?" Sarah asked.

"I've not kept you away from seeing our progress without purpose. I wanted it to be perfect for you the first time you enter. Allow me a dramatic reveal."

With an arm around her waist, he led her out of the woods and into the familiar clearing of the Waalebocht. He removed the blindfold. She was speechless as she stood in front of their brand new home.

It was certainly larger than their old home. The split Dutch door was open. The interior emanated light from the crisp white limewash. She hadn't realized how dark their old home was. She entered, drawn to the clean hearth, un-besmirched by years of soot and smoke.

Delft tiles decorated the back wall of their open-jamb hearth. She delighted in the little bucolic scenes and animals in the cobalt and ultramarine blues. Teunis also lavished their new home with an imported pendulum clock and two mahogany chairs with leather upholstery.

"I thought you would like those," he said with a pleased smile as she touched the tiles.

"Teunis... I don't have words... I adore it. All of it!" she whispered. Sarah's attitude completely changed. She finally *wanted* to move.

"For now, the oiled linen screens will do, but I ordered glazing for those two windows," he said.

"This must have cost a fortune..." She quickly regretted the utterance of practicality. She didn't want to spoil the moment.

"The sale of the exported clapboards will cover it," Teunis said, confident and quick. "I wanted you to have no hesitation in moving."

"I can't believe I will live in a place so fine." She couldn't stop her tears from falling. Suddenly, the nausea roiled up her throat, and she ran outside. She made it a few paces from the stoop before she retched up her midday meal.

"*Mijn kastanje*... are you all right?"

She wiped her face with her hands and realized her reoccurring nausea had nothing to do with the move. She was still crying.

"Nothing... is wrong... I'm with child."

He wrapped his arms around her and kissed her neck. Then, with a whooping cheer, he lifted her and twirled. He set her down after a full spin and brushed the stray hairs back from her face.

"I'm sorry. I shouldn't have done that. You poor thing. Having to pack a household and move while pregnant. No wonder you've been ill. I shouldn't have spun you so."

She wrapped her arms around his neck and buried her face in his chest, laughing through her tears.

"Spin me again! I think it helped send the contents of my stomach back down."

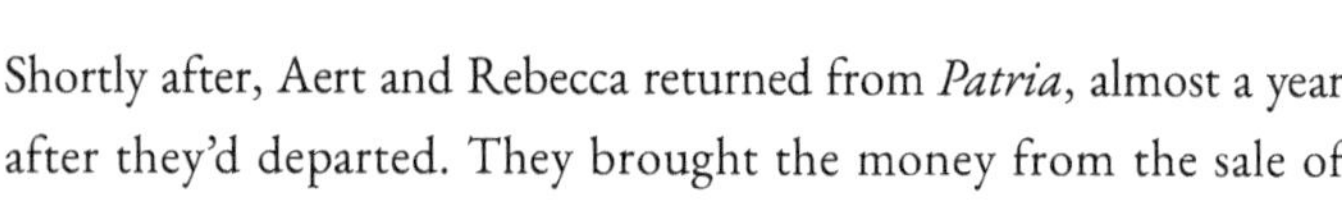

Shortly after, Aert and Rebecca returned from *Patria*, almost a year after they'd departed. They brought the money from the sale of Teunis's inherited land, letters and gifts from Teunis's family, and Rebecca was swollen with child.

"I'm shocked to see how much has changed while we've been away," Rebecca said, eyes wide, examining her parents' new home.

"I'm so relieved to see you. I prayed every day for your safe return," Sarah gushed as she kissed her daughter. She lovingly placed a hand on her daughter's large belly. "Tell me everything."

"Seeing this land from the sea was incredible!" Rebecca declared. "And Amsterdam was astounding! So large and crowded, you wouldn't believe it."

"Did you find Heykoop much changed?" Teunis asked Aert of their hometown he hadn't seen in nearly ten years.

"It's more changed here in the past year than there in ten! The fields and cows are the same, but the people have aged," he laughed. "Your sister was so glad that you named your daughter after your grandmother, though at first she boasted it must be after her. Their son Gysbert is sixteen years old! I hardly recognized him, but he still has the mischievous laugh. My father is not in good health, but it was a joyful reunion."

"And my brother?" Teunis asked, captivated.

"Abraham was regretful you couldn't make the trip. I told him all about the life you have here, and he understands. I'm sure he explains more in his letter I gave you, but he was much relieved to expand his estate as he's growing his family. His wife, Maeike, is a lovely sight—much prettier than when we were kids. Motherhood suits her. Their baby girl, named Aeltje, looks a lot like Neeltje. She's got the Bogaert brown eyes," Aert recounted.

Teunis looked wistful as he stared at the letter in his hands, thumbing the rag paper where it was creased.

"Your cousin Jan was there. He was most interested in details and opportunities in the colony. I daresay we may have him join us here," Aert said. Teunis perked up at that bit of news.

"I saw *Grand-Père* Joris as we landed at the pier. He's harbormaster now?" Rebecca asked.

"He was just granted the position last week. He was tired of watching the mayhem of vessels in the harbor," Sarah said. "He must have been very excited to see your ship come in."

"So what else did I miss while I was away?" Rebecca asked.

"Well, Aneken is now married! This past January, Jean Clerq finally wooed her," Sarah exclaimed.

"Ah, that's wonderful... They make an odd couple, though." Rebecca looked a bit puzzled.

Aneken took after Hans quite a bit. She was very tall, blond, and vigorous. Jean was born in the Dutch Brazil colony and had suffered an illness as a child that left him with a slight build and a limp. He made up for it with his wit and humor, which her siblings would say Aneken lacked.

"Perhaps they balance each other out. Teunis isn't so sure about him because he only highly esteems men 'from near Heykoop,'" Sarah said. Rebecca laughed.

"It's funny Teunis and Aert exalt Heykoop. It took us a day to travel there by cart from Amsterdam and I hardly knew we'd arrived. Heykoop looked no different from the surroundings. The entire area is flat farmland as far as the eye can see. I suppose that's why it's the people that they praise, not the land. They were all honest, hardworking, salt-of-the-earth folks. Teunis and Aert's family were incredibly warm and welcoming."

"Jean comes from a Walloon family. I'd esteem that just as highly," Sarah said in a hopeful, yet wondering tone. They both thought on that for a moment, wishing well for Aneken. "Some other news... I'm pregnant. Not as pregnant as you, though—clearly!"

Rebecca squealed and hugged her mother. "My baby will have a best friend the same age."

"Somehow it never worked out with your *grand-mère* and I to be pregnant at the same time. Mostly we alternated years," Sarah said, trying to remember each of her children's and siblings' births. It all blurred together.

"We stayed a little longer in *Patria* because I was so sick, then I realized it was the illness I saw you had at the beginning of each pregnancy," Rebecca said.

"You're already wiser than me. It took me ages to realize that caused my nausea this summer. The timing was such, it coincided with moving and had me befuddled. My poor daughter, you didn't even have your *grand-mère*'s tea to help with it," Sarah said, referring to Catalyna's raspberry leaf, mint, ginger, and lemon balm tea.

"Oh, she sent me with some," Rebecca laughed. "She has her way of anticipating those things."

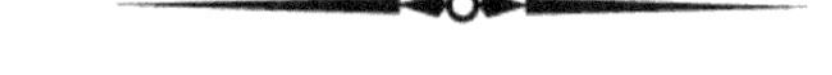

The following week, Teunis took their shallop to deliver three hundred clapboards to export on the ship *Hope*. He came back with their boat still full, barely controlling the anger that vibrated just under the surface of his countenance.

"Captain Emilius said his ship was already filled with cargo and backed out of the transaction. The dog!" Teunis said.

Sarah knew they needed that money to pay off the debts of their new house. She began to take stock of what fine new furnishing they could sell to pay the debt if the lumber sale fell through. Perhaps the Lord was chastising her for the pride she took in her new home. It would still be beautiful without the pendulum clock, the upholstered chairs, and window glazing. The clock especially made her uneasy. She never longed to know what precise time it was. The sun told her well enough.

CHAPTER 27

1661-1662

Foul weather tarried the ship *Hope*'s departure, giving Teunis the opportunity to take Captain Emilius to court. Sarah wanted to go with Teunis when he faced the captain, but Rebecca began her birth travails. She couldn't miss the birth of her first grandchild. Aert went in her stead. Sarah's mother also attended and won out on who would catch the baby.

"It's my first great-grandchild. It should be me," Catalyna stated. "Besides, I have the most experience."

Sarah agreed because her belly was large enough by then to be unwieldy. It was a surreal experience, watching her daughter in her birthing travails while feeling her own babe in her belly, fluttering with excitement. She held Rebecca's hand through the pain and remembered attending Phebe's first time birthing and her fear. Sarah reassured her daughter everything would be fine.

The new clock was actually quite handy in considering how increasingly close Rebecca's waves ran. Sarah ruefully acknowledged there was some use in having time precisely counted out.

She held her daughter's hand as they welcomed Sarah's first grandson, Theunis, into the world. He was named after Aert's father, as the variation of the name Antonis was exceedingly popular with Netherlanders from Utrecht.

Teunis and Aert returned triumphantly. They'd proved the sale was unconditional and must be paid out, whether or not there was room on the ship. Baby Theunis's arrival eclipsed their victory, though.

Teunis lit up with delight when he heard the name. Perhaps he felt it was partly for him, as his sister did about their Neeltje. It warmed Sarah's heart that it was also Rebecca's stepfather's name. It was the sign of a well-blended family.

Sarah gave birth in November to her and Teunis's fourth daughter, Aeltje. Sarah worried Teunis was disappointed he didn't have a son yet. If he did feel any chagrin, he didn't show it.

Teunis was naturally paternal with his stepsons, though. Jan, her eldest son, had been drawn to the sea-faring trade, like his father and stepfather. Teunis helped arrange an apprenticeship for him on smaller ships traversing up and down New Netherland that year. Jan looked like a grown man from the time he was about sixteen years old. He was tall and broad-shouldered, with light hair and amber-green eyes. Her son came back from his first journeys that summer with a determined resolve to become a captain. He never told Sarah about what transpired on those trips, but they'd transformed his confidence.

He was appointed captain of the ship *Sint Jan Baptist* at the age of only eighteen that fall. He departed for Amsterdam and would return with passengers and goods the following summer. Sarah and Teunis saw him off on the voyage. Sarah saw the misty look in her husband's eyes as they watched the ship leave the harbor of New Amsterdam.

When they returned home, Sarah's mother was just leaving.

"I came to tell you that Aneken's husband is ill. Jean claims it's the winter sickness which overtakes him every year. Aneken said his wet cough has only gotten worse for the past month. I made him a tincture, poultices for his chest, and herbal steam pots to put at his bedside."

"I'll take them some food. Maybe an herbal bone broth for Jean," Sarah said as she laid Aeltje in the bassinet. She went to the herbs she'd brought from their old kitchen garden, hung from the rafters to dry.

"No, take care to rest yourself, Sarah. Don't visit for a few days. I'm afraid it may be worse than a mere winter sickness."

Two months later, Sarah crept out the front door and gently closed it as her eyes adjusted to the dim light of the waning moon. The chill of the night made her inhale sharply.

She found Teunis sitting on their stoop, wrapped in a duffel blanket. He opened it to envelop her as she sat down next to him. He nuzzled his cold nose into her neck. She gasped at the shock of it, and he moved on to kiss her jawline. She drew him back into her neck, his breath quickly warming where he chilled her.

Almost every night, they'd sit on their stoop after the children went to bed and talk about their day. Even in winter. They talked over issues of their crops or animals, village gossip, or funny things their children said or did that day. Sometimes he sought her opinions on matters brought before him as *schepen*, though they were usually minor disputes.

"Sarah, I need your thoughts on a land matter. Rem wants to buy a portion of the meadow granted to you, not for his cousin Paulus, but for grazing his own animals. He offers a fair price in sewant or twice as much in blacksmithing services," Teunis whispered into her neck. Sarah reflected on the proposal. He pulled back to look at her.

"I don't see why not," Sarah finally said. "Rem's a good man. There's plenty we could use the money for, whereas that land is not even within sight of our new home. We could put the money toward the children's school fees or you could have him repair or remake the plow you've been complaining about."

"I expected it would be harder for you to part with it, on principle." He ran a finger along her cheek so she would look at him. "But I think it's the right choice."

"The principle of it has already served its purpose. I didn't have to worry over Paulus van der Beeck becoming our neighbor."

Aeltje cried out. They both froze and waited a moment. Sarah had just nursed her before she came outside. The cries ceased. Aneken was right there to console her and rock her crib. Aneken's husband, Jean, died six weeks earlier. She moved back home shortly after. She was sullen and quiet, but she devoted herself to helping with her new baby sister, Aeltje.

"In other news, it's confirmed that Breuckelen has had its first murder. Barent Jansen died this morning. The story I heard was that he was deep in his cups and was shouting unintelligibly at the Breuckelen ferry taphouse last night. He bumped into Albert Cornelysen Wantanaer, knocking his beer to the ground. Barent then attacked Albert for being in his way. Albert said he knifed him in his side out of self-defense."

"My goodness! Barent should have known a glove maker would keep a sharp knife! Will Albert be tried for murder, then?"

"Most certainly. He's out on bond, though."

"My friend, Susanna Negrin, was indentured to Albert before she got her manumission. She said he was a kind man to work for. He taught her to read. The court should find he was provoked to such an action, contrary to his character. Even so," Sarah shook her head, "a man was murdered. The first murder in Breuckelen."

"They'll likely try him in the New Amsterdam court for such a severe offense, so it will be a while before his judgment is upon him. I'm just glad I'm not the *schepen* in such a case. Makes me grateful for the petty cases I usually deal with," Teunis mirthlessly laughed. He continued, "To change the subject to something less grim... I've been thinking... it has only been a short while since Jean's death, and Aneken is rightfully still grieving, but it pains me to see her that way. I thought maybe we could have a potential suitor over for a visit, if only to give her a distraction?"

Sarah thought a moment of her reticence to entertain suitors after Hans died.

"No... I don't know. It's still so recent," Sarah said, but curious, she asked, "Who do you have in mind?"

"Dirck Jansen Hooglandt," he offered. "Dirck is a fine young man from—"

"Near Heykoop?" Sarah finished his sentence. Teunis gave her a sheepish grin as confirmation.

In the matter of marriages, she'd come to find Teunis always preferred a fellow Netherlander "from near Heykoop," which qualified them immediately in his eyes. She couldn't disagree on the point, though. Teunis had proved to be an industrious farmer and businessman, respected civic leader, devout church member, loving husband, and attentive father.

"Is he related to Dirck Cornelissen Hooglandt, my sister Lysbeth's sweetheart, the ferrymaster's son?" Sarah asked.

"Not that I know of, although perhaps distantly, as they're from the same place." He smirked, knowing she'd mock him if he said near his hometown one more time. "The Dirck I speak of resides in Midwout currently, not near the ferry. I suggest him because he has qualities similar to Jean."

"Like what?" Sarah asked, surprised.

"He's not tall, though he is quick-witted and talkative."

"Ah," Sarah said, agreeing those were Jean's attributes Aneken seemed to favor. "I suppose you could invite him to dinner sometime.

But don't broach the subject yet with either of them. It would be nice if they could feel it was a love match."

"Like us?" Teunis asked, jabbing her playfully with his elbow.

"Well, yes," Sarah said slowly. "Although I knew Phebe and Nys were setting me up. I really didn't want a new husband... but then you showed up, and I found it very hard to say no."

"How romantic," he said, teasing her.

"If I'm honest, I wanted you when I met you. They were right in thinking I would," she said, grabbed his face and kissed him. "Lots of people remarry quickly, but to me, it seems desperate if it's too quick and can show poorly on a woman's reputation. I wasn't desperate and Aneken isn't either."

"Once I met you, I was. Absolutely desperate to have you."

He pulled her onto his lap, wrapping the woolen blanket tighter around their bodies like a cocoon. She kissed him with abandon like she wished she had when they first met. His fingers laced into the hair at her nape.

Aeltje cried out. They both froze, lips locked. The pause of action only intensified their want of each other. After a moment of silence, Sarah released the breath she was holding. She felt guilty relying on her grown daughter for help. Although perhaps Aneken would remarry soon, and she should take advantage of the help while she had it. She kissed Teunis again, a moment longer, before going back inside.

Bringing home potential suitors for Aneken was put on hold as illness tore through the community that winter, not only at the Waalebocht but all the surrounding towns. Scarlet fever hit the Bogaert household. All of their children fell ill with the telltale bright red rashes, sore throats, and high fevers—all except three-month-old Aeltje. Luckily,

Sarah, Teunis, and the older children had already survived it when they were younger, and their symptoms were brief and minor.

By the end of a fortnight, most of their children had thankfully recovered, except two-year-old Neeltje. Her fever had burned so hot that her little body struggled to recover. Sarah bathed her forehead with cool water steeped with yarrow and did not leave her side. Neeltje was unconscious for days. Sarah continued to bathe her with yarrow water and prayed at her bedside. Her fever slowly went down, but she did not awaken. Teunis had a pained expression. It took him a long time to speak the words.

"*Mijn kastanje*, she isn't breathing. She's gone."

She had slipped away so slowly. Sarah couldn't believe it. She shook her and felt the unnatural stiffness. They wept and cradled their daughter's body.

The next day, Sarah went to the church in Breuckelen to pray. She wanted to be alone in her grief for a few hours. When she arrived and went in, she found she was not alone.

Her father knelt, eyes closed, in the front pew. He looked like he had been there a long time.

"*Papa...*" He didn't answer or open his eyes. She brushed his greasy salt-and-pepper hair from his forehead. He startled. She knelt next to him and slung her arms around him.

"I'm praying for your brother's recovery," he said. "I don't know how long I've been here... days?"

"I'm sorry, *Papa*. Jean died. Little Frederick, too... and my Neeltje."

Her father placed his head in his hands and shuddered with silent sobs. Jean was his eldest son. Frederick, Jean's son, was barely a year old. After a few minutes that felt like a painful eternity to Sarah, he sucked in a deep breath, stilled, then spoke.

"I should have been there, but I'm a coward in the face of disease. When I was a boy, the Catholic priest of Valenciennes told me that my parents died of the plague as a punishment for not being true believers. He told me I was conceived in sin and illegitimate. I wondered why the plague had not taken me as a baby, when it took my parents."

Sarah didn't know what to say.

"The priest was wrong, though. It is not a punishment. It is a test. I beseeched the Lord to spare our children. I bargained. I promised to serve Him. Now, He waits to see if I hold to my promise, despite loss, or abandon Him."

It was a heartbreaking start to the start to the year. By springtime and the planting season, illness had vanished, leaving a hollow bitterness in every family who had lost a loved one. Everyone mourned. Then they planted their crops. Bereavement wove into the continuous drive for survival.

CHAPTER 28

1662-1663

In April, Sarah's mother appeared at her door, brows knit. Clicks of her tongue punctuated exasperated short sighs. Sarah shooed her children to play outside so they could talk in peace.

"*Bonjour, Maman.* Do you want some rosehip tea? I've just made a pot. How are Maria and Michael?"

She knew her mother went to visit Cat's Wheel, now run by Sarah's sister Maria and her husband. They owned several properties on Pearl Straat, operating as inns and taverns. Catalyna visited monthly to review Maria's bookkeeping and the state of the place.

"I was in a foul mood today, made more foul by the lamentations of one guest at Cat's Wheel. That Danish woman, Annetje Kock, was crying and explaining the woes that brought her to rent the garret at Cat's Wheel. She said their landlord, Isaack Grevenraat, evicted them and is taking them to court over not paying their rent. They withheld their exorbitant rent because he hasn't followed through with conditions to improve the place. Grevenraat is a *schepen*, and she doubted they would prevail in court."

"What can they do?" Sarah handed her a mug of tea. Her mother set it down without drinking.

"I'll tell you! I went down to the *Stadthuys* to confront Grevenraat! I cursed him and told him to make the improvements or lower their rent. He told me he'll take me to court for slander. I don't care. Someone had to stand up for them."

"*Maman*, it's thoughtful of you to do that for a stranger—"

"Not a stranger, a guest at Cat's Wheel."

Sarah was worried about her mother. Everyone processed the grief of the past winter differently. Sarah knew her grief manifested in wanting to control the things that she could. She realized she inherited that trait from her mother.

Dirck Jansen Hooglandt visited often during that summer, in the guise of speaking with Teunis. Sarah saw, before long, that his visits cheered Aneken. He was a garrulous young man and made her smile. Sarah watched with delight when they started to sneak off for private walks in the fields or along the shore of the river.

"Another victory for a man from near Heykoop," Sarah laughed and whispered to Teunis after Aneken and Dirck announced their intentions to wed in October.

"Admit, there's something to it!" Teunis pinched at her ribs, making her giggle and blush.

"Well, you'd better hope they keep immigrating because we have a lot of daughters," she teased back.

"I was waiting to tell you," Teunis grew slightly more serious, "I've had news my cousin Jan is preparing to make the move next year. He's married with children, though." He smirked at her.

"Oh, that's wonderful!" Sarah exclaimed. "We're going to have to rechristen the Waalebocht as New Heykoop before long, aren't we?"

"God willing," Teunis said in jest, with a hint of wistfulness.

"How did my mother's court case go today?" Sarah knew they must have shared the ferry ride back from New Amsterdam earlier that day.

"Grevenraat had witnesses to Catalyna cursing him out. But he made the improvements to the lodging, so her curses were unfounded. She renounced her slander, agreed to pay him restitution, and promised not to repeat the offense."

"So, she won because he made the improvements."

"I suppose, although Catalyna had to pay for it..."

"It's the principle."

"Perhaps she should have just let them stay at the tavern. That's more the principle of profit for Cat's Wheel."

"It's not profit she wanted, it's what's right."

In March 1663, Sarah answered an urgent knock at her door. Her thirteen-year-old brother, Daniel, stood there trembling.

"Something is wrong with *Papa*. He's at the New Amersfoort Church for elections. Nys came to fetch *Maman* in a hurry. Will you take me?"

Sarah sprang into action. She saddled their new horse. Sarah hadn't ridden since she was a child. Women didn't ride horses, especially in their birthing years, but she felt that this was an emergency. She swung her little brother up to sit in front of her.

As they rode, she combed through the possibilities. After last winter's losses, everyone braced for another round of epidemic disease to stalk the countryside. But by February, it seemed it would just be the usual mild winter sickness of a runny or stuffed nose. "If you survive February, you'll make it another year," was a common adage.

They arrived at the church. As they entered, prayers greeted them, led by the Domine. Sarah, stricken with horror, realized it was the prayer recited when someone lies on their deathbed.

"Lord Jesus, holy and compassionate: Forgive Joris his sins. By dying, you unlocked the gates of life for those who believe in you: Do not let our brother be parted from you, but by your glorious power give him light, joy, and peace in Heaven where you live and reign forever and ever. Amen."

Her father was splayed on the floor, her mother by his side. He tried to speak, but the left side of his face was slack, and saliva drooled out of the corner of his mouth. Her mother wiped it as she whispered to him in French. Her father was nearly sixty but always had the vigor of a much younger man. The only giveaway of his age was the salt-and-pepper hairs sprinkled through his temples and mustache. The rest of his sandy dark-blond hair wasn't even balding. Now, with an ashen pallor, he looked much older.

Sarah and Daniel sank down beside their mother. Sarah saw her father breathed, and there was life in his eyes.

"*Maman*, let's take him home. We'll make him more comfortable and call a doctor."

"You can use my cart," a fellow congregant offered.

"I'll ride for a doctor," Nys said. Sarah pulled him aside.

"Try to find Surgeon Kierstede or De la Montagne... anyone other than Paulus van der Beeck, if possible."

They took him home, cradled in Catalyna's lap in the wagon. His condition didn't change for better or worse.

"Can you hear me?" Catalyna asked.

He squeezed her fingers with his good hand.

"Are you in pain? One squeeze for yes, two for no."

Two squeezes. She went on to ask if he was thirsty or cold or needed anything. He squeezed no to the first two, and after the third pulled her hand close to his heart.

Once home, they helped him into bed and tried to get him to drink some water, but much of it spilled out the slack side of his mouth.

Two hours later, Sarah was relieved Surgeon Kierstede was at their door. They told him what had happened.

"Hallo, Joris. You're suffering apoplexy. I need to ask you and your wife some questions, and I'll do what I can to alleviate the disease."

Sarah's father blinked rapidly.

"Did he eat and drink today?" Surgeon Kierstede asked.

"I think he had bread and butter… and peppermint tea."

"Did he have issue of the bowels?"

"Normal, I think."

"Joris, I'm going to start with bloodletting. Squeeze my hand if you'd like a draught to relieve pain."

He didn't squeeze. The doctor placed a bowl under Joris's weak arm. With a tiny knife, he sliced Joris's wrist. Her father didn't flinch. The blood flowed freely. Sarah could see the distress deepen on her mother's face. Catalyna avoided surgeons at all costs. She preferred her own tinctures and herbs, but Sarah knew her mother doubted their abilities and her healing skills since Jean had died. The magnitude of Joris's illness was beyond her. Sarah considered that it may also be beyond Surgeon Kierstede.

When the bowl was half full, the doctor bandaged Joris's wrist tightly with linen. The pallor in her father's cheeks worsened. His eyelids looked heavy.

"He should rest. I'll return tomorrow with some apophlegmatisms, if he's able to take them," Surgeon Kierstede said, packing his bag.

"What are apo…?" Sarah asked.

"It's a medicine. It will draw phlegm and bad humors away from the head."

By the time Surgeon Kierstede left, Joris was asleep. Catalyna curled up next to him.

"*Maman*, do you need anything?" Sarah asked.

"*Non*, come back in the morning."

Sarah couldn't eat or sleep that night. All she could do was pray and twist at the *sewant* bracelet her father gave her.

In the morning, Sarah went to her parents' house right away. Sarah's mother was perusing her herbs and tinctures with a faraway gaze. She spoke without looking at Sarah.

"He's still sleeping. No evident changes. He was awake in the middle of the night, and I tried to give him water. He has trouble swallowing as well as keeping it from spilling right out his mouth."

Just then, they heard him thrashing in their wooden *bedstee*, and they both rushed to him, along with her siblings, Daniel and Lysbeth. A fit wracked his body. He struggled to breathe, and then his body slackened. It looked like he was trying to speak.

Tears flowed from her eyes, but her mother's voice was steady and reassuring as she grasped his hands on his chest.

"Go not with fear, but content... We succeeded, Joris. Despite every peril, we prevailed. You live on in our children, and you will be remembered and honored, always... You are the great love of my life. Without you, nothing would have been possible... Tell Jacob and Jean that I love them."

Joris tried to speak again, but was unable. He clutched her hand with his and brought it to his cheek. He closed his eyes tightly, relaxed, and they did not reopen.

Sarah didn't leave her mother's side. Soon her grown siblings crowded the Rapalje home, encircling their patriarch and doting on their

matriarch. A pillar of all their lives, of the entire community, had crumbled. Everyone clutched each other to steady themselves.

Sarah held an arm around her mother as Joris was laid out on their table. Her mother hid her face in Sarah's shoulder and murmured, "In that last moment, holding him, I was transported back to the church in Leiden, when I first locked eyes with your father. It was during Jessé de Forest's speech recruiting settlers for this unknown land. The spark that illuminated my whole life... has been snuffed out."

Sarah didn't know what to say. She held her mother and they both quietly wept. The arms of her siblings surrounded them. Suddenly, her mother cleared her throat and pushed everyone away.

"Please go. I want to be alone... to wash and prepare him," her mother said, her voice breaking. "Sarah, inform Carel de Beauvois."

Monsieur de Beauvois had yet one more role, among myriad others, in the community: *aanspreker*. Dressed all in black, from his dark knee-breeches and doublet to a hat adorned with black crepe streamers, he went house to house, notifying and inviting families to the funeral of Joris Jansen Rapalje. He traversed the Waalebocht and Breuckelen. He notified the Domines of the New Amersfoort and New Amsterdam churches to make announcements.

The funeral was held two days later. Sarah's siblings and their children were so great in number, no one but immediate family could enter for the funerary mass inside the church. Domine Drisius exalted Joris's work in the church and community. Catalyna, Sarah, and each of her nine siblings read a passage from the Bible. Then they proceeded to the Waalebocht to bury him, amassed in the throngs of what seemed like the entire population of Breuckelen and the surrounding villages. There were so many pallbearers, it looked as if his coffin floated above a river of mourners.

They laid him in the ground of his favorite meadow. Everyone laid a stone until a cairn formed.

"It's a bitter irony that the death of your father brings such communion, never before seen among the scattered populous here," Phebe told Sarah. "If only he were here to see it."

"He sees it," Sarah whispered, choking back sobs, as she clutched the *sewant* bracelet he'd given her. She spun the beads as she thought of his fingers triumphantly holding each bead up, one by one, as they were successfully completed. White and purple, alternating good and bad on her wrist. How ironic the purple beads, meaning war, death, and sorrow, were more highly valued. If only he'd given her a bracelet of all white. If only a lifetime could contain only good.

CHAPTER 29

1663

Sarah's every thought was to care for her mother. Yet she had moments when her knees buckled in sorrow and days when she couldn't get out of bed. She hadn't noticed at first, but Teunis was always there to catch her or pull her back into the world.

He dutifully took on Joris's positions as deacon of the church and *schepen* of Breuckelen. Once she was over her initial shock of grief, he consulted her more often about court decisions. He would ask if she thought Joris would have agreed with his decisions. Eventually, he just asked what Sarah thought.

"Why do you consult me? You were elected to replace my father. Surely that means your judgment is trusted."

"I'm humbled and daunted by the idea of replacing him. How could anyone replace your father? You heard your father's wisdom, proverbs, and aphorisms more than anyone, plus you've lived here your whole life. You're most fit to make judgments. If you were a man, you would have replaced his positions. Yet, as a woman, you know more about people. Some may call it gossip or intuition, but I find it to be useful context," he told her. He gave her a sidelong smile. "Plus, I like to watch you deliberate. You bite your lip and narrow your eyes in the most beguiling way. You speak blunt facts with tact and grace. It really is a talent."

She blinked hard to hold back tears.

"Thank you, *mijn liefje*, but you sell yourself short. I don't know what I'd do without you."

"The other thing is... I keep asking what he would've said because... I miss him. I only knew him for ten years, but I loved him as much as my own father."

Now Teunis was blinking back tears.

"Well, as my father would say, 'You're not a hoe without a handle.'"

"'Don't mistake the horse droppings for figs,'" he shot back.

They both laughed. It felt good to laugh and cry at the same time.

Sarah trudged forth to sell her *passementerie* on a foul Saturday in early March. Hail assaulted those foolish enough, like Sarah, to take the ferry to Manhattan that day. Yet she was determined. She had taken weeks off from market days because of her father's death. Teunis's repeated requests for advice in court cases had helped her out of her melancholy and ill humor. She realized she was needed and that her father would not have wanted her life to end with his.

Sarah delivered *passementerie* pieces that had been commissioned and then ran into Margaret Hardenbroeck. She was getting married and was happy to place a large order for lace-trimmed household linens. It would certainly keep Sarah busy for the foreseeable future. Margaret paid half the agreed price up front. The commission assuaged her mood, but, as she walked, she still spitefully kicked the sleet accumulated on the ground. Someone called her name. She looked around and found Susanna Negrin waving to her across the market. She hadn't seen Susanna in a long time.

The two met and kissed each other's cheeks.

"I'm sorry about your father. There are no words I can say to bury that grief, but I walk with you in it." Susanna took her arm in condolence as they continued through the market.

"How is your midwifery practice?" Sarah asked.

"Babies are always being born, so business is steady. Another ship of Africans just arrived. The Company had me assess the health of the women. The Company officers asked questions like these women are nothing but heifers for breeding."

"Those women are lucky to have you to tend to them."

Susanna veered Sarah off the course of the market, toward Princes Graft. "I think we both deserve some distraction. Come with me. There's an auction of the land that used to be the sheep's pasture by the canal."

They arrived at the place, although there were few people gathered to bid in the foul weather. Domine Megapolensis was conducting the sales. They watched as the parcels were auctioned and the small pool of people further dwindled. Suddenly, Susanna raised her hand to bid. She was awarded a small plot.

The next parcel, next to Susanna's, came up for auction. Sarah impulsively made an offer, but a young man countered. Sarah raised her offer by two guilders. The young man hesitated to raise again, and Sarah won.

The entire amount she earned at the market that day would almost pay for it, but she was short. She could easily pay it later, but as she unconsciously turned the beads on the *sewant* bracelet that her father gave her, she realized she needed to use it. He gave it to her for this very purpose. *With this bracelet, you will always have teeth at the ready.* With tears in her eyes, she bought the land, in his memory. Teunis might be hurt she didn't consult him, but in their marriage contract he acknowledged she would conduct business in her own name. He'd be happy for the additional income of renting it out. It would give them a place to stay for the biannual cattle market.

She and Susanna grinned at owning a piece of land in the heart of New Amsterdam, an increasingly rarefied land right.

One hot, dry afternoon in mid-July, her sister Lysbeth's husband rode up as Sarah and her daughter Maria were boiling the wash and hanging it in the yard.

"Sarah, tell Teunis we see a ship coming in. He asked me to notify him when I saw a passenger vessel coming in. It's likely the *Bonte-Koe* by the look of her," Dirck called to her, not even dismounting. "I need to get back to the ferry. It'll be leaving in thirty minutes, and I still have cargo to load."

"Thank you, Dirck! He'll be on that ferry!" Sarah hollered as he turned his mare and rode away. Sarah momentarily had the urge to saddle up and fetch her husband herself.

"Jacob!" Sarah called to her ten-year-old son, Jacob, the eldest home at the time. He came running from their garden. "Take Lightning and go find your *Pater*. I think he'll be in the northern wheat field."

Their new horse, Lightning, was a cross between an English Thoroughbred and a Native horse. It was quite a bit faster than their Dutch draft horse Teunis had taken that morning. Jacob's eyes lit up. He loved riding the horses, especially if the aim was to go fast.

"Take care with her, Jacob," Sarah said sternly, as she carried the saddle over to the pasture where Lightning grazed. She secured the saddle for him. "Go quickly, but not carelessly. Tell him the *Bonte-Koe* is approaching, and the ferry leaves soon. He must hurry if he wants to go meet his cousin."

Not ten minutes later Teunis arrived on Lightning, wasting no time to strip his sweat-drenched shirt off to change into a fresh one that Sarah had waiting for him. Some minutes later, Jacob followed on their workhorse, Thundercloud, the horse which Teunis took to the fields that morning.

"I'll have a meal ready for them. They can stay here tonight and settle their things into their new home tomorrow," Sarah said. "Make sure Captain Jan comes too, of course." She'd taken to calling her son by his title to avoid the confusion of Teunis's cousin having the same given name. She still could scarcely believe Teunis's cousin crossed the Atlantic on the ship her son now captained.

"Of course. We'll have a grand reunion and a full table tonight!" Teunis said, breathlessly grinning, and kissed her. He hitched Lightning to their wagon and rode off. Sarah calculated he'd just barely get to the ferry in time, but Dirck would likely wait a few more minutes for him.

Sarah welcomed the frenzied distraction and was glad for the excitement Teunis had to welcome his cousin. She couldn't wait to see her son, but she wasn't eager to tell him that his grandfather had died while he was away.

Hours later, a breeze blew in as the sun lowered in the sky. Sarah nervously reswept their spotless stoop to look busy as she kept watch for her guests. Teunis pulled up in the wagon with his four passengers. They looked exhausted and relieved. Introductions were made.

Jan was a little older than Teunis. Sarah could see the family resemblance in his dark brown eyes and high cheekbones. That was about all that was visible, as the bottom half of his face sported a full, dark brown beard.

His wife, Cornelia, was Sarah and Teunis's age, with apple cheeks and a warm disposition. Her weary eyes and elation at arriving at their home told Sarah all she needed to know about their trip.

They had two children, seven-year-old Peter and four-year-old Lysbeth. Sarah's son, Jacob, peeled off with Peter to show him around, and her little girls gravitated to Lysbeth with their cornhusk dolls.

"Please come in. Is Captain Jan joining us?" Sarah asked, with more worry in her voice than she intended.

"Certainly, but he said he'd be late. He's overseeing the unloading of cargo to the inspection house, since his supercargo is unwell." Teunis told her. "Shall we start with a drink? We've got cider, beer, brandy, gin…"

"As guests, we brought something as a gift," Jan said. He went to the trunk they brought and pulled out a *vierdekijn* quarter cask. "A taste of *Patria*!"

"*Proost* to that, cousin!" Teunis replied as he helped Sarah set out their *roemer* glasses.

Sarah gulped hers and nearly snorted it out her nose. She forgot the beer from the homeland was much stronger. The delight on Teunis's face must be because this brew was from his region, but she found the taste difficult to discern from the strength.

"What a beautiful home! To see my little cousin so well established makes my heart fit to burst!" Jan threw his arm over Teunis, who beamed with pride.

"Are you very hungry? I have some bread, butter, cheese, and berries to nibble while we wait for my son," Sarah said, bringing tin platters to the table with the *hors d'oeuvres*.

"Oh, bless you," Cornelia said, her quickness to snatch raspberries at odds with the lightness of her tone. "Weeks of salted and dried foods has me craving anything fresh."

"Ah, I can imagine…" Sarah said, picking through her basket of garden produce. She cut a cucumber and dill fronds. "Have a cucumber slice with some cheese and dill on top. I think it's the most delightful treat on a hot summer day."

Cornelia tried it and closed her eyes. "This is the best thing I've tasted in weeks... maybe ever," she finally proclaimed softly, eyes teary once opened.

Suddenly, the sound of the girls fighting disturbed the moment. Sarah went to the stoop where they were playing.

Lysbeth brought a dolly with a porcelain face and plush stuffed body. Her youngest daughters, Aeltje and Catalyntje, jealously grabbed at it, fighting for who could touch the cool, hard face with rouged cheeks and painted lashes.

"Girls," Sarah said sharply, "Lysbeth is our guest and your cousin. We don't take our cousin's toys. We share with our family." She snatched the dolly away and watched as their eyes welled up with tears. "See, it's not nice to have your toy taken."

She gave the dolly back to Lysbeth.

Sarah felt guilty her children didn't have porcelain-faced dolls and annoyed that it had been introduced. Cornhusk dolls had been wonderful before they knew about such a fancy doll.

"I have an idea. Do you want to give your dollies some rouged cheeks?" Sarah asked. Their mood shifted from crying to interested. "Wait here, I'll get some rouge."

Sarah grabbed some berries and macerated them in a little wooden bowl. "Here," she said and dipped a pinky finger, touching it to the cheek of one doll. The girls, now animated in a task, did the same to squeals of joy. Lysbeth abandoned her porcelain doll to join in rouging the cheeks of cornhusk dolls.

Cornelia stood by, watching as Sarah handled the situation. She gave Sarah a knowing and approving grin.

"You handled that well. I'm sorry we didn't bring some dolls for your daughters," Cornelia whispered.

"That's all right. In the fall, I'll teach you how to make cornhusk dolls. Imported dolls are expensive. Your daughter can have dozens of cornhusk dolls for nothing."

They returned to the table where their husbands were deep in discussion, smoking their pipes.

"They said New Haarlem is ripe for settlement. That's where they're going," Jan was saying.

"Who's that?" Sarah said, sitting down and joining their conversation. Jan and Cornelia were a little taken aback at her so casually jumping into the men's discussion, but Teunis didn't miss a beat in replying to her.

"Some passengers on board with them," he explained.

"There's a war with the Esopus Natives right now, north of there. Last time there were settlements in that area was prior to the war with the Natives in '43. My friend's bowery and new house there were burnt down. Tell them to make an offering to the Weckquaesgeek for friendship and protection," she explained solemnly.

Jan and Cornelia sat sobered and bewildered at that bit of context.

"My wife was born here. She's a wealth of knowledge," Teunis said, smiling at Sarah and lightening the mood.

"I don't mean to scare you. My father would say that the Natives aren't different from Netherlanders. Some are our good friends and some aren't. Some are kind and others always seek to make trouble. Making friends with your neighbors is always preferable."

"We intend to settle in Boswijck for now," Jan said.

"Good, you won't be far from us. Our land borders the village there," Teunis said.

They heard Captain Jan ride up.

"Please, sit. I'll greet him," Sarah said and went out the front door and saw Jan's little sisters running up to him. The light was fading fast into sunset, and he appeared so dashing on his horse. He looked so much older than her mental image of him. Of course he does, she thought, and snapped herself out of maternal reverie.

"Jan!" she exclaimed and hugged him as he was barely off his horse. "Well done on another successful voyage."

"*Bonjour, Maman.*"

"Jan... I have sad news. *Grand-Père* died while you were away. He collapsed at church. It was sudden and he went quickly to the Lord."

"*Grand-Père* died? When?"

"February." Sarah held him at arm's length to look him in the eye. "He was a good man, and he died serving his church. His funeral procession was the largest seen on Lange Eylandt. He was very proud of you, Captain Jan."

"How is *Grand-Mère*?"

"She would be glad to see you. I invited her tonight, but she declined," Sarah said, the sadness in her voice giving away how Catalyna was doing. "Go see her tomorrow, but now, come inside and let's eat."

CHAPTER 30

1663

One month later, Sarah knocked her secret knock on Phebe's door. She wiped her brow anxiously. Arid July had turned into a humid August. Phebe answered the door. She hid her face in her hands.

"Phebe," Sarah whispered and wrapped her arms around her. "I came as soon as I heard."

Phebe crumpled into her embrace and Sarah sat her down on the stoop beside her. Phebe convulsed in sobs. Sarah held her that way for a long time. It felt like hours. Phebe's sobs would slow and Sarah thought she might speak, but the sobs would only begin anew.

"Do you want me to help you to bed? Perhaps you should rest," Sarah said after her sobs had slowed. She expected Phebe had exhausted herself. "Here, have a sip of water."

Phebe took the jug to her lips. Sarah helped her sip slowly.

"Nys is dead. I can't lie in the bed we once shared. I don't know what to do with myself."

"Do you want to talk about it? What happened?"

"My son came home yesterday with his father's enormous hat in his hands... the hat and his bloodshot eyes... I knew then."

"But how..."

"They were at the gristmill. My son said the millstone was catching, and his father went to investigate the cause. The mill shaft had splintered. Suddenly, it gave way. He was crushed to death." Phebe began to sob again.

Sarah tried hard not to gasp. Teunis told her it was a terrible accident. He didn't elaborate, but he urged Sarah to prevent Phebe from seeing Nys's body.

After some time, Phebe looked Sarah in the eyes and asked, "What do I do now?"

"Mourn your husband. Teunis is making arrangements. We'll have the funeral. Then ask again," Sarah said. "One day at a time... one moment at a time."

Two weeks after the funeral, Phebe sat across from Sarah at her table.

"What do I do now?" Phebe demanded.

"Eat the porridge I made you."

"I mean—"

"Settle Nys's estate," Sarah said. "Debts will likely surface. Go through his account books. You may have debts owed to you as well."

"I know we're richer in land than coin. Perhaps my son can run the gristmill, but he's still so young. He can't do it alone. I'm unequal to the tasks of being a widow."

"You're stronger than you think you are."

"I know you had qualms about remarrying, but... I have suitors. Do you judge me harshly for thinking about it so soon? It worked out for you. Teunis has been more..." Phebe stopped when Sarah put her head in her hands. "I'm sorry, I didn't mean..."

"*I'm* sorry, Phebe. It's still not easy for me to recall..." She looked up through thick tears. "...but your situation is different. I cannot judge you. You were so good to me during that time... after... You just listened to me spout ideas. I'm glad to return the favor."

Phebe finally ate some of the groats with milk and butter Sarah had made for her.

"Can we have some of that tea your mother makes to calm the nerves?" Phebe asked, smiling faintly.

"Of course." Sarah smiled. "If you'll tell me all about your suitors."

"There's only one I'm considering. Jan Cornelisz Buys. He's also recently widowed."

"And quite a few years younger!"

"I know what your father would say. He was not very fond of his uncle is Jan Damen..."

"My father was known to set aside his contempt for the man when he needed a loan. I suppose your suitor would be a secure financial choice if he has access to his uncle's favor."

"It's not merely for that reason I consider him. The conversations I've had with him have brought me comfort. He's a widower and loved his wife dearly. He doesn't have Nys's swagger or charm, but he understands me." Phebe blushed. She hid her face in the steam of the tea Sarah set in front of her.

"Sounds like you're rather charmed by him."

The blush rose to Phebe's ears. She changed the subject.

"In all the grief and turmoil, I forgot to discuss the news that your brother and my daughter were betrothed right before Nys died."

"I forgot as well! At least Nys blessed their union before he passed."

"Perhaps it will be a double wedding," Phebe said, smiling as tears fell down her cheeks.

A month after Nys's death, what could have felt like a solemn, perfunctory affair for Phebe became joyous with Sarah's brother and Phebe's daughter celebrating their marriage along with her. Jeronimus and Annetje's happiness rubbed off on everyone. Sarah noted that Phebe's eldest son wore Nys's enormous caster hat. It made her smile to see it had been passed down, as Nys wanted.

"It's so odd how life unfolds," Phebe had said to Sarah on her wedding day. "Who knew all my visits to the Waalebocht were making my daughter fall in love with your brother?"

"I suppose there's always a silver lining to be had," Sarah said, "and we shall be all the more grateful for it. We're officially family now!"

"Maybe we can pair a few more off to solidify our family connection?" Phebe jested, looking towards their little children playing together.

"They're a bit young, but consider it a standing betrothal," Sarah said, wrapping one arm around Phebe's waist. Sarah laid her head on Phebe's shoulder as they wistfully watched their little ones until Phebe's new husband snatched her up to dance.

She watched Phebe's expression. Phebe was happy, but in a different way than her wedding day to Nys. She knew it was tinged with sorrow, but also the relief from it.

Sarah thought of Hans, but then an arm circled her waist from behind, drawing her to stand. Teunis pulled her close and she kissed him before they joined the dance.

A few weeks later, Sarah's spirit was buoyant once harvest season was upon the Waalebocht. After such a hard year of losses, the land's bounty was finally a reward for persevering.

She followed Teunis and her sons, reaping the wheat. As she waited to tie up the shocks, her gaze fixed on the birch trees at the edge of the field. Their leaves had begun to yellow and the wind played in them, making them twinkle like gold coins. The maple leaves flitted dramatically, showing their undersides. That meant there would be rain that afternoon. She refocused on the task at hand.

She was so engrossed in tying up the shocks, she didn't see Weenji approach until she was twenty paces away. And she wasn't alone. Another woman joined her. A *sachem*, Sarah surmised from the elaborate breastplate she wore.

"Sarah, n*itap*!"

Sarah's heart lifted to hear Weenji use the term of friendship. She hadn't seen her for many seasons. Sarah reciprocated the greeting.

"Sarah, *nitap*. This is Quashawam, *sunksqua* of the Montaukett. She is daughter of the deceased Wyandanch, *sachem* of the allied eastern Lange Eylandt tribes."

Sarah hadn't been introduced to a *sachem* since she was three years old, when her father negotiated for land use at the Waalebocht. Her father told her she took her dress off and ran naked to the tidal pools and made the *sachem* laugh. Sarah doubted that would work now. She bowed her head and bent slightly at the waist. She glanced at Weenji, who did not show disapproval.

"Weenji, *nitap*!" Teunis shouted, barely ceasing his work.

"I think it will rain soon. Will you help me get the shocks up? Then we can speak without hurry while we eat," Sarah asked Weenji. "Quashawam, there is a bench by the kitchen garden if you wish to rest. We won't be long."

"We will both help with your harvest," Quashawam said.

Bruised clouds blew in as they finished the field work. As Sarah, Weenji, and Quashawam walked into Sarah's home, the sky cracked open with a hard rain. Teunis and Sarah's children were in the barn—and likely to stay there—until the rain let up. It gave Sarah privacy to talk with her guests. Sarah cut up fresh baked bread.

"If I knew you were coming, I would have baked a special bread. Rye bread will have to do," Sarah said, setting the bread, butter, cheese, and strawberry preserves on the table. She wanted to ask why they were there, but she waited for Weenji or Quashawam to speak.

They ate in silence.

"It is good," Quashawam said in Munsee as she finished eating. She turned to the reason for their visit. "I need a translator. There is a land dispute between my people and the English. I want to appeal to your *sachem* for help. The English plan to steal the lands of the Dutch as well. Will you translate for me?"

Sarah nodded.

"When do you need me to translate?"

"Tomorrow morning."

"You are welcome to stay here tonight."

The women nodded. Sarah studied Weenji. She had so many questions for her old friend. She knew Weenji joined the Montaukett after several in her village died of scarlet fever, including her mother. Many tribes, so diminished from their former size, banded together for strength, even with former adversaries. What was Weenji's role in her new community?

"Weenji, is your son well?" Sarah asked instead.

"Mehakachtey grows tall and strong."

Sarah, Weenji, and Quashawam took the ferry to Manhattan very early the next day. When they arrived at the fort, Sarah explained that the leader of the eastern Lange Eylandt tribes requested an audience with Director General Stuyvesant.

"*Mijn Heere General* has a very busy day. He may not have time to see you," his secretary explained. "He already spoke with two of the *sunksqua's* men last week."

"We'll wait," Sarah told him.

Sarah asked about the two men the secretary mentioned. Quashawam explained that she hoped a second appeal in person—and with a New Netherlander to translate—would make Stuyvesant listen this time. They waited until late in the afternoon. Finally, the secretary came to fetch them. He presented them before the council.

"*Mijn Heere General*." Sarah bowed her head. "I translate the words of Quashawam, *sunksqua sachem* of the Montaukett and allied tribes of eastern Lange Eylandt. The English population has increased and continues to grow. They sign deeds to buy tribal land, yet do not make payment. Their unfenced animals ruin the crops of the Montaukett. Furthermore, she warns that the English are planning an invasion of Dutch lands. She seeks an alliance with the Dutch."

"The English have staked their claim to the eastern part of Lange Eylandt. Her father, Wyandanch, made the agreement with them years ago. It is not for the Dutch to intervene."

"What of her warning that the English plan to invade Dutch towns? We need protection."

"I have been assured there is no such plan."

With that, they were dismissed.

"I'm sorry," Sarah told Quashawam and Weenji after she translated what Stuyvesant said. A sick tightening coursed through her chest and into her stomach. Stuyvesant declined to protect their tribal sovereignty. He would likely decline to help the Dutch on Lange Eylandt as well. She thought bitterly about how his solution was ordering them to concentrate their population in palisaded villages. They would have to fend for themselves.

"Sarah!" They passed a woman who turned and called her name. It was Judith Bayard, Stuyvesant's wife. "What are you doing here?"

Sarah stopped and greeted her. Judith was good friends with her mother. She decided to explain the situation to her. Perhaps she could persuade the Director's wife to advocate for them.

"I'm sorry my husband wasn't more helpful. Managing the encroaching English is like taming a Hydra, and with very little resources. He has to manage one threat at a time. My husband recently went to Boston to confront the governor about his unlawful declarations. They claim Dutch lands belong to the Connecticut colony. They forced the New Netherlanders to abandon their homes and gravely injured those who resisted. After speaking with the governor, he was not satisfied and, frankly, has been in a foul mood ever since."

"If you find him in a more opportune mood, would you suggest he consider protections for the people on Lange Eylandt? The New Netherlanders and the Natives?" Sarah asked. She nodded, giving Sarah a sorry look that did not give her hope.

When they ferried back across the river, Sarah tried to explain Stuyvesant's cold disregard of their plight. She found herself making excuses for Stuyvesant, as Judith did, even as a hollow roiling of dread and anger twisted in her stomach.

"Perhaps we could try again, after he's sorted the issues with Massachusetts and Connecticut. What will you do in the meantime?"

"If the Dutch are not interested, we'll find Englishmen to ally with." Quashawam said, chin raised.

PART FOUR: ESTEEM

1664–1685

Whatever locks itself shut has already petrified.
Does it feel safe and secure in its inconspicuous grey?
Wait – the hard warned by the hardest far away.
Woe betide – a distant hammer's lifted high!

Whoever pours himself like a spring, realization
realises him, will lead joyful to calm creation
that in opening closes, often ceases by starting.

– Rainer Maria Rilke –
"Sonnets to Orpheus"
Translated by Martyn Crucefix
Part 2, Number 12

Chapter 31

1664

Sarah and Teunis's favorite day of the week was Thursday, market day, in Breuckelen. During the forty-minute wagon ride, they discussed things they might want for a good price. It was a chilly March day, with snow still on the ground, half thawed in some patches. Sarah made use of a black rabbit muff that Teunis had bought for her on a previous market visit.

Today they hoped to sell early spring greens like endive, collard greens, chard, asparagus, ramps, and wood ear mushrooms, as well as smoked pork sausages, sacks of cornmeal, butter, and buttermilk. Sarah also took orders for *passementerie,* though she usually sold less at the Breuckelen market than New Amsterdam's.

They set up their wagon for display. They would take turns selling while the other perused what the different vendors sold that day. After parting with Teunis to make her rounds, Sarah found Phebe in the crowd and the two continued together, linked arm in arm.

"I have news," Phebe said with a sly grin. "There will be a new addition to our family."

"Phebe! That's wonderful," Sarah gushed, hugging her friend's arm even tighter.

"I'm sure, now. The past few years... with Nys... I had several false starts. I didn't want to curse myself by saying it aloud until I was certain," Phebe said solemnly. "I've only just told Jan this morning. He was so pleased. Of course, he yearns for a boy..."

The church bell clanged, not in its methodical tone to tell the hour or for service, but as a frantic warning. A man rode through the crowd on horseback, preceded by a drummer boy he almost trampled, and followed by a retinue of around one hundred men on horse and foot. Flanking the leader were two standard-bearers, each hoisting the English flag, a red cross on a white field. The lead horseman's jowls were framed by a long, curled, dark brown periwig. His mouth was pursed and his brow raised with haughty affection. He began shouting in English.

"I am John Scott, President of Long Island. This country you inhabit is unjustly occupied by your leader," he told them. "It belongs to the King of England and not to the Dutch. If you acknowledge His Britannic Majesty's sovereignty, you will be permitted to remain in your homes. Otherwise you will be forced to leave."

"He said he's John Scott, President of Long Island, and this land belongs to the King of England. He bids us to show allegiance," Phebe said, looking perplexed. Sarah had learned English from Phebe, but in her shock, she was grateful Phebe translated. She couldn't believe what she heard.

Secretary Van Ruyven stepped forward and said, "You may submit your declaration to our Lord Director General, Petrus Stuyvesant. Our allegiance is to the United Provinces of the Netherlands."

"Let Stuyvesant come here, and I will run him through with a sword!" Scott barked. Phebe translated for Sarah, but his reply was made clear by pantomime with his sword. "If anyone claims this is not his Majesty's land, I will cut the feet from under them!"

"What documents have you of your credentials and order?" Secretary Van Ruyven asked.

"I shall share them with Stuyvesant," Scott said dismissively.

Scott then dismounted and turned to Cornelis, the ten-year-old son of *Burgomaster* Kryger, who stood nearest to him. He commanded the boy to doff his cap and salute the royal standard. Cornelis either didn't understand or refused. He just stood there. John Scott slapped him across his face with his cane. At that, the bewildered crowd turned on the invading Englishmen and an outcry of injustice rippled through the onlookers.

One man shouted, "Try that with a man, not a child, you charlatan coward!" Scott's men seized him. He struggled free from their grasp and grabbed a copper bed-warmer pan from a nearby stall to keep them at arm's length. More onlookers took up impromptu weapons and stood beside the man. Everyone stood still and tense, waiting to see who would move first, until John Scott barked orders.

"There will be a time for fighting later! For now, there are more Dutch towns to we must inform. Onward, men!"

He remounted and signaled to his drummer boy. They marched toward New Utrecht.

Sarah and Phebe weaved through the bewildered throngs of people until they found Teunis. He was holding an informal meeting at the far end of the market street with other government officials of Breuckelen. When he saw them, he excused himself, tipping his hat to the *schepens* and *burgomasters*. Joining up with Sarah and Phebe, he directed them toward where their horse was hitched near their wagon.

"Let's get you ladies home. I don't know who that man thinks he is, but he ruined a good market day," Teunis said, trying to make light of the incident, but his eyes brooded. "Phebe, we can take you home on the way."

"Quashawam was right—the English mean to take over Lange Eylandt," Sarah said. "That damned fool Stuyvesant didn't listen. No Director has ever had the sense to heed a warning!"

"We'll draft a petition to Stuyvesant. It shouldn't be so easy for anyone with daft ideas to parade into our village and threaten us.

We can raise a militia, but it would be insufficient. We need more protection," Teunis told them once they were on their way.

"I can only assume that's not the last we hear from that windbag John Scott," Phebe said with distaste and a bit of worry. "Englishmen are ever so obstinate once they get a notion stuck in their mind."

Sarah was unsure of how serious the threat was. Scott made incredulous claims, for which he bore no proof. Teunis's plan of action to address Stuyvesant with his concerns reassured her. Perhaps the Director would listen to him. Since he'd taken the *schepen* position vacated by Joris, he'd grown into leadership as naturally as he had in becoming a father. For a mere son of a planter, civic duty seemed to suit him.

After receiving the petition from Teunis and his colleagues, Stuyvesant called a meeting of Lange Eylandt delegates. Teunis and two other men went as representatives.

"Tell me everything," Sarah demanded as soon as he returned.

"We recounted John Scott's parade and beating the *burgomaster*'s son. Stuyvesant had supreme authority and control in his voice and bearing, but his eyes revealed genuine worry. His secretary recorded our account. Stuyvesant said he would relate the transgression and our concerns to the Company board and the States General. He said he would request soldiers and munitions."

"What if John Scott comes back to threaten us in the meantime?"

"Stuyvesant said he'll meet with him and come to an agreement."

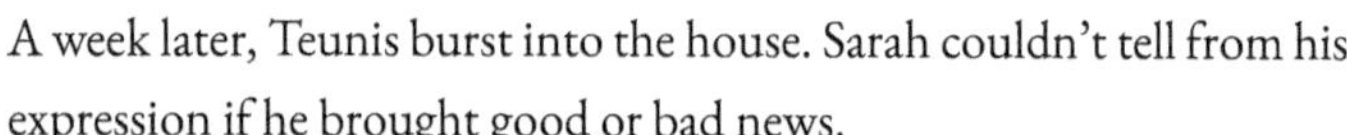

A week later, Teunis burst into the house. Sarah couldn't tell from his expression if he brought good or bad news.

"Stuyvesant has signed an agreement with the governor of the Connecticut colony, John Winthrop, Jr. Oostdorp was been given up, the Connecticut River relinquished, and with this last document, Mespat, Vlissingen, Rustdorp, Heemstede, and Gravenzande also fall out of Dutch control."

"In exchange for...?"

"The English won't harass *us* anymore. And certainly not by John Scott. Just after his meeting with Stuyvesant, Winthrop seized Scott and threw him in prison for 'stealing' land from him! As if it wasn't the Dutch they both stole it from!"

"And the Native's land... Weenji was here earlier. She said Quashawam gave Scott power of attorney. On Quashawam's behalf, he sued and demanded payment for all lands bought and not paid for. I told her I was glad the arrangement was satisfactory to them, but warned her to be wary of what the man's motivations are. She did not mention that he was imprisoned. I wonder if she knows..."

Sarah wrapped her arms around Teunis's neck and sighed. She melted into his scent of leather, fresh air, and faintly, their horse. A moment's peace from worry and a warm embrace were all she wanted. Just then, she had both.

In April, the melting snow of the hillsides drained into the river, as it did every year, but the higher elevations in the surrounding river valley had significantly more snow that year. Heavy rains then compounded the rising water for weeks. The river and tributaries spilled over their banks. The freshet threatened their planting season as most of their fields were saturated or completely under water.

Kip's warning years ago about the settlers at the Waalebocht becoming separated when the creek rose had come to pass. They had a bridge over the creek, but the water overflowed the banks and the bridge. The houses in their village became islands surrounded by water and mud. The cows sunk into the mud and their pitiful moos haunted Sarah's dreams. It took a long time to herd them to drier pastures and back to the barn at night. Teunis, being a pragmatic Netherlander, built up dikes to allow for passable high ground connecting the settlements and dry pastures. He and their sons made efforts to build up the dikes at low tide, but once it had risen again, the swell of water often reclaimed half a day's work.

"God created the world, but the Dutch created the Netherlands." Teunis quoted the saying that touted his people's ability to reclaim land from watery marshes of rivers and the North Sea via dikes and polders. They made slow progress.

Sarah had to admire Teunis's perseverance. Yet even he had his dark days. Their plow yoke split when the oxen strained to free the implement from the quagmire of mud. He had to dig the plow blade free with a shovel, but as he dug, the mud and gravel and water just flowed back into the hole. It was a Sisyphean task. When the rain worsened to torrents and he began cursing heaven above, Sarah dragged him inside. She peeled his drenched, muddy clothing off and gave him a basin of hot water to clean up with.

"Try again tomorrow. Let's pray for a break in the rain." She handed him lemon balm and chamomile tea with a generous splash of brandy.

Laundry became too much of a task. Some days she just dried the mud-caked clothing by the hearth and broke the dried pieces off in chunks, considering it then ready to wear again.

The next day Sarah noticed small animals floating, dead, in the eddies of the creek and pools in their fields. She shuddered, remembering the vision of her little brother Jacob on the creek bank, surrounded by dead mice, squirrels, rabbits, and birds. *The water is foul here... Come away with me, away from the dead.*

She warned her family and neighbors to only pull drinking water from the rain cisterns and barrels.

They pivoted to sowing fields in the far reaches of their land that were on higher ground or farther from the creek. Clearing that land was slow work, but the tree roots relinquished their grasp on the sodden soil with relative ease. Finally, some crops were planted with fervent prayers that they wouldn't rot in the ground.

It was a cheerless, exhausting month. A reprieve in the rain came in late April, and the following week showed some green shoots daring to break skyward. It was late and it wasn't enough, but after the beating April gave them, they clung to those little shoots with all the hope in the world.

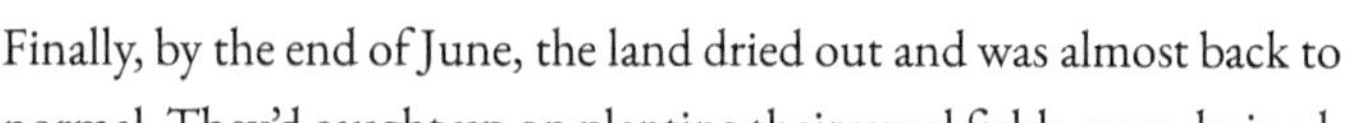

Finally, by the end of June, the land dried out and was almost back to normal. They'd caught up on planting their usual fields, now drained.

On a pleasant, sunny Wednesday mid-month, Sarah decided to take her three youngest daughters to look for wild strawberries and any other edibles they could forage. With crops sown late and the storehouse running low, foraging foods would be a necessity. If they found enough, they could sell some at the market the next day, too. Sarah shielded her daughters from her concern and framed the day as an adventure. It was a wonderful day to revel in the sun. They found a patch of blueberries, which were not ripe. Just beyond that, some downed trees flushed with frills of blue-gray oyster mushrooms.

They filled two baskets. Meandering further, they found a meadow of strawberries and lay down to eat their fill in the sun, like she and Phebe did when they were young.

Sarah missed Phebe. Her new husband moved their household to Midwout, so Sarah saw her less frequently. She missed Sarina too. She had seen her childhood friend so seldom in the last few years. Her life was quite different from Sarah's, especially since Isaac became a Great Burgher. Like Saartje, Sarina and Isaac were in a higher class now. She wondered what that was like, perhaps entertaining other important people over meals which servants prepared. Did their children ever get the chance to lie in strawberry fields? Or were their clothes too fine to lie about on the ground?

She was daydreaming and letting her mind wander, looking at great puffs of clouds in the sky. The girls said what shapes they looked like. A ship, a hat, a bear. Suddenly, the hair on Sarah's arms stood up. Something was wrong. The birds, one minute before sweetly singing, went silent.

A flock purged forth from the trees surrounding the meadow into the sky. The earth beneath them shuddered and the girls screamed. Sarah threw her body over her children, to defend them from God knows what. When the most violent of movements subsided after several minutes, they stood up tentatively. Sarah's knees trembled as much as the ground had moments ago. They gathered their baskets and ran home.

They entered the house and saw that whatever could topple, had. Brooms, tin lanterns, and the butter churn had fallen over, and one of the green *roemer* goblets lay on the floor, cracked.

Teunis rushed in the door not long after them. They all embraced at the center of their great room.

"Everyone all right?" he asked as he checked them over.

"*Ja, Pater*, but what happened?" Aertje asked.

"Earthquake. I've only experienced it once before, in *Patria*, and not nearly as strong. But we're safe. It's all right. It's over," he said, especially to Aeltje, who was still tearful and clinging to his leg.

"I thought it was cannon blasts hitting the island," Sarah whispered to him, hands on her cheeks.

"No, cannonballs would have to be hitting right next to you to feel like that," Teunis tried to reassure her, looking into her eyes, placing his hands over hers, kissing her pouted, trembling lips.

Teunis succeeded in distraction, asking the girls to show him what they had foraged. They calmed down, nibbling more strawberries.

"By the wrath of God, what is His displeasure with us in bringing floods and earthquakes?" Sarah whispered to Teunis.

"He also gives strawberries and mushrooms, and we do not implore Him for their meaning," Teunis tried to comfort her, but she could see that he too was disturbed by the significance of such foreboding cataclysms. "He reminds us we must take nothing for granted and He tests us to build our resiliency."

It reminded her of what her father said after Jean died. It is a test.

That afternoon, Sarah made a savory pie filled with the oyster mushrooms, dried sage, cheese, and milk. She christened it "trepidation *taert*."

By August, Teunis estimated their harvest would be as bountiful as usual. Perhaps even better, since they cleared and planted the additional fields. They stood in the field filled with mounds of the three sisters. They picked the beans that were ready.

"Everything is a little behind schedule, though. We must pray for a late frost this year," Sarah told Teunis.

He was not listening. He gazed over her shoulder. Sarah turned to see what took his attention. A lone horseman rode up to the Waalebocht palisade. Sarah was alarmed immediately once she saw it was Phebe's husband, Jan.

"Is Phebe all right?" Sarah panted after running to him.

"She's begun her birthing travails. All's well with her, though. Phebe's stepmother came to help, but she brought ill tidings from Gravenzande. There are four English warships anchored there and soldiers stationed ashore. They mean to capture New Netherland for England under orders of King Charles II. They say this land belongs to the king's brother, James, the Duke of York."

Chapter 32

1664

"Zounds! I want to defend our capital," Teunis cursed, frustrated by inaction in the days following Jan's warning.

The residents of the Waalebocht stayed inside their palisade. Waiting. Sick with anticipation. They numbered around eighty, but most were women and children. That left about fifteen men suitable to fight, if need be. That included Sarah's two teenage boys, Michael and Jorsey, who were as big as grown men. Sarah counted eight women who knew how to shoot a gun, but they didn't have enough guns or powder for everyone.

"*Mijn liefje*, we will defend our bowery. We will survive, even if New Amsterdam falls." Sarah tried to soothe Teunis while terrified at the prospect of the English ransacking the Waalebocht.

Sarah's mother and youngest brother moved in with Sarah for the time being. Teunis, her brother Daniel, and her sons Michael and Jorsey took turns keeping watch.

"We should be starting to reap the fields," Sarah told Teunis.

"It can wait a few days. Like you said, it's behind schedule this year. If we're waiting longer than a week, we'll post guards on those who venture out to harvest."

"What if they burn our fields? Or steal our harvest?" Sarah was having horrible flashbacks to Kieft's War, the last time their bowery was burned to the ground.

"Let them try! I'll blast them to hell!"

Two days after Phebe's husband alerted them to the imminent invasion, Daniel alerted the village that he heard men on horseback approaching from his post down the road. Everyone, except the children, waited at the closed gate of their palisade. Teunis, Daniel, and Michael had firelock rifles. Sarah had an adze. Catalyna wielded Hans's rapier. Their neighbors stood with them, likewise armed ad hoc—some with rifles, some with shovels.

They could see glimpses of the Englishmen through the gaps in the gate. They were not uniformed soldiers.

"Hark! We bring the English terms for surrender!" a man called out from beyond their gate in English. "Swear allegiance to his Majesty, King Charles II of England, and you will be afforded the liberty and independence granted to all Englishmen at home and established in the colonies. Henceforth, you will pay no tithes to the Dutch West India Company, nor obey Peter Stuyvesant. He is no longer your governor, not even a general, just a private citizen, like yourselves."

A handbill was shoved through the gate. A different man spoke in a deep, threatening tone.

"We offer fair treatment for those who surrender. If you decline, expect to be put to fire and sword, pillage and plunder. If you accept these terms, you will welcome and quarter us in your village."

Teunis did not know English well enough to understand.

"Allow us a moment to confer and consider the terms!" Sarah shouted, grabbing the handbill. She motioned for the Waalebocht residents to gather around her away from the gate.

Sarah read the bill aloud.

"In return for our surrender, we will peaceably enjoy whatsoever God's blessing and our own honest industry have furnished us with and all other privileges of His Majesty's English subjects."

Sarah and Catalyna exchanged a look. Sarah dared to believe they had the same plan.

"I say we fight!" Teunis cried out. "I'll not surrender! Those men aren't soldiers, they're farmers from the English towns of Lange Eylandt. We can beat them!"

"I say we let them in," Catalyna said. She was the elder of their village and most residents were her children, grandchildren, or great-grandchildren. "No bloodshed!"

"Surrender is for Stuyvesant to decide. We can quarter these farmers until we know if we're at war with them," Sarah suggested. "Those in favor of opening the gate, raise your hand!"

Sarah counted and shot Teunis a sympathetic look. They would let them in.

"You may stay in our village, but we await news from Director Stuyvesant for official surrender," Sarah said in English to the twenty men on horseback.

"You can quarter in my home, since I stay with my daughter," Catalyna volunteered. She turned and led them into their village. Sarah was sure she'd seen some of these men selling produce at the market in Breuckelen. She made Teunis draw down his firelock. Everyone else relaxed their stance after Teunis did.

"What are you thinking?" Teunis asked, disgusted, when it was just him and Sarah back at their home. Catalyna and Daniel took the Englishmen to their home, and the children stood gawking in the yard.

"My mother and I have a plan. Trust me. We are going to keep our village safe, but everything will depend on Director Stuyvesant's actions," Sarah said, rushing to the tinctures her mother had brought over days earlier.

Sarah chose their strongest sedative, a decoction of valerian root, chamomile, hops, and vervain. Sarah added in the linden tincture she used to put her children at ease when they were teething.

"These are not soldiers. They're farmers. We will keep them lulled and sedated. If Stuyvesant chooses to fight, they will be easier to subdue. If he chooses to surrender, these Englishmen will have fond memories of their relaxing stay at the Waalebocht," Sarah explained. "Can you retrieve a cask of beer that I can add this to?"

"I've said you were brave and bold in the past. I can only hope this is not more reckless than that," Teunis said. "Read to me again what the handbill says."

"I will, but please, get the cask. And a wheel of cheese."

"I'll get the beer, but none of our cheese!"

That evening the Englishmen enjoyed their beer, bread, and cheese, despite Teunis's protest. Sarah learned they were from Hempstead.

"Is your President John Scott still imprisoned in Connecticut?" Sarah asked one of the Englishmen. He was the youngest of them. Just a boy, really. He was probably around fifteen years of age, like Daniel and Jorsey.

"No, ma'am. He escaped from jail, but then was pardoned and ordered to the Caribbean, last I heard."

"You Dutchies give a good welcome," an older man said, ambling up beside the boy. Perhaps his father.

"Well, we are neighbors, aren't we? Better to be friends than enemies with neighbors," Sarah said with measured deference.

The Englishmen ate and drank themselves into a deep, snoring slumber that night.

The next day, September 5th, a uniformed English soldier arrived to the Waalebocht with a message that Stuyvesant yielded and negotiations of surrender took place.

Later, they received a message from Sarah's sister Maria, who lived near Fort Amsterdam. Maria wrote that Stuyvesant swore he'd only leave Fort Amsterdam if he was dragged out dead, but the Great Burghers, including Sarina's husband, petitioned and refused to bear arms. They'd rather surrender than perish, as they had no fighting chance. Stuyvesant's duty to the people ultimately prevailed. As they'd heard from the Englishmen quartered at the Waalebocht, the terms were favorable.

It surprised Sarah that stalwart Stuyvesant capitulated. She even felt empathy for how difficult that must have been for him. She swallowed that down, reminding herself how he'd ignored Quashawam's prescient warning and Teunis's petition for protection.

"Stuyvesant surrendered. My sister writes that hardly anything will change, except a king will rule over us instead of a company," Sarah informed Teunis.

Now it was Teunis's turn to run to the hedges to retch. He returned to her side, wiping his mouth.

"Sarah, I will never swear an oath to the English. *Mijn kastanje*, I cannot. I'd sooner die."

Sarah gasped at his hyperbolic response.

"Why? How could you say that?"

"When I was a sailor, I heard horrible stories from one man held captive by the English. Amongst the crewmen, we agreed we'd rather die than submit to English seizure."

Instead of arguing, she took his head in her hands. She circled his temples and smoothed his brow with her thumbs. He embraced her and buried his face in her neck. He shuddered and a single tear dripped down the hem of her back.

Three days later, they heard that the transfer of power took place. They lowered the Dutch flag from the fort, and Stuyvesant exited with his head held high. A man named Richard Nicolls was now their governor. He strode into the fort and raised the English flag. The city was officially rechristened New York, and the province, Yorkshire, after the King's brother, James, the Duke of York.

The English militiamen readied to return to their Hempstead farms, quite cheerful. They even paid Catalyna for quartering them.

The Waalebocht villagers breathed a sigh of relief, mixed with disappointment. Teunis went to Breuckelen. He wanted more information on what had transpired.

He returned some hours later.

"If we don't take the oath of allegiance, they'll allow us passage to *Patria*. I'd rather return than bow down to the King of England. Stuyvesant surrendered. I did not."

"I cannot believe you would seriously consider abandoning everything we've built here," Sarah said, taken aback.

"I am considering it…"

"You can swear an oath to King Charles II and you will still be Dutch. Our children will still be Dutch."

"And you?" he asked Sarah, looking at her like maybe he didn't truly know her at all.

She suddenly thought of him leaving clogs as a marriage proposal, something a Dutch woman would've understood. She'd failed that test. She remembered, as a young girl, how her schoolmaster criticized her French lisp and rid her of it. Yet she and her mother still spoke in French when they were alone. She thought of how she'd never been anywhere near Heykoop, Valenciennes, Amsterdam, nor London. And she knew she never would. They were just names of places other people were from.

"To the Natives, all Europeans are *Swanneken*," she said.

"I don't understand," he said brusquely.

"We're all just salt people who arrived in cloud houses."

He looked at her blankly.

"We're all the same to the Natives. We're all Europeans, pale as salt, who came from across the sea in ships that look like longhouses with billowing sails like clouds."

"You didn't arrive in a 'cloud house,'" he argued.

"Exactly. I was raised a French Walloon, became a Dutch New Netherlander, and soon I'll be an English New Yorker, I suppose," she continued slowly, building the layers, as the city itself had been built. "This place is my home. Whatever this place is, that's what I am. I'm not leaving."

CHAPTER 33

1665

Months went by. Sarah thought she made it clear to Teunis that she would not be persuaded to leave, but they argued on it daily. Tensions peaked when Teunis came home from the mill one day in the spring.

"Aert and Rebecca are leaving for the Netherlands. We're going with them."

Sarah did not cease chopping cabbage to argue with him.

"They're going because Aert's father is on his deathbed, not in defiance of becoming English subjects. The English haven't even made you sign the oath yet."

"What if they change their minds and take our land away to give to Englishmen? What if they make us pay them to live here? What if they disinherit women, like they do in the English colonies?"

"I'd react upon the time any of those things happen."

"What if they force us to speak English?"

"We will still speak Dutch at home and in church. It will always be our children's first language."

"*Nee.* I will never take the oath, on principle."

"Teunis, I can't travel."

"*Ja*, you will travel with me and all the children. The voyage is not so bad as you fear."

"I'm with child. Rebecca may have made the voyage that way, but at my age, I will not risk it. Is leaving more important than the safety of your wife and unborn child? Perhaps your son?"

He sighed. She knew how badly he wanted a son of his own. A wry smile spread across his face.

"You cunning, devious woman! I'd curse the timing, but I can't hide my joy at that news." He sighed in defeat. "*Nee*, I would not risk you or the baby."

She pressed his hand to her belly.

"How did I not notice?" he asked.

"You've been too preoccupied with thoughts of leaving to see what's in front of you."

The skies were clear blue on a beautiful June day. The full sun scorched, but a cool breeze was abundant. A wagon pulled up to the Waalebocht. Once Sarah realized it was Phebe, she stepped out from the shade of a peach tree. She flipped the brim of her starched coif forward to shade her eyes from the sun and waved from the orchard. She had been mowing stubborn patches of bramble around the trees with a scythe.

Phebe had her ten-month-old baby, Jacob, and her eight-year-old stepdaughter, Caryntje, with her. They met her out at the orchard.

"Phebe!" Sarah exclaimed and kissed her cheeks. "Miss Caryntje," she said and gave a curtsy to the shy young lady.

Caryntje bashfully smiled and curtsied back. Jacob stirred in Phebe's arms. He rubbed his eyes and chubby little cheeks.

"Sarah, you're mowing in *your* state? You look as if you've swallowed a watermelon whole!"

"Let's go sit over there. I'll lay out a blanket under the big apple tree," Sarah said as her girls rushed over, eager to see who was here. When they saw Caryntje, they excitedly grabbed her hand and took her off on a tour. They'd met her at church, but she hadn't been to their house yet. Caryntje was pleased to have some other little girls to romp with, but she gave Phebe a look to check if it was all right. Phebe nodded to her encouragingly.

"My goodness, Sarah. Look at you! Are you sure if you sit down, you'll be able to get back up?" Phebe asked skeptically. "Didn't you say you thought the baby would be born in August? You already look fit to birth, poor thing."

"*Bof*, I'm fine," Sarah said dismissively. Turning to Phebe, she clutched her forearm a moment, looking her in the eyes, and in a low voice said, "Double fine. I'm carrying twins."

They sat down on a blanket in the shade. The big apple tree had an expansive view of their house, garden, the horse pasture, stream, the other houses, and kitchen gardens in the Waalebocht village.

"Twins?" Phebe looked at Sarah with wide eyes, feigning surprise at what was obvious. She set Jacob down, and he quickly got on all fours to crawl around and explore.

"It feels the same as when I had Jacob and Catalyntje before. It feels like they're sharing a bed with a blanket that's too small. A movement on one side always gets a reaction on the other side," Sarah said as she sat cross-legged, holding her belly for support as she placed it like an egg in the nest of her legs. It was a pose that accentuated her belly, the folds of fabric from her loose, light-green linen skirt wrapped around and under her belly.

"I trust you to know. What is this... your fourteenth?" Phebe asked.

"If it's twins, it will be fifteen—counting Jacob, Catalyntje, and Neeltje—rest their souls," she said. "Every child is a blessing, of course, but I grow weary at the mere thought of twins. Hopefully, one is a boy. That may relax Teunis's fervor for more babies."

"By God, woman, you have the blessing, and curse, of fertility." She laughed at the jibe she would've considered blasphemy in her younger years. "It gets easier, in some ways. Jacob was my ninth and easiest yet. Most difficult was not knowing what in heavens was going on with the English conquest."

Jacob found a green apple that had fallen, and he rolled the orb between his chubby hands. He tried to bite it, and its bitter taste made him shudder and shake his head.

"I can't imagine how you must have felt, a new babe and the threat of hostile takeover," Sarah said, shaking her head. "How do you feel about it now? Living in an English colony again?"

"It's a much different English colony than the one I grew up in. In Boston, they were so harsh with their Puritan ideals and hostile in their condemnations. I'm utterly shocked by Governor Nicolls. I didn't know there were Englishmen who were not Puritanical tyrants," Phebe said in wonder.

"Stuyvesant left for *Patria*, likely to be rebuked before the Company board. I wonder if the Company preferred us destroyed, given their lack of support to defend ourselves," Sarah pondered. "*Maman* has visited often with Stuyvesant's wife, Judith. I think since *Maman* has seen so many changes in leadership here, she has great empathy and perspective to give her."

"I suppose our former Director intends to return since he did not take his wife with him?" Phebe asked.

"*Ja*, from what Judith says, he genuinely has a love for the city."

"Does Teunis still speak of returning to *Patria*?"

"Not since I told him I'm pregnant. Since the English haven't come to make us swear our oath of allegiance yet, I pray he's forgotten the idea. He's still performing his *schepen* duties, and he's building an addition to the house. It doesn't appear he's making plans to move, but I'm afraid that if the administrators came today to take his oath, he'd just as soon be on the next ship out. Rebecca and Aert left, chiefly because Aert received word that his father is on his deathbed. I think they'll return, eventually," Sarah said, but then changed the subject. "I'm famished. Let's find the girls and put together a midday meal. Help me up, please."

As Sarah's belly grew, her nonchalance at the thought of twins became less cavalier, and more worry crept into her mind. She thought of little Catalyntje, Jacob's twin, and how desperately she tried to get the girl to take her milk and willed her to live. As her belly grew heavier, she began to worry whether *she* would live through it.

Teunis forced her to rest and doted on her, but she resented being told what to do when she was increasingly irritable. She unconsciously put on a show of industriousness when he was around, not wanting him to see any lack of vigor as she thought that would cause him more worry. The rest of the summer they went back and forth that way, bickering over how much she should be resting. He said she should have been fine to take the ocean voyage with her stubborn vitality. That subdued her, somewhat. Her mother kept her supplied with her herbal tinctures, which she promised would make her womb strong enough for two.

One day, in mid-August, Sarah was grinding dried corn into fine flour with their household quern and felt pains. They progressed in a way unlike the usual pains of rotating the heavy quern stone.

"Maria, please continue for me," Sarah asked her fourteen-year-old daughter, gesturing to the quern. "Aertje, can you please boil some water?" she asked her nine-year-old.

Sarah went down on her knees on the braided rag rug in the center of their great room. Maria and Aertje gave each other a knowing look. On all fours, Sarah swayed her hips from side to side and stretched her back to relieve the wave of pressure. Three-year-old Aeltje thought her mother was being playful and got down on all fours too, pretending to be farm animals. Aeltje mooed and snorted, making Sarah laugh, until she too mooed with the next wave of pressure.

"*Moeder*, you peed," Aeltje said after Sarah's waters leaked through her skirts.

"Catalyntje, go fetch *Grand-Mère*," Sarah instructed her seven-year-old.

CHAPTER 34

1665

Catalyna was there in no time. Sarah's favorite thing about her mother attending her births was that she hardly spoke. She observed and reacted accordingly. Her mother saw Sarah's beaded brow and wiped her forehead with a cold, wet linen. She pressed on her hips during the height of the pressure waves and draped a hot, damp linen over Sarah's lower back to ease the cramping.

Sarah also loved that it was a brief time when she was treated like a child needing comfort, instead of her role as the mother, always providing it.

Sarah stayed on all fours on the braided rug for a long time before she reached for her mother's help to get up. Catalyna helped take off her wet dress. Her mother had placed extra linens down in their bed, which is where Sarah ended up going. She lifted one knee up onto the bed and stopped, as another wave came on.

Sarah felt quite good in that one-legged standing position, her head, belly, and other leg resting on the bed. The next wave came quickly and was more intense.

"A head," Catalyna told her, waiting to catch, by her side. "Should we call for Teunis?"

"Nooo," Sarah forced out. She didn't want him there if anything went wrong. She would spare him from witnessing it.

The first baby came at the end of the next wave. A big baby girl. Catalyna passed her to Maria. She gingerly wiped her new sister's face with a warm cloth while the other sisters looked on, cooing their welcome to their new baby sister.

It was a moment of relief and then a shift in pressure. Sarah was in more pain now. She angled her body to find a better position. She ended up holding the corner of the bed frame in a squat for the next several waves that quickly proceeded. The fifth wave gave the second twin. Another healthy baby girl.

They didn't have to call for Teunis. Shortly after Sarah birthed the *arrière-faix* and was helped into bed with her two babies to nurse, Teunis arrived unaware, looking for his midday meal.

Finding his wife and two new babies in bed, Teunis whispered, "Praise be," and Catalyna led the girls to her house to prepare some food and give Sarah and Teunis some time alone.

"Sarah..." Teunis said, eyes welling with tears, as he kissed each of his new babies and her. "How did you do such incredible work, all before midday?" He laughed through his tears. He stroked Sarah's hair back and watched the babies, both latched to a different breast. Sarah expertly held them like two stacks of firewood under her arms. After a minute, she shifted and nodded to him.

"She was born first. Have a look at her and tell me if she looks like a Neeltje," Sarah said. According to tradition, one would be named after their sister who passed away. Sarah repositioned the second baby and looked at her more fully.

Teunis gently rocked the first twin for a long time. She groggily cracked one eye open to look at him and promptly closed it again. She was the larger twin, born with slightly more wispy flaxen hair.

"This is Annetje," he finally said.

"Then here is Neeltje," Sarah said definitively, looking at the baby already asleep in her arms, still suckling in her sleep even though the pap was now absent.

Sarah sank down from sitting upright. She motioned for Teunis to join her in bed. Lying on their sides with the girls in the middle, Sarah and Teunis formed a wall between their babies and the outer world. Sarah fell asleep immediately. Teunis could not bring himself to close his eyes. He watched over his twins and his wife with awe.

The following Sunday, they traveled to the chapel on Stuyvesant's bowery, just north of the wall, for the baptism of their girls. Stuyvesant was still in *Patria*, but his wife Judith hosted. Judith and Tryntje Roelofs, Saartje's little sister, would be sponsors for the girls' baptism.

During his sermon, Domine Megapolensis took the chance to expound on their unfaltering Dutch values, despite the English takeover. There was a second Anglo–Dutch War in Europe, and his sermon was a thinly veiled exaltation of Dutch prowess. He spoke on, venerating Sarah as a model Dutch wife and mother.

"Sarah, firstborn of our beloved New Netherland, gave birth at forty years of age to healthy twins, while already having produced eleven living children... She is an aspiration of the fertility and proliferation of the church," Domine Megapolensis boomed. Sarah's cheeks burned, hearing herself as part of the sermon, and bowed her head.

The Domine explained the meaning of baptism as passing over from the darkness to the light, just as the Israelites had in Exodus. He called Sarah, Teunis, their babies, and their sponsors to the altar. Her brother Jeronimus and brother-in-law Pieter van Nest stood with Judith Bayard and Tryntje Roelofs as sponsors. The girls were sprinkled with water. Then the congregation made two rows down the aisle and raised their hands together to make a tunnel through which the baptismal party passed under. The Domine then dismissed them with a command to serve the Lord in the outside world.

Judith Bayard held a reception afterwards at the impressive brick home of the Stuyvesant bowery. Annetje and Neeltje's baptism turned into a grand celebration. The great lawn and orchard were filled with the Dutch residents of the city.

Judith pulled Sarah aside.

"I was a bit surprised the Domine revealed your age during the sermon. I gave birth to my sons at an advanced age, after my own mother claimed I'd be a lifelong spinster. Perhaps it goes without saying, but I would have added to the sermon that, beyond producing many children, you've raised them well."

Sarah smiled at her kind words. She was aware the baptism was used as a bit of a foil for Dutch patriotism and an excuse to gather and celebrate after their former Director's capitulation. Since her husband left for the Netherlands, Judith had taken every opportunity to strengthen the morale of the Dutch community. Some had taken up the offer to return to *Patria*. It was disheartening to see them go.

Sarah hoped the celebrations and praise from the Domine buoyed Teunis's spirits enough to convince him to stay. Sarah felt honored. She was still sore from birth, wearing a woolen clout to catch blood, and exhausted by the needs of her two newborns, but seeing people invigorated her.

When Sarah saw Sarina and Isaac among the well-wishers, her face lit up. Sarina came to sit on the bench next to her, where Sarah cradled Annetje, and wrapped her arms around them.

"Oh, my dear Sarina," Sarah whispered, "I've missed you."

"It's so good to see you, Sarah. Congratulations!" Sarina exclaimed and pulled back to look at little Annetje, who was asleep. Teunis held Neeltje, who was barely awake. Sarina peeked at Neeltje and smiled. "I can't tell with the one sleeping, but I think this girl has your eyes, Sarah."

Sarina had her two-year-old, David, and eight-year-old, Hendrick, with her. Isaac joined them and gravitated to Teunis.

"Hallo, boys, aren't you handsome and well behaved," Sarah said to David and Hendrick. "How is the rest of the family, Sarina?"

"We've been well. Susannah just married Pieter de Riemer." Sarina spoke with pride of her eldest daughter's marriage.

"Congratulations!" Sarah said.

"Our son, Jan, is a bit of a handful, but he's improving. He's decided he wants to be a surgeon." Sarina continued, nodding toward the edge of the crowd on the lawn, "And it looks like he's taken a liking to Susannah Varlet."

Sarah saw Jan flirting with Judith Bayard's niece. The girl laughed at what Jan whispered to her, cheeks flushed.

"She's a nice Huguenot girl," Sarah said.

"Yes, much better than some other company he's kept in the past," Sarina said. "Is Phebe here?"

"No, unfortunately. She hasn't been feeling well."

Sarah was very worried about her. She'd been ill for some weeks and had lost a lot of weight. She hoped Sarina could sense she didn't want to discuss it further.

"Teunis, congratulations to you as well!" Sarina said when he had a break in his conversation with Isaac.

"Thank you, though I can hardly take any credit," he said, beaming at Sarah. "I'm a very lucky man."

"With three girls already, I bet you were hoping for a son?" Sarina asked, curious.

"I'll take what the Lord deigns to give," he said, smiling genially. "And He was quite generous this time."

"Quite," Sarah emphasized.

At the beginning of December, Sarah convinced Teunis that, despite the bad weather, she had to go see Phebe. The last news she'd heard was two weeks ago, that a surgeon tried bloodletting, with no success. She had a terrible feeling time was of the essence to see her friend. Her nineteen-year-old son, Michael, agreed to take her in the wagon, pulled by Thundercloud. Maria and the twins joined them.

It was an awful day for travel. A fine snow fell, making it difficult to see. The road was rough between the Waalebocht and Midwout. The mud of November had frozen into a mess of hard ruts that were like bumping over endless tree roots, sending their wagon jerking and reeling. Sarah thought she might have to stop to purge her stomach, both from worry and the jostling, but thankfully she held herself together. One good thing was the twins slept through the entire ride, held by Sarah and Maria.

When they arrived, Phebe's husband, Jan, welcomed them in. He looked tired, his eyes puffy and forlorn.

"How is she?" Sarah whispered.

"No better, sadly," Jan said.

"Can I see her?" Sarah pleaded.

"*Ja*, I hope it will do her well to see you. She often says your name in her sleep. I'm grateful you're here."

Sarah opened the doors of the *bedstee*. Phebe lay under many layers of woolen blankets and furs, covered up to her chin. Her face was beyond pale and gaunt. In the shadowed caverns of her eye sockets, it was difficult to discern that her eyes were closed. Sarah lay down next to her in the bed, embracing her. After a moment, she stirred, opening her eyes to Sarah.

Phebe opened her mouth to speak, but nothing came out except a rattle of breath.

"My dear Phebe, I'm here," Sarah said. She rose and dipped a cloth in the basin of water next to the bed. She dripped some water into Phebe's mouth.

Phebe closed her eyes again for a long moment. She then opened them and croaked out, "Sarah."

"I'm here," Sarah replied and lay down next to her again. After several minutes, with much effort, Phebe turned towards her.

"Sarah..." She still struggled to speak, but there was more clarity and determination. "Look after my children."

"Of course, Phebe. Don't worry about that," Sarah said, wanting so badly to sob at the thought.

She braced herself and redirected the conversation.

"Let's think of pleasant times now. We had many," Sarah said, trying to ease her friend's worry. "I wish we could be lying in a field of strawberries on a clear, summer day like we used to as girls... Or swimming in the creek, floating without a care in the world..."

Phebe's eyes squeezed shut. Papery folds radiated from the corners of her eyelids, but the corners of her mouth upturned in a small smile.

"When you first showed up with your father at our tavern, you were so clench-jawed and sullen. You would scarcely meet my eyes when we spoke, but I just knew we would be best friends. And then you utterly transformed over only a few years. You looked so beautiful on your wedding day to Nys. You radiated like a glowing ember... Motherhood only kept that ember burning, reignited by each of your children... I don't know what I would have done without you after Hans died... Thank you for insisting I meet Teunis. Where would I be without you? Being with you always renewed my spirit, especially when I was at my wits' end, many times. I can't thank you enough for that."

She turned to Sarah, heaving with sobs.

"I love you," Phebe labored to say.

"I love you, too. Shhh, shhh." Sarah held her through the piles of blankets. "Don't worry, Phebe. You must be among the blessed, otherwise why would the Lord have made you such a blessing to your husbands, your children, and me?"

They lay there together in silence for a long while. When she knew Phebe was asleep, she got up quietly. The twins were probably hungry, and they should start their journey back home. Her heart felt leaden at the thought of leaving her friend. What more could she do or say? It was cruel. Phebe was forty-one years old. She knew her friend would leave her soon—too soon—and she would miss her so much. She tried to focus on the blessing it was to have known her at all. An English girl and a French Walloon in a Dutch colony: improbable but happiest of odd couples.

A few days later, Monsieur de Beauvois, dressed as *aanspreeker*, came to Sarah's door in his black attire and crepe ribbons blowing in the snowy wind. She let him in to carry the news, even though she already knew.

Phebe had died.

"You may stay here as long as you like," Sarah told the five youngest of Phebe and Nys's children. They came to stay with her after Phebe's burial. She took them in to give Jan time to grieve and form his own plans. He kept their two-year-old Jacob and his daughter Caryntje with him.

Elsje was seventeen and had found a position as a housemaid for Sarah's former neighbors in the city. She would leave soon. Femmetje was fifteen and had asked Sarah if she could continue to live there. That left Denys, Jan, and Cornelis, who were twelve, eleven, and eight years old. Teunis urged the boys to stay. He could use more help on the farm, and he'd had such brotherhood with Nys that he felt paternally obliged to them. One day, over breakfast, the boys announced they'd like to stay, if it was all right with their stepfather.

Sarah went to visit Jan and broached the subject. He was thirty-seven, twice widowed, and wanted to remarry. In fact, he already had plans to marry Willempje Thyssen. He did not take umbrage with the Nyssen children's choice.

"You're the closest thing they have to a mother now. It's what Phebe would have wanted," Jan said.

Having the additional mouths to feed was a small price to pay for the solace they gave Sarah in fulfilling her promise to her dear friend. She couldn't mourn like she might have, by lying in bed, crying. In comforting and mothering Phebe and Nys's children, she couldn't allow herself to sink into the mire of grief.

The liveliness of the household gave little room to be contemplative and gloomy. Her eight children and Phebe's four had grown up together and were used to the dynamic. It felt exciting for the children, like a sleep-away night that never ended.

They were all thankful for the addition Teunis built. Even expanded, the house felt full to the brim.

Chapter 35

1667

Sarah followed Teunis as he wound his way through the forest at the back of their property. He had told her to follow him on a walk, but not what the destination was. She brought a basket, hoping they'd find some morels, but all she seemed to spot were pinecones disguised as the ephemeral spring mushrooms.

They spoke little and walked softly enough that they came upon a doe and fawn in a clearing. They stood back as the deer lazily nibbled the forest floor. The fawn doddered along after its mother's lead. Teunis had his rifle, but spring wasn't the season, especially for a doe with such young offspring. Fall was best for deer hunting. Sarah remembered how the Natives used to set fires to burn parts of the forest in the fall to clear the underbrush and make hunting easier. Their tactic was less common now as land was sold for farms, and burnings were seen as a hazard and aggression to the settlements.

The deer caught their scent and bounded off, their white tails raised like flags merrily waving adieu. Sarah and Teunis went to the clearing to discover what they had been nibbling. They found beheaded nettles but also untouched fiddlehead ferns. Sarah gave a soft whoop as she found a few morels. She nestled them into her basket, along with some young nettles the deer hadn't gotten. Teunis helped her gather the fiddleheads with his small hip knife. They still didn't speak as he motioned for them to continue onward.

Their silent sojourn reminded her of when she went hunting with her father as a child. The sacred silence. She enjoyed getting away from their settled village, cultivated fields, and gardens and into the natural world that was here before they were. *It was still here.*

They ascended the hillside, zigzagging up a deer path that also served to sluice runoff when the snow melted. It was dry now and easy to hike up. It was a steady incline though, and Sarah's cheeks flushed.

Teunis looked back at her, checking if she was all right. She answered by dodging past him and racing to the next serpentine cutback. She panted, smiling, as he caught up. He looked amused but resumed leading the way without stopping.

Finally, they came to a big rocky outcrop. He led her to the edge, facing the river, their land, and the trail they'd come up. It was a sight Sarah had never seen. The Waalebocht was visible, the Mespaetches Kil swampland running down beside them to the East River, and Manhattan behind it. Sarah realized she'd seen this rocky crest from afar, but she'd never thought to scale it. The budding green on the trees would soon obscure this view in the summer.

"See this?" Teunis stood behind her, tracing a line with his finger around parts of the Waalebocht, Bedford, Boswijck, and Breuckelen. "That's officially ours, signed by Governor Nicolls. You're married to one of seven Lange Eylandt *patroons.*"

Sarah thought about what that meant. The patent had been in Hans's name and transferred to her after his death. They'd had the patent for twenty years. That was nothing new. Unwelcome questions darted through her mind. Now under English rule, it was officially recognized as theirs, and Teunis was given the honorific title of *patroon.* The English didn't allow women to own property. So, it wasn't *theirs*, it was Teunis's. By English inheritance laws, it would go to the eldest son. She and Teunis had all daughters. Would the land inheritance go to the eldest of Hans's sons?

She looked out on the landscape and breathed deep. *Stop thinking and just look.* She decided now wasn't the time to squabble over English law. This was a remarkable sight that Teunis had been so thoughtful to show her. It felt powerful to view their vast acreage from above. She suddenly realized the other implication in his statement.

"You signed the oath of allegiance?"

"*Ja.*"

"So, you don't want to return to *Patria*?" she asked.

"I realized my home is wherever you are. I thought of you when I signed the oath, not the King of England."

She looked back at Teunis. He had taken his hat off, and his wavy brown hair, with some stray gray strands, ruffled in the breeze. She smoothed it back and kissed him. She turned again to the expanse, with his arms wrapping around her.

He pulled her closer and spun her around again to kiss her deeply. His hand caressed up to her breast and she gasped in pleasure as she kissed him back. Moments for intimacy were scarce with such a full household. He guided her to a seat-height stone, sat down, and pulled her onto his lap as they kissed. He unbuttoned his breeches, and she pulled up her skirts. She kissed his neck, her hips pressing against him, as she looked out at the overwhelming vista. She never had so many pleasures combined.

They descended the trail with naughty grins few husbands and wives can have after so many years and already having so many children. But they returned with the spoils of morels, fiddleheads, and foraged greens, so no one suspected their cheer was for more than that.

Some time later, Sarah realized she was pregnant again. She reveled in the thought that it was the moment she and Teunis experienced together on the cliffs that would give them another child. She told Teunis the news as they sat on their stoop one night.

"What wonderful news, *mijn kastanje*," he whispered into her ear as he held her close.

"What's wrong?"

She sensed a melancholy behind his eyes.

"My news is not as happy as yours. This morning in town, I heard the English and Dutch have signed a treaty. The United Provinces officially conceded our colony to the English in exchange for Suriname in South America, Fort Cormantin in Ghana, and Run in Indonesia. They traded us for sugar plantations, a way station for enslaved Africans, and a monopoly of nutmeg." He sighed. "I know it's ungracious, but... I just realized this will be our first child born in an officially English colony. I'm at peace with staying here, but it still sickens my heart."

The concerns at the back of her mind about inheritance and English law finally had an opportunity to be shared.

"I have a sickening feeling, too. The English said they would allow us to keep our land and customs. Yet they do not. The patent they confirmed in your name had been in my name, as Hans's widow. The fact they don't allow women to own property makes me worry about our children's inheritance. According to the Duke's Laws, the eldest son receives two-thirds of the estate and money. I worry for our daughters," Sarah told him. "If your death precedes mine, I will be forced out of our home after forty days and given only a third of our estate. The Duke's Laws are a dreadful change for women."

"I was too preoccupied by them confirming our ownership. I did accept your land as my own, but I will also give freely of it, come the time any of our children want their own plot. I don't know how long they will allow Dutch wills to abide, but you should inherit all that is ours, if I were to pass before you. After we both pass, it should be split among all our children equally. I don't see how they can ignore our wishes, clearly made jointly in our will. Perhaps, if our daughters are married, it will be in their husband's name, but it will still be theirs to enjoy, and pass down to their children."

"I trust you, Teunis. I just don't know if I trust the English," Sarah told him warily. "I feel silly questioning the English now, when I was so quick to surrender... and now that you've signed your oath."

"I understand why you worry," Teunis told her, "but they have been true to their word so far in letting us Netherlanders keep our lands, laws, religion, and trade. But... we can always move to Heykoop..."

He gave her a sly smile. She couldn't help but smile and elbow him for the jest.

"*Nee*, I still would never leave. I just want to protect everything we've worked so hard for. I want our children's lives to be easier because of it."

"*Ja*, I know. I worry for our children, too."

"Also, there's the land I bought in New Amsterdam, on Princes Graft, after my father died. It's in my name."

"I'll see to it that you retain the patent. We'll insist it remains in your name. Perhaps having that done will assuage your fears," Teunis offered. She was glad he would help, but it irritated Sarah that Teunis would have to speak for her, as if she was a child.

CHAPTER 36

1667

Two weeks later, their appointed court date arrived.

"Remember, I must appear as your guardian and representative. Perhaps they will be humored enough by your demure manner in court that they will confirm the patent in your name," Teunis said, running his fingertips over her starched, bleached coif as they prepared to leave for court that morning. He chastely kissed her forehead. She bristled but practiced staying silent.

He scuffed his boot on the way out the door and stopped to buff it. He had spent much of the previous evening polishing them.

The three English court officials were the epitome of refined men of wealth and political stature. Their long, curled periwigs, capped with impressive castor hats, were each embellished with an ostrich feather.

Sarah stood a pace behind Teunis, and after her initial assessment of the officials, she fixed her gaze at the foot of the ornate turned-leg table they sat behind.

"Your Honors, I bring before you a request to confirm the land patent granted to Sarah, widow of Hans Hansen."

He brought forth the original patent document, signed by Domine Megapolensis. The secretary, a young Englishman whom Sarah had seen living in New Amsterdam before its seizure, translated for Teunis and read the document aloud. The officials conferred.

"Under the Duke's Laws, this widow's land shall be affirmed as the property of her eldest son," one official said to his colleagues.

"Your Honors," Tunis interjected. "The Articles of Capitulation state: 'All people shall continue as free denizens and enjoy their lands, houses, goods, ships, wherever they are within this country, and dispose of them as they please.' Also, that 'The Dutch here shall enjoy their own customs concerning their inheritances.'"

Sarah was a bit staggered by Teunis's knowledge of the Articles. She looked up and glimpsed the paper he read from. Had he consulted a lawyer? The officials shifted in their seats.

"So it does. I was giving you the courtesy reminder of the laws set forth by his Majesty's brother. The patent shall be affirmed as written, translated into English." The official struck his gavel. "For now," Sarah thought she heard him say under his breath.

As soon as they were out of the courtroom, Sarah squeezed Teunis's arm, silently. Once in the street, she couldn't contain herself.

"Well done, *mijn liefje!*"

"I'm sorry I presented you as a widow and not my wife. I suspected they would have affirmed the patent in my name if I had."

"How did you know to invoke the Articles of Capitulation? I hadn't thought of that."

"I spoke with some of my fellow Breuckelen officials. They connected me with Stuyvesant's lawyer who drew up the document. His secretary wrote me a copy of the articles that would help." He paused, eyes drawn down the street. "I'm sorry, *mijn kastanje*. Will you wait here a moment? I see someone I should speak with about their order of clapboards."

"*Ja*, of course."

Sarah, still a bit stunned and completely elated, looked around the street. She was drawn to a glazier's shop window. It was beautiful. So clear and large, without the waving distortions most windows had. She found herself distracted by its perfect reflection. She saw the familiar city life bustling behind her. The city continued as it always had, at first glance. The *huisvrouw* scrubbing the entrance to her home. The fishwife, calling out in her brash voice, as if the smell of her basket didn't announce her. But then, a pair of English soldiers appeared. Sarah eavesdropped. One complained about a "bread and cheese man" he had to deal with the night before. His tone dripped with contempt. Sarah surmised he meant "bread and cheese man" as an insult for a Netherlander, but it made her laugh.

She saw a familiar face. One that had once both inspired and intimidated her. Margaret Hardenbroeck, the she-merchant. She turned and greeted her.

"Hallo, my lacemaker," Margaret said. Their interactions were usually transactional, so it surprised Sarah when Margaret looped her arm through hers and asked, "Will you walk with me?"

"Of course. How are your children? And your business?" Sarah asked. She heard Margaret and her husband were now the wealthiest merchants in the city.

"Both have their joys and annoyances. How are yours?"

"I'm pregnant, and I just had a land patent confirmed in my own name," Sarah blurted out before she thought better of her immodesty. She continued to speak to distract from what she had just said. "Have things changed much for your business since the English took over?"

"Congratulations on your good news. I'm glad to hear it. As for the English... Governor Nichols recently told me that New York is his favorite city in the colonies, then informed me I will have a quota of three shipments per year. Only three! The Englishmen praise my husband, attributing all our wealth and success to him, even though I often manage as supercargo on trade voyages... And all *I* brought to our marriage... I bite my tongue for now. I bite it so often my lips must be red."

"It's foolish to restrict your shipments if they want the city to grow and prosper."

"These Englishmen look to the former New Netherland to grow their wealth just as the Company did. That has not changed. I think they would have imposed more changes on us already if they didn't find us profitable. Take comfort you live outside the city. They will make us English eventually, but it will come more slowly for those of you across the East River. I think I'll mainly reside in my lands north of Manhattan. Less Englishmen there."

During the first days that truly felt like summer, Sarah's son Michael came to her as she was alone in the kitchen garden, picking caterpillars off their cabbages and mercilessly crushing beetles between her fingers. She plunked the caterpillars into a tin pail to be used as fish bait.

"*Maman*," Michael said with his hat in his hands, looking bashful. Sarah looked up at her tall son. Was he blushing, or was it the sun on his cheeks from working in the fields? "I want to marry Femmetje. I love her."

Sarah was touched by the way he plainly spoke about it. The name Femmetje was the Dutch version of Phebe. She was, in many ways, a Dutch version of her mother. She had the same almond-shaped face and perceptive brown eyes, but she'd inherited Nys's voluminous curls, as many of the Nyssen children had.

"Does Femmetje share your feelings?" Sarah asked. She knew Femmetje did, but she wanted to see if he'd open up more.

"*Ja*," he blurted. After a moment, he stammered, "At least, I think so. I wanted your permission to ask her, since she doesn't have her parents and you knew them best."

"*Ja*, you should ask her. I'll speak to your *Pater*. I'm sure he will be happy to give you some land and help you build a house," Sarah said, smiling, excited by the idea.

"I have my twenty morgens of land that Stuyvesant allotted to *Pater*, Aert, Jan, and myself. I plan to make our home there and expand as we are able," Michael said firmly. He'd clearly thought this through.

"Nys and Phebe would approve," she told him and then whispered, "I think Femmetje will too."

Sarah was gladdened that Michael wanted to stay near home. His older brother, Captain Jan, was still committed to sailing and not ready to settle down.

Femmetje joyfully accepted Michael's proposal. His stepfather and brothers helped build their house. Following the harvest, they were wed. It had been a very good harvest year, and it bode well for the young couple.

Sarah's belly grew quite large by the time the harvest was done. It was not as large as with the twins, so she felt more at ease with it. She didn't try to prove her vigor so much, but she stayed busy with tasks of preserving, pickling, and storing the harvest. Savoring the later stage of pregnancy, feeling the baby moving, she wondered if it might be the last baby she'd carry. She thought something was different this time. Her belly shape was lower, but that may have resulted from the twins stretching her womb. She was also craving cheese and crunchy pickled vegetables, while with all her girls, she craved jam, *koekjes*, and sweets.

On Saint Nicholas Day the children all received treats from Sinterklaas. They now used stockings hung from the hearth, since the number of clogs was too much of an obstacle to using the fireplace. Sarah was preparing a feast for dinner that evening.

She was skinning and eviscerating six pheasants that Teunis, her sons, and the Nyssen boys hunted down the previous day. She suddenly felt lightheaded. Sarah was practiced at butchering animals and had never been squeamish at the task. She sat down and then felt her stomach lurch, so she ran outside.

Maria ran after her. Sarah was on all fours, retching into the snow.

Her daughter wiped her mother's forehead and mouth with a washrag. Sarah's hands, bloodied from butchering, left two red prints in the snow. Maria helped wipe her hands clean and got her mother back indoors. Sarah went to their bed to lie down. She asked Maria to fetch Catalyna.

By the time her mother arrived, Sarah was bleeding and her birthing waves had begun. She was surrounded by her daughters that, although young, knew the procedure. They'd placed extra linens and a fresh basin of boiled water by the bed. Catalyna looked alarmed at the blood. Sarah knew so much bleeding so early in her travails wasn't normal for her. Her mother pressed Sarah's stomach, feeling for where the baby's limbs and head were. She then pressed her ear to Sarah's belly to check the heartbeat.

"Maria, tell your father to fetch a midwife," Catalyna whispered to her granddaughter.

She let Sarah go through two more waves before she checked between her legs. Her mother's face paled.

"What is it? What's wrong?" Sarah gasped through the pain.

"Sarah, it will be all right. Stay calm, but... I think the baby is mispositioned. I think upside down."

Sarah was in a great deal of pain. Catalyna gave her the red trillium tincture she'd brought.

An hour later, Susanna Negrin appeared at the door.

"Thank heavens, Susanna! Please help..."

Susanna felt Sarah's stomach.

"Sarah, it's all right. I've delivered perfectly healthy breech babies. You will need patience. It is not so different from any other birth. Let's move you to your hands and knees." Susanna's voice was even and patient. Sarah felt a modicum of relief.

A hand took hers and it was only then she realized Teunis was there. She held his hand and wouldn't let go.

It took many more waves that felt like an eternity. The baby's buttocks presented first. One more wave of pushing and the shoulders were free.

"It's a boy!" Sarah's mother cried out. Teunis let out a sob and gripped Sarah's hand.

"Very good, Sarah. Next wave of contractions, I need you to give a great push. God willing, it will be the last," Susanna said.

Sarah could see the baby as she looked between her legs. Susanna wrapped linen around the child and instructed Sarah's mother to support the lower part as she prepared to free the head.

The time for the final push came. Sarah strained so hard she felt she'd turn herself inside out. White hot pain and then release. The baby was free with a sickening pop, like a knuckle cracking.

He didn't cry.

Sarah's mother scooped up the silent baby. Sarah watched, upside down, as another wave took her. Her mother wiped the baby's face and rubbed his breastbone with her knuckles. She sucked bloody mucus from his nose with her mouth and spat it on the floor. Upon that action the baby heaved a great breath and thrilling cry. Sarah's daughters, who stood silent with bated breath, also let loose a loud cheer. Her mother's face, exultant, smeared with blood, fixated on the wailing baby.

"Sarah, Teunis, you have a son," her mother said. "And a very large one at that!"

"Gysbert," Sarah whispered. They'd planned to follow Dutch naming conventions and call him by Teunis's father's name. She looked at Teunis. His eyes welled with tears and relief.

"My son," Teunis murmured.

"Gysbert, you are already proving to be a naughty boy, coming into the world rump first," her mother chided with a smile as she handed him to Sarah.

Gysbert latched to Sarah's pap with a liveliness that calmed Sarah's worries immediately. They were all silent as Susanna prepared to cut the cord. She waited until it turned white, tied it off, cut it, and cleaned up. She prepared to leave.

"Susanna, thank you. If the baby had been a girl, the name would've been Susanna," Sarah said.

"You hardly needed help."

"On the contrary. I needed *all* the help this time. I needed my mother, my midwife, and my husband."

"*Ja*, thank you, Susanna. And Catalyna..." Teunis's voice broke. "Sarah, I didn't think I could revere you more, but this demands it. I have a son!"

They settled in for the winter, everyone's spirits raised by the new baby. Sarah was the center of the world for the twelve of them living with her. She allowed herself to bask in their love and attention, enjoying the chaotic, full house she had. She realized they would all be grown one day, and the house would be quiet.

This was the best time of life, she thought. Even though exhausted and pushed to her limits, there was always someone there to help carry the load of running the household. She could run out of stamina, but she'd never run out of love.

CHAPTER 37

1671

Nearly four years later, her thoughts muddled by upsetting news, Sarah sprinted toward the river. Teunis hollered her name and chased after her. She'd had a head start and fury propelled her.

Sarah reached the water and saw their canoe half aground at the water's edge. Without pause, she scooped her skirts into the hull, heaved the vessel off the shore, and jumped in with one fluid motion. She was a good distance into the river before she looked back and saw Teunis at the shoreline, holding the paddle.

Sarah scanned the hull, realizing she had nothing with which to propel herself. The only other thing in the *wey schuyt* was a fishnet.

She took a deep breath. *This is foolish, but anything to avoid the conversation with Teunis.*

The canoe drifted out farther, continuing with momentum from her pushing off. The sun was high, the September breeze crisp and refreshing. Far ahead of her was Manhattan. Autumn just started to turn the trees into a myriad of rich, warm tones. The distorted undulations of the sun dancing on the water were hypnotic. She should be figuring out what to say to Teunis, but her thoughts flitted and slipped like a gleam upon the waves.

She was so angry, not with Teunis, but his unwelcome news of a mysterious debt that should have been buried in her past. It was pulling her back in time and making her act like a child.

First problem to solve was the current predicament she put herself in. She could not just drift forever. She needed to get back and discuss it with Teunis.

I will need to swim back. Swimming has always calmed me. The cool water will douse my anger.

Undressed to her linen chemise and stays, she tied her woolen partlet around her middle to keep herself warm in the cold water. She thought it might help her float until it became sodden. She tied the fishnet around the woven bow seat, grabbed the other end, deeply inhaled, and slipped into the river.

The water was shockingly cold at first, as she expected. She wound the fishnet around her hand and floated on her back, pulling the canoe along with her. The surface water was warmer. As she got used to it, it was even pleasant.

She floated and kicked her feet in small, quick motions while she looked at the sky. Pulling the canoe slowed her down, but she wouldn't abandon it. She checked to make sure she was going in the right direction. Teunis was undressing. She kicked persistently, wanting to savor the swim and moment to herself, but she wanted to stop Teunis from getting in the water. He wasn't a very good swimmer. Sailors were not supposed to swim.

I don't want to be saved... I don't need to be saved...

She made it to the shore. Teunis waded in, scooping her up in his powerful arms, as she surrendered her cold-numbed body to his warmth. Their amused children watched quizzically from afar until Teunis yelled, "Children, secure the *wey schuyt!*" as he slipped Sarah's wrist free from the fishnet.

"All right, Teunis. Let's dry off, pour ourselves a drink, and we can speak on it," Sarah said in begrudging consent as he carried her in the house. Her teeth chattered.

Once they were in dry clothes, she sat down beside him at the table and took up the wooden mug of hot cider and rum.

"You're not supposed to blame the messenger," Teunis said, chiding her.

Remorse made her stomach churn. The look of hurt on his face was like a knife peeling away her rind of obstinacy.

"Why are you so beautiful, even while you're so tempestuous?" He stroked her hair back, brows furrowed, eyes searching hers with unspoken questions.

His compliment and eager love crushed her. *He should be outraged. He should regret marrying me.*

"I don't blame you. I am sorry I made you wade out after me," Sarah said quickly. "I needed a little time. I'm angry! How could the Company bring up this debt eighteen years later? And what in the heavens was it for?"

"Seven hundred and seventy-eight guilders is quite a sum. I thought Hans was a successful man in his carpentry and crops," Teunis said, then looked directly in her eyes. "I don't know what things were like back then though," he said, willing her to tell him.

In the seventeen years that she and Teunis had been married, Sarah hardly ever said Hans's name aloud. Other than things about her children, she said very little at all about the period of her life before she had married Teunis.

"Looking back, I guess he was quiet about business. He didn't discuss things." She sighed. The dam opened. "Times were difficult after Kieft's War, when we had to start over. We had to buy grain from Rensselaerswyck and rebuild our house. I could make a hundred guesses, and none might be true as to why he owed the Company so much. He worked for them for years. When times were dire, they coldly cut his wages. It just seems dubious they claim this debt now, seven years after they lost control over the colony, almost twenty since he died. Hans is dead, yet I never saw a body. How can they collect on a man who the family never buried?"

"I'm sorry, *mijn kastanje*. Debts and death are the only reliable things in life," Teunis said, "and it's never a good time for either."

"I need to find out what it was for. I'm not going to blindly pay off a ledger that might be incorrect," Sarah stated. "Can we pay in crops?"

"They said guilders or beaver skins, but it's not the season for obtaining pelts in a hurry. Not in that number. Nor do we have the guilders," Teunis said, pondering.

"They'll accept *sewant*. They must if they want to be paid," Sarah said, unconsciously reaching to spin the beads on the *sewant* bracelet which she no longer had. "I have a box of *sewant* from the sale of our house on Pearl Straat. Back then, I think it was worth around eight hundred guilders."

It pained her to empty the coffer of her children's inheritance, but better that than they inherit debt.

"It's all right, Sarah. We've been doing well the last few years. I've reinvested everything into our farm, but there are certainly things we could sell. Plus, the crops this season will make up for it," Teunis said, putting his arm around her.

"I'm still angry about it though," Sarah snapped, but leaned into Teunis's embrace.

"I'm not going to have to swim for you again, am I?"

"No, next time I'll check there's an oar," she said, defiant, but grinning at him.

The Company purser sent to retrieve the debt said he did not have an itemized summary of what it was for, just a total sum.

"Perhaps it was for his passage? Or his land grant?" the Company man guessed.

"He worked over fifteen years as a shipwright for the Company. How could he have still owed money for either?"

The Company man shrugged.

Sarah went to Govert Loockermans. An African woman opened the door.

"The master's taken ill abed," the woman replied after Sarah asked to see him.

"What is the ailment? I *must* speak with him. Will you tell him the widow of Hans Hansen Bergen is here? My husband died while working for your master."

"Whatever ails the master, his end is near. Best to speak with him today. Wait here."

The woman disappeared. When she returned, she motioned for Sarah to follow her. Sarah noted Loockermans's well furnished home. The shrewd merchant had done well for himself. He had been appointed *burgomaster* and served his civic duties as *schepen*, fire marshal, and orphanmaster.

The servant reappeared and led her into a parlor. Loockermans reclined on a chaise, eyes closed, with his wife embroidering at his side.

"I'm sorry to disturb you," Sarah said.

Loockermans opened his eyes. His wife rose to greet her.

"He's sedated, but you're welcome to speak with him."

"I'm Sarah Rapelje. Do you remember me? Widow of Hans..."

He nodded.

"A substantial debt Hans owed to the Company has come due, without explanation. I was hoping you may know something. Did Hans ever mention it?"

He nodded, and with a growl, cleared his throat.

"*Ja*, it's why he continued the trade runs for me," Loockermans said in a raspy voice. His wife brought him a glass of water.

"What was the debt for?"

"At first, it was a debt for rebuilding your bowery at the Waalebocht. But then, Hans was caught smuggling a time before the incident that led him to court. He bribed the official to keep silent on the matter. He paid the debt off slowly, but then he found out the official kept the money, yet added his debt to the Company ledger. The official said it was part of their deal that he owed the amount to him *and* the Company. Hans was working on paying it off when he died."

"Who was the company official? Couldn't he have exposed him?"

"Cornelis Van Tienhoven. Hans couldn't expose him without Van Tienhoven charging him with smuggling."

"Why didn't you pay the debt if Hans was caught while working for you?"

"It wasn't for me. It was for another privateer who had already left the colony. I helped Hans when he was caught smuggling for me, remember?"

"Van Tienhoven's dead or disappeared. That vile scoundrel! Why should I pay for his blackmail?"

"No one is left to say what that debt is for, unless you dispute paying it. Do you really want it on the record that your husband was involved in smuggling and bribery?"

She hung her head.

Sarah returned home to Teunis. How could she explain what she'd learned? She preferred Teunis stay ignorant of the struggles in her life before she knew him. He was free to romanticize the evolution of the colony instead of the ugly reality. But he caught her as she staggered in, crying.

"*Mijn liefje...* My past has caught up with me. I was fourteen years old when the most vile, conniving man in the colony sought to wed me. Hans saved me from him, but that vile man never let go of his grudge. He found a way to blackmail Hans years later. That's what the debt is from. I can't dispute it. I can pay it with the *sewant* from the sale of our New Amsterdam home."

"*Mijn kastanje, nee.* I took your husband's wife and land. I'll also take his debt. Let's be done with it."

Sarah sobbed. She was still angry at Van Tienhoven, the Company, and Hans. Did this mean Hans was truly in her past? Why did her sorrow feel as raw as if he had just died? She felt the old shame stoked at finding comfort in the arms of Teunis, yet he said all the right things. She buried herself in his embrace as solace from that feeling.

A fortnight later, the court took payment of double the guilder debt in *sewant*, in place of pelts or guilders. Commissioner Isaac Bedloe accepted the *sewant* since the debt was not Teunis's own.

Chapter 38

1672-1673

The following fall , Sarah went to the market in New York to buy fabric and ribbons to make her daughters' new dresses. The girls had completed their Bible studies and were to perform the Heidelberg Catechism in a few weeks, becoming full church members. She was inspecting a bolt of fine linen when she overheard soldiers discussing news from Europe.

"... year of disaster in the Netherlands..."

She dropped the cloth and followed them to eavesdrop, then left straightaway to return home.

Sarah found Teunis immediately after she returned.

"I heard English soldiers speaking with one another at the market... France attacked the United Provinces. They took Heykoop... they've overtaken everything but the coastal provinces," Sarah said, breathless with panic. "Aert and Rebecca... your family..."

Aert and Rebecca were still in Heykoop with their five children. The last letter from them said Aert's father's estate had been settled after his funeral. They had plans to return to New York.

Teunis was stunned. He thought for a moment.

"They will be all right. Aert will protect Rebecca. My family will take care of them," he said. "The English will defend the United Provinces. This aggression from France cannot stand."

"King Charles II is allying with the French. He's broken his treaty with the Dutch."

Teunis lost his composure. His eyes narrowed and darkened.

"Damn that oath breaker king I swore loyalty to," Teunis growled.

"The soldiers say France grows too strong. King Louis XIV overreaches too deeply into England's pockets. They say Parliament will not continue to fund the King's endeavors," Sarah said. "What does that mean for Aert, Rebecca, and the children? Will they not be allowed to return here?"

"Heykoop is such a small, rural town. They'd be better off to tuck in and wait out this conflict rather than risk a voyage. All we can do is pray they are well, until we hear otherwise."

The sun set on what had been a blazing hot day in early August 1673. Sarah and Teunis sat on their stoop after their evening meal. They watched the sun's reflection of fiery brilliance on billowing blankets of clouds. Swallows and bats swooped low to feast on swarms of midges at the water's edge.

Michael came riding up on his horse in the hazy twilight.

"Hallo, Michael!" Teunis called out. "You just missed dinner."

"I'm not here for dinner but to share news," her son said as he dismounted and joined them on the stoop. His siblings, who had been playing nine pins in the yard, gathered around. Sarah knew Michael went to Manhattan that day. She'd hoped he brought news of Aert and Rebecca.

"The Dutch fleet of twenty-one ships that were sighted off Staten Island a few days ago have come to retake the city! Captain Anthony Colve sent a proclamation to assure us we will be unharmed if we agree to submit again to the States General of the Netherlands," Michael said, breathless, grinning with the news.

"What was Governor Lovelace's reply to that?" Teunis asked.

"He's in Albany," Michael replied. "The Dutch have a force of six hundred soldiers, and the English only have one hundred at the fort, in any case. Captain John Manning is in charge of the fort and is stalling, hoping more English troops will arrive."

Sarah laughed at the reversal of Nicolls's conquest nearly a decade ago. She was so worried it was bad news about Aert and Rebecca. It was a relief. Teunis looked weary, but the corner of his mouth curled into a smirk.

"They won't face resistance from me," Teunis said, leaning back and stuffing his pipe.

"I'm going back to the city in the morning. I want to be there to see the English surrender," Michael said, eyes wide with anticipation.

"You are your *Pater*'s son," Sarah said. For his heritage being Walloon and Norwegian, Michael was most fiercely a New Netherlander.

Teunis smiled, proudly gazing at the young man he helped raise.

The next morning, the fleet had drawn closer to Manhattan. A brief volley of cannon fire could be heard all the way to their bowery at the Waalebocht. Sarah, Teunis, and their children went about the day as usual. Their village did not prepare itself as it had when the English frigates appeared, but they eagerly awaited any news.

That evening, Michael returned to share what had transpired.

"The Dutch fleet drew close to the fort and fired. The fort's guns fired back, but neither did any damage because they were out of range," Michael began. "Then they sent a landing force north of the city and they marched down Brede Wegh to the fort. All the citizens were cheering as they marched. I and many others joined in marching with them. When we arrived at the fort, they drew up the white flag to signal their surrender. The English troops marched out of the gate and laid down their arms in front of the fort."

"Remarkable!" Teunis commented.

"Captain Colve is an inspiring leader. He treated Manning honorably," Michael declared. "He's an Orangist, so he renamed the city New Orange."

Michael referred to those in *Patria* who supported Willem III, Prince of Orange. He was the nephew of King Charles II. Orangists wanted Willem to become *Stadtholder,* their national leader. Many Protestants heralded Willem as a champion of their faith, since he'd fought in wars against the Catholic French.

"Captain Colve put out a call for citizens to join his militia. I volunteered," Michael said proudly.

"Well done," Teunis said. "He should be happy to have such a capable son of New Netherland join him."

Sarah was less enthusiastic about Michael's zeal for service. The English would likely try to recapture of their city at some point. She thought of her son's wife and baby at home. She worried, but stayed silent on it for the moment.

The following March, a convention was held under Governor Colve as to the best interests of the colony. Teunis attended as a delegate of Lange Eylandt.

"Colve is as inspiring as Michael says," Teunis had told Sarah. "He's very diplomatic and open to the will of the people. It's the type of

Dutch leadership we always seemed to lack before. He has more of a mind to listen to the citizens."

But then, of course, the winds shifted in Europe and shook everything up again. Not even two months later, New Orange heard news of the Peace of Westminster, a treaty in which New Orange would be exchanged to the English again for Suriname. The Dutch resurgence had only lasted a year.

"*Bof*," Sarah said, annoyed. "What difference has it made, Dutch or English? The cows don't produce more milk, nor are the harvests any better, nor the winters any shorter under one or the other." In her heart she was disappointed, but her husband needed her to be stoic.

Teunis looked heartbroken, but he nodded at Sarah's argument. He and Sarah were both nearly fifty years old. Stability was more attractive than a continued struggle.

CHAPTER 39

1678

"I have a surprise," Teunis told Sarah, mischievous and giddy as a child. "I can't hide it from you. Come with me."

Sarah's eyes lit up, and with a restrained smile usually reserved for the antics of her children, she followed him out to their storehouse.

When he got to the door, he bade her to wait a minute before coming in. She waited, dutiful but impatient, until she heard him rap on the wall.

She entered to see Teunis seated with a beautiful violoncello. She drew in a breath of surprise. As she entered, he drew the bow across the strings and a deep sonorous timbre struck Sarah to her core. He played a short melody, soft and deeply moving. Sarah was astounded. She had tears in her eyes. He placed the violoncello in a little velvet-padded wooden cradle box that allowed it to stand upright next to him.

"That was beautiful! What in the heavens, Teunis? You play the cello?" she exclaimed, drawing closer to examine the finely made instrument. Her fingers grazed its curving silhouette.

"Not very well. My father played, and I learned a little, as a child. I told Aert I wanted one when he left for *Patria* again. He's staying until spring, so he sent it ahead. I want to play for the wedding celebrations next summer. Clearly, I need the time to practice."

They'd been planning a joint wedding for two of their daughters. Maria was marrying a man named Jacob Rutsen. He was born in

Albany, but his father was "from near Heykoop." Their daughter Catalyntje was betrothed to Phebe and Nys's son, Jan. Again, not from Heykoop, but his father was. Sarah's heart swelled, not only with the joy of planning wedding celebrations, but with this new dimension of her husband. They were both fifty-three years old and had been married to each other for nearly half their lives.

"Teunis, I can't believe you never told me you were a musician! All this time, I thought I married a planter."

She teased him, but she still had tears in her eyes as she looked over the sensuous form of the instrument in its velvet cradle. He was silent, and she glanced at him. He had tears in his eyes, too.

"It's not the most practical thing to play music when you need to survive off the land." He shut his eyes tightly with an attempt of a smile at the corners of his lips. She wrapped her arms around him. After a moment, he continued, "My father would play sometimes with my mother singing an accompaniment. They're some of my happiest childhood memories. But then... after my mother died, my stepmother berated my father for such an indolent pastime. He stopped playing."

"I wish I met your parents. Such an extraordinary man must have had extraordinary parents," she said, flipping what he'd said when he asked to meet her children two decades ago. He buried his face into her neck. She could feel his choked breathing and decided to lighten the mood. "Legend is, my father was a drummer for the Company for one day, but he was asked not to return because he had no rhythm."

Teunis laughed. "I thought Joris was good at everything!"

"As he liked us all to believe," Sarah quipped. "But how are you going to practice without the girls learning your secret talent before the wedding?"

"I found some other musicians that will play with me for the wedding. They agreed I can leave my instrument in the space where we'll rehearse. I had to tell you though, since I'll need to sneak off to the city to practice."

"Thank you for telling me your secret. I'll cover for you. Don't worry." She looked him in the eyes and winked.

In December, a curious omen appeared.

Teunis noticed it first. In the southwestern sky, an emanation of light smaller than the sun but greater than a star appeared. It was truly odd to behold in the daytime. That evening the sky clouded over and it was lost.

"Bright as the day was, I swear, I saw a strange light in the sky," he told Sarah that evening.

The following evening at twilight it could be seen again in the west. At night, the great streamer following it was visible as it stretched across the sky, looking frozen in imperceptible motion. Sarah and Teunis sat wrapped in a blanket on their stoop. Four-year-old Gysbert lay across their laps. He'd fallen asleep gazing at the night sky.

They'd heard at church that some called it the Dreadful Comet, certainly threatening God's judgments and vengeance. The congregants beseeched their Domine for answers. He suggested prayer and fasting.

The evening of the Sabbath, they sat again on their stoop, watching it, squinting to decipher its meaning. Sarah thought it was beautiful. She thought there couldn't be anything dreadful about a light appearing in the darkest months of the year. It seemed hopeful to her.

"The Natives believe the spirits of the dead travel across the sky to the west, with the setting sun... Can you imagine...? Do you think my lost babies, my father, and brothers might be riding it to Heaven?" Sarah asked Teunis. A long silence followed.

"Yes, I can imagine them," he answered, smiling at her.

"What happens to it after it dips beyond the horizon?" she asked Teunis, laying her head on his shoulder.

He considered for a moment.

"They keep riding until they reach Heaven. Their radiance persists, even if we no longer see it."

In July, Sarah's daughters were married at the Dutch Reformed Church in Flatbush in a small ceremony, with Sarah, Teunis, and Jacob Rutsen's parents. Sarah held Phebe and Nys in her thoughts as their son Jan married Catalyntje. She imagined clutching Phebe's hand and whispering that the long-standing betrothal they joked about had come to pass. There were some tears of grief she passed off as tears of joy.

Afterward, they returned to the Waalebocht, where the celebrations were held. It was an enormous affair. Sarah coordinated with their neighbors, and the Waalebocht had been transformed into a village-wide party. Everyone brought their tables outside, lined up, to create a grand banquet in the orchard. The feast ranged from sea to forest, providing anything one would want to eat. Pig, venison, goose, and sturgeon were spit roasted. Sarah organized a *koolsla* contest among the *huisvrouwen*. Whichever housewife had the least *koolsla* left at the end of the night, reigned queen, but also had to share her recipe. Sarah's mother entertained the children with folktales from the old country. Casks of beer, wine, rum, and brandy were tapped and flowing. The aroma of *oliekoeken* filled the air. Now, the tears welling up in Sarah were only for joy and pride. Only a small pang of grief needled her heart, missing those who would not attend, but it was offset by her hostess duties as she welcomed their family and friends.

"Sarah, I must tell you the story of how I took your advice," Teunis's cousin, Jan, told her excitedly when he greeted her. "After we moved to New Haarlem, I found a surprising way to befriend our Weckquaesgeek neighbors. A young Native child was crossing the ice of the creek when he fell through. I pulled him to shore with a branch. His clan has been bringing us venison ever since!"

"I'm glad to hear that, Jan. I told you—they make better friends than enemies!"

Sarah saw Sarina and excused herself to speak with her. She came alone. Her husband, Isaac, had died the year previous. She had not remarried and told Sarah at his funeral she never would.

"Congratulations, Sarah! What a magnificent celebration you've put together."

"I'm glad you came, Sarina. It's been far too long since we've had a chance to see each other."

"I wanted to say goodbye. I'm leaving soon to live with my daughter in Albany. Come visit, if you ever get the chance."

Neighbors approached Sarah, asking if she'd plan the wedding celebrations of their children. One neighbor nominated her as the social director of Lange Eylandt. Sarah blushed at their flattery, but she eagerly agreed—any excuse to devote herself to more celebrations.

She was happy to see Mehakachtey attended. He played horseshoes with her sons. Dressed in a linen shirt and deer-hide breeches, his attire reflected his ease traveling between cultures. She wished Weenji could have been there, but she died from the winter fever over two years ago. Another needle to her heart amidst the revelry.

Susanna Negrin was there. She fussed over Gysbert when he dropped a horseshoe on his toes. Over the years, she liked to check in on him. She said she did so with every baby she helped deliver. Sarah doubted she checked in as often with every child, or she'd have no time for anything else.

As the sun set and everyone had eaten, torches were lit, and the musicians appeared. The moon rose across the river. *Kandeel* was brought out for a special toast from the father of the brides. Sarah was transported, momentarily, to when her father gave the toast at her and Hans's wedding. A lifetime ago.

"To my daughters, whom I love with my whole heart, and to my new sons-in-law, whom I welcome with my whole heart, let us toast to your future. May your roof be tiled with *taerts*. May you multiply like the rabbits of Konijn Eylandt. May your love be burnished with age to shine bright. May you never think you're too old to learn new songs. *Proost!*" Teunis quickly downed his *kandeel* and, to his daughters' delighted astonishment, joined the band at his waiting cello.

"Let's dance!" Sarah shouted, full of hope that her children would create their own families and flourish in this land that she loved.

AFTERWORD

Sarah lived sixty years, toiling through the hard labor of a frontier woman: working in the fields and kitchen, birthing, and raising her children. She died September 16, 1685. She had sixteen children over twenty-eight years, including two sets of twins. Thirteen of her children lived to adulthood. This is the strongest "evidence" of her strength and fortitude, although I try to portray things that don't always show up in records—ways she found strength with other women, advocating for herself and for what she believed in, buying land on her own, running her own business—things which women in New Amsterdam did. The Dutch colonial period stood out to me as a time where women were wives and mothers, but that wasn't the sole extent of their domains.

Sarah's mother outlived her eldest daughter by four years. Catalyna gave several testimonies in her golden years, which crucially served in lieu of existing records of the first settlers and affected the boundaries of Pennsylvania and Maryland. Jasper Danckaerts, a Labadist missionary, wrote of Catalyna in his journal in 1678: "She is worldly minded, living with her whole heart, as well as body, among her progeny, which now number 145, and will soon reach 150. Nevertheless she lived alone by herself, a little apart from the others, having her little garden, and other conveniences, with which she helped herself."

Catalyna and Joris had twelve children—eleven of whom lived to adulthood—and Rapalje descendants are estimated to number more than one million Americans today. Catalyna's descendants include railroad and shipping magnate Cornelius Vanderbilt, Northern Pacific Railway head J. M. Rapelje (founder of Rapelje, Montana), fashion designer Gloria Vanderbilt, and CNN celebrity newsman Anderson Cooper. Sarah's descendants include the actor Humphrey Bogart, NBC news anchor and journalist Tom Brokaw, and politician Howard Dean. There are also merchants, artists, writers, and many salt-of-the-earth farmers.

Some of their progeny would stay in New York City for generations. Many would continue to be pioneers, moving west, first to New Jersey, western New York state, the Midwest, Montana, as well as the Pacific coast, and Canada. They took their customs and traditions with them.

In 1684, women's rights regressed under the English. Women were no longer allowed to purchase land or conduct business in their own name and primogeniture meant the eldest male son was the defacto beneficiary of inheritance. It's ironic that by essentially confining women to the domestic domain, the English inadvertently made women the last to give up the Dutch language. It remained the "mother tongue" of most Dutch-descended families well into the 19th-century and even into the 20th-century.

Considering it's been around 400 years since the beginning of the relatively short-lived period of Dutch colonial America, it's remarkable that echoes remain present in the United States today. It's even more surprising their history is not as widely known as the Pilgrims in American founding mythology, because it resoundingly reflects in the spirit of what our nation, and especially New York City, became. The Dutch influence paved the way for toleration of different cultures and religions (in pursuit of capitalist interests), gender inclusive rights for business and property, the first bold pushes for representative governance and freedom of religion, the position of district attorney in our legal system. And also Santa Claus, waffles, doughnuts, cookies (not biscuits), coleslaw, and pumpkin spice.

Author's Note

You may be wondering—which parts are true and what's fiction?

This novel is a work of fiction based on records (marriages, baptisms, court cases, testimonies, etc.) joined with the broader historical context. I happened to find these intertwined records because several of the main characters are my ancestors, including Sarah Rapalje, my eighth great-grandmother. There's a great deal to connect and yet much left to the imagination to make a narrative.

I tried to stick to the facts as much as I could, but creative license was taken to make this novel entertaining as well as educational. Sarah did claim she was the "eldest Christian daughter of New Netherland" in a court case when she requested a land grant and tax remittance. Catalyna's case against Paulus van der Beeck was taken from court records, though it's not clear if it was Sarah or one of her sisters that was struck by the barber surgeon.

One source said, "Sarah was a woman of great talent and vigor, acknowledged as social head of Brooklyn." There's no evidence Sarah or her mother were lacemakers, but it's plausible. *Passementerie* and needlework was something taught to most young women. Many Walloons worked in textile production. Joris worked as a *boratwerker*, or wool worker, before emigrating. Catalyna's surname, Trico, may be a reference to her family working in the production of tricot, a fabric similar to jacquard.

Phebe Seales is also my eighth great-grandmother. Three of her children married Sarah's children, and one of Phebe's daughters married Sarah's brother. From this, I supposed they were friends. I imagined that a French-speaking Walloon and an English girl forming a bond in a Dutch colony typified the "melting pot" for which New York would later be renowned. Phebe was indeed released from indentured servitude just before her master's expulsion from the Massachusetts colony. Her master, John Coggeshall, was a supporter of Anne Hutchinson, a central figure in the Antinomian Controversy that rattled Massachusetts's theocratic governance. Phebe and Sarah's husbands were both named Teunis, from the province of Utrecht in the Netherlands, and both had been sailors in the Company's employ. It's easy to imagine they were friends, too.

There are two genealogical books written by descendants of both of Sarah's husbands, the Bergen and Bogart families. Each is peppered with wonderful snippets of family lore, like the story of Hans lulling hostile Natives with a song. Records provided the plot points of Hans petitioning to attack the Long Island Natives and his court case for smuggling. Hans's mysterious large debt was real, but his rivalry with Van Tienhoven is fictional.

Van Tienhoven never proposed to marry Sarah, but all other characterization of him came from records. He was a well-educated man who put himself at the right hand of every Director General since he arrived in the colony. The story of him dressing like a Native and chasing girls around came from a written history. He was often at the inciting events of conflicts with the Natives. His adulterous scandal and mysterious death were taken from written histories.

Sarina (Sarah) du Trieux, Isaac de Forest, and Saartje (Sarah) Roelofs Kierstede are based on real people. I changed the names of these "Sarah"s to avoid confusion. Their stories are equally fascinating and may be explored in future novels.

Susanna Negrin, as a character, began with a mention of her as Sarah's neighbor in a land patent confirmation. I then found she was the only African church member prior to 1664—meaning she was not only baptized but had passed an examination of her faith. Her parents were freed in Kieft's manumission in 1644, but not Susanna and her siblings. I don't have evidence of Susanna's manumission, but a Domine later wrote that he did not want to continue to baptize Africans because they would only use it to gain freedom. That sounds like baptism had previously helped gain freedom for some. New Netherland never codified slavery into law, which meant that the colony never established clear parameters to human bondage. Nor did the courts limit the enslaved Africans' participation in the judicial system, thus allowing them to own property, receive wages, use the courts, and legally marry. There are many accounts of enslaved and free Africans advocating for themselves and their family members in court records. There are no records that Sarah or her parents owned slaves, although subsequent generations did.

Weenji, Wunita, and Cholena are completely fictional characters, but reflect records that hint at the Rapaljes' relations with the Natives. Records state that Joris made a land deal with chiefs of Keschaechquereren for his bowery at the Waalebocht. In Catalyna's account of the early days in the colony, they had peaceful and free trade relations with the Natives. There's family lore that, as a child, Sarah (or her sister) was ferried in a washbasin across to Nutten (Governors) Island by a Native nursemaid. A dissertation on New Netherland mentioned in the footnotes that Sarah Rapalje worked as a Munsee translator for Peter Stuyvesant. Weenji's name is an homage to a Lenape descendant, Weenjipahkihelexkwe, or Nora Thompson Dean (1907–1984). She dedicated her life to the preservation and sharing of Lenape culture. Quashawam was a real Montaukett chief who made deals to solidify her people's security. She really did warn Stuyvesant of the impending English attack and made deals with John Scott that protected land for her people.

John Scott is a historical character worthy of his own novel. His parade through the Dutch towns, claiming he was the President of Long Island, is based on recorded histories.

The Dutch colonial period only lasted fifty-five years (1609-1644), yet the Dutch certainly left their mark. I plan on continuing to tell their stories, so they aren't forgotten among America's founders.

THE END

Please take a moment to rate and review on Amazon or Goodreads. It really makes a difference for an indie author like me.
Thank you

Please visit my website, www.fawnbrokawdoyle.com, for a bibliography, character list, family tree, a free prequel short story, and blog posts that explore my research for this novel.

ACKNOWLEDGEMENTS

I owe a great deal of gratitude to the New Netherland Institute and Charles Gehring for tackling the translation of twelve thousand pages of Dutch-language administrative records. The court records that informed the framework of this book came from their ongoing, immense contribution of translation. Thank you to the New Amsterdam History Center, The New York Historical, New York Genealogical & Biographical Society, and the Society of Daughters of Holland Dames for their dedication to preserving and sharing Dutch New York history. Many thanks to historical authors Russell Shorto, Jaap Jacobs, Firth Haring Fabend, Joyce Goodfriend, and Susannah Shaw Romney. Their books are at the top of my list of indispensable histories of the period.

Thank you to the people who personally broadened and enriched my research: the staff of the Wyckoff House Museum, Crailo Historic Site, Historic Huguenot Street, historical podcaster Chance Kelly, historian Bertrand Van Ruymbeke, genealogist and historian Sandra Robinson, Pamela Howard at Historic Albany Foundation, and historical fiction authors Lana Waite Holden and Bill Greer. My thanks to The History Quill for being a wonderful community and resource for indie historical fiction authors.

Special thanks to those who helped me craft a better story: my development editor Kelly Urgan, copy editor Sarah Dronfield, critique partners and fellow authors Pat Advaney and Martha Bush, and many beta readers (especially Ava Mack and Marcy McNally).

Acknowledgment is due to the many Native tribes who inhabited (and whose living descendants are still connected to) their ancestral lands that the Dutch colonized: the Lenni-Lenape (Delaware), Muhhekunneuw (Mohican), and Haudenosaunee (Iroquois). The myth of Manhattan being sold for $26 worth of goods is inaccurate and not accepted by contemporary descendants. The "sale" was a European interpretation of a deal to peacefully share the land and trade, with gifts of goodwill, not payment. Thank you to delawaretribe.org, the Museum of the American Indian, Misty Cook, Brent Stonefish, and Brent Michael Davids.

My gratitude to Ann Foster, writer and host of the podcast Vulgar History, who inspired me to take the leap into writing this story. Thank you to my kindergarten teacher, Mrs. Hill, who told me I would write books. Whenever I felt self-doubt, I thought of your confident words. Thank you to all the people (including many newfound cousins) who share my enthusiasm about this history and cheered me on during the writing process.

Finally, my deepest gratitude to you, my readers!

ABOUT THE AUTHOR

Fawn Brokaw Doyle is a lifelong history nerd and writer with degrees in Communications and Industrial Design. While researching her genealogy, her creative spirit ignited to share the story of her 8th-great-grandmother, Sarah Rapalje.

By day, she's a flatware designer, wife, and toddler mom who enjoys traveling, state parks, historic sites, and learning handicrafts, herbalism, and mycology.

By night, she is a genealogist, historian, and novelist.

Historical fiction is her favorite genre because it's transportive and connects modern readers with the human experience of history. She loves exploring lesser-known eras and short, intriguing side notes that inspire and deserve a fully rendered story arc. She plans to continue writing historical fiction with that focus.

Salt People of the Cloud Houses is her debut novel.

Glossary

abécédaire – French – alphabet tablet used for teaching

aanspreker – Dutch – a person who goes door-to-door announcing a death

arakun – Algonquian – raccoon

arrière-faix – French – the placenta or afterbirth

baas – Dutch – master/governor/boss

bedstee – Dutch – a cupboard-like box bed

bowery – Dutch – large farm

burgomaster – Dutch – mayor, chief magistrate, or executive of a city or town

de rigueur – French – fashionable according to strict etiquette

Domine – Dutch, from Latin – priest, reverend, or minister of the Dutch Reformed Church

fardegalijn – Dutch (English: farthingale) – a hoop structure that gave shape to skirts

huisvrouw – Dutch – housewife

Jonkheer – Dutch – young lord

kandeel – Dutch – celebratory cocktail made with cream, sack wine, eggs, sugar, and spices

kast – Dutch – a tall, wardrobe-like cupboard with double doors

klompen – Dutch – clogs

kleinbier - Dutch - a low-alcohol lager beer

knottedoek – Dutch – an embroidered linen dowry cloth

koekje – Dutch – cookie

koolsla – Dutch – coleslaw, chopped cabbage salad with butter

kruidnoten – Dutch – cookie (similar to a gingersnap)

kwey – Algonquian – greeting

Maman – French – mother

ma petite puce – French – my little flea; term of endearment

meisje – Dutch – little girl

Mevrouw – Dutch – Mrs./madam

mijn liefje – Dutch – my darling/sweetheart

mijn herre – archaic Dutch – my lord

mijn kastanje - Dutch - my chestnut

min kvinne mitt alt – Norwegian – my woman my everything

Moeder – Dutch – mother

morgen – Dutch – unit of land measurement that is equal to about two acres (0.8 hectares)

nitap – Algonquian – friend

oliekoeken – Dutch – doughnut

partlet – a sleeveless garment worn over the neck and shoulders, worn for warmth or to fill in a low neckline; they could look like a cropped cape or a dicky

passement – French – passement is an early French word for lace trim (passementerie worked in linen thread is the origin of bobbin lace)

Patria – Latin – the Fatherland (United Provinces of the Netherlands)

patroon – Dutch – a landholder with manorial rights to large tracts of land

Pays-Bas – French – the Low Countries (northern France, Belgium, Netherlands, and Lichtenstein)

roemer – Dutch – a glass goblet studded with decorative prunts, raised decorative dots that improved grip, on the stem

sachem – Algonquian – chief

sappaen – Algonquian – corn porridge

schepel – Dutch – measurement of grain, ¾ of a bushel

schepen – Dutch – a municipal court official, similar to an English alderman or town councilor

schout – Dutch – a local official appointed to carry out administrative, law enforcement, and prosecutorial tasks, similar to a modern district attorney

sewant – Dutch (English – wampum) – beads made of shell that served importance to Natives

Stadthuys – Dutch – state house

sunksqua – Algonquin – *elevated woman* – female sachem, or leader

Swanneken – Algonquian – salt people; name used for European colonists

taert – Old Dutch – a sweet or savory pie

usus – Latin – In 17th-century New Netherland, women had the option of choosing between two types of marriage: manus and usus. Under manus, a wife was considered subordinate to her husband and lost her legal identity. In contrast, a usus marriage allowed women to retain all the rights they had as single women, including the right to own property.

Waalebocht – Dutch – Walloon's bay; curve in the river

wey schuyt – Dutch – canoe

wilden – Dutch – wild men or savages

wunneet – Algonquian – *it is good* – phrase used when exchanging trade goods

vlieger – Dutch – a formal cape worn by married women

vly – Dutch – valley where water collects; swamp